MONSIEUR PAMPLEMOUSSE OMNIBUS

VOLUME 1

THE AUTHOR

Michael Bond decided to become a writer while serving in the army during the Second World War. The result was Paddington Bear, now a household name, who was born after a shopping trip one Christmas Eve when he spotted a small, solitary bear in a large London store. *Monsieur Pamplemousse* was his first adult novel. Such was the success of his inspired blend of comedy, crime and cuisine that a whole series of books featuring Pamplemousse and Pommes Frites followed.

Monsieur Pamplemousse Omnibus

Volume 1

Michael Bond

a&b

First published in Great Britain in 1998 by
Allison & Busby Ltd
114 New Cavendish Street
London W1M 7FD
http://www.allisonandbusby.ltd.uk

Monsieur Pamplemousse
first published in 1983
by Hodder and Stoughton Limited

Monsieur Pamplemousse and the Secret Mission
first published in 1984
by Hodder and Stoughton Limited

Monsieur Pamplemousse on the Spot
first published in 1986
by Hodder and Stoughton Limited

A catalogue record for this book is available from the
British Library

ISBN 0 7490 0352 9

Printed and bound in Great Britain by
Mackays of Chatham Plc
Chatham, Kent

Monsieur Pamplemousse

1

MONDAY EVENING

Monsieur Pamplemousse dipped a little finger surreptitiously into the remains of some *sauce Madère* which had accompanied his *Filet de Boeuf en Croûte* and licked it reflectively before making a note on a small pad concealed beneath a flap in his right trouser leg.

Repeating the first part of the operation, he held his hand momentarily below the level of the table-cloth and felt the familiar roughness of a warm and appreciative tongue reach up to lick it clean.

A moment later there was a gentle stirring, followed by the padding of four large feet as Pommes Frites rose into view and made his way slowly across the floor of the restaurant.

A loud lapping sound coming from the direction of a water bowl situated just inside the entrance doors confirmed Monsieur Pamplemousse's worst suspicions. He underlined the note he had just made and then returned the pen to an inside pocket.

If Pommes Frites agreed that the *sauce Madère* was too salty, then too salty it was.

Strange that it should be so in such a renowned establishment as the Hôtel-Restaurant La Langoustine. In all the years he had been visiting St. Castille such a thing had never happened before. It could mean only one of two things; either an inexperienced and over-generous hand had been at the salt cellar in the kitchen—which seemed unlikely—or Auguste Douard, the chef-patron, was 'taking precautions'.

Putting salt in the Madeira to prevent staff from imbibing too much on the sly was an old trick, but in this case, with La Langoustine already the proud possessor of two Red Stock Pots in *Le Guide*, and well on its way to the supreme accolade of a third, such a move seemed not only unwarranted but positively foolhardy. Unless . . . Monsieur Pamplemousse resolved to keep a watchful eye on the situation. Over-indulgence of liquor was a recognised occupational hazard in the culinary world, but it was a hazard which needed to be resisted at all costs if one wished to scale the heights of the profession. It would be a disaster of the first magnitude if Monsieur Douard himself were to succumb to the bottle at this stage in his career.

Nevertheless, one had to be firm. There were standards which, once set, had to be maintained and lived up to. Working for *Le Guide* had taught him one thing: never to relax, never to take things for granted, always to savour, to analyse and compare.

The fillet of beef had been admirable; tender and lightly cooked beforehand to ensure that its juices were properly sealed within before being encased in its envelope of flaky pastry. As for the pastry, as ever it had been a miracle of lightness; the two together had made a magnificent, a heavenly combination. A slightly reckless choice for a first course, especially in view of what was to follow, but the journey had been a long one and there were two mouths to feed. Besides, it had been a very small portion—just enough to taste and report on. As things turned out he was glad he'd chosen it, for the accompanying sauce had definitely been below par.

Having justified the matter in his mind, Monsieur Pamplemousse helped himself to a solitary olive, mentally deducting another point from the restaurant's total for having failed to remove the plate when the first course arrived, and a further point from his own personal tally for being so weak.

Choosing a moment when all the waiters had their backs to him, he poured a quick glass of wine from a bottle cradled in a large, carved wooden sabot standing nearby, then he slipped the cork under the table for Pommes Frites to examine.

An approving sniff came from somewhere below the folds of the cloth. Given the choice, Pommes Frites much preferred Bordeaux, but he was no mean judge of Burgundy either. If it were possible to translate a sniff into oenological terms, then Pommes Frites' verdict was: 'If you *must* have a Côtes du Rhône instead of a decent Pauillac—and seeing we are more or less in the area, why not?—then what better than a '73 Hermitage?'

Monsieur Pamplemousse swirled the deep red liquid around in the glass, held it to his nose and sipped. The bouquet was superb, the taste complex and full of character. The vineyard must have escaped the late hail storms of that year. It promised well.

Pushing aside the sabot, he tucked his napkin firmly inside his shirt collar in preparation for the next course, then turned his attention to his surroundings, reflecting as he did so that only in his beloved France could a restaurant combine all that was best in food with the worst excesses of interior design.

La Langoustine had reached its present eminence largely on account of its food. That, and an attention to detail in the hotel itself which was beyond reproach. The freshly cut flowers and the confiseries placed in all the rooms to welcome the guests when they arrived, the bowl of fruit beside every bed and the assortment of soaps and perfumes and after-shave lotions in the bathrooms, more than made up for any deficiencies in the décor.

But having said that, it had to be admitted that in other respects the hotel was a veritable monument to bad taste. Bad taste which had its roots in the days when wood was as plentiful and easy to come by as plastic is today.

Like her forbears, Madame Sophie Douard was deeply into wood and she, too, had added to the general effect in no mean way. Apart from the sabots and a large collection of old fire bellows which adorned the heavily panelled walls, wood in all its possible shapes and sizes and colours filled the dining room. But even these decorations were dwarfed by a trolley of positively heroic dimensions which occupied a position of honour in the centre of the room. Mounted on a pair of old cartwheels, it made the serving of sweets a hazard to both diner and waiter alike.

The Hôtel-Restaurant La Langoustine had stood in its present position for something like two hundred years. Founded by Madame Hortense Douard, who had won brief fame during the Revolution by delaying the approaching hordes by methods best left unreported, and whose memory was enshrined by a statue in the square outside, it had survived two world wars and between whiles prospered in its own quiet way.

When Auguste, fresh from catering college, met and married Sophie, he changed his name by deed poll so as to preserve the continuity of the Douard family. After a period of several years away from St. Castille, during which time he served his apprenticeship with some of the great names in French cuisine, he returned to take command following the death of Sophie's father, and from that day on La Langoustine had never looked back.

As Auguste's reputation spread far beyond boundaries never dreamed of by its founder, it began to cater for a more cosmopolitan clientele, and a further sign of the changing times lay in the fact that Madame Hortense's statue now boasted a fountain with twin jets which gushed forth from points neither nature nor its original creator had ever intended.

Lately, in anticipation of receiving his third Stock Pot, Auguste had taken to dropping his christian name in favour of plain Douard, and rumour had it that a cookery book—*Cuisine Douard*—was already in preparation, ready to be launched when the big moment arrived.

Work had lately begun on modernising the hotel—converting cupboards into extra toilets and box-rooms into en suite bathrooms, and plans were under way for an extension to the building. Already cranes were poking their noses over the rooftop as a group of old outhouses at the rear was demolished to make way for the new.

Perhaps, by the time he came again, the postcard which he sent home as always, marking his room with its view of the garden, would be redundant. Monsieur Pamplemousse hoped not. He had the resistance to change which came with middle age.

The restaurant was beginning to fill up; a sprinkling of tourists—he was pleased to see an English couple deep in their copy of *Le Guide*, and at a table next to them two earnest American ladies, schoolteachers by their appearance, were busy working out where they had been on their gastronomic tour of Europe, and where they were going to next. For a moment he marvelled at the way such slender frames could emit such piercing voices and accommodate such vast quantities of food into the bargain. Perhaps the dissipation of all that energy in talk and travel enabled them to burn up the excess calories gained en route? Several tables were occupied by prosperous-looking business-men, bemoaning the iniquities of governments past, present and future, and yet wearing their prosperity with accustomed ease; others by scientists from the nearby solar energy station. There was a courting couple who were paying more attention to each other than they were to the food. A young man at a crowded table in the middle of the room was making great play with his knowledge of wine—probably the son of a wealthy vigneron, for he spoke with authority.

And in the far corner, partly cut off from the rest of the diners by a wooden screen, sat the blonde girl and her partner who had been responsible for the unpleasantness earlier in the evening.

Monsieur Pamplemousse stole a quick glance at her. Tall and slim, her clothes bore the unmistakable air of quality which only the very wealthy as opposed to the merely well-off can afford.

It had all been over in a matter of moments, but it had left a nasty taste in his Kir Royale. Certainly there was no trace of forgiveness in her pale blue eyes as they momentarily met his and held them. Eyes that matched her too impeccable accent; utterly without warmth. She looked as if she wished him anywhere but where he was sitting. He was unmoved.

The visit to the Hôtel-Restaurant La Langoustine was, for Monsieur Pamplemousse, an annual event, a way of killing two birds with one stone. The combining of business with pleasure was normally frowned on by the powers that be at *Le Guide*. Strict and unbiassed anonymity was the rule. But Monsieur Pamplemousse had been visiting the hotel for many years, following the rise in its fortunes with a friendly eye and an appreciative stomach, and each year he combined a brief holiday with an up-to-date report. Others would have to follow on, of course, to confirm his findings, particularly now it was in line for a further Stock Pot. That would mean a visit or two from Monsieur le Directeur himself. But his annual stay there was acknowledged to be sacrosanct.

He always occupied the same room, on the first floor at the back of the hotel, overlooking the garden and away from the noise of traffic in the main square.

Pommes Frites had a space reserved for his inflatable

kennel below the window—not a bone's throw away from the kitchens, where he had many friends. Above all, they had their own special table in the restaurant. Monsieur Pamplemousse was a creature of habit; he needed certain parameters to which he could relate on his travels. It was the only way one could do the job and retain a degree of sanity and a healthy digestion.

He liked his table in the corner. From it he could watch the goings on in the rest of the room and yet remain relatively unnoticed. He could observe the arrival and departure of the other guests and keep a watchful eye on the staff as they bustled to and fro between kitchen and dining room. Above all, he was close enough to the entrance to overhear snatches of conversation when people left; little titbits which were invaluable when it came to making out his report.

All the more reason then, to feel deeply aggrieved when he came downstairs that evening and found the blonde girl engaged in a bitter argument with the maître d'hôtel on the subject of *his* table.

Normally accommodating in such matters, Monsieur Pamplemousse had politely but firmly stood his ground.

Fortunately Pommes Frites had taken the situation in at a glance and put an end to the discussion by settling himself down with such a proprietorial air it left no room for further argument.

All the same, it had been very disturbing while it lasted. The girl had taken it with particularly bad grace, and if the look she'd flung at Monsieur Pamplemousse as she and her companion were ushered to another table could have been translated into deeds, a certain part of his anatomy would by now have been sizzling merrily away in the sauté pan, destined for the doubtful privilege of appearing on the menu under the heading 'Dishes of the Day'.

Monsieur Pamplemousse shifted uneasily in his chair at the thought. And yet . . . despite, or perhaps because of her ill-temper, which had brought a becoming flush to her cheeks and a disconcerting rise and fall to her breasts, she had a certain fascination which he was not alone in appreciating. He'd noticed others in the room casting curious glances in the direction of the screen from time to time, obviously in the hope of catching another glimpse.

Monsieur Pamplemousse couldn't resist taking another quick look himself. As he did so he gave a start. Until that moment he'd hardly given the girl's companion more than a passing glance. He seemed a perfectly ordinary young man. Dark, possibly Italian from his looks; whereas he'd put the girl down as German or Scandinavian, her accent had been just a little too perfect. Discreetly dressed, obviously deeply embarrassed by the whole affair, he'd done his best to merge into the background, hardly uttering a word. Hands in his jacket pockets, he'd seemed only too anxious to escape behind the screen. Now Monsieur Pamplemousse could see why.

As he watched, the young man reached across the table to hand a dish to the girl. Almost immediately there was a crack like a pistol shot and it broke in two. The reason was simple. In place of a normal hand he had what looked like a steel claw, not unlike the grab on one of the mechanical excavators outside.

But there was worse to come. Brushing aside a waiter who rushed to his aid, the young man reached up with his other hand and revealed a second claw, identical to the first. Monsieur Pamplemousse drew in his breath with an involuntary gasp. Poor devil. What possible disaster could have been responsible for such a dreadful misfortune?

To his surprise the girl hardly seemed to notice, let alone offer to help. Instead, she had her eyes firmly fixed on the door leading to the kitchen as it swung open and a waiter bearing a large silver dish covered by a matching silver top entered the room and headed towards Monsieur Pamplemousse, where he placed it reverentially on a serving table in front of him.

The maître d'hôtel hurried forward.

Monsieur Pamplemousse looked at him with concern, the couple in the corner forgotten for the moment. The man looked as white as a sheet.

'Is anything the matter, Felix?'

'No, Monsieur Pamplemousse . . . that is to say . . .' Casting an anxious glance towards the kitchen, he wiped a bead of sweat from his brow. Then, seemingly reassured, he spread his hands out in the gesture of one whose fate is not of their choosing; a mixture of fatalistic acceptance of things past and apology for other events to come.

Monsieur Pamplemousse resolved to ignore everything in favour of concentrating on the task in hand. Everyone had their problems and doubtless all would be revealed in due course. There were more important things to think about. Already he could feel a stirring at

14

his feet as Pommes Frites' nose inched its way out to investigate the arrival of the pièce de résistance.

One of the specialities of La Langoustine, in fact it would be true to say *the* speciality, was *Poularde de Bresse en Vessie Royale*; a whole chicken from Bresse, the best in all France, specially reared for Monsieur Douard and marked with his personal number by a private breeder, corn fed to precise instructions from the moment it was hatched to the day on which it was ready for the table, at which point it was carefully prepared with slices of truffle slipped beneath the skin and stuffed with seasoned foie gras. Placed inside a freshly scraped pig's bladder, which had been cleaned with salt and vinegar, it was then sewn up and cooked in a pot of chicken consommé for two and a half hours.

A dish fit for a king. Indeed, Auguste Douard had first prepared it for a minor royal personage who had chanced on the hotel, and it had remained on the menu ever since.

'*Voilà*, Monsieur!' Felix removed the domed lid with a flourish and then stood back mopping his brow again.

Monsieur Pamplemousse felt his mouth begin to water as the smell reached his nostrils. Pommes Frites gave a snuffle of anticipation, knowing full well that even his master couldn't tackle the whole of a dish which was normally meant for two.

The maître d'hôtel picked up a carving knife and a fork and stood with them poised, one in each hand. For some reason or other he seemed to have a strange reluctance to cut open the envelope where it had been sewn together. First he put the knife down, then he picked it up again, and each time he did so he gave a little moan.

Finally, unable to contain himself a moment longer, Monsieur Pamplemousse jumped to his feet. 'I do not know what has come over this restaurant tonight,' he exclaimed. 'Nor, at this stage, do I greatly care. Allow me. It is not going to bite you. At least, I sincerely hope not.'

For some reason his words had a devastating effect on Felix and his voice when it came was a barely audible croak. 'As you wish, Monsieur.' He backed away and clutched at the sweet trolley for support.

With the assurance of one who has seen it done a thousand times before, Monsieur Pamplemousse took the implements and with one deft movement pierced the bladder along its seam with the carving knife, at the same time pulling the gap apart with the fork. Then he stood back to admire his handiwork as the balloon-like outer casing collapsed on to the dish, revealing the contents for all to see.

As he did so the blood drained from his face. For a brief moment there was silence and then a woman screamed.

Monsieur Pamplemousse took a quick look round the room, noted in passing that the couple behind the screen were nowhere to be seen, then he sat down and gazed at the dish in front of him.

To say that the head looked vaguely familiar would have been a gross exaggeration in the circumstances. It was too misshapen to be readily identifiable as anything other than that of a man, perhaps, to judge by the matted covering of black hair, in his early thirties . . . and yet . . .

As if to sum up the feelings of all those present in the room, Pommes Frites lifted up his head and gave vent to a loud howl.

'Please,' said Monsieur Pamplemousse wearily as the sound died away, 'will someone cover up this monstrosity before I make a similar noise.'

And then, instincts born out of years spent in not totally dissimilar situations coming to the fore, he stood up again and raised his hand for silence.

'I must ask that you all remain where you are for the time being. No one is to move until the police arrive.'

'I protest!' A man at a nearby table jumped to his feet and glared at him. 'My wife is upset. I demand to be allowed to leave. By what right . . .'

Monsieur Pamplemousse decided to take a chance. Reaching into an inside pocket he withdrew a small wallet, flicked it open, and flashed a card briefly through the air. 'By this right, Monsieur. And when I say no one,' he continued, 'that is precisely what I mean. No one.'

Monsieur Pamplemousse spoke with an air of quiet authority. An authority which many people over the years had good cause to remember, often to their cost. As he flicked the wallet shut and returned it to his pocket a faint smile crossed his face. Really, it was quite like old times.

*   *   *

'You realise that impersonating a police officer is an offence?'

'Impersonating?' Monsieur Pamplemousse raised his eyebrows in mock protest. 'Not for one single instant did I say I was a police officer. I merely showed them my American Express card. If they chose to . . .'

Inspector Banyuls brushed aside the words. His point had been made; his authority established. Leaning back in his chair he examined his fingernails. It was a meeting of opposites. The dislike had been mutual and instantaneous.

'I accept that you acted in what you considered to be the best interests. Nevertheless . . .' he looked up with a gesture which indicated that from now on, he, Inspector Banyuls, was in charge.

'Who would you consider most likely to wish to do you some harm?' The implication that the list could be a long one was not lost on Monsieur Pamplemousse.

'I have been retired from the Sûreté for several years now,' he began.

'Ah, yes . . .' Inspector Banyuls couldn't resist the opportunity. 'I remember now. It was in all the papers at the time. What was it they called it? The Case of the Cuckolded Chorus? Almost the whole of the line. How many girls were involved? Twenty-two?'

'Fifteen,' growled Monsieur Pamplemousse. 'It was a trumped-up charge. Besides, anyone who wanted to do me harm would have done so long ago.'

'Some husbands have long memories . . . As for lovers . . .'

'Were I still in Paris, perhaps . . . but in this part of the world?'

'It has all the marks of the Mafia. A warning perhaps?

18

Keep off . . . next time . . .' Inspector Banyuls made the classic throat–cutting gesture. Despite himself, Monsieur Pamplemousse couldn't help but feel a shiver run down his spine. Banyuls was right.

'These things . . . the Mafia, they are more of the South than of the North.'

'Nevertheless, you say you recognised the head?'

'It looked familiar, that is all.'

Inspector Banyuls tried a different approach. 'Why are you here?'

'It is a private matter. One that need not concern you.' Monsieur Pamplemousse returned the other's gaze without blinking.

'And you are leaving, when?'

'I have yet to decide. It depends.'

'Depends?'

Monsieur Pamplemousse refused to be drawn. Instead he cupped his hands round a large balloon-shaped glass to warm it and then sniffed the contents with an air of well-being.

'Would you care to join me in an Armagnac? It is the '28. A great year. I can recommend it. It is the patron's Réserve d'Artagnan. A whiff of Three Musketeers country. One can taste the oak from the forest of Monzelun.' Even as he spoke he knew he was saying the wrong thing.

'I wouldn't know, Pamplemousse. The pay of an inspector in the French police does not allow for such pleasures—even before retirement. One day you must let me know how you manage it. And now . . .' he rose, 'there is work to be done. There are others to be questioned. I must thank you again

19

for your foresight in retaining them. Perhaps some will have a better memory of the event than you appear to.'

Monsieur Pamplemousse acknowledged the words with a nod. He'd been about to remark on the absence of the young couple, but he decided against it. Why should he put himself out? The problem was Inspector Banyuls' concern, not his. Had he been Inspector Banyuls there were a number of questions which would have required an answer.

Where, for example, was Madame Douard?

In all the years he'd been visiting La Langoustine she had never been absent from her post, greeting guests as they arrived, visiting all the tables to make sure everyone was happy. He hadn't seen her all the evening. It was very odd.

Monsieur Douard was also conspicuous by his absence. Busy though he always was, he was never too busy to pop out for a quick greeting. Tonight he was nowhere to be seen.

Then there was the extraordinary behaviour of Felix.

Last, but not least, there was the matter of the head.

Lifelike though it undoubtedly was—or had been before the application of heat—the inescapable fact remained that it was made of plastic, pinkish brown, shiny plastic, something he'd realised straight away on closer inspection.

Alors! He turned his attention to the Armagnac. 1928. The year of his birth. Was that why he had chosen it? Or was it some perverse and rather petty desire to score over the inspector; to show that although he might be retired he certainly wasn't yet out of the running? If so, it was an unworthy motive—one which would have disappointed the makers had they been present. Such ambrosial spirit was meant for higher things.

It was also meant to be savoured in peace and quiet. Really, the noise in the restaurant had reached an intolerable level. Even Inspector Banyuls seemed to have lost something of his cool as he did battle with the rest of the occupants, each trying to get a word in first.

Watching him run a distraught hand round the inside of his shirt collar, Monsieur Pamplemousse felt a pang of sympathy. Perhaps, despite his dislike of the other, he should have been more co-operative. Fuelled by the warmth of the liquid now at work in his veins, his feeling of remorse grew. He felt a sudden desire to mount a rescue operation; to create a diversion. A wicked gleam came into his eyes.

Rapping his empty glass sharply on the table, he stood up and cleared his throat. Almost immediately the room fell silent.

'Everyone,' he said, choosing his words with care, 'seems most concerned about the *Poularde de Bresse en Vessie Royale*—or perhaps in the circumstances I should say the *Tête en Vessie Royale*—with which I was served earlier in the evening, but which, I hasten to add, I did not touch. Not a morsel passed my lips. But no one yet seems to have considered the fact that the head of this unfortunate young man was once attached to a body and that a body has many parts.'

Here Monsieur Pamplemousse paused for effect, conscious that all eyes were on him.

He turned to a woman nearby. 'I notice, Madame, that you ordered the *Pâté de Cervelle en Croûte*—brains in pastry. I trust they were to your liking? Not too smooth?

'And you, Monsieur, did you enjoy your liver? Or do you now wish you'd ordered the *truite*?

'As for you, Monsieur, I believe you had the hearts?'

Pressing home his advantage remorselessly, Monsieur Pamplemousse looked towards the American ladies. 'I couldn't help overhearing you ask for your leg of lamb to be well done. A wise decision. If it had been too rare it might have acquired even more of a nightmarish quality in the years to come.'

He glanced down at the menu. 'I see they have *andouillette*. Now, that would have been quite an experience . . .'

Monsieur Pamplemousse was enjoying himself. Now that he was beginning to warm to his theme there were all sorts of exciting possibilities.

But his pleasure was short-lived. The silence which followed his remarks was broken by a loud crunching sound. It came from a spot somewhere near his feet.

'*Sapristi!*' Monsieur Pamplemousse turned and gazed at the empty dish on his serving table. 'Oh, my word! Oh, my very word!'

Pommes Frites gazed unhappily around the room, a rivulet of pinkish gravy running down his chin. He liked an audience and one way and another he'd been feeling pretty left out of things. Not only that, but he'd been getting more and more hungry. Now, both situations had been well and truly rectified; the former in a way which left little to be desired, the latter in a way which left a great deal. Never in the whole of his life had he tasted anything quite so disgusting.

On the other side of the room someone was noisily sick.

Monsieur Pamplemousse was pleased to see it was Inspector Banyuls. At least when Pommes Frites disgraced himself he gave value for money.

2

TUESDAY MORNING

Pommes Frites was fed up. Fed up and in disgrace; or fed up because he was in disgrace. It amounted to much the same thing in the end. Everywhere he went in St. Castille he left a trail of 'Oooh, la la!'s, as passers-by pointed him out and recounted their version of the previous night's escapade.

And as he continued his perambulations so the story was repeated and handed on, growing in horror and complexity, until by the time he got back to the Square du Centre mothers were running out into the street to grab their protesting children and drag them indoors lest his appetite and taste for blood got the better of him again.

Convicted on circumstantial evidence, that's what he'd been.

Inspector Banyuls had not been pleased. If Inspector Banyuls had had his way, banishment to an open-ended kennel in Siberia during the depths of winter would have been among the least of his punishments. There had been talk of arrest and charges of consuming vital evidence with criminal intent.

Just because he'd happened to be standing near the empty dish at the time and happened to have gravy on his chin. It wouldn't have been quite so bad if he'd enjoyed his meal, but he couldn't remember ever having eaten anything quite so unappetising before; he could still taste it. If he, Pommes Frites, had any say in the matter not only would La Langoustine be out of the running for a further Stock Pot, they would lose the two they already possessed.

Unkindest cut of all, in all the excitement he'd been sent to bed supperless. It was a good job he'd remembered a small cache of bones buried in the garden during a previous visit, otherwise he might have starved to death. Then they would have been sorry. It was not quite what his taste buds had been expecting, but in the circumstances better than nothing.

Even his master's defence of his actions had seemed a little half-hearted. But at least he had tried, bringing to bear such arguments as he could muster to make the point that Pommes Frites couldn't be blamed for giving way to what were, after all, only his animal instincts.

Animal instincts indeed! In his time Pommes Frites had dined at some of the best restaurants in France, and although he wouldn't, and most certainly didn't, ever turn up his nose at the odd biscuit or two when they were offered, there were limits.

To show the extent of his displeasure he left his mark against the side of the fountain and then confirmed everyone's worst suspicions by baring his teeth at a small boy who had come to watch, adding a rather satisfactory growling noise for good measure.

As the child ran off screaming, Pommes Frites began to feel slightly better. He made his way across the square towards the hotel and peered in at the bar in the hope that his master might have finished breakfast and be ready to join him in another stroll.

But Monsieur Pamplemousse was deep in conversation with the patron. In fact, had the question been put to him in so many words, a walk was not high on Monsieur Pamplemousse's agenda at that moment in time. He had other things to think about. One way and another he'd spent a sleepless night and while listening to Monsieur Douard he was fortifying himself with an early morning *marc* over his coffee, strictly for medicinal purposes, of course. It was the least he could do for his nerves.

Pommes Frites hesitated, torn between the thought of another stroll and not wanting to miss anything. In the end curiosity won the day and he curled up comfortably at his master's feet, pretending he was asleep but in reality keeping a weather eye open for possible clues which might help him to redeem his lost reputation.

'Such a thing has never happened before!' Monsieur Douard, his head buried in his hands, was going back over things for the umpteenth time.

'Always I am down in the kitchen in good time for the evening's work, while Sophie gets ready to welcome the guests . . . and yet, last night . . . I do not know what came over us. One moment we were awake, I in my room, Sophie in hers, the next moment . . . poof! . . . we were out like a light. No one could awaken us. Thank heaven for Pierre.

'Pierre is my new chef de cuisine. He trained in much the same way as I did—at the same school, in fact. Mark my words, a spell with Bocuse, or perhaps the Troisgros brothers, and one day he, too, will have his own restaurant. Perhaps he will be the first to win three Stock Pots in his native Brittany. The kitchen of a restaurant is like the bridge of an ocean liner—it can, and often does, function without its captain. Nevertheless, things are not quite the same. Pierre is good, and in time he will be even better, but he has been brought up by the sea—he has it in his blood. I tell him, sometimes he is a little too fond of the salt. He is also lacking in fire. If I had been in my kitchen last night those *maquereaux* would not have got away with it as they did.'

Monsieur Pamplemousse breathed a sigh of relief. He decided to try one more test.

'Will you join me in a *marc*?'

Monsieur Douard raised his hands in mock horror. 'I have a busy day ahead of me. Later, perhaps, but if I were to start now . . .'

Things were beginning to fall into place. The absence of Madame Douard at dinner. The non-appearance of Auguste. The general air of things not being quite as they should have been. The over-salted *sauce Madère* . . . only one more item remained unexplained. No doubt Inspector Banyuls had already posed the question, but there would be no harm in asking it again.

'I still don't understand how the change round of dishes came about. It couldn't have been easy.'

Auguste Douard made a clucking noise. 'Ah, poor Felix. I fear we shall not be seeing him before tonight. He has taken to his bed. He was attacked in the pantry earlier in the afternoon by an armed assailant—disguised, would you believe, as a waiter?'

27

Monsieur Pamplemousse felt that by now he would believe almost anything.

'While the kitchen was empty,' continued Auguste dramatically, 'this same man forced him at gun point and under threat of death, to substitute a dish he had brought with him for the real one. As you know, *Poularde de Bresse en Vessie Royale* has to be ordered in advance.'

'And how many were ordered last night?'

'Five others besides your own. I supervised their preparation earlier in the day.'

Monsieur Pamplemousse fell silent. So the one which had arrived at his table had not necessarily been meant for him.

'I have a theory.' Monsieur Douard forestalled his next question. 'It is my belief that someone wishes to bring disgrace on the house of Douard. As you will understand, I have many rivals, some of whom would stick at nothing.'

'Isn't that a bit extreme?'

'Extreme?' Auguste Douard dismissed the thought. 'You have no idea of the rivalry, no idea. Especially,' he cast a sidelong glance at Monsieur Pamplemousse, 'especially when it is an open secret that La Langoustine is in the running for a third Stock Pot.

'There is big money involved. To have three Stock Pots in *Le Guide*, or three stars in Michelin, or even four toques in Gault Millau, is an open-sesame to other things; a pass-key to many doors which would otherwise remain closed. One reaches another plateau. Have you ever been in a restaurant on the day they receive news of their third Stock Pot? The telephone doesn't stop ringing. There are offers for lecture tours, television programmes, books . . . merchandising rights . . . many men would give their right arm for such opportunities, and equally many would stop at nothing to prevent others reaching that goal. As in all fields, success brings its problems. For every person who reaches the heights there are others waiting in the wings. Alors . . .'

Monsieur Pamplemousse gave him an oblique glance. Auguste Douard clearly wished to say something, but equally clearly he was unsure whether it was safe to or not.

He decided to test the water. 'You have something on your mind, Monsieur?'

Auguste took a deep breath. 'You are a man of the world, Monsieur Pamplemousse, accustomed to eating in the best restaurants, staying at the best hotels, drinking the best wines . . .

'Suppose . . . suppose, for example, you had been in the position last night of having to pass judgment on La Langoustine? A judgment that might well affect its entire future. How would you be feeling this morning in the cold light of day?'

Monsieur Pamplemousse busied himself with his coffee. So his secret was out. *Merde*! What would they say back at headquarters if they knew? It would be a black mark. Monsieur le Directeur would not be pleased.

Auguste Douard read his thoughts. 'You must understand that any man who dines regularly by himself and orders with an air of authority is an object of interest, particularly at this time of the year when all the guides are being prepared. The man from Michelin we usually recognise because he is for ever drawing little symbols in his diary and going through the menu to make sure there are no spelling mistakes—they are very meticulous, those ones. The man from Gault Millau, on the other hand, is much more concerned with his nouvelle cuisine and after he has left we find many notes torn up in the waste bucket. They are very fond of their purple prose. Those from the English guides ask "What is for breakfast?" Whereas . . .'

'Whereas?' Monsieur Pamplemousse prodded him gently.

Auguste Douard looked round carefully to make sure they were alone before replying.

'Monsieur Pamplemousse, you are an honoured and most welcome guest in our hotel. You and Pommes Frites. It has always been that way and I trust it will remain so in the future. Your reputation in the Sûreté as a man who never gave up on a case, often and sadly to his cost, has gone before you. Your taste in food and in wine is something I have observed with pleasure over the years, and your approval is a reward in itself. I ask for nothing more. In matters of cuisine I am content to be judged by what is set before you. In the end there is no other way. Your secret is safe with me.

'But I will not conceal from you the fact that last night's affair came as a great shock, not simply because of its nature, but because of its timing. As you know, we have many plans for the hotel; many commitments. We have much at stake.

'To win the approval of Michelin is a great honour; to gain a further toque in Gault Millau, that, too, would be good. But to receive a third Stock Pot in *Le Guide*—the oldest, the most respected in all France, that would mean so much I cannot possibly put it into words. I repeat, I ask no favours as far as your judgment on the food is concerned. I would not insult either you or *Le Guide* by suggesting such a thing. However, if there is some way in which you can help to solve this mystery I shall be more than grateful.'

Monsieur Pamplemousse considered the matter for a moment or two, conscious that the other was watching his every movement.

'Were what you have just said about me true,' he hedged, 'it would have been even more unfortunate if I had recommended last night's dish as a speciality. Think what that might involve in the future.' He chuckled at the thought and then immediately repented. Monsieur Douard was obviously in no mood for such frivolities.

'Rest assured, Auguste,' he placed one hand on the other's arm and allowed himself the luxury of familiarity, 'if it is within my power to help in any way during my stay here, then I shall be happy to do so. I must confess my curiosity has already been aroused. As for the other matter, if I were in a position to pass judgment then in no way would I allow what happened to influence my decision.'

He clasped the other's hand warmly in his own and then rose from the table. For some reason or other Pommes Frites had become increasingly agitated, and glancing out through the door he could see why. The young man with the artificial hands was crossing the square. He was by himself and he seemed in a hurry.

His companion—the girl—aloof as ever, was heading towards the main part of the town carrying a shopping bag. Gucci by the look of it.

'Thank you, my friend.' Auguste waved as Monsieur Pamplemousse made his way outside. 'I feel better already. A man should not enter his kitchen in a mood of despair. He should be in a state of grace. Tonight I shall prepare something very special indeed—just for you!'

But Monsieur Pamplemousse scarcely heard. His mind was already on other things. Crossing the square, he was just in time to see steel-claws, as he'd mentally christened the young man, round a corner near the P.T.T. and disappear up a side street.

Signalling Pommes Frites to heel, he waited for a moment or two and then hurried after him.

Like many towns in the region, St. Castille had been spared the outer sprawl of industrialisation. It began and ended abruptly, almost as if surrounded by an invisible moat. Once past the grey, gaunt building of the hospice which marked the boundary they were in open country.

Hardly slackening speed, the young man began the steady climb up a narrow road leading towards the plateau which lay at the foot of the hills and mountains to the east.

Once, early on, a car shot past, scattering Monsieur Pamplemousse and Pommes Frites as it took a bend ahead at high speed.

Breathing heavily as he jumped down from the boulder which had acted as a temporary refuge, Monsieur Pamplemousse shook his fist after both car and driver as they disappeared up the hill in a cloud of dust. Whoever was at the wheel might know the road, but he was no respecter of persons.

Beyond the treeline some miles ahead he could see a cluster of buildings which he guessed must be the new solar heating station, St. Castille's contribution to the march of progress. No doubt they were deriving pleasure and profit from the warmth of the day—which was more than he could say. Even Pommes Frites was beginning to flag a little and he hung back for a moment to slake his thirst noisily from a brook, babbling its way down the hill. Some bees from a nearby cluster of hives buzzed their disapproval at the intrusion and then settled down again.

Monsieur Pamplemousse mopped his brow while he waited. It was pointless indulging in any sort of cat and mouse game. Apart from a few olive trees and the odd clump of gorse, the countryside ahead offered little or no cover.

A lizard appeared as if by magic on a nearby stone, froze, and then carried on its way. Overhead a bird hovered for a moment and then it, too, went on its way.

Throwing caution to the wind, he quickened his pace as they set off again. He had no wish to turn the whole thing into a cross-country race, but if he didn't catch up by the time they reached flatter ground that was what might happen.

But the young man seemed to be displaying no interest whatsoever in his surroundings. Hands thrust deep into his pockets, just as they had been in the restaurant the night before, he went on his way—

looking neither to the right nor to the left. And yet Monsieur Pamplemousse was left with the curious feeling that not only did he know he was being followed, but he actually wanted it.

Already the terracotta rooftops of St. Castille were far below, lost in the morning heat haze. Apart from a few sheep and the solitary figure of a man with a shotgun slung over his shoulder on a rise to the right of them—doubtless a farmer trying to fill the evening cooking pot—they could have been alone in the world.

In other circumstances Monsieur Pamplemousse might have enjoyed it more. As it was he was beginning to wish himself back in Paris. The sheer scale of it all; the grandeur of the distant Alps outlined against the perfect blueness of the sky, the hum of the insects, the smell of the wildflowers, were lost on him. Head down, he found himself wondering what had ever possessed anyone to build such a road in the first place. Where on earth had they been going and for what purpose? Come to that, what was he doing there? What would his colleagues at headquarters think if they could see him now? He'd really only set off on a whim. For a second or two he toyed with the idea of turning back. It was all rather ridiculous.

Occupied as he was with these thoughts, he failed to notice his quarry had stopped until he was almost on top of him. By then it was too late to do anything about it.

'Will you please stop following me?' Steel claws sounded over-wrought. 'I know what you're going to say.'

Monsieur Pamplemousse took out a handkerchief, already wet with perspiration, and mopped his brow again while he played for time. He was momentarily at a loss for words. To be truthful he hadn't the least idea what he'd been going to say.

'You were going to ask about these, weren't you?' The young man held up both hands. They glinted in the sunshine.

'What about them?' If that was what he wanted it was as good an opening conversational gambit as any.

'I knew it! I knew it! You're all the same. Why can't you leave me alone?'

Monsieur Pamplemousse felt somewhat aggrieved. To give him his due, although the matter of the mechanical hands was not without interest, they hadn't been uppermost in his mind. He certainly wouldn't normally have been so unfeeling as to pose a direct question on the subject without being prompted.

'You don't *have* to tell me.'

'You're not going to believe me if I do. No one ever does.'

'You could try me if you wish,' said Monsieur Pamplemousse gently.

The young man sat down on a stone at the side of the road and gazed out across the valley. 'I used to work for a large catering firm,' he began at last. 'Grimaldi. You may have heard of them. Refrigerators . . . deep freezes . . . kitchen equipment . . . that sort of thing. Waste disposals . . .'

Monsieur Pamplemousse caught his breath. 'You don't mean . . .'

The young man nodded miserably. 'The trouble is I've never been very good with my hands.' He broke off. 'That's a laugh as things turned out.

'Some people are mechanically-minded, some aren't—never will be. I was demonstrating our latest model—the Mark IV industrial size with the last-for-life bearings and the optional U-train recycling attachment, when something went wrong. I should by rights have sent for a mechanic, but it could have been a big order so I tried to fix it myself and that's when it happened. I put my hand down inside and whoosh! There it was—gone!'

They fell silent as Monsieur Pamplemousse tried to picture the scene.

'It must have been a very big machine,' he ventured at last. 'I mean . . . to accommodate two.'

His companion gave a shrill laugh. 'That's what's so ridiculous. That's the bit you're really not going to believe.'

'You mean . . .' Monsieur Pamplemousse shuddered at the thought. 'You didn't do it a *second* time?'

'There was a big investigation, you see . . . afterwards. All the pezzi-grossi from Rome were there. They asked me to show them exactly what went wrong, so I put my other hand inside and . . . and . . .'

Monsieur Pamplemousse gazed at the young man. He was glad he'd been spared the second 'whoosh'. To paraphrase that great Irish writer, Oscar Wilde, losing one hand was a misfortune, losing two in the same manner was downright careless.

'You've no idea, *no idea* what it's like . . .'

Monsieur Pamplemousse shifted uneasily. He

realised he had been standing perfectly still for some minutes, hanging on the other's every word. That, combined with the long, uphill walk had brought on a certain stiffness; his shins felt quite painful. What could he say? What words could he possibly find to meet the young man on common ground? What personal misfortune could he conjure up to even begin to match the other's?

He was a kindly man at heart and as he pondered the matter an outrageous thought entered his mind; one which had he dwelt on it for any length of time he would have dismissed out of hand. As it was, almost without thinking and with the highest possible motives, he found himself giving voice to an untruth.

'Monsieur,' he said simply, 'I do not know your name, but fate seems to have thrown us together for a short while and I have to tell you that you are not alone. You do not have a monopoly on misfortune.'

The young man stared at him. 'What are you trying to tell me?'

Monsieur Pamplemousse tapped the secret compartment in his right trouser leg, the one containing his precious note-book. It gave out a hollow, wooden sound.

'Does that sound like flesh and blood to you?'

'You don't mean . . . it isn't?'

Monsieur Pamplemousse nodded. Then, having embarked on a certain course, decided that he might as well be hanged for a sheep as a lamb.

'And that is not all.'

'Not . . . both?'

Monsieur Pamplemousse nodded again. Conscious

that Pommes Frites' eyes were following his every movement, he avoided the direct lie. It was totally idiotic, but there it was. There was no going back.

'That's terrible. I'm sorry. I would never have known.' It was the young man's turn to be tongue-tied. For one moment Monsieur Pamplemousse thought he was going to cry.

'By the way, it's Giampiero.'

'Giampiero?'

'My name.' The young man thrust out his right hand for Monsieur Pamplemousse to shake and then withdrew it hastily. 'I'm sorry. I'm always doing that. I still haven't got used to it.'

For some strange reason Monsieur Pamplemousse found himself registering the fact that before his accident Giampiero must have had very long arms; almost apelike. Perhaps that was what had brought it about. Perhaps if they had been two or three inches shorter it wouldn't have happened.

'Fancy having *two* wooden legs. I don't know what to say.'

'Poof!' Monsieur Pamplemousse waved his own hand carelessly in the air. Then, as he caught sight of it, immediately felt guilty.

There was an embarrassed silence. 'That is life,' he continued. 'Don't ask me how it happened. Like you, I would really rather not talk about it. Besides, it all took place long ago. I merely wished to show that however bad things may seem, there is always someone a little worse off. No one is entirely without their private sorrows.'

He broke off. Out of the corner of his eye he could

see Pommes Frites stalking off towards a large gorse bush by the side of the road. On its own, not an unusual occurrence. What distinguished this particular occasion from previous ones was the fact that he would have sworn on oath the bush in question hadn't been there when they had first arrived. It was most odd. Perhaps he had been standing out in the sun for too long, or maybe he'd over-indulged himself with the *marc* at breakfast. Auguste was right; one should take care. Nevertheless . . . Monsieur Pamplemousse dismissed the matter from his mind, putting it down as a momentary aberration; a summing-up which would have echoed Pommes Frites' feelings almost exactly had he been able to put them into words. Such things did not happen.

Even so, as he investigated the bush Pommes Frites couldn't help feeling a certain amount of surprise that it smelled strongly of bay rum instead of gorse. Just as he was in the very act of raising his right leg his attention was caught by something else strange. The bush was beginning to rotate very slowly on its axis in a clockwise direction. Pommes Frites gazed at it in astonishment for a moment and then hurried round the back in the same clock-wise manner in order to keep up with his chosen spot. He had a wide experience of bushes in all shapes and sizes, but he couldn't remember such a thing ever happening before.

As the bush settled down again he decided to have another go, devoting all his attention this time to the job in hand, lest it began playing any more tricks. Balancing on three legs while at the same time keeping a watchful eye open for possible attackers from the rear demands a certain amount of concentration. A moment's relaxation, especially if the bush happens to be of a thorny variety, can be very painful.

Pommes Frites concentrated, and as he did so he became aware of something else that was odd. It was a large bush and it wasn't planted in the ground as were most bushes he'd come across, it was being held by someone; someone moreover who appeared to be clutching a long, shiny object in his other hand. Only an inch or two away from the end of Pommes Frites' nose there was a large expanse of blue, pin–striped suiting. He blinked several times in order to make quite sure that he was seeing aright, but the object was definitely made of some kind of material. Material, moreover, that was stretched almost to bursting point by virtue of the fact that whoever was inside it was bending over.

Never one to let an opportunity slip by, Pommes Frites gave the material an exploratory sniff.

As sniffs go it wasn't one of his best efforts. In his time he'd done many better, but the effect left absolutely nothing to be desired.

To his astonishment the object of his attentions suddenly leapt into the air and went off bang—right in his face.

Without waiting to find out the cause of this extra-ordinary occurrence, let alone complete his *renverser la vapeur*, Pommes Frites took off like a sheet of greased lightning. He was vaguely aware of shouts and cries and the sound of a car being driven off at high speed, but by the time he peered out from his hiding place all was quiet again.

Assured that whatever had caused the phenomenon had gone on its way, he emerged and noticed for the first time that although his master was more or less where he'd last seen him, he was now lying on the ground with one leg in the air. Pommes Frites decided it was obviously one of 'those mornings', and he hurried across the road in order to take a closer look and see if he could find out exactly what had happened.

Monsieur Pamplemousse could have told him. Monsieur Pamplemousse could have told him in no uncertain terms what had taken place as seen from the other side of the bush. The whole thing was indelibly imprinted on his mind. Pommes Frites' view had been from the wings as it were—a peep behind the scenes; his role that of prompter. Monsieur Pamplemousse, on the other hand, had viewed it all from stage centre and had, when he thought back over the chain of even s later that day, played t' e leading role, escaping death or at the very least being maimed for life by a matter of millimetres.

It had all happened in a flash, although at the time it seemed more like a bad dream taking place in slow motion. He'd been vaguely aware of seeing Pommes Frites amble off in the direction of the bush. He'd also felt there was something 'not quite right' when he'd seen him disappear round the back, but he'd been taken up with other matters. Then all at once the bush had taken off like a missile from its launch pad. There had been a flash of sunlight on metal, followed by a loud bang, and then something hit him in the right leg, knocking him off balance and causing him to fall to the ground.

41

Like Pommes Frites he'd also been aware of a figure running from the bush and the sound of an engine starting up, but by the time he'd recovered himself sufficiently to do anything about it the car was already almost out of sight and it was too late to catch its number.

He felt the top of his leg. The trousers were torn and peppered with small holes, but by some miracle which could only have been arranged by his own personal guardian angel—the one who had watched over him all the years he'd been in the force—the shot seemed to have been taken fairly and squarely by his note-book.

'Mamma Mia!' Giampiero returned from an abortive pursuit of the car. He seemed remarkably calm in the circumstances. More relieved than upset. 'That was a bit of luck!'

'Luck?' Monsieur Pamplemousse could hardly believe his ears.

'Well, I mean your having a wooden leg. Think what it would have been like otherwise. It could have been very nasty.'

Monsieur Pamplemousse clambered to his feet and dusted himself down. Not for the first time that morning he was finding difficulty in expressing himself.

'*Merde!*' he muttered under his breath. '*Idiot! Imbécile!*'

As he stomped off down the road he felt a pain in his leg, or rather a series of tiny pains rolled into one, rather as if someone had hit him with a wire brush. Some of the shot had obviously penetrated the skin. Who knew what vital organs they might have made contact with had they spread any further? Organs that might have required the surgeon's knife.

'There's a very good carpenter in the town,' called Giampiero. 'Madame Sophie will give you his name.'

But Monsieur Pamplemousse was already out of sight round a bend in the road and taking stock of the situation. Settling himself down behind an outcrop of rock he gazed sadly at the tattered remains of his note-book, his aide-mémoire, while Pommes Frites busied himself licking the wounds. What months of hard work, what meals they had consumed were recorded within its covers. Now it looked more like a kit of parts for a cardboard colander.

Someone, somewhere, was going to pay dearly for this. If he'd had any doubts before about the wisdom of staying on in St. Castille, they had now gone for ever.

Pommes Frites looked up from his ministrations and wagged his tail in anticipation. He knew the signs.

3

TUESDAY EVENING

Auguste Douard removed a large earthenware marmite from his oven, placed it on top of the 'piano' which ran the length of the kitchen, and gave the contents a stir with a long wooden spoon. Having tested the result to his satisfaction, he slid the pot further along towards the cooler end and then turned to Monsieur Pamplemousse.

'For you,' he said, 'I am preparing a *tian*. It is not a dish you will often find in restaurants. It belongs more to the home . . . it is a family dish. In some of the smaller villages up in the mountains it is still sent out to be cooked in the oven of the *boulanger*. It is a *gratin* of green vegetables; spinach, chard, courgettes—all finely chopped and then cooked in olive oil. After that, some rice, beans, a few cloves of garlic, some eggs to thicken and a coating of breadcrumbs and Parmesan cheese. Up here, away from the coast, we also add a little salt cod to taste or some wild asparagus when it is in season.'

He smacked his lips. 'I think you will enjoy it. It is a good, peasant dish and it will need a good, robust wine to accompany it. A Cornas from the Rhône valley would go well. I have a friend there who has land on the steepest part of the slopes. It is sheltered from the

Mistral and he makes wines of great power. He always keeps a little to one side for me. It needs to be ten years old at least.

'Afterwards, perhaps a Banon or a Bleu d'Auvergne. It is a good time of the year for it. The milk is from herds high up in the mountains and we know a very special farm where it is made. Unpasteurised . . . the best!'

Monsieur Pamplemousse found himself envying Auguste his circle of friends. It was really partly what it was all about: knowing the right places to buy. He glanced around the kitchen. He never ceased to be surprised by the quietness of it all. Far removed from the popular image, where it was all shouting and noise. In most big kitchens he'd been lucky enough to enter, only the chef himself had a right to speak and when he did everyone jumped to it.

He wondered idly if Monsieur Douard's choice of a dish which had to be cooked in a stockpot was intentional, a hint. Then he dismissed the thought as being uncharitable. Auguste Douard was one of nature's gentlemen; he would not be so devious. His next words confirmed the thought.

'My poor friend. All these years and until today I had no idea. From your walk no one would ever have guessed. Although I have to admit that now I do know I detect a slight limp.'

Once again Monsieur Pamplemousse found himself regretting the story he'd concocted on the spur of the moment. He'd done it with the best of intentions, but throwing out a crumb of comfort for Giampiero was one thing—deceiving others who trusted him was something else again. The only consolation was that the limp Auguste detected was very real. His leg was still smarting from the attentions of the local chemist.

But Auguste already had other things on his mind. Sensing that Monsieur Pamplemousse did not wish to discuss the matter he changed the subject rapidly.

'Oh, what a day it has been!' He ran his eye briefly over the clipboard to which the first of the evening's orders had already been attached, then briefly gave out a few orders with hardly a change of voice. 'First the examining magistrate poking about here, there and everywhere—trying to sound important, then Inspector Banyuls. And they all expect their little *pourboire*. As if they were doing *me* a service! How would they like it if I went into their offices and helped myself to the stationery? Just because I happen to run a restaurant they feel everything should be on the house. Honesty has strange boundaries, even with the law itself.

'Now they have decided to leave someone permanently on guard in case there is another incident. What a way to greet one's guests—an armed policeman in the hall!

'I sometimes think only a fool would go into this business. A fool, or someone who is born with eyes in the back of his head.' With a wave of his hand he embraced the whole of the kitchen. 'They are all good people—the best; but at the end of the day it is not their head which is on the chopping block, it is mine. Each and every day—twice a day—my work is offered up for examination and discussion and analysis. Unless I watch their every move and check this, taste that, add a little here, take away a little there, there will be a sauce which is too thick, or a steak which is overdone, or vegetables that have not been properly cleaned. How can I be expected to watch out for criminals in the pantry as well?'

Monsieur Pamplemousse excused himself. More orders were starting to arrive; the pace was quickening. It was no place to linger.

Pommes Frites was waiting for him in the hall, keeping a watchful eye on the gendarme. Pommes Frites and gendarmes didn't always see eye to eye. Together they made their way into the dining room where Felix was waiting to usher them to their table.

'A bad business, Monsieur. You are happy? You would not like to sit elsewhere?'

'Very happy, thank you.' He wasn't going to give up his table for anyone. Apart from anything else he welcomed the opportunity to take stock of the restaurant again.

It was less full than usual. News had obviously travelled fast. No doubt there were many who had been put off, at least for the time being. They would be back—it would be their loss if they didn't return. There would probably be fewer orders for the *Poularde en Vessie*. If Monsieur Douard had not prepared the *tian* he might have been tempted to order one out of sheer bravado.

One or two of the diners nudged each other as he sat down. Some stared quite openly. He noted that Giampiero was already seated with his girl friend, if that was what she was—he must check to see if she was wearing a ring—but there was no hint of recognition.

47

He mentally shrugged his shoulders. If that was the way they wanted it, then so be it. They must have started their meal early, for they were already on the cheese course.

Felix came between him and his line of vision, flicked open a serviette, and with rather more ostentation than usual held it out for Monsieur Pamplemousse to take.

Once again he appeared to be behaving rather oddly. It crossed Monsieur Pamplemousse's mind to wonder if he was in for a repeat performance of the previous night's occurrence, but he dismissed it at once. Auguste was on duty in the kitchen. Besides, he'd seen him plunge the spoon deep into the *tian* with his own eyes. If there had been anything untoward inside it would undoubtedly have been revealed. All the same, he had to admit the thought was not a pleasant one.

What on earth was the man doing? Either give him the serviette or not. Each time he reached for it Felix danced away like a matador who has seen better days.

'A note, Monsieur Pamplemousse,' hissed Felix.

Monsieur Pamplemousse gave a start. Sure enough, partly concealed within the folds of the white serviette, and held in place by Felix's thumb, was a piece of lined paper.

'It is from the gentleman in the corner. The one with whom there was the unpleasantness last night. It is a matter of the utmost discretion.'

Monsieur Pamplemousse nodded. 'Leave it on the table. I will look at it in a moment.'

But he needn't have worried. There was no question of either Giampiero or his companion taking the slightest bit of notice. They were much too busy talking.

Monsieur Pamplemousse reached for the wine list and under the pretence of studying it unfolded the paper. The note was short and to the point. It said, quite simply, in large anonymous letters: MUST SEE YOU. CAN'T WAIT. SUGGEST RENDEZ-VOUS.'

He thought for a moment and then, entering into the spirit of the game, took out his pen and added a suitable reply in like hand. The only rendez-vous he could think of without going into great complications was his own room later that night.

He signalled to Felix. 'Tell the sommelier I will have a bottle of the Cornas,' he said in a loud voice.

'See that the note is returned,' he added quietly. 'It is inside the wine list; near the front—in the champagne section.'

'A wise choice, Monsieur, if I may say so. It will go well with your meal.' Felix gave his approval with scarcely a change of expression as he took the wine list. 'I will leave it for him in reception.'

Shortly afterwards he disappeared out of the dining room. He wasn't a moment too soon, for no sooner had he returned than the couple rose from their seats.

As they passed by his table Giampiero's eyes flickered for a fraction of a second. Monsieur Pamplemousse gave an answering signal that all was well and then they were gone.

By leaning forward he was able to follow their progress. He breathed a sigh of relief as he watched Giampiero make his own way across the hall and take both a key and the note from a pigeon-hole to one side of the reception desk.

There was a moment's anxiety when the girl, showing signs of impatience, paused on the stairs and said something to him, but Giampiero had everything under control. One second the note was in his hand, the next it had gone. It was like a conjuring trick.

As they disappeared together up the main stairs Monsieur Pamplemousse turned his attention to a plate which had just arrived on his table. It bore a large slice of *Pâté de Canard*, made as only Auguste could make it, with white Bresse duck, white fillet of pork and foie gras.

The wine was all he'd been led to expect. It was dark. It must have been almost black when it was first made. It tasted of the hard work that had gone into it and it augured well for the *tian* to come. Monsieur Pamplemousse winced as he jotted down a few notes before his main course arrived. He wished he'd thought to apply a little padding beneath his freshly repaired trousers. The ladies in the *nettoyage* had been most intrigued and he'd had to concoct yet another story.

He gave the wine a gentle swirl in the glass to open it out a little more. It was good that Auguste had chosen a simple dish in response to his request for something out of the ordinary. It was a point in his favour. All too often restaurants with two Stock Pots were guilty of over-embellishment; of too great an addiction to the cream jug with their sauces. They had grown up in an age when rich sauces were part and parcel of *haute cuisine,* and in many cases they were so steeped in tradition they would probably never change their ways. It was the younger generation of chefs who had tried to break away from tradition. More and more they were laying claim to a third Stock Pot—and deservedly so. Without succumbing to the worst excesses of *nouvelle cuisine*, where colour and presentation often took precedence over all else, many had returned to the recipes of their forefathers and a simplicity which was wholly admirable in a land which was rich in meat and fish and fresh vegetables. It was a move which won his wholehearted approval and the *tian* in front of him was a blissful example.

Monsieur Pamplemousse looked forward to observing Pommes Frites' views on the matter, although if the lip-smacking going on under the table was anything to go by, the result was a foregone conclusion.

Waving aside the offer of a second helping, he issued instructions for a portion to be kept warm until they retired; an unnecessary request since Pommes Frites' reactions were much sought after and appreciated everywhere they went. A clean plate and a satisfied licking of the whiskers were accolades in themselves.

His cheese over and done with, Monsieur Pamplemousse decided against a coffee and opted instead for a *tisane verveine* in his room. To be truthful he had eaten more than enough, and a couple of involuntary sneezes came as a warning sign that his liver needed something more than the Vichy water to keep it in good working order.

A turn round the square with Pommes Frites was indicated. Apart from anything else there was work to be done and he needed to marshal his thoughts. The attack earlier in the day had been worrying to say the least; the more so as he still wasn't sure who had been the prime target—himself or Giampiero. Although the latter had brushed it aside at the time, there was something in his manner which didn't ring quite true. It crossed his mind that Giampiero might even have wanted to be followed that morning.

As they left the hotel he took a look around. It was already dark. A few people were taking their coffee on the hotel terrace. On the other side of the square the sound of laughter came from the Café du Centre. Somewhere a radio blared forth and then just as quickly cut out again. It was replaced by a rasping sound. Metal against metal. That, too, stopped again as suddenly as it had begun. Monsieur Pamplemousse was too old a hand to feel nervous, but there was a noticeable quickening of his step as he set off, carefully avoiding the shadowy areas of the little streets leading from either side of the Hôtel de Ville.

His feelings were obviously shared by Pommes Frites. After his nasty experience with the bush he directed his activities very pointedly at man-made objects, such as the fountain in the middle of the square. Pommes Frites was definitely off nature for the time being. After his nasty experience that morning even the plane trees surrounding the *boules* area were objects of suspicion. You knew where you were with stone. Stone stayed where it had been put.

His inspection and the call of nature complete, Pommes Frites took a last sniff and then led the way very firmly round the back of the hotel towards the kitchens. He felt hungry and supper was long overdue. Unlike some people, he only had two meals a day— give or take a snack or two in between.

Monsieur Pamplemousse undid the boot of his 2CV,

removed a small canvas bag and metal cylinder, and connected the two together with a length of flexible tubing. He turned a knob on the cylinder, there was a hiss of escaping air, and seconds later a miniature house began to take shape, emerging from its container like a butterfly shedding its cocoon.

A deft tug at a zip fastener holding the front door in place, the spreading of a blanket on the floor, and the kennel was complete and ready for occupation.

As if on cue, a waiter emerged from the back of the hotel carrying a bowl containing the remains of the *tian* and another full of water. Soon Pommes Frites was busy with his supper.

Monsieur Pamplemousse knew better than to interrupt. From the expression on his face it was clear that Auguste's choice met with Pommes Frites' approval, and after a brief good-night pat on the head, he left him to it and turned back inside.

Pommes Frites' kennel was a great boon. The invention of a rubber specialist in Paris, who normally devoted his talents to more esoteric items, it made travelling around France much less of a problem than it might have been. Not all hotels welcomed dogs, and some charged accordingly. It also saved the embarrassment of having Pommes Frites suffer the indignity of being 'relegated' to the back of the car, as had sometimes happened in the early days. There were some things in life that were hard to explain to a dog. There was also the fact that after a heavy meal Pommes Frites was apt to snore rather loudly and, much as he loved him, sharing a room was not always the happiest of arrangements.

Closing the door behind him, Monsieur Pamplemousse made his way to the reception desk in order to collect his room key and to see if there was any mail.

Drawing a blank as far as mail was concerned, he picked up his key from the receptionist, confirmed his order for the *tisane* and turned to go upstairs, treading warily round some buckets and other paraphernalia left by the builders who were doing things to the downstairs facilities.

As he did so he became aware of some sort of activity going on in the little room which served as an office for Madame Sophie Douard.

Under the pretence of getting himself entangled with the handle of a bucket, Monsieur Pamplemousse gazed at Madame Douard in astonishment. Hidden from the watchful eye of the receptionist, she was standing just inside the doorway to her room and behaving in the most extraordinary manner. Both hands behind her neck, rather as if she was searching for something she had dropped down the back of her dress, she was rolling her eyes and running her tongue round her lips as if in the throes of some kind of a fit. For a moment he was irresistibly reminded of the seduction scene from a very bad film, then just as quickly he dismissed the thought. It was unthinkable.

He had never given the slightest cause for such behaviour.

Madame Sophie was probably having trouble with her zip fastener—either that or she'd had a bad attack of hiccups and had been trying to cure it by means of a cold key down her back. He was about to offer to go to her assistance when there was the sound of voices heading their way. Almost immediately Madame Douard sprang into action. Removing her hands from behind her neck, she straightened her dress and pushed the door shut with one swift movement.

By that time Monsieur Pamplemousse's problems with the bucket had become very real. All the same, in the brief moment between first hearing the voices and the slamming of the door, he could have sworn she'd winked at him. Moreover, it had been no ordinary wink, confined merely to the closing of one eye. It had been a full-blooded, no-holds-barred, voluptuous, uninhibited wink of a kind he'd only previously encountered during his days on the beat in some of the seamier areas of the Paris underworld, when invitations to stray from the straight and narrow had been many and varied.

And yet, even that was not a true analogy, for there had also been a certain childlike innocence about the whole thing which had totally removed all trace of lewdness.

'Are you all right, Monsieur?' He suddenly realised the waiter with the *tisane* was standing behind him.

Reflecting that there was nothing in the world so strange as people, Monsieur Pamplemousse led the way upstairs. His note-book was waiting for him. Before dinner he had begun the painstaking task of carrying out some running repairs and he was anxious to complete them before the night was out.

Thanking the waiter, he lifted the tiny pot from its charcoal burner and poured himself a cup, savouring the sweet smell as he did so.

The more he examined his note-book the more he

realised how lucky he was to have escaped so lightly. The pages looked as if they had been ravaged by some wood-boring beetle. He shuddered to think of the agony he would have had to endure had those same holes been in his leg. The few pieces of shot that had by-passed the leather cover of the book had only been peripheral, but had he caught the full blast . . . it didn't bear thinking about.

He became so absorbed in his task he soon forgot not only Madame Douard's strange antics but his appointment with Giampiero.

It wasn't until a sharp, metallic knock on the door brought him down to earth that he remembered it.

'One moment.' He hastily hid the pages under the bedcover. It wouldn't do for them to be seen.

But he needn't have worried. Giampiero hardly glanced at the bed as he entered the room. After a brief exchange of greetings he crossed to the balcony and looked outside for a moment. The moon was already high and as he stood silhouetted against the sky Monsieur Pamplemousse suddenly realised where he'd seen his face before. Or rather, to be more exact, where he'd seen a reasonable facsimile. It had been on his plate the previous evening. There was the same curly hair, the same Italian features.

As if reading his thoughts, Giampiero turned back into the room.

'You realise, of course, that it is me they are after, not you?'

'They?'

Giampiero gave a gesture of impatience. 'They . . . him . . . it . . . what does it matter? Had Eva and I been sitting where you sat last night you would have been spared the experience. I've been thinking about it all day. That man in the bushes this morning. Had it not been for your dog, who knows where the blast would have landed?' He glanced down at Monsieur Pamplemousse's legs. 'You are all right?'

'A mere flesh wound. It is nothing.'

'More like a bark wound, I should have thought.' Giampiero laughed. It struck Monsieur Pamplemousse that he sounded slightly drunk. Either that or he was nervous about something. He chose to ignore the remark, which he thought was slightly lacking in taste anyway.

'But why should they . . . he . . . it . . . be after you?'

Giampiero shrugged. 'The money, I suppose.'

'Money?'

'The only good thing about my accident . . . the insurance . . . a record sum. It took a long time, mind. At first there was a great deal of discussion. It was bad enough after the first accident, but later, when I had the second, there were all kinds of legal arguments. They even tried to say I only did it for the sake of the insurance.' He gave a shrill laugh. 'They should try putting themselves in my place. Fortunately I had a sympathetic judge. Now I am waiting for the note.'

'The note?' Monsieur Pamplemousse began to feel the conversation was getting a little one-sided. 'What note?'

'Don't you see? These things that have happened. They are all warnings. I have thought about it. The plastic head last night . . . the shooting this morning.

57

If they had really wanted to kill they would have used something more powerful than a shotgun.

'Next, there will be a note saying, "Pay up, or else . . ." If you want my advice you will leave as soon as possible.'

'I'm afraid that is not possible,' said Monsieur Pamplemousse firmly. 'Anyway, if it is you they are after I see no point.'

'All right, but don't say I didn't warn you.' Giampiero made as if to run a hand through his hair and then stopped just in time. 'I suppose I shall get used to it one day. I don't know what I would do without Eva. She has been marvellous. Despite everything, she married me. It is no life for a young girl.'

'You were engaged when it happened?'

'No . . . we didn't even know each other. We met by accident some while later.' Giampiero gave a wry smile. 'One of my better accidents as things turned out. But just lately . . . things have been different. We are always on the move. I can't seem to settle. I find myself skulking in corners . . . wanting to be alone. Sometimes I feel I would like to end it all . . .'

'You mustn't think such things.' Monsieur Pamplemousse broke in as he felt a wave of sympathy come over him. Really, it was almost like father and son. He wished he could reach out and embrace Giampiero. 'What has happened must make life very difficult, but not impossible. Think of Renoir . . . in his old age his hands were so gripped by rheumatics he had to have his brush tied to them in order to work . . . but such work. Take Van Gogh,' he continued, warming to his theme. 'He lost an ear, but he still carried on.'

Giampiero shot him a strange look. 'What difference did losing an ear make?'

'Well, it couldn't have been easy.' Monsieur Pamplemousse felt a trifle hurt.

'I know. You are right.' Giampiero went out on to the balcony again and gazed across the valley. 'We share the same view, you and I. Our room is a little further along. Eva noticed it last night. We saw you just before you went to bed. Every evening we stand on our own balcony and every evening I think, despite everything, it is good to be alive.' There was a metallic clunk as Giampiero suddenly leaned forward and gripped the railings. 'If I were to paint, that is . . .'

Monsieur Pamplemousse opened his mouth to interrupt. His mind was suddenly full of questions, but for the time being at least they were destined to remain unasked. Instead, he found himself staring at the spot where a moment before Giampiero had been standing.

He rushed to the balcony as the night air was rent by a loud howl; a howl which was a mixture of surprise, terror and almost total disbelief. Peering gingerly through the gap where a section of the rail had once been he saw Giampiero clambering unsteadily to his feet some ten or twelve feet below. He looked shaken but otherwise unharmed.

Beside him, Pommes Frites, obviously in a state of considerable shock, gazed unhappily at the remains of his kennel as, to the accompaniment of a long drawn-out sigh of escaping air, it sank slowly to the ground beneath the weight of the section of railing. From the look of things Pommes Frites had been even luckier to escape injury than Giampiero.

Monsieur Pamplemousse bent down and examined the balcony rail. Accident-prone though Giampiero undoubtedly was, and powerful though his mechanical hands must be, it was inconceivable that they could have cut through several centimetres of metal. A quick glance confirmed his suspicions. On either side of the gap, plainly visible in the light from his room, were two fresh saw-cuts, and on the stonework below there were traces of metal filings. As he stood up he felt rather than saw a movement from a balcony further along. But when he looked there was nothing to be seen. He looked over the edge of his own balcony again. The kitchens were in darkness, as was the rest of the hotel. Pommes Frites, having given voice to his feelings on the matter, was busy licking his wounds. Giampiero was looking up.

'Wait there,' he called, somewhat unnecessarily in the circumstances. Neither Pommes Frites nor Giampiero looked as if they had any immediate plans to go anywhere. 'I will be right down.'

As he made his way along the corridor leading to the back stairs Monsieur Pamplemousse noticed a chink of light coming from beneath a door at the far end where the Douards had their quarters. Otherwise there was no sign of life. No voices. No doors opening to see what had happened.

Incredibly, apart from the breaking of the metal and Pommes Frites' howl, the whole episode had taken place in almost complete silence. Miraculously, the kennel must have broken Giampiero's fall, otherwise it would undoubtedly have been far worse. Perhaps he had a lucky streak after all.

It was a shame about Pommes Frites' kennel. If the worst came to the worst he would have to come up-stairs and spend the night under the bed. Not an ideal solution—especially after the *tian*. Auguste hadn't stinted himself with the beans.

As he turned to go down the stairs, Monsieur Pamplemousse glanced at the light again. He wondered if he should have knocked on the door in case he needed help, then decided against it. There would be tedious explanations.

It was a decision which, had he but known it, spared him yet another shock—at least for the time being. The light, as it happened, came from beneath the door to Madame Sophie's apartment, and despite the lateness of the hour, Madame Sophie was very definitely at home to callers. Not to put too fine a point on it, had Monsieur Pamplemousse entered her room at that moment the chances of him making the ground floor before daybreak would have been very remote indeed. As it was he went on his way, blissfully unaware of his narrow escape.

Freshly bathed and powdered, Madame Sophie stood in the centre of her boudoir, contemplating her reflection in a massive carved giltwood framed mirror with an air of satisfaction.

True, there were a few odd wrinkles here and there, a line or two etched in beneath her chin, but on the whole nature and the passing of the years had been more than kind to her.

In the warm glow from the pink-shaded lamps which dotted the room, with its thick carpeting, its Louis Quatorze furnishings, its chintz curtainings, its silk

61

hangings, and its massive four-poster bed, Madame Sophie bore a striking resemblance to her distant relative in the square outside. But there the likeness ended, for Hortense was made of stone; cold, hard and unyielding stone, and there was nothing cold, hard or unyielding about Madame Sophie at that particular moment.

As she reached forward to open a drawer in her tulipwood *table de toilette*, her flesh vibrated like a pink blancmange. Allowing a moment or two for it to settle down again, she removed the golden head of Queen Alexandra from one of a pair of Stanley Hall of London silver perfume jars—a present from a past admirer, an English visitor whose stay at La Langoustine had been enriched by an unexpected bonus over and above those already mentioned in his travel brochure, one for which even Monsieur Michelin would have been hard put to find a suitable symbol. Adding a touch of scent here, another two or three there, Madame Sophie began putting the finishing touches to her toilette in places which might have made the figure depicted on the other half of the set raise one if not both of his royal eyebrows.

Her fumigations complete, she addressed herself to an array of undergarments laid out on her bed, chose a black, silk *porte-jarretelles* and then, with a total disregard for the film of powder which every movement of her ample buttocks distributed around her, seated herself on a Falconnet giltwood canapé and proceeded to draw on a pair of black silk stockings with an air of loving care given only to those for whom work is also a pleasure and a joy.

For a moment or two she considered the possibility of donning a matching pair of hand-embroidered knickers, then tossed them to one side as being an unnecessary gilding of the lily. If all went well she would only have to take them off again and she would need all her energy.

Crossing to her dressing table, Madame Sophie pulled open another drawer and took out a small package purchased that very evening from the local *bricolage*. After first making sure it was folded inside out, she slipped it beneath the top of the *jarretelles* and stood for a moment running her hand sensuously up and down the polished surface of a carved mahogany standard lamp, savouring its every curve. A deep sigh escaped her lips. Already she could feel the blood coursing through her veins; blood that had been still for far too long, several weeks in fact.

For what seemed like the hundredth time that evening, she picked up the note she had found lying on the floor outside her office where it had fallen and ran her eyes over the words—even though she knew them off by heart. 'MUST SEE YOU. CAN'T WAIT. SUGGEST RENDEZ-VOUS. MY ROOM WHEN COAST CLEAR. P.'

The writer had obviously been hard put to contain his excitement as he penned the billet doux, for towards the end the writing began to change. Letters that had started off firm and bold became almost spidery as the hand trembled.

There was only one 'P' staying at the hotel. The 'P' who, on retiring to bed that evening had ordered a *tisane verveine*, which, as everyone knew, was noted for its aphrodisiacal effects. Who would have thought it? Still waters ran deep. All the times he had stayed at the hotel and never a word; hardly a glance even. That same 'P' who had become so over-excited earlier that evening he'd stepped in a bucket of whitewash.

Ignoring the incongruity of white upon black, Madame Sophie slipped into an embroidered silk nightdress, ran her tongue over lips already moist with anticipation and headed for the door.

If Mohammed was too shy to come to the mountain, the mountain certainly had no inhibitions whatsoever about visiting Mohammed. She had never been to bed with a wooden-legs before. It was an opportunity too good to be missed.

A moment later, like a galleon in full sail, she set off down the corridor carrying all before her with an air of regal splendour which would not have disgraced Madame de Pompadour herself.

4

TUESDAY NIGHT

Pommes Frites stirred uneasily in his sleep as a creaking in the corridor outside Monsieur Pamplemousse's room entered his subconscious and nudged him into wakefulness.

One way and another he hadn't been enjoying a very good night. When the bombshell in the shape of Giampiero landed on top of him he'd been in the middle of a particularly good dream—all about an inexhaustible supply of bones he'd discovered in a cave in the Dordogne. To have it broken into before he'd had a chance to take so much as one bite let alone hide any away for future use was bad enough, but then to see his kennel, his pride and joy, collapse before his very eyes—that was the end.

He'd tried giving the nozzle at the back a few hopeful chews, as he'd seen his master do on the odd occasion when the supply of compressed air had given out, but blowing into it was quite beyond his powers and in the end he'd given it up as a bad job, resigning himself to having to spend the rest of the night indoors.

Pommes Frites wasn't too keen on sleeping indoors during the summer months. The winter was a different matter entirely. During the winter it was nice being able to snuggle up in a warm bedroom close to the radiator. But there was nothing to equal waking early on a summer's morning and enjoying the freedom of a pre-breakfast stroll before anyone else was around. He would also miss the little titbits Monsieur Douard invariably brought him before he left for the market. The morsel of *Boeuf en Croûte* that morning had been especially nice; he almost preferred it cold. It had been one of the few good things about a day that had got steadily worse as it progressed.

Apart from that, rooms were inclined to be stuffy; you couldn't go to sleep with your head sticking out of the door as you could in a kennel. They were even more stuffy when you were expected to sleep under the bed; especially, it had to be said, when the bed belonged to someone like his master. Monsieur Pamplemousse didn't let little things like other people falling from balconies disturb his routine and he'd fallen asleep almost as soon as his head had touched the pillow. And once asleep, Monsieur Pamplemousse was inclined to snore. Tonight was no exception.

Then there was the question of the pain across his middle. Pommes Frites wasn't sure whether it had to do with Giampiero landing on top of his kennel, or whether it was something he'd eaten. It might have been the *tian*. There had been rather a lot of that. Or it could have been the soufflé dish he'd been given to lick clean. Whoever ordered the soufflé obviously had eyes that were bigger than their stomach. There had been a lot left over. It was unlikely to have been the pâté—rich though that had been. Nor the *Carré d'Agneau* he'd had for lunch—he could have eaten two lots of that and then come back for more if his master hadn't got there first. As for breakfast—that was much too long ago, and anyway breakfast didn't really count as a meal.

That was another thing about being outside. When you were outside and not feeling very well there were usually blades of grass to eat. Pommes Frites was a great believer in blades of grass as an antidote to all ills. Not that there was much in the way of green grass in St. Castille at that time of the year, but it was better than nothing.

He pricked up his ears again. He could definitely hear creaks in the corridor; creaks and heavy breathing. They seemed to be coming from right outside the door. By now he was thoroughly awake.

Normally Pommes Frites would have been on his feet and investigating the matter in a brace of shakes, but he suddenly realised that he was quite literally pinned to the floor. The pain in his stomach came not from its having been landed on earlier in the night, nor from an over-indulgence of the good things in life during the day. It came about because there was a large bulge in the mattress above him; a bulge in the shape of his master.

Wriggling was possible, if slightly painful; bounds were definitely out of the question.

Pommes Frites closed his eyes again and hoped that the noises, whatever they were, would go away. But he was doomed to disappointment.

A faint click from the direction of the door heralded a welcome draught of fresh air. It was followed almost immediately by another click and as the door closed there came a strong smell of talcum powder and he heard the sound of breathing again, closer this time and much heavier, then a soft rustle of silk as something white and filmy landed on the floor beside him.

Pommes Frites blinked at the object in astonishment, but before he had time to work out what was going on let alone do anything about it, the breath was suddenly knocked clean out of him for the second time that night as a heavy weight landed on top of the bed.

But if Pommes Frites was taken by surprise, Monsieur Pamplemousse was positively devastated. Unlike Pommes Frites, he was unable to claim that he'd been in the middle of a particularly pleasant dream; rather the reverse. He'd fallen asleep with a confusion of thoughts in his mind; thoughts which eventually began to form themselves into a small cloud on the horizon. A cloud which then turned and began to head in his direction, growing inexorably larger and all-enveloping with every passing second. Seconds, which at the time seemed like hours, but which he realised afterwards were all contained within the brief period between sleep and waking.

All he was aware of was a dreadful feeling of trying desperately to raise his leaden arms to ward off the cloud and being unable to move them. As he forced open his eyes, heavy with sleep, he realised to his horror that somewhere along the line the dream had turned into reality and that the amorphous mass on top of him had taken on human shape. A shape which was at once warm, voluptuous and all-embracing. A shape whose lips were showering him with endearments as they sought his own. Moist, sensuous, urgent lips, belonging to a body which seemed to possess more than its fair share of hands; hands which caressed and searched and stroked and squeezed.

Taking advantage of a momentary lull in the proceedings as his assailant raised herself and drew breath for an instant, Monsieur Pamplemousse managed to free one arm. Reaching out in desperation to the table beside his bed, he grasped the first thing that came to hand—a heavy, carved wooden candlestick.

No one would be able to say he'd gone down without a struggle.

But the moment of respite was short-lived. Before he had time to transfer his grip from the base to the top in order to make better use of it as a weapon, he felt himself being embraced yet again. Limbs stretched out, pinning both his arm and the candlestick between them.

Monsieur Pamplemousse steeled himself for a second assault, racking his brains as he did so for an explanation as to who his assailant might be and what possible circumstances could have triggered off such a bizarre event.

But the assault never came. True, the moans and groans and the intermittent cries of ecstasy continued unabated, but they had taken on a more regular pattern. He realised with a start that the pleasure being enjoyed by his intruder was not of his making, nor indeed was it of a kind that in his wildest and most boastful dreams could he possibly have emulated. Lying there, gathering his senses, Monsieur Pamplemousse had to admit to a faint feeling of regret that he was unable to share in the obviously all-pervading delight being enjoyed by his companion. For one wild moment he contemplated a little sleight of hand; a substitution of instruments. Then he dismissed the idea. In his present state of shock he would never get away with it. Far better to lie back and let matters take their course.

At last the movement ceased and with a long drawn-out gasp his visitor collapsed panting by his side.

'*Chéri.*' The whispering voice on the pillow beside him brought him to his senses with a bump. He suddenly realised where he'd heard it before.

'Never . . . never, never, never have I experienced such a moment. Such . . . love . . . such . . . manhood. I didn't realise it could be possible. If only I had known before. When I got your note . . .'

Monsieur Pamplemousse's mind raced ahead of the words. Note? What note? He had sent no note.

As the arms entwining him relaxed he took advantage of the moment and shifted his position.

Madame Douard appeared to be searching for something. Whatever it was she seemed to have found it, for she relaxed again. 'My little wooden legs . . .' her voice took on a girlish note as she turned to him again. 'Let me caress them in my own special way . . .'

Any doubts Monsieur Pamplemousse might have had as to what was going to happen next were resolved as a searing pain suddenly shot up his leg.

Merde upon *merde*! It could not be true. It was not possible. The pain hit him again. This time a little higher up. It *was* true! Madame Douard was sand-papering his right leg! By the feel of it the paper was *très gros* quality at the very least.

Summoning all his strength, he gave a tremendous heave and leapt out of the bed, crossing to the door in a single bound, determined at any costs to escape the clutches of this daughter of the Borgias.

Once outside he hurried down the corridor as fast as his legs would carry him. Mindful of the fact that Madame Douard's knowledge of the hotel was infinitely greater than his, he took the stairs leading down into the hall two at a time and headed towards the toilets. Surely, inflamed with passion though she was, Madame Douard couldn't possibly follow him into the *Hommes*.

Rounding a corner, he narrowly missed the pile of builders' material and paused in order to peer up at the doors, trying to decipher in the dim glow of the emergency night lighting which was which. It was a long time since he'd used them.

As part of its modernisation, La Langoustine's public toilets were undergoing extensive changes. A feature which obviously gave Monsieur Douard particular pride when he'd been describing it over breakfast was the installation of a system of automatic flushing in the *Hommes*, operated by means of an electric beam. All very well, but in the circumstances he wished they'd devoted a little more of the money to buying some proper symbols for the doors. In the half-light it was hard to tell whether he was looking at a man wearing an extra long jacket or a girl in a very short dress.

He was about to give up and take a chance when he noticed a relic of earlier times which had yet to be removed; some carved wooden letters high up on the door which spelled out the word 'ADA'. By process of elimination, the second door along had to be the one he wanted. A moment later he was safely inside.

As the door closed behind him he looked around and saw facing him a long shelf, surmounted by a mirror, running the length of one wall, and below it a row of hand-basins and stools.

Gazing at his reflection in the mirror, Monsieur Pamplemousse realised several things in quick succession. First of all, in his haste he had come away without his pyjamas. Not that there would have been either the time or the opportunity for such niceties. The weather was warm and they were still in his suitcase. Second, also reflected in the mirror, was a long line of cubicles, but nowhere was there any sign of the urinals Auguste had described so graphically that morning.

His heart sank. He was in the *Dames* after all. *Merde*!

The appositeness of the expression suddenly struck him. At any other time it might have brought a smile to his lips, but he froze as he heard the sound of footsteps approaching. High heels on stone flooring. On the principle of any port in a storm he made a dive for the nearest cubicle. Pushing the door shut behind him he collapsed on to the seat and held his breath. He wondered whether or not to risk drawing the bolt and then decided to play it by ear and await developments.

The outside door opened and swung gently to again. He caught a faint whiff of perfume. The smell was expensive, discreet, subtle. Whoever it belonged to it certainly wasn't Madame Sophie; he would remember hers for a long time to come. The wearer was obviously looking for something. He heard a murmur of impatience as a cupboard door was opened and then closed again. He felt his heart miss a beat as the footsteps came in his direction and paused, then he relaxed again as they entered the next cubicle along.

He waited gloomily for further developments. It was the Follies all over again. No one would believe him a second time if he said he'd gone through the wrong door by mistake. He would be branded as a Peeping Tom for ever. He could almost see the headlines. NUDE INTRUDER STRIKES AGAIN!

He pricked up his ears. Whatever else was happening in the next cubicle he was sufficiently a man of the world to realise that it didn't point to the occupant having been taken short.

There was a heavy clunk which sounded like someone removing the top from the cistern. A moment later there was a splash followed by an even heavier clunk as the top was replaced. After a moment's pause there came the sound of rushing water as the toilet was flushed.

After what seemed like an interminable wait while the cistern refilled the cubicle door opened again. There was a rustle from the paper-towel dispenser, the sound of a wastebin lid being lifted, a faint squeak from the outer door, then the clip clop of feet as whoever it was disappeared again as swiftly as she had come.

Monsieur Pamplemousse waited for a moment or two, counting his lucky stars that he had remained undiscovered, then gingerly pushed open his cubicle door. Something very odd was going on and he was determined to get to the bottom of it.

Mindful of his narrow escape, he decided to make sure the coast was clear before going any further. It wouldn't do for whoever had been in there to return and catch him red-handed.

Opening the door to the corridor he stuck his head through the gap and peered out. All was quiet.

He was about to withdraw inside again when he felt rather than saw a pair of eyes boring into him. Focusing his gaze on the far side of the entrance hall he became aware of a faint glow from a lighted cigarette, and below it, merging into the darkness of a deep armchair, a figure in uniform.

'*Bonne nuit!*' Much to his annoyance, Monsieur Pamplemousse realised his voice was a shade higher than he'd intended. He cleared his throat and pointed up to the sign. 'I seem to have made a mistake. It is not easy in the dark.'

The figure in the armchair didn't move. There was a sucking noise, almost like a sigh, and the cigarette momentarily glowed brighter. From its light Monsieur Pamplemousse made out the by now familiar figure of the gendarme. He stifled his annoyance. He'd totally forgotten about the gendarme.

Summoning all his dignity, he emerged from the toilet and headed back towards the stairs, conscious as he did so of a pair of eyes watching his every movement.

As he reached the first floor landing he quickened his pace. The possibility of meeting anyone else at that time of night was slight, all the same . . . he paused outside his door and listened. Suppose Madame Sophie was still there, awaiting him with open arms? *Mon Dieu!* What a night!

Bending down, he applied his eye to the keyhole

and then realised that it was a waste of time. The light was still off. As he stood up he caught a glimpse of a uniformed figure at the top of the stairs. It ducked out of sight, leaving behind a trail of cigarette smoke.

Taking the bull by the horns, he flung open the door and marched deliberately into his room, reaching for the light switch at the same time. As the room flooded with light a form on the bed lifted its head and stared at him reproachfully through eyes red from lack of sleep.

'*Pardon!*' Monsieur Pamplemousse flicked the switch which operated the lights over the dressing table and then turned off the overhead ones. In all the excitement he'd forgotten about Pommes Frites. But from the look on his face it was clear that Pommes Frites had not forgotten his master.

The whole disastrous evening was imprinted for evermore, not only on Pommes Frites' mind, but on most of his body as well. One way and another it had taken quite a battering that night. Having his kennel collapse on top of him had been bad enough, but that had all been over in a matter of seconds. Being incarcerated under the bed had been much, much worse—never-endingly worse. The combined weight of his master and Madame Sophie had strained the springs to their utmost and when the activity was at its height it had felt for all the world as if he'd been trapped beneath a giant pile driver.

Pommes Frites had no wish to pass judgment on the morals of others, least of all his master, but he wished they'd carried out their frolickings elsewhere.

Battered and bruised, when the coast was clear and he was at last able to crawl out from his hiding place,

Pommes Frites sought refuge on top of the bed. There he intended to stay until he was removed by force. Not that he felt totally safe even then. He wouldn't have been at all surprised if the ceiling suddenly fell in. Nothing would have surprised him any more.

At least . . . he fixed his master with a stare. He had been expecting some kind of an apology, a word of cheer or a friendly pat, but Monsieur Pamplemousse obviously had his mind set on other things. During the course of their life together he, Pommes Frites, had been witness to many strange goings on. Had he been equipped for the task he could have written a book about them. A book which might well have reached the best sellers list in *Animal Ways*, but . . . he blinked in order to make sure he was seeing aright— never before had he seen his master acting quite so strangely.

Suddenly aware of Pommes Frites' unwinking gaze, Monsieur Pamplemousse turned his back on him. Pommes Frites had a very disconcerting gaze when he chose and he wasn't in the mood for explanations; he had enough problems as it was.

Madame Douard's shapely form, fashioned by nature in one of her more generous moods, had been made even more luxurious over the years by its owner's pursuit of good food. The two combined meant that the nightdress she had left behind fitted him like a glove. And like a glove, putting it on was not as easy as it looked—especially as he didn't want to run the risk of damaging it irreparably in the process. Bending over would be hazardous in the extreme.

However, something untoward had taken place in

the *Dames* and he was determined to get to the bottom of it before the night was very much older.

Taking a large, white handkerchief out of a drawer, he tied a knot in each corner and then slipped it over his head like a makeshift bonnet.

'Good boy!' With a reassuring wave to Pommes Frites he made for the door and hurriedly shut it behind him.

'*Good boy!*' Pommes Frites stared suspiciously at the closed door for quite a long while. He was used to the various nuances in his master's voice, and the guilt-ridden tones of the last remark had not escaped him. It was the kind of voice Monsieur Pamplemousse usually reserved for Madame Pamplemousse on those occasions when he arrived home late without a reasonable excuse, reasonable in Madame Pamplemousse's eyes, that is . . . Part apologetic, part defiant, with a dash of apprehension mixed in for good measure.

Pommes Frites heaved a deep sigh. In his haste his master hadn't even bothered to turn out the light.

He was about to try and resume his slumbers when something else happened to delay matters. A piece of blue paper came sliding underneath the door. A piece of blue paper, moreover, which had a border of flowers round it. Even without moving Pommes Frites could see them: large brightly coloured flowers. Also without moving he could smell a scent; a scent which he recognised at once. It belonged to the other half of the two people most responsible for his present aches and pains.

Pommes Frites tensed himself lest the paper should be a prelude to yet another attack, perhaps this time on his own person. Then he relaxed again as he caught the sound of retreating footsteps going back down the corridor.

Unaware of the happenings on the floor above, Monsieur Pamplemousse made his way towards the toilets in a curious crablike shuffle. Negotiating the stairs had taken rather longer than he'd bargained for, partly on account of his having to take them very carefully one at a time lest he burst the seams of Madame Sophie's nightdress, but also—although he wouldn't have admitted it to anyone—wearing it was having a delayed but pronounced effect on his ardour.

He toyed with the idea of assuming a disguised voice and saying good night to the gendarme, then he rejected it. That might be pushing things a little too far. In any case the man seemed to have disappeared for the time being.

Breathing a sigh of relief, he pushed open the door to the *Dames*, noting as he did so the outline symbol on the door and above that the original sign 'EVE'. It wouldn't do to make a second mistake and compound the felony by getting himself trapped in the *Hommes* dressed in his present garb.

Once inside he lost no time. Making straight for the cubicle where all the activity had taken place, he lifted the top from the cistern and peered inside.

A look of satisfaction came over his face. Clearly visible at the bottom was a long piece of metal with a polished wooden handle. Pulling up a sleeve of the nightdress, he reached down into the water. It was as he'd suspected; a small, single-ended saw, equipped with a fine-toothed blade of the type used for cutting metal. The blade, which was new, bore signs of having recently been used. Its blueness had been worn away and fragments of metal clogged the middle section of teeth.

Wrapping the handle in a piece of toilet paper, he laid it carefully on the floor while he replaced the cistern top. Then he picked it up again, unbolted the cubicle door and made for the exit. Altogether, he could hardly have been in there for more than a minute or two.

'*Bonsoir*, Pamplemousse.' He jumped as a familiar figure detached itself from a pillar in the hall and came towards him.

'Or should I say, *bonjour*?' Inspector Banyuls gazed at him coldly. Making no attempt to hide the contempt in his voice, he looked Monsieur Pamplemousse slowly up and down, taking in the saw as he did so. The construction he placed on the meeting was obvious. A saw was for cutting wood. Holes cut in wood were for looking through.

He turned to the gendarme. 'You did well to call me, Lesparre. But as it is late I suggest we leave further enquiries until morning. As for you . . .' He turned back to Monsieur Pamplemousse and held out his hand. 'I will relieve you of that, if I may.'

'Now, look here.' Monsieur Pamplemousse made a half-hearted attempt at bluster. 'Before we go any further *I* suggest you question your subordinate on who else has used the toilet within the last half-hour. I am not the only one.'

'Is this true?'

The gendarme gave an indifferent shrug. 'How should I know? I have my rounds to do. I have seen this man twice. Once as naked as the day he was born, and now . . .' He left the sentence unfinished, but his opinion on the whole sordid matter was all too obvious.

Monsieur Pamplemousse knew better than to argue. He had met the type many times before in his career. Fine if they were on your side, but there was no getting through if they weren't.

'All right.' He handed the saw to Inspector Banyuls, who tucked it inside his jacket with an air of satisfaction. 'But it could be to your advantage to have it checked for finger-prints as soon as possible. With luck the water may not have destroyed them, in which case you will find other ones than mine on the handle.

'As for my being here in the first place, you will no doubt be aware of the fact that certain alterations are taking place. Obviously the toilet facilities for the *Dames* are being enlarged. That is why they now have two rooms. One,' he pointed to the sign on the door he'd just come out of, 'one is marked "EVE" and the other "ADA". Naturally, when I first saw the one marked "ADA" I assumed this one was for the men. It is a mistake anyone might make.'

He was pleased he had treated the matter in a dignified way. Others might have tried to think up a cock-and-bull story. It paid to tell the truth in the end.

Inspector Banyuls was looking at something on the floor. He followed the direction of his gaze and dimly made out a small piece of carved wood.

'I'm sorry. I don't have my glasses and unfortunately I am unable to bend down at the moment.'

'Boasting again, Pamplemousse!' The inspector bent down, picked up the object and held it in the air between thumb and forefinger.

It was obvious what it was, but clearly he was determined to get his pound of flesh.

'I am surprised that an ex-member of the Sûreté should be so easily taken in,' he said. 'I think you will find, although I am sure you already know, that the toilets are as they have always been . . . "ADAM" and "EVE". It is simply that the letter "M" has fallen off the end of the "ADAM".

'Also,' he added, pressing home his point remorselessly, 'next time you feel an overwhelming desire to dress up as a woman, I suggest you either confine your activities to your own room or you first shave off your moustache. It does not go well with your costume.'

Monsieur Pamplemousse reached instinctively to his face and then, conscious of a barely suppressed snigger from the gendarme, turned on his heels. He knew when he was beaten.

Aware this time of not one, but two pairs of eyes boring into him, he made his way slowly back up the stairs. Halfway up the worst happened. Over-reaching his step, he felt the material start to give. The sound of tearing silk echoed round the hall, but he was determined not to give the others the satisfaction of seeing him hurry. Never had a flight of stairs seemed so long.

As he let himself wearily into his room he caught sight of the note on the floor and, regardless of the harm he was doing to the rest of the nightdress, bent down to pick it up.

'My shy one of the darkness,' he read. 'You have no need to run away as you did tonight. You have made me the happiest woman in the whole world. Sleep well, and gather your strength for the morrow. I will make sure you have need of it. I shall be counting the seconds until we meet again. Your ever-loving, ever-wanting, ever-needing, ever-lusting . . . S.'

Too tired even to bother removing the nightdress, Monsieur Pamplemousse flopped down on the bed alongside Pommes Frites. Gazing up at the ceiling he offered up a silent prayer, thanking the good Lord that Sophie did not plan to return that night. At least it gave him some sort of respite. He glanced at the candlestick. Things were in a mess and no mistake. It would take some sorting out.

As he reached back over his head to turn out the light a warm tongue sought out his arm. He immediately felt better. There was something very reassuring about Pommes Frites' tongue in times of trouble.

In no time at all their snores mingled. Both were out for the count.

They were still in the same position when the chambermaid opened the door with her pass key next morning, illuminated by a shaft of sunlight sneaking in between a gap in the shutters.

Putting a hand to her mouth to stifle a scream, she stood in the doorway drinking in the scene. A dog—a large dog, and a man dressed in a woman's silk nightdress, ripped all the way down the back—and what was he clutching? A candlestick! '*Mon Dieu!*'

It was the kind of thing she had read about in *Dimanche-Soir*, but never in her wildest dreams had

82

she expected to see such goings on at La Langoustine. In her time she'd come across many strange sights, but this one capped the lot. It had all the ingredients of a first-rate scandal. She would have something to tell the others when she got back home, my word she would!

Quietly, she closed the door behind her and turned the card on the handle to *occupé*.

5

WEDNESDAY MORNING

'*Attendez, s'il vous plaît.*' With the briefest of signals to Pommes Frites, Monsieur Pamplemousse entered the telephone booth outside the Hôtel de Ville, placed a large pile of coins neatly on one side of the shelf and a carefully folded copy of *Ici Paris* on the other, then drew a deep breath as he mentally prepared himself for the first of three calls, all of which were, to a greater or lesser extent, of a confidential nature. The bedrooms of La Langoustine were not yet equipped for direct dialling and he had no wish to be listened-in to by the girl in reception, still less Madame Douard if she happened to be around.

The first of his calls was to his wife, Doucette. He'd been having qualms of conscience about Doucette. Doucette, who stayed at home looking after the running of the flat, doing the washing and ironing, watering the plants, dusting, standing in supermarket queues, while he, Pamplemousse, was away on his travels— often for weeks or months at a time.

If only he could explain to her the loneliness of it all. The sheer boredom of having to eat meal after meal on behalf of *Le Guide* and its readers, some of whom probably couldn't tell a *Tivoli aux Fraises* from a *Bombe Surprise*. Awarding marks for a *sauce Béarnaise* one day, taking them away on the morrow for an overcooked *sauce Périgourdine*. Having to stuff himself with *Écrevisses à la Bordelaise* followed by *Pêches à l'Aurore*, when all he really craved for was a simple underdone steak and salad, with perhaps a *glace vanille* to round things off. She would never understand. The grass was always greener on the other side of the fence.

As the phone began to ring at the other end of the line he brushed a crumb from his coat sleeve and made a mental note to add croissants to the growing list of bonus points for the hotel.

Breakfast had been a little later than usual—mainly because in all the excitement he'd forgotten to leave his order card outside the bedroom door. But in the event it had been one of the most delicious croissants he'd eaten for a long time. Or, if he were to be absolutely honest, *three* of the most delicious croissants, for they had been very more-ish. Warm, buttery, with a satisfying lightness, they had positively melted in the mouth. A perfect accompaniment to the large glass of freshly squeezed orange juice and the slightly acrid but flavoursome coffee, not to mention the bowls of home-made *confiture*, the berries of which were as juicy and full of fruit as the day on which they had been picked; a miracle of preservation. Altogether a most rewarding start to the morning. The slice of lemon in Pommes Frites' water bowl had been a pleasant touch as well.

For a moment the memory of it all brought about another twinge of conscience and he toyed with the idea of asking his wife if she would care to join him for the rest of the stay. But only for a moment. A click as the receiver was lifted at the other end brought him sharply back to earth. In the circumstances such thoughts would never do. He had enough problems as it was. He must not weaken. He told himself Doucette would not enjoy the experience. Apart from all the undercurrents at work the rich food would play havoc with her diet.

'Couscous, is that you?' He put out a tentative endearment to test the water. '*Oui. Oui, oui, chérie*, it is I, Aristide . . . *Oui*, we are still in St. Castille . . . *Chérie*, how strange . . . I was only thinking to myself a moment ago how nice that would be, but unfortunately something important has come up . . . No, Doucette, I think it would be better if you didn't. Really, I do. I cannot explain for the moment, but I have to remain here a little longer, you understand? Besides, it is not like being on the coast and you know how much you dislike the cold. The mountain air . . .'

Holding the telephone receiver away from his ear, Monsieur Pamplemousse gazed at it distastefully. It was all too clear that Doucette didn't understand. He decided to play his trump card. The one that never failed.

'In that case, *chérie* . . . if you would *really* like to . . . I will make immediate arrangements. You can catch an afternoon train. I will arrange to have it met. You will be here by . . .'

The reaction was as he had predicted. How could she possibly leave Paris when there was so much work to do? Who would take care of the flat? The *plombier* was arriving on Thursday to put a new washer on the kitchen tap—something he couldn't possibly do even if he was there to do it—which he wasn't. Besides, she was in the middle of making a new dress . . .

Monsieur Pamplemousse stifled his relief and allowed his attention to wander across the square. Even Pommes Frites seemed to have caught the general mood of the conversation, for he was standing bolt upright with his ears pricked and his legs wide apart as if ready for the off at a moment's notice.

'No, *chérie*, I do not know for how long. Perhaps it will be for one more day, perhaps two. Maybe a week.' He lowered his voice. 'It all depends.'

Almost immediately he regretted placing so much emphasis on the last phrase.

'No, no, no, Doucette, of *course* there is no other. I promise you on my honour, I have been faithful.'

Catching sight of a priest entering the church on the far side of the square, Monsieur Pamplemousse hastily crossed himself and turned back into the booth. Looked at in a certain light what he had just said was un-doubtedly true. He, Pamplemousse, had been faithful. Faithfulness was largely a matter of intent. Was it his fault if others, less strong, had forced themselves on—or even *upon* him? Might it not be true to say that it was only consideration for others, a desire not to disturb them in their sleep by calling out, that had stifled his protests? The Americans, as ever, had a neat way of putting it. What was the expression they used? Brownie points. Did he not at the very least deserve a few Brownie points for his unselfishness?

'And how are the window boxes, Couscous?' he enquired. 'Have you given them plenty of water? You know how quickly they dry out in this hot weather . . . It is raining in Paris! how strange! Here the sun is shining. It is like . . .'

A loud click brought the conversation to an abrupt end—at least as far as Madame Pamplemousse was concerned.

Merde! Women! Monsieur Pamplemousse replaced the receiver with rather more force than he had intended and prepared himself for the second call of the morning.

It was brief and to the point.

'*Bonjour*. Pamplemousse here. May I have the office of Monsieur le Directeur, please?'

'Certainly, Monsieur Pamplemousse. At once, Monsieur Pamplemousse.'

'Chief, Pamplemousse here. I have a slight change of plans. It will necessitate a few more days in the area.

'Ah, you have already heard? A strange business. It was in the *Poularde de Bresse en Vessie*.

'Yes, chief. Thank you, chief.

'*Oui*, I will take care.'

'*Le Guide* needs you, Pamplemousse. You must be in Rouen by next Sunday at the latest. There is a deadline to meet. There have been bad reports of their *Mille-feuille de Saumon au Cerfeuil*. I would go myself but I cannot spare the time.' The directeur of *Le Guide* spoke in the clipped tones of a general preparing his troops for battle. Tones which, try as he might, Monsieur Pamplemousse always found hard not to imitate when they were holding a conversation.

Catching sight of an elderly woman peering at him through the glass he realised with a start that he had been standing rigidly to attention. Turning his back on her he tried to relax.

The truth of the matter was that the whole organisation of *Le Guide* was planned like a military operation. The walls of headquarters were covered in maps, each of which was festooned with flags. The operations room itself—the holy of holies, to which admittance was gained by green pass only—was staffed by uniformed girls who pushed little bronze figures around on giant tables with croupier-like efficiency. Monsieur Pamplemousse knew that provided he filled in the correct forms all would be well and his request granted, but woe betide him if his reports were late. It would mean some pretty heavy field-work in the weeks to come—possibly entailing two *dîners* a night. He blanched at the thought. Thank heaven for Pommes Frites.

'Hullo . . . Pamplemousse . . . are you there?'

'*Oui*, Monsieur le Directeur.' This would never do.

'My regards to Pommes Frites. Oh, and Pamplemousse . . . if you stay more than three days don't forget your P189.'

'*Oui*, Monsieur le Directeur. *Merci. Au revoir*, Monsieur le Directeur.'

Monsieur Pamplemousse replaced the receiver and mopped his brow. And now for the most delicate, and yet if he intended to stay another night in St. Castille, probably the most important call of the three. He took out his spectacles, wiped them clean, and checked a ringed number on page fifteen of *Ici Paris*—just to make doubly sure.

'*Poupées Fantastiques, à vôtre service.*' The voice at the other end sounded unctuous in the extreme; soft and oily, like an over-dressed aubergine. Monsieur

Pamplemousse recognised it at once. It belonged to the proprietor, Oscar. Voice and owner matched perfectly. Nothing changed.

He cleared his throat. 'I wish to place an order,' he said briskly. 'I need it urgently so I am prepared to pay whatever is necessary.' That should do it.

'Certainly, Monsieur. One moment, Monsieur, while I find a pencil.'

Monsieur Pamplemousse began issuing his instructions. 'That is correct. The Mark IV. As advertised in *Ici Paris*. The de luxe model.'

'An excellent choice, Monsieur. I can assure you it is impossible to do better. Our customers are worldwide and we guarantee complete satisfaction. All our Mark IV models are individually tested before they leave our work rooms.'

Monsieur Pamplemousse suppressed a shudder. 'It is not for me . . .' he began.

He was interrupted by a fruity chuckle. 'That is what they all say, Monsieur. If I were to tell you the names of some of our clients . . . However, I can assure you of our complete discretion. All records of orders. are in code and kept under lock and key.'

'I wish,' said Monsieur Pamplemousse, trying to sound as blasé as possible, 'for the male version. Battery driven, but with certain modifications.'

'Certain modifications?' Monsieur Pamplemousse almost felt the hand go over the mouthpiece at the other end. He took a deep breath.

'I would like it to have wooden legs.'

'*Wooden legs?*' The man seemed to take an unnecessary delight in repeating the words as slowly and loudly as possible. So much for the discretion of *Poupées Fantastiques*.

Monsieur Pamplemousse looked uneasily over his shoulder. The woman outside appeared to be doing something to her deaf aid. Probably turning up the volume.

'Is it or is it not possible?' he barked. The conversation had already gone on far too long for his liking.

'Monsieur, all things are possible. As you can see from our advertisement we cater for all tastes. Nothing is too bizarre or *exotique*. Although I have to admit . . . would this be for Madame?'

'No, it would not!' thundered Monsieur Pamplemousse. 'And another thing . . .'

'*Another?*' The man could hardly keep the excitement from his voice.

'I want delivery today.'

'Today? Monsieur is joking, of course.'

'Listen, you.' Monsieur Pamplemousse decided to play it rough. 'I said today and I mean today. I do not mean yesterday, nor do I mean tomorrow. There is a high-speed train leaving Paris at fourteen twenty-six hours. It should arrive in Orange at about eighteen hundred. I shall be there to meet it. If it is not on that train I shall take immediate steps to have your premises closed down and you with them. Now, do I make myself totally and absolutely clear or do I have to spell it out in words of one syllable?'

There was a long silence at the other end during which Monsieur Pamplemousse stole a quick glance at the outside world. The woman with the deaf aid was almost wetting herself with excitement. She had been joined by two others.

'What name shall I put on the parcel, Monsieur?'

'Pamplemousse.' He tried to speak as quietly as possible.

'Pamplemousse? Not *the* Monsieur Pamplemousse? Pamplemousse of the Sûreté?' A note of respect had entered the voice.

'*Late* of the Sûreté. An early retirement . . .' He wished now he had used a nom de guerre.

'Ah, yes . . .' A whistle came down the line. 'I remember now . . . there was all that trouble with the girls at the Follies. Thirty-three wasn't it?'

'Fifteen,' sighed Monsieur Pamplemousse.

'Tell me, Inspector.' Oscar began to regain some of his earlier confidence. 'What is she like? Do you have any photos? We pay good prices for the right kind of negatives.'

'The fourteen twenty-six TGV!' Monsieur Pamplemousse decided he had had enough. For the second time that morning he was about to slam the receiver down, then he had second thoughts.

'One more thing.'

'*Oui*, Inspector?'

'I would like a plastic inflatable dog kennel. King size.'

'A plastic inflatable *dog kennel* . . . *King size? Mon Dieu!*'

'If you consult your records you will find I purchased one some four years ago. I had it made specially.'

Monsieur Pamplemousse felt in a better mood as he

left the telephone booth. His last request had clearly given him game, set and match.

'*Pardon*, Monsieur.' The woman with the deaf aid, her bloodless lips made ever thinner by being tightly compressed in disapproval, pushed past him and began ostentatiously cleaning the mouthpiece of the telephone with her handkerchief, much to the enjoyment of her friends.

Avoiding their gaze, Monsieur Pamplemousse looked around for Pommes Frites, but Pommes Frites was nowhere to be seen. That was all he needed. He could think of nothing he wanted to do less at that moment than hang about outside the telephone booth. Quite a small crowd had collected and they were eyeing him with a mixture of interest and downright disbelief.

Reaching into an inside pocket he withdrew a small whistle and blew into it hopefully several times.

His audience broke into a titter as they waited for the blast and none followed. Much to Monsieur Pamplemousse's embarrassment, Pommes Frites was clearly out of range. For a moment or two he toyed with the idea of trying to explain the basic principles of silent dog whistles to his audience, but then he thought better of it. They didn't look as if they would be terribly receptive. Instead, he pretended to study a poster in the window of the P.T.T. No doubt Pommes Frites would reappear in his own good time. He always did.

*   *   *

Unaware of his master's predicament, Pommes Frites made his way along the Grande Avenue Charles

93

de Gaulle looking more than a little pleased with himself.

Not even one of his most ardent admirers—and he had a great many—would have credited him with an over-abundance of grey matter. Generosity, an un-rivalled and highly developed sense of taste in matters culinary, a capacity for love and affection, steadfastness, tenacity; he had many things going for him. But when it came to such mundane matters as, for example, the putting of two and two together and making four, it took him a little while to get things sorted out in his mind. In short, equations were not one of his strong points. Simultaneous ones even less so.

On the other hand, by remaining blissfully unaware of his mathematical shortcomings he was able to sail through life without the additional worries such knowledge often brought to others.

Two and two could sometimes make five, at other times three; it depended entirely on circumstances. And in Pommes Frites' view it didn't really matter much anyway.

On this particular morning, however, there was a gleam in his eye and a resolute angle to his tail which showed beyond all shadow of doubt that he, Pommes Frites, had reached a decision. And once Pommes Frites reached a decision there was no diverting him. It was a decision, moreover, that had to do with the safety of his master. Than which, in his eyes, there could be no finer cause.

Nose to the ground, he ignored the rather tasty looking *tranche* of *Terrine de Sanglier* which Monsieur Hollard was placing in the *charcuterie* window to his right, turned a blind eye towards a ginger cat disappearing down an alleyway to his left, and closed his olfactory glands to the smell of freshly baked bread wafting down the street from Madame Charbonnier's *pâtisserie*.

Pausing only to leave his mark on a concrete flower tub standing on a corner of the newly completed pedestrian precinct, he hurried on his way, following a trail which led him up some steps towards the Place Napoleon. There was a purposeful expression on his face; an expression which boded ill for anyone who attempted to get in his way without a very good reason.

It had taken Pommes Frites some little while to reach the conclusion that all was not well, and having reached that conclusion he was determined to do something about it.

The sound of Madame Pamplemousse's voice through the glass door of the telephone booth had set him worrying. There had been something in the tone of her voice, not to mention the way Monsieur Pamplemousse regarded the end of the telephone receiver as he held it out at arm's length, which pointed to the fact that 'something was up'. What happened shortly afterwards had clinched matters in his mind.

Pommes Frites knew several very good reasons why Monsieur Pamplemousse was reluctant to leave town; and one of those reasons, had his master but known, passed within two feet of him shortly after he entered the telephone booth.

The encounter had been a chance one, for the man in question reacted in a way which could only be described as furtive in the extreme. Pulling a black Homburg down over his forehead, he'd turned his back towards Monsieur Pamplemousse and crept past the telephone box until well clear, before disappearing up the Grande Avenue Charles de Gaulle as if his very life depended on it.

All of which, given the fact that it was a hot day and there were other equally interesting things happening in the square at the time, might not have occasioned anything more than a passing glance from Pommes Frites, had it not been for the smell; an unusually strong and clearly recognisable scent which set his nose twitching and made him jump to his feet with all his senses racing.

Not for nothing had Pommes Frites been born a bloodhound. Bloodhounds were good at smells and he'd met that same one before—to be precise, in, on and around the bush he'd encountered up the hill the previous morning, and it had remained firmly fixed in his memory ever since.

Apart from having a personal score to settle, he had a feeling he might be able to kill at least two birds with one bite—and he knew exactly where he intended placing it if he got half a chance. Hopefully, if all went well, he could also do something to put his master back in favour with Madame Pamplemousse. And with these thoughts uppermost in his mind, he set off in hot pursuit.

Not that Pommes Frites disliked Madame Pamplemousse. Her complaints regarding the amount of hairs he left behind when he rose from his afternoon nap had about as much effect on him as did water on a duck's back. Pommes Frites was not one to fly in the face of nature. There were things he could do something about and there were things he could do nothing about. Loose hairs happened to be something he could do nothing about. As for complaints about the state of his paws when he came indoors after a walk in the rain, people who worried about such trifles ought not to polish their floors. It was a matter of differing temperaments.

Monsieur Pamplemousse understood about such things. Monsieur Pamplemousse often came under fire himself for much the same reasons: crumpled cushions, stray hairs, muddied shoes. It was a case of like gravitating towards like and there was an understanding and a bond of affection between them that mere words could not describe.

Besides, Pommes Frites owed Monsieur Pamplemousse a great debt of gratitude.

It dated back to the occasion of Monsieur Pamplemousse's early retirement from the force.

It so happened that around the same time Pommes Frites, who'd been on attachment to the Eighteenth Arrondissement where Monsieur Pamplemousse lived, was made redundant following a government cut-back.

Although it was a simple matter of last in first out, it wasn't a nice thing to happen to a dog of Pommes Frites' sensibilities, especially so early on in his career. Trained to the peak of perfection, passing his course with flying colours, only to find himself discarded like an old slipper.

Word had reached Monsieur Pamplemousse, who'd rescued him in the nick of time from being sent to the local dogs' home; a journey from which there would probably have been no return.

A nicer retirement present Monsieur Pamplemousse couldn't have wished for, nor could Pommes Frites have dreamed of a happier turn of fate. It was the kind of thing a dog doesn't forget in a hurry.

All these and many other things might have entered Pommes Frites' mind that morning had he been given to deep and philosophical thoughts, and if he hadn't had his attention firmly fixed on more important things.

As it was he bounded up the remaining steps leading to the Place Napoleon, ignored a sign which proclaimed that 'CHIENS' were 'INTERDITS', threaded his way in and out of the various stalls dotting the square, and hurried towards number 7-*bis* on the far side.

The smell was growing stronger with every passing moment, and as he pushed open the door with his nose Pommes Frites paused and sniffed appreciatively. The scent had now taken on a slightly different flavour. Along with the odour of bay rum, there were overtones of sweat and . . . yes, there was definitely more than a trace of fear. Instinct told Pommes Frites that he had the advantage of his prey.

Licking his lips in anticipation, he headed towards a flight of stairs immediately facing him.

Number 7-*bis* was old and rambling, and sadly in need of repair. High up on the outside wall overlooking the market an inscription recorded the fact that the Emperor Napoleon himself had once stayed there for lunch (from twelve fifteen until a quarter past two) during his long march across the Alps. But that had been a long time ago, on the 23rd June 1815. Since that happy day it had fallen into neglect, and had even escaped the attentions of the present progressive mayor—he of the 'CHIENS INTERDITS' sign, who was endeavouring to bring back to the town of St. Castille some of its former glories.

Pommes Frites had to pick his way very carefully up the ramshackle wooden staircase in order to avoid making any kind of noise; or even, for that matter, to avoid falling through it in some places.

On his way up he peered in at some empty rooms. In one there was a table with the remains of a meal, in another a couple of unmade camp beds. As he reached the third landing an ominous metallic click from somewhere close at hand caused him to stop in his tracks. He froze for a moment, then quickened his pace. Not for nothing had he attended a two-day seminar on ballistics; the only dog of his particular year to gain maximum marks and the coveted Golden Bone.

The sound meant only one thing. There was someone on the floor above with a gun, and if the heavy breathing was anything to go by, that someone was in a hurry.

Covering the remaining stairs at something approaching the speed of sound, Pommes Frites struck, and having struck, held on for all he was worth.

As he sank his teeth into the posterior of the figure on the far side of the room, a most satisfactory noise emerged from its other end; the first of a whole series of satisfactory noises.

It was an amalgamation which would have brought tears of joy to even the most fastidious of recording engineers in search of the esoteric in the way of sound effects. Not, perhaps, destined for the Top Ten, but assured of a place for ever more in the libraries of all self-respecting drama studios the world over.

Cataloguing would, of course, always present a problem, for it was hard to pin-point the dominant theme. Put at its simplest it was the cry of a man of Italian extraction, leaning out of a third-floor window in a small French town and taking aim at a distant target with a high-powered rifle. (Sounds of busy market nearby and hum of distant traffic in background.) Being attacked by fierce dog. Assorted barks and growls. Tearing of cloth. Cries of pain. Firing of rifle, followed by more cries of pain and alarm (mostly in Italian) as man falls from window and lands on second-floor balcony below. Sound of balcony giving way. More cries, some in It., but predominantly Fr. as man lands on barrow of fruit and veg. in street below. (12.5 secs.)

Pommes Frites stood with his paws on the window-sill and gazed down at the scene below. He felt slightly disappointed about the balcony. It hadn't entered into his calculations and it marred what might otherwise have been a perfect operation; one which he knew would have won the approval of his master.

Talking of which . . . looking up, he noticed a gap in the buildings opposite. Through it he had a clear view of the Square du Centre, La Langoustine, and—on the far side—a familiar figure standing outside the telephone booth. Even from that distance Monsieur Pamplemousse looked somewhat impatient.

It was time to go. Already he could hear footsteps and voices on the stairs. Being no fool Pommes Frites decided to avail himself of a second flight of stairs at the rear of the building.

A few minutes later he ambled into the square looking as if he hadn't a care in the world.

'Pommes Frites!' Monsieur Pamplemousse's voice held a touch of asperity. 'And where have you been?' He wagged his finger in mock reproof. 'The *boucherie, n'est-ce pas?*'

Pommes Frites gave a sigh. The *boucherie* indeed! Why was it that even the best and nicest of humans always suspected the worst. Really, there was no justice in the world. No justice at all.

He had half a mind not to give his master the present he'd brought him, but after a brief struggle his good nature and early training got the better of him. Reaching up, he dropped a small, shiny object into Monsieur Pamplemousse's outstretched hand.

It was cylindrical in shape, 7.5mm in diameter and despite its sojourn in Pommes Frites' mouth, still had the strong and unmistakable smell of cordite, a fact which did not go unnoticed or unrewarded by its recipient.

Pommes Frites wagged his tail as his master reached down to pat him. He couldn't have wished for a nicer reward.

6

WEDNESDAY EVENING

'*Merde*! *Sacrebleu*! *Nom d'un nom*!' Monsieur Pamplemousse gazed in frustration at the unwrapped contents
of a parcel which littered his bed. He was not in a good
mood.

For a start, the journey to Orange and back had
taken much longer than he'd anticipated. At any other
time it would have been a pleasant way of passing an
afternoon. First the drive through the great lavender-
growing area of the Vaucluse; at this time of the year
the plants already cropped and looking for all the world
like row upon row of freshly barbered hedgehogs on
parade and ready for inspection. Then the drop down
through the Gorge de la Nesque via the D942 to the
melon country of Carpentras, with the opportunity of
making a short detour in order to sample the delights
of a glass or two of the delicious sweet Beaumes de
Venise. It would have been a good way of combining
business with pleasure, for as well as commenting on
food *Le Guide* also offered advice on the best and most
enjoyable ways of getting from one restaurant to the
next.

But things had not turned out as planned. The rot had
set in at Orange itself with the discovery that the TGV
high-speed train didn't stop there. Not only did it fail

to stop, its specially laid track enabled it to ignore the city altogether and head straight for Avignon at a speed of something like 260 kilometres an hour.

Wondering what the Romans would have thought about this slight to a city they had helped to create and make beautiful, Monsieur Pamplemousse hurtled after the train in his 2CV, covering the first half of the thirty or so kilometres at a speed which would have caused M. André Citroën to gaze in wonder had he been alive and able to witness the event.

Unfortunately, wonderment was not one of the emotions shown by a gendarme when he came off the *autoroute* at Avignon Nord. The stern, implacable disapproval etched into his face left no room for other, finer feelings as he compared the entry time on Monsieur Pamplemousse's card with that indicated by his watch.

The practice of holding spot speed checks on the *autoroute* was something Monsieur Pamplemousse was aware of but had never actually encountered before, and he wished it could have happened at any other time.

Arguing was a waste of time. He went on his way eventually with a wallet which was considerably lighter than when he'd first set out, and reached the *gare* at Avignon long after the train had arrived and gone on its way again. That, in turn, meant his parcel received rather more attention than he would have liked.

The discretion in the filing system about which *Poupées Fantastiques* had boasted obviously did not extend to their labelling department. Either that or Oscar had deliberately tried to get his own back, for he'd seldom seen quite such a blatant advertisement on the outside of a package. An over-zealous official behind the counter refused delivery until it had been opened and its contents put on display for all to see. Trying to brazen things out by pulling his old rank had been a mistake too. The man had called his bluff.

The whole affair had been so upsetting he'd lost his way taking a short cut somewhere up in the mountains on the return journey and both he and Pommes Frites had arrived at La Langoustine tired, late and hungry.

Pommes Frites had been no help whatsoever. Normally Pommes Frites liked car rides. He enjoyed nothing better than bowling along with his master at the wheel and the side window open so that he could poke his head out from time to time and feel the cool breeze on his face and whiskers.

But today was an exception. He was still feeling the effects of the previous night's encounters. A certain stiffness had set in, a stiffness which hadn't been helped by all the exercise that morning. In short, Pommes Frites would much sooner have stayed where he was, recovering. However, he hadn't been given any choice in the matter. Without so much as a by-your-leave, he'd been bundled into the car and had had to endure over 340 kilometres of winding roads—more if you counted the extra kilometres they'd travelled trying to find the right one back, and it had put him into one of his difficult moods. Having refused to wear his seat belt, he kept leaning against Monsieur Pamplemousse every time they went round a right-hand bend, and threatening to burst open the offside door every time they rolled in the opposite direction. In the end Monsieur

Pamplemousse put his foot down metaphorically as well as in practice and banished Pommes Frites to the back seat, an indignity he suffered in silence until just before St. Castille, when he'd been sick.

The only consolation to show for the afternoon—and Monsieur Pamplemousse was man enough to admit it—lay in the fact that the model itself, seen in all its inflated glory, was a masterpiece of the *poupée* maker's art. A symphony in wood and rubber. His warning must have gone home—for an unknown hand had even gone to the trouble of turning it into a rough likeness of himself with the addition of a moustache. An optional extra which made even Pommes Frites look twice. Perhaps—who knows?—it might have been someone he'd come up against in the old days and done a good turn for. Whatever the reason, ten out of ten for initiative.

It had been a strange experience, blowing it up with the aid of Pommes Frites' gas cylinder and seeing it grow into his own shape before his very eyes. Pommes Frites had been most surprised—seeing an effigy of his master instead of the usual kennel. It wasn't at all what he'd expected and he spent some time sniffing the result and wondering what on earth was going to happen.

Where they had managed to get the wooden legs from at such short notice, Monsieur Pamplemousse neither knew nor cared. It was sufficient that the job had been done to his satisfaction. Although it wouldn't have fooled anyone in the cold light of day, at night—with the lights turned out—who knew? It was worth a go.

He found his pyjama jacket and put it on over the top half, smiling to himself as he pulled back the bed cover. In one respect at least, *Poupées Fantastiques* had done him a great compliment. Madame Sophie, when she returned that night, would certainly have nothing to complain about—provided the electric mechanism stood up to the strain.

Making some final adjustments to the position of the model, he inserted one end of a long lead into a socket at the base of the spine—the one which according to figure fifteen in the instruction manual connected to the pressure-operated *membre*, and ran it carefully up the bed and over the end of the mattress, passing it underneath to a point about halfway down, where he looped it round one of the bedsprings for good measure.

It was as he paused to consult the instruction manual again before connecting the free end to a large battery box that his jaw suddenly dropped. The battery box, said the manual, in the casual terms reserved for such matters, will require eight 1.5 volt rechargeable batteries. He searched through the wrapping paper. They had not been included.

'*Imbéciles!*' Where was he to get eight 1.5 volt batteries in St. Castille at this time of night? It would be bad enough trying to get one battery. One battery he might be able to borrow from someone's torch, or two even—but eight—rechargeable ones at that!

For a moment or so he toyed with the idea of getting into his car again and going in search of a late-night garage. There must be one in the area. On the other hand . . . Monsieur Pamplemousse's knowledge of things electrical was not of the highest, but he did know that a car battery contained considerably more power in just one of its cells than a whole drawerful of torch batteries. He well remembered having once seen a car go up in flames because of a short-circuited battery; once they got going there was nothing to stop them. In the circumstances, a car battery might be an ideal power source for Madame Sophie's needs. If the worst came to the worst he could always get it recharged in the morning.

Some ten minutes later Monsieur Pamplemousse staggered up the back stairs carrying a large object wrapped in a car rug.

Shortly afterwards, having bared the ends of the lead, he twisted them round the two terminals, added some adhesive tape from his first-aid kit for good measure to make doubly sure they didn't come adrift in the heat of the moment, and pushed the battery under the bed.

Now for the big moment. The *moment critique*.

Closing the shutters in case he was being overlooked, he turned off all the lights except one and, under the watchful gaze of Pommes Frites, approached the figure on the bed.

Turning back the sheets, he gave the *membre* a tentative tweak. Almost immediately there was a click followed by a faint humming sound and things began to happen.

The result was beyond his wildest expectations. My word, but things had progressed since the old days. In the old days he'd heard tell of inflatable models being exported for the benefit of lonely guardians of what

107

remained of the French colonial empire, but they had been of the opposite gender and certainly not—at least in his experience—readily available on the home market.

The whole thing was a miracle of ingenuity. Those areas which needed to contract, contracted. Those which needed to expand, grew large, gathering speed with every passing moment, vibrating in sympathy with the heaving buttocks, while the mouth opened and closed in random fashion emitting such lifelike moans and groans that even Pommes Frites' hackles began to rise.

Madame Sophie was in for a high old time that night. He wouldn't have minded being a fly on the pillow. If all went well she would be able to add her name to *Poupées Fantastiques*' list of satisfied customers in the truest sense of the word.

He consulted the instruction book again. There was no sense in wasting the battery. Besides, all the heaving and moaning was making him feel restive. Finding the right diagram at last he reached for the pressure-operated switch which controlled the vital organ. The humming died away.

He tried it several more times—just to make sure everything was working properly. It really was most intriguing. A tweak in one direction and the model relaxed with a hiss of escaping air. A tweak in the other and it started up again.

But if Monsieur Pamplemousse was fascinated by the gyrations of the figure on the bed, Pommes Frites was beside himself with excitement. He couldn't believe his eyes. Firmly convinced that it was some new kind of everlasting bone dispenser he began running around in circles, giving vent to growls of anticipation. He'd been given an everlasting bone once at Christmas and it had kept him going for several weeks; he couldn't wait to sink his teeth into it.

It was as the hubbub was at its height and he was nearing his fiftieth lap of the bedroom, barking his head off with delight, that he suddenly skidded to a halt and stared at the door. Or rather, he stared at the spot where the door had been the previous time round. Now it was open.

'Monster! . . . Pervert! . . . Unhappy man!'

Monsieur Pamplemousse jumped to his feet, but it was too late for explanations, if indeed he could readily have thought of one. Before he had a chance to open his mouth the door closed and the chambermaid disappeared, but not before she had ostentatiously removed the requirement notice from the handle and placed it outside. As far as she was concerned the room could stay *occupé* for all time. Such depravity was quite beyond belief. If she hadn't witnessed it with her own eyes she would not have thought such things were possible.

Feeling as deflated as the figure on the bed, Monsieur Pamplemousse gave the wiring a final check and then pulled the cover into place. All good things come to an end sooner or later and even Pommes Frites seemed somewhat sobered by the experience as he exchanged glances with his master.

Shortly afterwards, freshly bathed and with the dust of the journey removed, Monsieur Pamplemousse emerged from his room and with Pommes Frites leading the way headed down the stairs for a much needed dinner.

Madame Douard was busy at the reception desk with a late arrival. As he passed their eyes met briefly and he felt the colour rise to his cheeks. Madame Sophie had large eyes. Large and round, a strange mixture of innocence and promise. At the moment they were full of promise.

Monsieur Pamplemousse mopped his brow as he entered the dining room. *Mon Dieu*! If only he'd been thirty years younger. Alas, such opportunities had never come his way when he was eighteen; or perhaps they had and he'd been too shy to take advantage of them. Life could be very unsatisfactory at times.

On the other hand, only that very morning when he'd been out for a walk with Pommes Frites he'd caught sight of Madame Sophie disappearing into the local *bricolage*—no doubt to replenish her supply of sandpaper, probably with a coarser grade. Far better to devote his energies to safer things. He'd noted earlier in the day that *Loup* was on the menu; *Loup en Croûte Douard*—one of the patron's specialities. Perhaps he would indulge himself. *Soupe aux Moules Safranées* to begin with; the whole washed down with a Meursault—the '76. He felt his taste buds begin to throb; the kind of throbbing which could only be assuaged by a Kir Royale. One made with his favourite champagne: Gosset.

There was a thump, thump against his right leg as Pommes Frites wagged his tail with anticipation.

110

Monsieur Pamplemousse was not the only one with active taste buds.

*   *   *

'Great minds discuss ideas, average minds discuss events, small minds discuss people. Me, I discuss none of these things. I am a chef and I talk of food.'

Monsieur Douard's booming laugh echoed round the deserted square. 'That is also why I do not wish to discuss Sophie. In her own way she is a good wife. She runs the hotel like a dream. Nothing escapes her eye. She looks after the money. The bills are always paid on time. The customers go on their way happy, and she leaves me alone to get on with my work. What more could a man wish for?'

Monsieur Pamplemousse was tempted to say a wife who didn't jump into bed with the clients at the drop of a hat, but Auguste forestalled him.

'If she has her little peccadilloes on the side, that is her affair. It does no great harm.'

Thinking of his aching muscles, Monsieur Pamplemousse came to the conclusion that harm, like most things in life, was only relative. All the same, picturing what was safely tucked in his bed upstairs, he couldn't help but wish the conversation would take another turn. Monsieur Douard was obviously trying to tell him something he would really rather not know about. Worse still, it was getting late and it would be an even greater embarrassment if, on his way to bed, Auguste met Sophie en route to her assignation.

'The great sadness of life,' he said, trying to change

the subject, 'is our ignorance when young that first love can ever end.'

'My friend,' Monsieur Douard was obviously reading his thoughts with uncanny accuracy. 'Do not distress yourself. To tell you the truth, I am grateful. When one is at work all day in a hot kitchen there is little time left over to take care of other things.'

Monsieur Pamplemousse forebore to comment that in his travels he'd met a good many chefs who found their appetites more than whetted by the time they'd spent in their kitchen. Hotted up, in fact. In life, if you really wanted something you made time for it.

'Most mornings,' continued Monsieur Douard, 'I am up at five. I have to go to the market to make sure I get fresh vegetables. I have to go to the butcher to make certain the meat is as I wish it to be. Then I have to see what fish is available so that I can come back and prepare the menu. Then there are many people to see; the *négociant* about the wine; people who have been supplying me with cheese over the years—small farmers from up in the mountains, representatives from the big suppliers; people I know who grow fruit for me specially and who bring it when it is exactly right for picking, not a day too early and not a day too late.

'Then, and only then, can I really begin work. At the end of the day it is nourishment I require—not punishment. It has always been that way—ever since we were first married. Sophie understands my feelings and I respect hers. She is a woman with an abundance of love—some might say an over-abundance, and she loves to give. It is her nature.

'Over the years there have been many. In the beginning the *sous-chef* had to go. He was never at his post. Then there was the *garde-manger*, guests, the *facteur* . . . in their time they have all drunk their fill, including the odd-job man. *Especially* the odd-job man. She has a strange proclivity for wood. She should have been in a circus. Give her the smell of sawdust and she is away. There is no stopping her. There are things I could tell you . . .'

Monsieur Pamplemousse rather hoped he wouldn't. He felt doubly glad he'd placed his order with *Poupées Fantastiques*. He hoped it would stand the strain.

But Auguste was warming to his subject. He waved towards the statue in the middle of the square. 'She is a true descendant of Hortense and no mistake.'

Monsieur Pamplemousse followed his gaze. Whoever had sculptured Hortense had been fortunate enough to capture her in what could only be termed an unguarded moment. Bending over in order to pick some flowers, on what was presumably a summer's day, for she was totally unclothed, the pose had afforded ample opportunity to highlight what were undoubtedly her best features, her *derrière* and *doudounnes* enhanced still more by the forces of gravity. In the moonlight, and seen from a certain angle, Monsieur Pamplemousse had to agree that the figure bore a striking resemblance to Madame Sophie, although he was too much of a gentleman to say so.

Monsieur Douard broke across his thoughts. 'She is very beautiful, that one. The story goes that she is under a spell . . . that she is waiting . . . has been

113

waiting all these years for someone to come and . . . release her. Someone, that is . . . who understands.

'Poof! It is all nonsense, of course. But there are some things—like Papa Nöel—in which it is nice to believe.' He gave a nudge. 'Perhaps it is the same with Sophie. Perhaps she, too, is waiting. She will not have long, *n'est-ce pas?*'

Monsieur Pamplemousse gave a nervous laugh. In spite of himself his voice sounded cracked and dry. He licked his lips and downed the last of the Armagnac.

'Another?'

He shook his head. 'No, thank you. Pommes Frites and I may take a stroll before we retire.'

Monsieur Douard stood up and held out his hand. 'In that case, my friend, forgive me if I don't join you. I have to be up early. Enjoy yourselves. It is a beautiful night.'

As Auguste disappeared into the hotel a figure rose into view from beneath a nearby table, stretched, and then joined Monsieur Pamplemousse at the top of the steps leading down from the terrace.

Together they set out across the square. Monsieur Pamplemousse paused by the fountain and glanced up. Douard had been right. Hortense *was* beautiful. Deliciously, delightfully, provocatively beautiful. Surveying the world through half-closed eyes, her lips were parted slightly as if she was about to be kissed. Better still, as if she wanted to be kissed. She appeared to be staring straight at him, and there was about her an air of voluptuous, ill-concealed abandon, which caused strange stirrings inside his stomach.

At that moment a car came round the corner of the

114

square, its headlights picking out the statue momentarily as it shot past. For a brief moment Monsieur Pamplemousse had a feeling that one of Hortense's eyes had closed in a wink, then it was gone—a trick of the light.

He shook himself. It was totally and utterly ridiculous. Perhaps the Armagnac had been a mistake.

'Pommes Frites,' he said. 'You and I are going for a very *long* walk.'

Pommes Frites indulged his master with a wag of his tail. As far as he was concerned there was nothing stopping them. A statue was a statue was a statue. They were made of stone and having said that you'd more or less covered the subject. He'd already left his mark more than once on the side of the fountain belonging to this one, *and* slaked his thirst into the bargain. He saw no particular reason to linger any longer.

Somewhere not far away there was the sound of a car turning. From the way the engine was being revved the driver was obviously in a great hurry. Probably a late-night traveller who'd taken the wrong turning and was cursing his luck. It seemed to be heading back the way it had come. There was a squeal of tyres as it rounded a corner and entered the square.

Expecting it to follow the normal line of traffic anti-clockwise round the statue, Monsieur Pamplemousse was about to move out of its way round the other side when some sixth sense signalled an urgent warning. Shouting to Pommes Frites to get out of the way, he made a leap for the safety of the fountain. Jumping on to the edge he was propelled forward by his own momentum and only saved himself from falling into the water by clutching the back of Hortense.

He felt the draught from the car as it hurtled past, its driver clutching the wheel while two white faces peered out at him from the back window. It was the same car that had followed him up into the hills the day he'd met Giampiero.

Looking round, he breathed a sigh of relief. Pommes Frites had managed to scramble clear as well.

Glancing over his shoulder he could see the lights of the car as it disappeared up the hill the way it had come. Pushing against Hortense's shoulders he inched his way slowly downwards until he was clasping her bottom. After a pause for breath he gave a heave. As he did so he felt a faint rocking movement. *Quelle horreur!* He would never be able to show his face in St. Castille again if he pushed the statue off its perch and Madame Hortense broke in two. He held his breath and tried again. There was an ominous creak from somewhere below.

Very slowly he turned his head and caught sight of Pommes Frites standing some distance away staring at him; or rather staring, he realised, at something a little way beyond him.

Equally slowly he turned his head back the other way and then suppressed a groan as he saw a familiar figure watching him.

'Testing the legend, I see. How very romantic.'

Monsieur Pamplemousse glared at the speaker. Inspector Banyuls seemed to have perfected an uncanny knack of appearing at the least opportune moment. He must spend most of his waking hours lying in wait.

'*Péquenot!*' he muttered under his breath. There was no other word for it. That was what he was . . . *un péquenot*. A hick. He wouldn't last two minutes in somewhere like Paris.

Taking the bull by the horns, he pushed against Madame Hortense with all his might. Better a broken statue than suffer the indignity of Banyuls' stares a moment longer than was necessary. As he toppled backwards he was mortified to feel a helping hand reach out in the nick of time to prevent him falling back into the road.

Regaining his balance he jumped to the ground and glared at the inspector as he brushed himself down.

'Instead of just standing idly by,' he growled, 'you would be better employed in the pursuit of the car that forced me up there in the first place.'

'Car? What car? I saw no car.'

Monsieur Pamplemousse glared at him. 'If you won't go after it,' he bellowed, 'then I will.'

Signalling to Pommes Frites, he strode across the square to where his own car was parked, climbed in, slammed the door and pressed the starter.

In the silence that followed he felt rather than saw a shadow loom up against the side window. There was a tap, then the door opened.

'Well?' said Inspector Banyuls sarcastically. 'Don't tell me you have changed your mind.'

'Someone,' said Monsieur Pamplemousse with as much dignity as he could muster, 'seems to have taken my battery.'

'What!' A sudden change came over Inspector

117

Banyuls. He reached inside his pocket and took out a note-book. 'This is serious.'

Monsieur Pamplemousse gazed at him. How could anyone be such an oaf as to ignore what he was convinced amounted to yet another attempt on his life and yet spring into action on hearing about a missing battery? He'd been nearly poisoned, shot at, had his balcony railings sawn through, escaped death by inches from a maniac in a car . . . words failed him. The man's mind was an arid desert.

'I will give you a clue,' he said slowly and distinctly. 'It is my belief that the person who took it is not a million miles from this very spot, and if you meet him I should treat him with the greatest respect. He is undoubtedly highly dangerous and may well render you grievous bodily harm.'

Deriving what little satisfaction he could from the parting shot, he climbed out of the car again and with Pommes Frites at his heels set off briskly towards the Grande Avenue Charles de Gaulle. Pommes Frites had long since given up trying to follow what was going on. He was wearing his mournful expression, the one he kept for occasions when things promised—like after-dinner walks—took a long time to materialise.

Monsieur Pamplemousse felt he could delay matters no longer.

It was late when they got back. Pommes Frites had been determined to get his pound of flesh. The clock over the Hôtel de Ville already showed past midnight, and by the time Monsieur Pamplemousse had inflated the new kennel and said good night the half hour had also struck.

Finding the rear entrance locked, he made his way round to the front of the hotel and with a nod to the gendarme who was still on duty just inside the doorway, crossed the hall to the stairs.

Halfway up he thought he heard a muffled explosion coming from one of the floors above. He sniffed. There was a smell of burning coming from somewhere not too far away. Rubbery, rather like a vacuum cleaner which is about to give up the ghost. That was all that was needed to round off the evening—a fire!

Hurrying up the remaining few stairs he was about to turn on to the landing when instinct told him to slow down. Luck was with him. Peering round the corner he was just in time to see Madame Sophie leaving his room. She was, to say the least, in a state of *déshabillé*. Her hair hung about her shoulders in ringlets, most of her front appeared to be covered by some kind of black deposit, and from the brief glimpse he had of her face it wore a glazed expression like that of a believer who has just been awarded the honour of the last waltz with her favourite guru. Oblivious to all about her, she turned and groped her way along the corridor, finally disappearing into her quarters at the far end like someone in a trance.

As soon as the coast was clear Monsieur Pamplemousse hurried after her. As he drew near his door the source of the smoke was only too clear. Wafts of it were emerging from the gap at the bottom. Holding a handkerchief over his nose he pushed it open and went inside. It was even worse than he had expected. It smelt and looked like a charnel house.

Gasping for breath he crossed to the shutters

and flung them open, then turned, prepared for the worst.

His bed was a sorry sight. Rumpled sheets were one thing, and in the circumstances not unexpected, but of the *poupée*, apart from the two wooden legs and a motley collection of wires, rods and sundry items of unidentifiable electronic devices, little remained but a smouldering heap of blackened rubber. Like the rim of an all too active volcano, they surrounded a large hole in the centre of the mattress.

Through it he could see the twisted remains of his car battery. Placing it immediately below the bedsprings had obviously been a cardinal error. He'd taken no account of Madame Sophie's weight, nor her enthusiasm once she got going. She must have cut through the wire and caused a short circuit. If Banyuls knew what had really happened to the battery he would have filled his note-book a dozen times over. How he would ever face the chambermaid again he didn't know.

While he was thinking the matter over, Monsieur Pamplemousse heard a slight sound at the door. He turned and saw a sheet of notepaper lying on the carpet. It had a familiar look.

The words confirmed his worst fears.

'Dearest one of the darkness,' he read. 'You who remain so silent and yet have so much to give. When I left you tonight you seemed strangely deflated, and yet . . . and yet, each time we meet . . . is it only twice? . . . each time is more exquisite than the one before. I thought I knew you, but tonight was different again. What will tomorrow bring? I cannot wait . . . although I know I have to. Until then . . . your loving S.'

Merde! Monsieur Pamplemousse sat down on the end of the bed and buried his head in his hands. Now he was really *dans le chocolat*. A dying sizzle came from somewhere underneath, but he ignored it. It was no good. Tomorrow he would have to go through the whole rigmarole again. What next? Perhaps . . . perhaps the Mark V—the one with the optional extras—whatever they might be.

He opened his suitcase and reached inside for the catalogue which had been enclosed with the parcel from *Poupées Fantastiques*. Sleep would not come as easily as usual that night.

7

THURSDAY AFTERNOON

At fourteen hundred hours precisely on the following day, Monsieur Pamplemousse, replete from a most satisfactory *déjeuner* at the Bar du Centre, picked up his receipted bill and set off across the square towards his hotel.

He felt at peace with the world. The word *cuisine* had many meanings and variations, but in his humble opinion one of its most rewarding peaks lay within a freshly baked *baguette*, split down the middle, lightly buttered, with perhaps a dash of *Moutarde de Dijon* to taste, and then filled with slices of ham—preferably from the Ardennes and tasting of the smoke from the trees of the forest and the maize and acorn diet on which the pigs had been reared. When it was washed down with a bottle of local wine, such as the Chateau Vignelaure he'd been privileged to drink that day, there was nothing finer.

It was a view with which Pommes Frites heartily concurred. Apart, that is, from the mustard. Pommes Frites didn't like mustard. It made his eyes water.

Monsieur Pamplemousse made a mental note to confirm the Bar du Centre's entry in *Le Guide*. Not with a Stock Pot—they would neither expect it nor thank him for it, but certainly with a wrought iron table and chair—the symbol which denoted a good place to stop en route, and a cut above the award of a mere bar stool.

One way and another it had been a busy morning. There had been the ordering of a new *poupée*—the Mark V this time complete with batteries, to be sent direct to the hotel without delay. That in itself had taken a great deal of argument and had used up most of his small change. Oscar had not been keen on the idea at all. In the end he'd had to resort to threats again, but it had left him feeling weary. Arguments always did.

Then he'd had to change his car battery. The plates on the old one were buckled beyond hope. That had taken most of the morning. The Citroën agent was at the other end of town, too far to carry the old one. And when he'd finally got it there on the back of a borrowed bicycle he'd encountered a distinct lack of enthusiasm about taking it in part exchange.

Halfway across the square he heard someone call out his name and turned to see Giampiero hurrying towards him. He looked worried.

'Is it true about last night?'

Monsieur Pamplemousse stifled a sigh. The chambermaid must have been talking. Not that he could blame her—she probably couldn't wait.

'I heard the car going past from my room. I rushed to the end of the corridor but by then it was too late. I saw you and Inspector Banyuls by the fountain, so I guessed you were all right. Then, soon after, I heard a bang . . . it sounded as though it came from the direction of your room. After that I smelt smoke . . .'

Monsieur Pamplemousse hesitated, wondering

whether to tell the full story, then thought better of it. 'It wouldn't be the first time someone has tried to do away with me.'

'Perhaps.' It was Giampiero's turn to hesitate, then he, too, seemed to change his mind. 'But take care.' He held out his hand. 'It is possible we may be leaving soon. Eva is getting restive. She wishes to move on.' Again there was a slight hesitation.

'I'm sorry.' Really there was little more to be said. In any case he was anxious to be on his way. It was kind of Giampiero to bother about his well-being and although it was true that it wouldn't be the first time someone had been out to do him harm, that was long ago. He felt more than able to take care of himself. Besides, it was nearly five past the hour.

Entering the garden behind La Langoustine by a side gate, he made his way towards a small hexagonal iron and glass gazebo standing in the centre of a small patch of rough grass which served as a lawn. He was pleased to see that it was still empty.

As he sat down a waiter emerged from the rear of the hotel carrying a silver tray on which reposed a silver pot filled with coffee, a cup and saucer, and a large balloon-shaped glass containing Armagnac.

Having placed it on the table in the centre of the gazebo and made sure that all was well, he retired gracefully from the scene, nursing the forlorn hope that the other occupants of the hotel might emulate Monsieur Pamplemousse and take their after-lunch drinks on the terrace, in the garden, or even—sparing Monsieur Pamplemousse—in the gazebo itself. Anywhere, so long as he could get on with clearing the tables. The waiters from La Langoustine were playing netball against a team from an hotel in the next village that afternoon and time was of the essence.

At fourteen-o-eight, Pommes Frites, having decided that there was nothing to be gained from hanging about, wandered off for a post-prandial nap, leaving his master to cogitate on life in general and the after-taste of sandwiches *au jambon* and Armagnac in parti-cular. It was hot in the gazebo and if he was going to have a nap he preferred to do it in the comfort of his kennel.

Monsieur Pamplemousse looked forward to his half hour or so of peace and quiet every afternoon. The gazebo was a new addition—so new it still had the steel ring on top which had been used to lift it into place—but it was ideal. It was amazing how quickly one settled down to a new routine. A few days in a place and it began to feel as though you had always lived there.

He would have been somewhat put out had he been able to read the waiter's mind. Fond of company when the occasion demanded, Monsieur Pamplemousse also placed great store on moments when he could be alone with his thoughts, which was quite a different matter to being lonely. Loneliness was often being by oneself in a crowd. Being alone of one's own choice was in its way a great luxury, so when he saw the girl from reception heading his way he pursed his lips with annoyance. From the agitated way she was behaving he could tell she was not the bearer of good news.

'A telephone call, Monsieur . . . from Paris.'

Monsieur Pamplemousse grunted. Who could it be,

telephoning him in his lunch hour? 'Did they not give their name?'

'No, Monsieur. It was a man. He said it was urgent.'

'I will take it in my room.' Downing his Armagnac at a gulp, Monsieur Pamplemousse clambered to his feet and followed the girl back into the hotel.

At fourteen fifteen precisely, while he was making his way up to his room—a moment marked by the striking of the clock over the Hôtel de Ville—Albert, a *clochard* whose abode was rarely fixed and then usually at the whim of Inspector Banyuls or one of his subordinates, polished off the remains of a litre of a *vin* whose ordinariness needed to be tasted to be believed. Climbing unsteadily to his feet, he smacked his lips, which he then wiped on the sleeve of his tattered raincoat, crossed the street, and made towards the *chemiserie* of Madame Peigné, which was about to open for business.

Standing outside he opened his raincoat wide, thus exposing himself to Madame Peigné, who was about to unlock the door, and proceeded to go about his own business by the simple expedient of relieving himself on the glass panel.

Madame Peigné, who'd only had her windows cleaned that very morning, gazed at the sight open-mouthed. Registering the fact, without being totally aware of it, that there was something very odd about Albert's anatomy, she uttered a short prayer and reached for the telephone on her counter.

Having many times rehearsed how to call for help in the dark in the event of an emergency, she was able to dial the correct number without missing a single moment of Albert's performance. She had read of such things. She had—let it be said—even dreamed of such things, although not nearly as often as she would have liked, but never had she expected to see what she was seeing in the flesh as it were. Albeit, and thankfully, it was separated from her by a sheet of plate glass—but there it was, as large as life if not twice as beautiful. Her feeling of relief that she hadn't actually got as far as unlocking the door was only outweighed by her desire to make the most of the situation. It was better than anything she had ever seen on television.

Inspector Banyuls tried to keep a straight voice. 'He is doing *what* with it?' he asked.

Madame Peigné gulped. 'He is brandishing it at me. And . . . and . . .'

'And *what*?' Inspector Banyuls tried not to sound too impatient.

'He . . . he has a balloon tied to the . . . the end of it. A large, red balloon.'

'May I have a description?'

'You mean . . . for the identification parade?' The voice at the other end could barely suppress its excitement. 'One moment while I get my glasses.'

Having posed the question, Inspector Banyuls immediately regretted it. His words had obviously been misinterpreted. He put the receiver down, signalled to one of his subordinates, and made one of his very rare jokes.

'It seems,' he said with a thin smile, 'that St. Castille is *en fête*. Please go at once to Madame Peigné in the Rue Vaugarde. She is having trouble with the decorations.'

127

It was the last joke he was to make that day. He'd barely put the telephone down when it rang again.

This time it was Monsieur Dupré, outfitter, clothier, and senior partner in the firm of Dupré et fils, an establishment almost as ancient as La Langoustine itself, and whose windows had suffered—were still suffering if the occasional sound of breaking glass was anything to go by—indignities of an even more basic and destructive nature than those of the previous complainant.

'A brick?' repeated Inspector Banyuls. He glanced at his watch and entered the time—fourteen eighteen—on a pad in front of him. 'What sort of brick?'

His question unleashed a veritable torrent of abuse. A torrent which made it difficult to sort out the wheat of plain, unadorned truth from the chaff of uncontrolled indignation.

It seemed that Monsieur Dupré had been enjoying his usual leisurely lunch on the pavement outside the Bar du Centre on the other side of the square—a *steak frites* with salad, followed by a *crème caramel*—when, before his very eyes, a miscreant of the worst possible kind had struck, not once, but several times, leaving a hole in the window large enough to climb through.

'*Déshonorant! Scandaleux! Action sans intermédiaire!*' were just a few of the phrases Monsieur Dupré barked with matching gestures down the telephone at the back of the bar, while at the same time keeping a watchful eye on the goings on in his shop window across the square.

The *lourdaud* was even now trying on a pair of shoes—several sizes too small by the way he was

128

mincing up and down. The backs would be broken for certain.

'Yes, yes, I will send someone round as soon as possible.' Inspector Banyuls' voice sounded wearily over the line. 'No, I cannot come myself. I cannot be in two places at once and I am needed here. There are many things happening at the moment and my forces are depleted.'

'I warn you, Banyuls, I am not without friends in the higher echelons.' Monsieur Dupré, his face growing redder and redder, gripped the telephone receiver rather as he might have gripped the throat of the transgressor on the other side of the square had he possessed the necessary courage. Even as he did so there was a click. He gazed at it disbelievingly for a moment. The impossible had happened. Banyuls had hung up on him.

There was another crash of breaking glass. Monsieur Dupré's uninvited guest was enjoying himself. It wasn't often one could break the law and be paid for doing it. Never one to question good fortune when it came his way—the Lord alone knew how rarely *that* was—he had accepted with alacrity a fat fee and the promise of free transport out of town at fourteen thirty-five hours if all went according to plan. No doubt in the fullness of time the law would catch up on him, but in the meantime he had a new jacket, a pocketful of socks, several ties and handkerchiefs, and a new pair of shoes. Sadly, two left-fitting ones, for Monsieur Dupré was not one to take chances and never left complete pairs on display in his window. But beggars could not be choosers; the trousers went very well with the jacket, and the shirt couldn't have been a better fit. As for the tie—he looked at his reflection in the mirror. It was many years since he'd last sported a tie.

Covering his arm for protection with another jacket, he enlarged the hole in the window and clambered out. The few passers-by who had stopped to watch, tempered their outrage by their very active dislike of Monsieur Dupré, who had grown fat and rich at their expense over the years. Reaching inside the window for a hat as a last-minute embellishment, the intruder waved goodbye to his audience and set off out of town towards his rendez-vous. It was now twenty-two minutes past the hour by the clock across the square and he would have to hurry.

In his office at the Commissariat de Police, Inspector Banyuls also checked the time, registered the fact in his mind that the *autobus* from Forcalquier had just passed his window on schedule, and reached for the telephone as it began to ring again.

What would it be this time? He couldn't remember ever having had a day like it before. Apart from the matters he had dealt with personally, reports were coming in of other strange happenings in various quarters of the town. No part of St. Castille was without its problems. There was the mysterious affair of the old crone with six—or was it seven?—children, all of whom had decided to squat in the middle of the main road to Digne and were refusing to budge. They had better be moved before the *autobus* went on its way or there would be hell to pay. Already he could hear the sound of irate car horns.

Then there was the case of old Madame Ranglaret.

She'd emptied an entire bucket of slops over some American tourists who'd been taking a stroll round the old part of the town and had had the misfortune to pass under her window at the time. In fact, not just one bucket, but, according to all accounts, three! One bucket might have been an accident—but three! Where she'd got them all from goodness only knew. Madame Ranglaret had probably never owned more than one bucket in the whole of her life.

As for Dupré. He regretted hanging up on him. He would have to make amends in some way. On reflection, he, Banyuls, would deal with the matter personally. Not for nothing had Monsieur Dupré contributed to the police funds over the years.

It was going to involve a lot of paperwork. As if he didn't have enough on his plate already.

He picked up the receiver. 'Banyuls here.'

But if Inspector Banyuls hoped for some kind of respite from his problems he was unlucky. As the voice at the other end spluttered forth its indignation he reached for a pad.

'One moment . . . let me get that down. You say you are playing *boules* against a team from Digne . . . their *pointeur* had just committed a *pousse-pousse*.'

Inspector Banyuls was no *boules* player, but he knew enough about the game to appreciate that in some circles, the very serious circles—and St. Castille was in line to win the area championship, bowling a *pousse-pousse*—the act of making your ball end up as close to the *cochonnet* as possible and at the same time intentionally knocking your opponent's ball out of the way—was considered *de trop*.

He could picture the scene in the Square du Centre; the strip of gravel under the plane trees behind the fountain; the group of elderly citizens with their berets, their Gauloises, and their own personal locker against the wall; perhaps a sprinkling of younger bloods privileged to join in; the click of the balls and the grunts and imprecations and arguments as the play went first one way and then another. They were all probably too engrossed in the game to even notice the outrage being perpetrated in Monsieur Dupré's shop. Some, no doubt, were already looking forward to the traditional *pan bagna* after it was all over.

Placing his other hand over the receiver, he raised his eyebrows for the benefit of anyone who happened to be passing, and then realised that he was alone in the station. He must concentrate. It wasn't easy, for his caller was more than a trifle incoherent.

'Yes, yes, I understand. Your *tireur* was about to throw a *carreau*.' He gave a sigh. Why was it that in all walks of life a certain mumbo-jumbo had to be created in order to add to the mystique? Why couldn't the man simply say that the best thrower in the team was about to hurl his ball and try to knock his opponent's one for six, leaving his own in its place? It would be much simpler.

'Yes, I *do* know that Jean can crack a walnut at twenty paces, but I really do not see . . .' It was hard to tell where the conversation was leading. *Boules* was undoubtedly an important matter, but . . .

'What? You have lost your *cochonnet*? Do you mean to say you have been talking to me all this time about a lost ball? Really . . .

132

'*What?*' Inspector Banyuls jumped to his feet. 'Would you mind repeating that? A man came out from the crowd of sightseers, picked up the *cochonnet* and did what with it? . . . He placed it in the letter box outside the P.T.T? The *Autres Régions* section? . . . Yes, yes, I know the P.T.T. does not reopen until fifteen hundred hours. I will be with you immediately.'

Slamming the receiver down, Inspector Banyuls reached for his belt and revolver.

Forces were at work in St. Castille which for the moment were beyond his understanding. There was a feeling of near anarchy in the air. But he would get to the bottom of it.

It was an unprecedented situation. Such a thing had never happened before. Not in his memory. The entire police force of the town was fully occupied. For the first time in its history he was going to have to lock up the station and leave it unattended.

Noting the time on his pad—fourteen twenty-three—he turned the key in the station door and made his way quickly towards the square. If he wasn't careful there could be a lynching. Already a large crowd had collected.

Ahead of him, the *autobus* had disgorged its passengers and was making ready to leave again. Reluctantly, for the driver was craning his neck to see what was going on. A solitary female figure in a fur coat was just disappearing with some luggage into the Hôtel Langoustine. From behind the hotel there were sounds of activity—a crane was moving into position, its jib turning and the giant grappling hook swinging through the air as it set to work. Close by a lorry was backing through a gap in the wall, revving its engine impatiently.

In his room on the first floor of the hotel Monsieur Pamplemousse was taking his call.

'. . . sorry to trouble you, Aristide. I wouldn't normally have telephoned, but we only got the news this morning. It is terrible. Terrible.'

'What news?' For a moment Monsieur Pamplemousse couldn't think what the other was talking about. Then he remembered. Time flew.

'Oh, it wasn't so bad. A bit of a shock at first. It was unexpected. It isn't every day one finds a head on one's plate. However, it's kind of you to ring.'

'A head?' It was the turn of the voice at the other end to sound puzzled. 'What head? I was telephoning about your accident. It is terrible news. Terrible. Both legs, I hear. The boys are arranging a collection.'

Monsieur Pamplemousse suppressed a groan. He wished he'd never thought of the idea. It seemed as though he would be plagued with it for the rest of his life; all for the sake of a momentary act of goodwill.

'They can't!' he exclaimed. 'They *mustn't*.'

'Nonsense! It's the least we can do.'

'But it isn't like that.' Monsieur Pamplemousse hovered between telling the truth with the risk of revealing all and embroidering his tale still further. If rumours could fly one way they could certainly fly the other. Perhaps a transplant? It was amazing what they could do these days. He would be able to return to Paris a new man. But *two* legs, and from whom? Two different ones? Perhaps one male and one female? Or

even two female? Now, *there* was fuel for thought . . .
A voice in his ear reminded him that the other was still
speaking.

'There, is talk of applying for a wheelchair through
the Ministry. With your background . . .'

'Look,' he broke in, 'I am saying there is no truth in
the story—no truth whatsoever. But for the moment,
while I am still here in St. Castille, I would rather it
wasn't spoken about. I will explain it all when I get
back to base.'

'No truth?' The voice at the other end sounded
almost disappointed.

'I swear on my copy of *Le Guide*. The two legs I am
standing on at this moment are not only flesh and
blood, they are my own, as they always have been. As
for the collection—you must give the money back at
once. All of it. It would be most embarrassing . . .'

'Oh, that's O.K. No trouble there. You know how
it is . . . the end of the month . . . most people out on
the road . . . the Directeur always in conference. To
tell you the truth, we haven't actually got very much
yet. Everyone sends their felicitations, of course. The
thing is . . .'

'Well?' Monsieur Pamplemousse tried not to sound
aggrieved.

'That's the other reason I'm phoning. To warn
you . . .'

'Warn me?'

'I wouldn't be in your shoes right now, that's for sure.
Hey, can you stand a shock?' Monsieur Pamplemousse
could have sworn the voice at the other end was about
to break into a chuckle. He glanced at his watch

impatiently. It was almost half past two. His coffee would be stone cold.

'Speak up, do.' He could hardly hear for the noise outside. The builders must be back at work earlier than usual. Apart from the rattle of the crane there was an infernal roar from one of the lorries. Above it all he suddenly heard a long drawn out howl from Pommes Frites.

'One moment.' Holding the receiver at arm's length he crossed to the balcony. As he reached out to pull the shutters closed he glanced down into the courtyard below. Pommes Frites appeared to be struggling to free himself from his kennel. For some reason or other—perhaps a nightmare following his lunch—he must have stood up too quickly. He looked for all the world like an arctic explorer dressed in one of those bulbous waterproof jackets that were all the rage. As he watched, Pommes Frites managed to struggle free at last and ran barking across the garden, peering up-wards as he did so.

Monsieur Pamplemousse followed his gaze and suddenly became transfixed at the sight which met his eyes.

There, not a stone's throw away, rising inexorably into the air on the end of the crane's cable, was the gazebo. The very same gazebo in which he'd been sitting only moments before. The hook on the end of the cable had been slipped through the steel ring which surmounted it. Miraculously his coffee things and the empty Armagnac glass were still in place on the table.

But it wasn't any of these trivial details or the

mournful sound of Pommes Frites' howls that caused him to blanch; it was the sight of a solitary white-faced occupant, clutching a parasol with one hand and the side of the gazebo with the other as it swung in a circular motion while the crane shunted back on its rails.

Before he had a chance to call out, the jib moved away from the window. The movement sent the hut spinning, as with more haste than finesse it began lowering it on the other side of the garden wall.

'Hullo! Hullo!' A series of whistling noises brought Monsieur Pamplemousse back to earth again with the realisation that he was still holding the telephone receiver. He held it up to his ear.

'Ah, there you are. What on earth's going on? As I was saying, this may come as a bit of a shock, but you see . . . when your wife heard the news she left for St. Castille at once. There was nothing we could do to stop her. She should be with you any moment now. I thought I had better warn you . . .'

The rest of the words were lost as there came a roar of an engine. Monsieur Pamplemousse gripped the receiver in his clenched hand as he leaned out of the window across the balcony to see what was happening.

'Doucette has not only arrived,' he said grimly, 'she has already left again. She came past my window not ten seconds ago in a gazebo, and at this very moment she is on the back of a lorry speeding God knows where . . . Pommes Frites is about to set off in pursuit, but I fear the worst.'

They were the last words he was to utter for some

while. Straining to the utmost in order to follow the progress of the lorry he made a grab for the rail and realised all too late that it was no longer there. He felt himself falling. Halfway down he remembered he'd moved Pommes Frites' kennel. Then everything went black.

8

FRIDAY MORNING

'I am sorry to disturb you.' Monsieur Pamplemousse stirred and shook himself awake. Ever since his fall he'd been confoundedly sleepy, hardly able to keep his eyes open for more than a few seconds at a time. His mouth felt dry. He suspected drugs but had no recollection of being given any.

He sat up and gazed at Inspector Banyuls, poised at the side of the bed, note-book in hand.

'What time is it?'

'Eleven thirty in the morning.'

Monsieur Pamplemousse concentrated his thoughts. 'It can't be,' he said at last. 'I remember very clearly having lunch at the Bar du Centre . . .'

Inspector Banyuls allowed himself one of his rare smiles. 'That was yesterday—Thursday. Today is Friday. Friday morning. As I was saying, I do not wish to disturb you . . . for obvious reasons.' He nodded towards a large mound at the bottom of the bed. 'But if we are to have any success in our search we must have a description.'

'Friday?' Monsieur Pamplemousse looked instinctively for his watch. A lighter patch of flesh marked where it had been. He had a momentary feeling of panic, as if a lifeline had been cut off. Then, to his relief, he saw it on the table beside the bed. Alongside it was his favourite Cross pen. He reached for the watch, checked Banyuls' statement, and slipped it back on his wrist. Things were slowly swimming into place. The telephone call. The gazebo. Doucette . . . the broken balcony . . . Pommes Frites barking as he ran off in pursuit of the lorry . . .

'I repeat. We must have a description.'

'Of course . . . I understand. Let me see . . .' This was no good. No good at all. He must concentrate.

'Fairly large, I would say. Tall, that is . . . not in weight. The weight is about forty-five to fifty kilograms. Deeply sunk eyes—a mixture of hazel and yellow. Large ears. Looks rather sorrowful. The hair . . . the hair is a mixture of colours. Black and tan with a little red here and there, flecked with white on the chest . . .'

Inspector Banyuls carried on making notes for a moment or two. His writing was like his moustache; small, thin, precise and well cared for. When he finally caught up with his words and read through them he let out a whistle.

'*Morbleu*! She sounds *formidable*. No wonder you holiday alone. Tell me, how long have you been married?'

Monsieur Pamplemousse gazed at him pityingly. '*Married*? I am not talking of my wife. I am talking of Pommes Frites.'

Inspector Banyuls seemed to have some difficulty in swallowing. Tearing off the page, he screwed it up into a tight ball and tossed it into a wastebin.

'I am not,' he said at long last, 'I never have been,

and I never will be interested in Pommes Frites. I have better things to do with my time than look for stray dogs. Besides, he ate my best clue.' He made it sound like a schoolboy complaining about a lost ball.

Monsieur Pamplemousse glared at him. 'And I,' he said, drawing himself up as high as he could in the circumstances, 'have better things to do with my time than talk to nincompoops. How dare you talk of Pommes Frites in that way! You are not fit to tread the same ground he walks on. If you were lost together in the Sahara desert you would not deserve a sip at his water bowl. The sad fact is that he would readily allow it whereas it wouldn't even cross your tiny mind to share yours with him. If he is not found and found quickly I shall hold you personally responsible. And if any harm comes to him in the meantime I would not care to be in your shoes.'

Monsieur Pamplemousse sank back into his pillow, exhausted by the effort of his outburst, and awaited a return barrage. But to his surprise, the reply when it came was unusually mild.

Inspector Banyuls snapped his note-book shut and fastened it carefully with an elastic band. 'I realise,' he said, 'that you are a little overwrought after your . . . experience, therefore I shall ignore those remarks. I will return later in the day when you are more amenable to conversation.'

He crossed to the door and then paused and looked curiously at Monsieur Pamplemousse. 'Tell me,' he said. 'Why are you here? What exactly *are* you doing in St. Castille?'

'I have already told you. I am here on holiday.'

Inspector Banyuls shrugged. 'I ask,' he said, 'because when you were brought in, this,' he reached into an inner pocket and withdrew another note-book which he tossed on to the end of the bed, 'this was found strapped to your . . . er . . . leg.' Once again Monsieur Pamplemousse was aware of an odd hesitation. 'It appears to contain entries about various rendez-vous— St. Castille included. All written in some kind of code. It is also,' he continued pointedly, 'full of holes.'

Monsieur Pamplemousse breathed a sigh of relief. To have had his true identity revealed would have been bad enough, but to have lost his precious note-book into the bargain would have been much, much worse. Its accumulation of riches would be hard to replace even though much of it had found its way into *Le Guide*.

He thought quickly. 'I am conducting a survey of the police forces of France,' he said maliciously. 'The holes are where I feel improvements could be made. If you look closely you will see there is a large one opposite St. Castille.'

But he was addressing a changed Inspector Banyuls. For some reason best known to himself he refused to be drawn. In any case, before he had time to reply the door opened and there was a rustle of starched linen as the ward sister—a nun—entered the room, signalling that it was time to leave. The door closed again and he heard a murmur of voices in the corridor outside. The sister appeared to be laying down the law regarding something about which Inspector Banyuls, to judge from the sceptical tone of his voice, remained unconvinced.

Monsieur Pamplemousse took stock of his surroundings. Obviously he was in some kind of hospice. Probably the one he'd seen on the edge of the town. From the view through the window he judged himself to be on an upper floor. A half-open door led to an adjoining bathroom. His suitcase was on a stand just inside the door. Slipping out of bed he crossed to it and lifted the lid. Everything appeared to be intact. Clothes, neatly folded, some untouched reading matter. A smaller case bearing an embossed stock pot on its lid, containing among other things his Leica R4 and Trinovid binoculars, property of *Le Guide*, was safe. The directeur would not have been pleased if on top of all else that had been lost. He unlocked the case, slipped the binoculars out of their compartment, and crossed to the window. His guess was correct. He was on the fifth floor. The window faced the mountains, affording much the same view as the one he'd enjoyed at La Langoustine. Somewhere out there in all probability was Doucette. Doucette and Pommes Frites.

He put the binoculars away again, relocked the case and climbed back into bed, slipping his feet beneath the wire cage which was the cause of the large lump at the bottom. He couldn't imagine why it was there. He felt his legs. Apart from a slight soreness where he'd been hit by the shot and the aggravation caused by Sophie's sandpapering, they seemed fine. In fact, taken all round, give or take a little stiffness here and there, he felt remarkably fit; none the worse for his fall.

He took a closer look at the room. On the wall near the door was a sampler. 'GOD GIVE ME PATIENCE', and underneath the words, 'BUT

PLEASE MAKE IT SOON'. He was definitely in the hospice. The humour bore all the signs of a Catholic mind at work.

By his bed, on top of the cupboard, there was a glass and a bottle of Vichy water.

He sniffed. There was an all-pervading smell of flowers in the room, and yet he could see none.

Climbing out of bed for the second time, he pulled aside a screen across a corner near the window and identified the source.

Back in bed he stared at it, trying to decide what it could possibly mean. To say that he had been sent flowers was the understatement of the year. It looked like the entire stock of a *fleuriste*. There were flowers in vases and in jugs; there were posies, arrangements— someone had obviously gone to a great deal of trouble. In the middle of them all—the centrepiece in fact—was a large, glass-fronted cabinet containing, of all things, his wooden legs. He recognised the charred ends where the bed had caught fire. But why on earth had they been put inside a glass case? And why all the flowers? Above it there was a carved figurine of the crucifixion. It was like a shrine.

Monsieur Pamplemousse lay back pondering the matter for a while and he had almost fallen asleep again when he was woken by a tap on the door.

'Come in.' He sat up, rubbing his eyes drowsily and opened them to see a young novice coming towards him carrying a large parcel and some smaller mail: a packet and two postcards. She hovered uneasily beside the bed and then placed the parcel gingerly on the counterpane as if it was some kind of a bomb about to explode. Stepping back quickly, she blushed and then crossed herself. Her expression seemed to be a mixture of disbelief and disappointment. Rather as if yet another illusion in her young life had been shattered; her choice of calling confirmed.

He saw why. The parcel was from *Poupées Fantastiques*. The label would have been recognisable a kilometre away.

'Merci.' There seemed nothing else to say.

Monsieur Pamplemousse followed the girl with his eyes as she turned towards the glass cabinet, crossed herself a second time, and then fled from the room as if the Devil himself was behind her. Thank the Lord he was fit and well and not in there for treatment. If all the staff crossed themselves every time they did anything, woe betide anyone who was in there hoping for a quick operation.

He read the first of the two postcards. If the writing was familiar the words were equally so. It bore a Paris postmark and it was from Doucette in reply to the one he'd sent her when he arrived at La Langoustine. His own card, as always, had taken a good deal of time to write. He remembered it very clearly. 'This is a picture of my room (the one marked with a cross) and below it is the garden. Now they have a gazebo where every lunch time I sit and have my café and think of you.' Doucette's was brief and to the point. 'It is the same room you always stay in! Do they have no other cards?'

Monsieur Pamplemousse turned to the second one. On the front there was a picture of the Roman theatre at Orange and on the back another message from Doucette, this time full of regrets and wanting to see him. It must have been written while she was waiting for the *autobus* to St. Castille. Poor Doucette.

The packet was marked 'CONFIDENTIEL' and looked official. He tore the envelope open. The contents would have confirmed Banyuls' worst suspicions about his presence there. From a friend in ballistics, it dealt with the bullet case Pommes Frites had brought him the morning of the shooting in Place Napoleon.

It told him nothing that meant anything. It was much as he had expected. The cartridge was a 7.5 × 54 m.m. match quality. Probably fired from a French FR–F1 Tireur d'Elite sniper's rifle. Ten-shot, manually operated, bolt action. Now obsolete. There was a lot of other information about availability of silencers and other accessories, mostly technical and mostly meaningless. It was of a type common in the French Army, and doubtless on the black market as well; an observation confirmed by a newspaper cutting which was attached, reporting a recent raid on an Army barracks in the South where amongst others fifty such weapons had been stolen.

Monsieur Pamplemousse turned his attention to another newspaper cutting. This time from an Italian newspaper. There was a picture of a familiar figure waving two bandaged hands jubilantly in the air. Italian wasn't his strong suit, but as far as he could make out the cause of the celebration was the winning by Giampiero of his claim for damages against his employers. No figure was mentioned, simply the fact that a settlement had been reached out of court for a sum believed to be in excess of five thousand million Italian lire . . . that was . . . he did some quick mental arithmetic . . . that was more than twenty million French francs. No wonder Giampiero had said there was a lot at stake.

He stared at the cutting for a moment or two. Strange, but it was not quite as he had explained it. Giampiero hadn't mentioned it being settled out of court. He checked the date at the top. It was almost a year ago to the day. He looked at the item again. Unusually for an Italian paper, there was no human interest angle—just the bare facts. Perhaps by then the whole thing was already *passé*.

He lay back again and closed his eyes. In his mind he had already accepted the possibility that Giampiero was right and that he had become the target for, to use the well worn phrase, 'persons unknown'. There was no other explanation. Despite the fact that over the years he had on more than one occasion been the subject of an attack of revenge it had always been little more than a storm in a tea-cup. A temporary mental derangement of someone with a grudge to bear. If you carried on as usual it went away again, but this was different. The present series of attacks bore all the hallmarks of the Mafia; there was obviously more than one person involved—several in fact. The head he had been served up with on the first night had obviously been meant as a warning. Quite probably the attack on the hill the next day was meant that way too. If they had intended to kill him they would have used something more powerful than a shotgun.

The episode with the car? That was another matter again. It had been a narrow squeak, but he doubted very much if they had been out to kill him.

The sawing through of his balcony rails? Somehow that didn't fit in with the rest. It was an inconclusive thing to do, more the act of someone who wanted to get him out of the way for some reason or other.

He had his own theory as to the identity of the person responsible. The perfume that night in the toilet had been unmistakable, unique. The wearer, he knew, had the cold hard eyes of someone quite capable of wielding a hacksaw to good effect if the occasion demanded. Proving it would be another matter. Something Banyuls could have got his teeth into if he'd felt inclined, which he obviously didn't; his mind was on other things.

As for the bullet—the spent case for which even now lay on his bed—that, too, could have been an intended warning. Pommes Frites must have thought it important since he'd brought it back for him, and he trusted Pommes Frites' judgment in these matters.

His thoughts turned to Pommes Frites. He would never forgive himself if anything happened to him. Not that he thought for one moment that anything would. Pommes Frites was well able to take care of himself. Doucette he was even less worried about. Since he was so clearly the target, he and no one else, he couldn't believe that they would do her any harm. More than likely she would give as good as she got and they would be glad to be rid of her. Doucette had a sharp tongue when she was roused. All the same, he wouldn't get any peace until he saw both of them again alive and well.

Another strange thing was the lack of any note. If what Giampiero had guessed at was true there should by now have been some kind of demand. At the very least after the first evening.

He wondered for a moment about Giampiero's relationship with Eva. On the surface it seemed an unlikely combination, and yet both in their own way were shadowy figures. Apart from a few brief encounters in the restaurant he'd hardly set eyes on the girl since he arrived; at least he had talked to Giampiero. Of the two he instinctively liked and trusted Giampiero, and yet . . .

Monsieur Pamplemousse picked up his pen. It was time for a list. A setting out of all the relevant facts in chronological order, beginning with his arrival on the Monday evening.

What day did Banyuls say it was now? Friday? It was incredible to think that he'd been in St. Castille for less than four whole days. So much had happened it felt more like a month.

But before he had time to marshal his thoughts, let alone put pen to paper, he heard the sound of approaching voices in the corridor. Lots of voices. They paused outside his room. It sounded like some kind of delegation. *Mon Dieu!* What was it now?

He hadn't long to wait. The door burst open and a flood of white-coated students poured through. Led by the large and authoritative figure of a surgeon and accompanied by the sister and a younger nun carrying some X-ray plates, they headed towards his bed.

Totally ignoring him, they gathered round the foot and waited expectantly while the sister untucked the top sheet.

'*Voilà!*' Taking the end from her, the surgeon threw

it back over the top of the cage like a conjuror demonstrating his latest and most ambitious trick.

If a flock of pigeons had emerged Monsieur Pamplemousse couldn't have been more taken aback, and he was hardly prepared for the response accorded this relatively simple act.

The applause as the audience bent down to take a closer look was spontaneous and genuine. Mingled with it there was a feeling of awe, almost as if those present felt they were witnessing some big breakthrough in the medical world; a moment of truth to which they had been admitted as privileged beings.

Given the cool draught which had suddenly blown up beneath his nightshirt, Monsieur Pamplemousse felt he hardly warranted such appreciation, gratifying though it was.

But his moment of glory was short-lived. Leaving the bedclothes to fall where they might, the surgeon strode across to the window and signalled for the X-ray plates.

Levering himself up in bed, Monsieur Pamplemousse strained in vain to get a better view. Nor, for that matter, could he catch more than a few passing words, and those that did come his way were hardly reassuring.

Lowering his voice in the manner of doctors the world over when discussing the fate of their patients, the surgeon held forth while the others gathered round him like members of a rugby scrum. If Monsieur Pamplemousse had thrown a ball in—or better still, the bed pan—he felt sure it would have come flying out again.

There were a lot of sucking-in noises as one or two

of the students drew breath in surprise and several times he caught the word *amputer*. It was a word that seemed to bother the sister almost as much as it did him, but for very different reasons. It wasn't so much that she was against the idea; she didn't want it to happen before the arrival of the *évêque*. Though what he would want with a bishop, or a bishop with him, Monsieur Pamplemousse had no idea.

A second school of thought seemed to favour a series of exploratory operations in the interim period. *Découvert* was the word used.

Monsieur Pamplemousse had a profound mistrust of the medical profession. They had a habit of removing things without so much as a by-your-leave, or even a second's thought as to whether or not they could get them all back in again, and he had no wish to be tampered with unless there was a very good reason.

Finally, he was unable to stand it a moment longer.

'When, or how, or why I arrived in this hospital,' he bellowed, 'I have no idea. But I arrived with at least one of everything to which I am entitled, two where there should be two, and that is how I intend leaving. I demand to see whoever is in charge immediately. I know my rights.'

Silence greeted his outburst for a second or two. Even the surgeon was momentarily struck dumb. Obviously, the thought of a patient having any kind of rights was an entirely new concept, and one outside his experience.

The sister hurried forward, anxious to pour oil on troubled waters. 'Now, now, we mustn't behave like that.'

'*We?*' barked Monsieur Pamplemousse. '*We* are not. *I* am. And I repeat, I am having no more tablets, no more injections, no more talk of exploratory operations, no more anything until I learn exactly what is going on.

'As for you, Monsieur.' He glared across at the surgeon. 'If you or any of your colleagues come within a kilometre of me with one of your wretched knives, or if I hear the word *amputer* once more it will be you who are in need of a transplant, not me. I hesitate to go into details while there are ladies present, but by the time I have finished you may well wish to join them in taking the vow.'

Not displeased with his effort, Monsieur Pamplemousse lay back in his bed again with his hands clasped and watched while his visitors filed out looking suitably cowed.

As soon as they had disappeared he reached over and poured himself some Vichy water. Being in hospital was improving neither his temper nor his liver.

He was about to return to his list when there was yet another knock at the door. He closed his eyes. Let them all come. It was getting to be like the Gare de Lyon at the start of the holiday season. Who was it to be this time?

The answer was framed in the doorway. It was Inspector Banyuls again. The new, conciliatory Banyuls. A Banyuls, nevertheless, who, catching sight of the parcel on the bed, couldn't resist a dig.

'*Sacrebleu!*' he exclaimed. 'You never give up, Pamplemousse. Even in hospital, you never give up.'

Monsieur Pamplemousse tried mentally counting up to ten. He wondered whether the inspector had taken some sort of course for saying the wrong thing or whether it just came naturally. If he had taken a course he must undoubtedly have come out top of his year.

The inevitable note-book appeared. 'You will be pleased to know, Pamplemousse, that progress has been made.'

Monsieur Pamplemousse felt his heart miss a beat. His opinion of Banyuls went up. 'You mean . . . Doucette? Pommes Frites has found Doucette?'

Inspector Banyuls shook his head. He seemed to find the interruption annoying. 'We have found your car battery!'

'My battery?' Monsieur Pamplemousse repeated the words as if in a dream.

'I thought you would be pleased. It appears to have been damaged in some way. I doubt if it is usable. We found it in a local garage. Whoever was responsible for the theft brought it in on the back of a bicycle and changed it for a new one suitable for a Deux Chevaux.

'What is more, we have a very full description of the person. Make no mistake. We shall bring him to book.'

Monsieur Pamplemousse lay very still, trying to make up his mind whether the inspector was being serious or not. He decided that incredible though it was he had yet to match the description in his note-book with the patient in front of him. But Inspector Banyuls obviously had other things on his mind.

153

Putting his note-book away, he approached the end of the bed.

'May I?' he enquired. And without waiting for a reply he lifted up the counterpane and peered underneath.

'Curious,' he said. 'Most curious. You will not mind if we send someone round to photograph them?'

'Them?' A dreadful thought entered Monsieur Pamplemousse's mind. Perhaps he had suffered some terrible injury. An injury so bad no one had dared tell him. He dismissed the idea, but only with difficulty.

'Let them all come,' he said, putting on a brave face. 'I am past caring. All I wish for at the moment is that someone should tell me what is going on. Not a single person comes into this room without they lift up my bed-sheets. I am beginning to feel like some side-show in a travelling circus.'

It was Inspector Banyuls' turn to look puzzled. 'You mean . . . you really do not know?'

'That is exactly what I mean.'

Inspector Banyuls crossed to the window and stood for a moment looking out in silence, then he turned. When he spoke again he was obviously choosing his words with care.

'The people in this part of the world are people of the mountains. They are insular—like islanders. Suspicious of strangers, and very superstitious.'

Monsieur Pamplemousse listened with interest. He couldn't for the life of him think what the other was leading up to.

'Some say one thing, some another. Rumours are rife. There are those, like the good Mother Superior,

154

who maintain that it is the work of God. Others say the opposite. Already a maid in the hotel has come forward to give evidence of things she has seen. She has produced part of a mattress with a hole burned in the middle to substantiate her views. A statement has been taken. Speaking for myself, I am keeping an open mind.'

Monsieur Pamplemousse ground his teeth. 'Banyuls,' he said, slowly and deliberately, 'you are a good man, but will you please stop beating about the bush and answer my question. Why am I being kept in here?'

The inspector moved away from the window and placed himself in a strategic position between the bed and the door. He pointed towards the glass case in the corner. 'You are here,' he said, 'for the very simple reason that yesterday afternoon when you fell from your balcony you were a man with two wooden legs. Moments later, when you were found, you had two real ones. It is not every day the people of St. Castille are privileged to bear witness to a miracle in their midst.

'There is, of course, a third faction—the disbelievers, or should I say the *agnostiques*.' He shrugged. 'But then, there always will be, whatever the subject.'

Monsieur Pamplemousse couldn't resist the obvious question.

'And you, Banyuls, to which faction do you belong?'

'I am a policeman. I deal in facts. I am also by nature suspicious and I keep an open mind. What do you say, Pamplemousse?'

Monsieur Pamplemousse clasped his hands in front

of him and assumed one of his most beatific smiles. Now that he had recovered from the initial shock of the inspector's revelation a certain something inside him felt he might enjoy the almost unlimited possibilities of his new role.

'Peace be with you, my son,' he intoned. 'For blessed are they who have not seen and yet still choose to believe.'

As the bang from the door echoed and re-echoed down the corridor he relaxed again. The smile faded as he returned to his list. Baiting Banyuls was all very well but it didn't solve any of his problems; rather the reverse.

Tearing off the top sheet of his note-pad he wrote the words 'I MUST BE KIND TO BANYULS' in large letters and attached it to the light on the wall behind his head. In that position it would announce to all the world that deep down his heart was in the right place and yet it would retain the advantage of not being permanently in his line of vision.

9

FRIDAY AFTERNOON

Unbeknown to Monsieur Pamplemousse, his feelings about Inspector Banyuls were being echoed at that very moment by Pommes Frites. If someone had posed the direct question, 'Hands up all those who wish they had been kinder to Inspector Banyuls,' Pommes Frites would have lost no time in raising his right paw. Pommes Frites was in a situation where he could have used some assistance. Something in the nature of a fan-out by the local gendarmerie would have gone down very well at that moment in time, for although his early training with the Sûreté had taught him many things, the art of being in more than one place at the same time had not been included in his course syllabus.

Had Pommes Frites been in the habit of keeping a diary, he would undoubtedly have headed the day in large, capital letters: 'BLACK FRIDAY'. One way and another it had been a fitting follow-on from 'DARK GREY THURSDAY', 'BROWN WEDNESDAY', 'OCHRE TUESDAY' and 'PUCE MONDAY'.

Not that he was grumbling. On and off, he'd had quite an enjoyable week. The taste of some of the meals at La Langoustine still lingered, and there had been some pleasant strolls round the town itself. But the ratio of good moments to bad had followed a downward curve as the week progressed, culminating in his present dilemma. To paraphrase Shakespeare's *Hamlet*, it really boiled down to a question of, 'To go or not to go? Whether 'twas better to keep a watchful eye on Madame Pamplemousse and suffer the possible slings and bullets of her outraged captors, or, having spent most of a day and a night on the job, hot foot it back to town by the shortest possible route.'

His pursuit of the lorry had got off to a bad start. At first he'd been so taken aback at seeing Madame Pamplemousse take off in the gazebo he'd hardly been able to believe his eyes. Then, when the full import of what was going on finally sank in, he'd stood up too quickly in his excitement and got himself entangled with his kennel.

His state of shock had been compounded when his master had, quite literally, landed at his feet. For the second time in as many days he'd found himself staring at the remains of his house. The only consolation to be gained was that in struggling to free himself from his kennel he'd quite by chance pushed it into exactly the right spot to break Monsieur Pamplemousse's fall and save him, if not from death, at least from serious injury.

By the time he'd checked things out and assured himself with a few well chosen licks that his master was still breathing, he had lost even more time and the lorry was nowhere in sight.

Pommes Frites was good at trails, but in the absence of any kind of scent he'd had to rely on instinct, and in the end instinct hadn't let him down.

He knew that the lorry had gone in roughly the same

158

direction as the one he and his master had taken the morning of the attack, so he took a chance. There was certainly a smell of lorries. Not that there was anything unusual in that. There was scarcely a ditch or hedgerow in the whole of France that didn't bear silent witness to the fact that lorries in one form or another passed by every day of the year, but the smell he chose to follow was unhealthily fresh.

The first part of the journey took him up the same road, past the very same bush which had caused all the trouble. Pommes Frites had given the bush a wide berth, even though it was now lying on its side, its foliage turning brown. He had no wish to repeat the experience.

All the same, it gave him his bearings, and he was able to take a short cut over the brow of the hill until a point in the road where it suddenly branched into two.

It was here that luck deserted him temporarily. Taking the right fork—the one that appeared the most used—he went on up the mountain towards the site of the new solar heating station. There he'd spent a fruitless day sniffing around domes and bits of metal and vast areas of glass and getting hotter and hotter in the process.

Hotter and hotter, that is, until the sun had gone down. After which he'd got colder and colder. The temperature dropped considerably and Pommes Frites spent a sleepless night wondering what to do next.

But all had not been in vain. In fact, if he hadn't gone off on a false trail and reached his vantage point he might never have seen the flash of morning sun reflected from a piece of glass on a neighbouring hill. It had to be the gazebo.

Pommes Frites made his way back down to the fork and then set off again, happy in the knowledge that what goes up must eventually come down again, and that since the road, which had now become a track, didn't seem to go anywhere other than up, anything like a lorry would have to pass him if it came back down again. It was a tenuous piece of reasoning, but when you are running hard reasoning comes in short spurts, and Pommes Frites had been running very hard indeed.

It all took much longer than he had expected and it wasn't until he was almost at the highest point of the next hill that he rounded a bend and suddenly stopped dead in his tracks. There in front of him, large as life and parked outside a small stone building, was the lorry. Crouching down behind a boulder, he surveyed the scene, taking it all in bit by bit and building up a picture in his mind. Somehow or other it wasn't quite as he had expected.

True, the gazebo had been unloaded from the lorry. It had been manhandled down some planks which still rested on the tailboard, and it was now ensconced on a nearby hillock.

But it wasn't the lorry or the gazebo that caused Pommes Frites to give the bloodhound's equivalent of a double-take; it was the sight of its lone occupant.

He could hardly believe his eyes. He'd been prepared for practically anything but what he saw. He tried looking away again and then refocusing his gaze, but it was still exactly the same.

Far from being in a distressed condition, Madame Pamplemousse appeared to be enjoying herself no end. The door of the gazebo was wide open and she was sitting in the middle, basking in the rays of the morning sun as it beat down on her through the glass roof and sides. She even had her coat off which was most unusual. Pommes Frites couldn't remember ever having seen Madame Pamplemousse out of doors without a coat before. He was too far away to see exactly what she was doing, but if it hadn't been quite so hard to believe he would have sworn she was knitting. By her side there was a breakfast tray.

While he was watching a man came out of the hut carrying another tray which he took across to the gazebo. He was followed by a second man who hurried on ahead to prepare the way. There was a flurry of movement and then a short scene which Pommes Frites immediately recognised. It was one he'd seen enacted many times before. He knew it off by heart. The straightening of the back, the wagging finger. He could almost hear the sniff which punctuated the monologue. The men were being told off for entering the gazebo without first wiping the dust from their shoes. Even as he watched one of them bent down and began wiping the floor with his handkerchief.

Madame Pamplemousse might have been abducted, but she was quite definitely in charge, and it was equally clear that she was perfectly happy to stay where she was—at least for the time being.

Taking advantage of the moment, Pommes Frites crept nearer still, wriggling along on all fours, body close to the ground, until he was in a position to get a better view and hear what was going on.

It was hard to know exactly what was being said—a lot of the conversation seemed to be conducted in sign language, but the gist was clear enough: Madame Pamplemousse was being invited to return to St. Castille the way she had come. Equally clearly Madame Pamplemousse had no intention whatsoever of doing anything of the sort. Madame Pamplemousse had had quite enough of travelling on the back of lorries. She was never going to travel on the back of a lorry again. Either they provided her with proper transport or she would not go at all. And if she didn't go at all then it would be the worse for all concerned.

There was a hurried conference. Lesser beings might well have been left to their fate, but Madame Pamplemousse was not, in any sense of the word, a lesser being. Madame Pamplemousse was not to be trifled with. What Madame Pamplemousse said went.

Under other circumstances Pommes Frites might well have enjoyed the sight of his adversaries being so thoroughly cowed, but he had various things on his mind.

Apart from being a bit fed up at having spent a night without food and shelter on the mountain, he was beginning to wonder how his master was getting on. For the time being, Madame Pamplemousse seemed in no great danger, and at least he now knew where she was, which was more than he could say for his master. There was no knowing where he might be.

Something else was beginning to bother him as well, another mathematical problem. Of the two men, he recognised one as the man who had sprung out of the bush at him—the one who had gone off bang so unexpectedly. The second man had been driving the car the night when he had very nearly been run down, of that he was sure. Pommes Frites had a good memory for faces. But one and one made two, and there had been three people in the car. The one who was missing was the man who had appeared briefly as the waiter on their first night. Of the three Pommes Frites trusted him least of all. He had a nasty feeling his absence might have something to do with his master, but first he had to find Monsieur Pamplemousse, and to find Monsieur Pamplemousse he had to get back to St. Castille, and quickly. Pommes Frites' thought processes might have been slow but they were thorough; they left no stone unturned, and once he'd sorted things out in his mind he was quick to take action. A moment later he was on his way back down the mountain as fast as his legs would carry him.

*　　*　　*

As it happened, Monsieur Pamplemousse's thoughts at that moment were occupied by much more mundane matters.

Hardly had Inspector Banyuls left than a trolley arrived bearing his lunch. After an evening and a night without food, Monsieur Pamplemousse was more than ready for it; now he was regretting his haste.

Not even several copious draughts of Vichy water helped to assuage the pain which had settled heavily in the middle of his chest, a pain which was only relieved by getting out of bed and walking around.

He crossed to the window and gazed out gloomily. One day he would have to persuade the directeur to allow him to conduct a survey of food in institutions. One day. It would hardly be a labour of love. The string which had held his *poulet* together had been better cooked than the bird itself. As for the soup that preceded it . . . what was it the Prince of Gastronomes, Curmonsky, had said? A good soup should taste of the things it is made of. If the one he had just eaten fulfilled that criterion he shuddered to think what its ingredients must have been.

In the courtyard below him people were hurrying to and fro. An ambulance drew up and disgorged its occupants. There was a sprinkling of nuns. Monsieur Pamplemousse's gaze softened as he looked at them. They were good people, devoting their lives to others. They always made him feel a trifle inadequate. A car drew up a short distance away from the others and a woman in black got out. The sight of all the comings and goings made him feel restless. The whole thing was quite ridiculous, but having said that the question arose as to what he should or even could do about it.

To walk out of the hospital was one thing. To leave quietly without setting up a great hue and cry was another matter entirely.

He crossed to the door and opened it. A long corridor running the full length of the building stretched out before him. The stairs and lifts were at the far end, on either side of a glass-fronted room inside which he could see the sister busy at her desk. As she looked up, sensing a movement, he dodged back into his room.

Glancing at the crumpled bed with its cage for his legs and the pile of pillows, a thought struck him; memories of childhood pranks and days at summer camps. A momentary diversion was all that was needed and he could be away.

He was on the point of stripping off the bedclothes when another idea occurred to him. A refinement which might make all the difference between success and failure. Once again *Poupées Fantastiques* could come to his rescue.

Bereft of Pommes Frites' gas cylinder, Monsieur Pamplemousse had to resort to what amounted to mouth-to-mouth resuscitation and by the time he had finished he was red in the face and panting from his exertions.

All the same, it had definitely been worthwhile. *Poupées Fantastiques* had excelled themselves. True, they had omitted the wooden legs this time, but in the circumstances that suited his purpose very well. If things carried on at the present rate they must be considering going into mass production. He would have to demand a royalty for the use of his image. He was pleased to see that they had taken note of his complaint and this time they had included the batteries. Twelve, no less! And he could see why. The Mark V differed from its predecessors in details only, but those details had obviously inspired the designers to give full rein to their fantasies. A fact which was readily apparent when he operated the switch.

He drew the blinds and then, to complete the picture, slipped out of his nightshirt. It was as he was in the act of pulling it over the head of the dummy that he heard voices outside.

Flinging the model on to the bed, he made a dive for the safety of the screen in the corner of the room. No sooner was he behind it than the door opened and he heard the voice of the girl who'd brought the mail earlier in the day.

'There is a lady to see you, Monsieur Pample-mousse . . .'

The voice broke off in mid-sentence and he heard a gasp. Peering through a join in the screen he saw the white face of the novice gazing in horror at the figure on the bed. In his haste he must have left the motor switched on.

'Oh, *Mon Dieu!*' Crossing herself, the girl fled from the room, leaving Monsieur Pamplemousse's visitor to her fate.

A moment later there was a click as the door was gently closed. His visitor clearly didn't share the novice's inhibitions. A thought crossed Monsieur Pamplemousse's mind. Could it be . . .? He shifted his position to try and get a better view and received an impression of blackness, a black veil, a black hat, and a long black dress reaching right to the ground.

Whoever it was, it certainly wasn't Sophie; and yet, even as he watched there was a flurry of movement and before his astonished gaze the unidentified visitor picked up the hem of her dress with both hands and began to raise it. Monsieur Pamplemousse crouched rooted to the spot. If it wasn't Madame Sophie it must be a near relation. An aunt perhaps? It was incredible, the woman hadn't been in the room more than a minute. He wondered if it had something to do with the mountain air.

But if Monsieur Pamplemousse was expecting to witness an action replay of the occurrences in his own room he was doomed to disappointment. Instead of revealing a set of frilly underwear, the first thing that caught his eye was a matching pair of blue trouser legs, rolled up to calf length and held in place by a pair of clothes pegs. The second thing, dangling from a fastening concealed beneath the dress, was the ominous shape of a Walther 9mm submachine-gun. It was a type Monsieur Pamplemousse had once fired during an attachment to the West German police; he remembered it well.

Slowly and deliberately the owner swung the stock into position, cocked the gun, slipped the lever above the pistol grip to fully automatic and pointed it towards the bed.

With a rate of fire of 550 rounds a minute, the full magazine took a mere seventeen seconds to discharge, nevertheless it seemed to last an eternity. It gave Monsieur Pamplemousse time to thank his lucky stars that he was where he was and not still between the sheets. Had he been in the bed . . . his stomach turned to water at the thought.

Luckily the gun was equipped with a silencer or the noise would have been deafening. Even so it was loud enough for Monsieur Pamplemousse to expect to hear running feet at any moment, but none came. Perhaps, for once, the sister had deserted her post.

The assailant was in no great hurry. If anything he seemed to be acting as if he had all the time in the world. For a full thirty seconds he gazed through the smoke at the remains of the figure on the bed. Although Monsieur Pamplemousse had no means of knowing it, his would-be assailant had just received the answer to a question that had often been a subject for discussion among those who worried about such things. If a man died at what might be called a *moment critique*, did he or did he not retain his enthusiasm for matters of the flesh. The answer in this particular case was definitely no. He had never seen anyone's manhood quite so destroyed. It was all very satisfactory. It was a pity the matter had to end this way, but that was life—or, in this case, death. You won one—you lost another. His instructions in the beginning had been to warn, to intimidate, but not to kill. However, there came a time when matters got out of hand, when tidiness was important, This was one of those occasions. He would have to wait a little while longer for his rewards, but he had all the time in the world. Waiting—in the company of 'a certain person', would have its compensations.

He smiled grimly beneath the veil, then as slowly and as deliberately as when he'd entered the room, he detached the umbilical-like cord from the gun and placed it on the floor. Walking would be much easier without it—he had no wish to have a hot barrel between his legs. A moment later he crept out of the room as silently as he had arrived.

Monsieur Pamplemousse let a decent interval elapse before he came out from behind the screen. The air was heavy with the smell of cordite. Avoiding the cartridge cases that had been ejected on to the floor, he crossed to the window, threw up the blind and leaned out.

Taking a deep breath of the fresh air he turned back into the room. As he did so he saw the door handle turning. Suddenly conscious of his vulnerable state now that his nightshirt had been destroyed by gunfire, he made a dive for the safety of the screen. He was only just in time.

'At it again, Pamplemousse?' Inspector Banyuls made no attempt to conceal his disapproval. 'Is there no limit to your depravity? I have received a serious complaint from the Mother Superior. It seems that you have been exposing yourself to one of the novices. These young ladies have taken the vow . . .'

The voice broke off in mid-flight. Very gently Monsieur Pamplemousse lowered himself to the floor in order to get a better view. But he needn't have worried about making too much noise. The inspector's attention was totally riveted by something just out of the line of vision.

For a moment or two Monsieur Pamplemousse wondered what could possibly be of such paramount importance it took precedence even over the contents of the bed. Clearly, it was having a deeply emotional effect on the other.

Then he remembered. It was his 'thought for the day'; the one he had fixed to the wall before lunch. 'I MUST BE KIND TO BANYULS.'

He hesitated, wondering whether to make his presence known, but before he had time to make up his mind there came the sound of a car starting up. It was followed almost immediately by an instantly recognisable barking.

The spell was broken. Inspector Banyuls pulled

himself together, rushed to the window and looked out. Then, moving at a pace which Monsieur Pamplemousse would not previously have given him credit for, he disappeared out of the room like a man possessed.

As the pounding of feet died away Monsieur Pamplemousse hopped over to the window and peered over the edge. He was in time to see the car which had arrived earlier bearing his would-be assassin disappear out of the gate at high speed. A moment later Inspector Banyuls emerged from the main entrance, hurled himself into his own car and followed after it.

'Pommes Frites! Pommes Frites! *Asseyez-vous!* *Asseyez-vous!*'

Monsieur Pamplemousse's voice coming from on high caused Pommes Frites to skid to a halt. Pommes Frites liked chases and he'd been about to set off on yet another one. Hopefully it would have ended with him being able to slot a further piece of his jig-saw puzzle of a problem into place, for it took more than a frock and a veil and a hat to disguise the fact that he'd been in the presence of the last member of the gang.

But hearing his master's voice and knowing that he was safe and well was much more important. That took precedence over all else.

He was pleased that on the off chance he'd followed Inspector Banyuls. Having drawn a blank at La Langoustine as well as several other likely places in the town, he'd begun to get worried. It had been something of a forlorn hope, but the inspector did have a habit of turning up unexpectedly and he'd had a feeling that where he was his master wouldn't be far away.

Now all he had to do was find out where the voice was coming from.

He hadn't long to wait. There was a clattering of feet and Monsieur Pamplemousse came out of the hospice to greet him.

For a moment or two all was panting and licking tongues. Then Pommes Frites bounded towards the gate, narrowly missing being run over by an ambulance that was coming the other way.

As he rushed off up the road barking his head off, Monsieur Pamplemousse hesitated. Short of phoning for a taxi and saying 'Follow two cars which went that way about ten minutes ago,' he wasn't at all sure what to do next.

Pommes Frites was sure. As he came bounding back to his master and nuzzled up to him, licking him in no uncertain way, he made his feelings very clear. Pommes Frites was hungry.

Monsieur Pamplemousse looked at his watch. Lunch came early in the hospice; his own had been shortly after mid-day. It was now approaching two o'clock. In the circumstances it might be best to leave the next moves to those whose job it was to worry about such things.

He wondered whether they should eat at La Langoustine or the Bar du Centre, then reached for his note-book. If his memory served him correctly, there was a little place up in the mountains—about twenty minutes drive away, where they often had *Lapin au Gratin* on the menu. Rabbit marinated in white wine, then cooked gently for an hour or so with thyme and garlic, before being coated thickly with white breadcrumbs and cheese and browned under a hot grill. If he was lucky they might have it today. He'd be interested in seeing Pommes Frites' reactions. His taste buds began to water. He was glad he'd left most of his chicken. Hunger was the best sauce in the world.

As for the other matter; no doubt all would be revealed in the fullness of time and he was perfectly content to wait.

10

SATURDAY

Monsieur Pamplemousse was whistling as he left the offices of the P.T.T. Returning his *poupées*—one charred beyond belief, the other full of holes—had been a symbolic act; like the tearing up of papers and the tidying of his desk in his days at the Quai des Orfévres when he'd reached the end of a case.

The idea had come to him when he found a packing slip in the second parcel. 'In case of complaint,' it said, 'return within fourteen days and your money will be refunded.' He wondered what *Poupées Fantastiques* would make of them, not to mention the two burst kennels. Not for one moment did he expect to get his money back, but the action made him feel better and at least it solved the problem of what to do with the remains.

The whistling was also a sure sign that it was nearly time to move on. Pommes Frites recognised the fact at once, even if his master didn't.

Outside in the square things were much as usual for a Saturday morning. A couple waiting for the *autobus* recognised them and nudged each other. Their interest communicated itself to others in the queue and there was a ripple of turning heads. An old woman in black came out of the mini *super-marché* pushing a chariot

173

laden with packets of soap powder, crossed herself when she saw them and turned up an alleyway. He took a quick photograph before she disappeared from view. A small boy came running up to ask for an autograph. Monsieur Pamplemousse obliged, thinking himself lucky he wasn't a pop star having to do it all the time. With a name like Pamplemousse he'd soon get writer's cramp. The boy thanked him and then looked disappointed when he saw the paper, as though he'd been expecting something more. Perhaps he ought to have added Pommes Frites' paw print for good measure.

He glanced at his watch. Ten thirty. Time for a quick stroll before his meeting with Giampiero, time to put together a picnic.

As they made their way down the Grande Avenue Charles de Gaulle for the last time they received more curious glances. A café went quiet, then started up again as soon as they were past. Some people crossed the road to take a closer look, others made efforts to avoid them. Monsieur Pamplemousse found himself walking self-consciously, in much the same way as he always did if he was involved in any kind of theatricals. He couldn't have felt more awkward if he'd actually possessed wooden legs. Madame Peigné was looking hopefully out of her shop window. Pommes Frites obliged, drawing on some of his infinite reserves.

By the time they got back to the Square du Centre the *autobus* had been and gone. There was a large van outside Monsieur Dupré's. Four men, looking like mime artists as they struggled with their invisible load, were fitting a new window into place.

Monsieur Pamplemousse climbed up the steps to the hotel terrace, selected a table a little apart from the others, and ordered *café* for two. He had a feeling Giampiero would be on time. Pommes Frites had a quick drink from the fountain, repaid some of it in kind on the side, then joined him.

Inside the hotel, through one of the dining room windows, he could see the staff getting ready for a wedding party that afternoon, arranging flowers, setting tables together in a long row, lining up the glasses meticulously. He caught a glimpse of Madame Sophie supervising. Doubtless it was a scene which was being enacted all over France that morning. It was the time of year for weddings.

He thought of Doucette and wondered how she was getting on. Despite all the activity in the hotel, Auguste had still found time to take her back up to the gazebo after breakfast on the pretext that he wanted to check on his property. Monsieur Pamplemousse suspected he wanted to pump her on the subject of his Stock Pot rating. Knowing Doucette he wouldn't get very far. They rarely discussed such matters anyway.

Auguste had returned with the news that it would need a small crane and a lorry to get the gazebo back down again and reinstalled. In the meantime Madame Pamplemousse was happy. She was hoping to finish another sleeve before lunch.

At eleven o'clock precisely Giampiero appeared on the steps of the hotel. Monsieur Pamplemousse noted regretfully that he was alone. He'd been hoping to meet the delectable Eva, but he had a feeling that was now something which wasn't to be.

Giampiero looked like a new man, as indeed he was in at least one respect. It gave them something in common.

He held out his hand in greeting as he came towards the table. Monsieur Pamplemousse grasped it warmly in his own, retaining his hold for perhaps a fraction longer than he normally would have done, making sure it was real. Not to be outdone, he crossed his legs as he sat down, revealing a few inches of calf. It didn't pass unnoticed.

Giampiero settled down beside him. 'And Madame Pamplemousse, how is she this morning? None the worse for her experience, I trust?'

'On the contrary. She hasn't enjoyed herself so much in years. It is quite like old times. She is spending the day at what she calls her "mountain retreat". I swear it is the first time I have seen her take her coat off out of doors in the twenty years we have been married. Not only that, but she will be able to do her meditating in peace. It is like having her own little temple on top of a mountain. She is determined to stay there until it is taken away.'

The words came out automatically. It was like the beginning of a fencing match; there were little preliminaries to be got through, niceties to be observed, whereas in truth there were so many things he wanted to know he was dying to get on with the main purpose of the meeting.

'And you? You are still planning to leave?'

'Pommes Frites and I have another appointment,' said Monsieur Pamplemousse non-committally. He tossed the question back. 'How about you?'

'I shall return to Rome. I, too, have another appointment. I may take a few days off to get used to these again.' Giampiero lifted up both hands and flexed his muscles. The fingers looked pinched and white where they had been compressed by the steel claws, as if he was suffering from advanced anaemia.

'It is surprisingly difficult. I keep reaching for things and stopping short. Shaving is the worst. I suppose you get used to anything in time, but it has given me a new outlook on life. I shall never again pass by a beggar without arms.'

'If it were me I think it would take more than a few days,' said Monsieur Pamplemousse.

Giampiero shrugged. He gazed out across the square. Already a group of men were getting ready for a game of *boules*, surveying the ground; kicking aside stones, polishing their equipment with pieces of old towelling.

'I shall also have to get used to being "single" again.'

They both fell silent, each busy with his own thoughts.

The revelation when they'd met earlier that morning that Giampiero worked as an investigator for one of the big Italian insurance companies had not come as too much of a surprise. It fitted the facts. Now that his work was over he'd slipped into his normal character, much as Monsieur Pamplemousse might have donned a favourite sports jacket.

What still staggered him, though, was the business of the steel claws; the fact that the hands had been artificial in all senses of the word. It took a bit of getting used to. Giampiero looked naked without them. Like a man who has just shaved off his beard.

He gazed curiously at the other. The world of insurance was an alien one to him. He'd once put in a minor claim after a burglary, but it had been turned down on the grounds that he'd left his window open—a window on the seventh floor! Since then he'd treated all insurance companies with suspicion; they were a law unto themselves, the very first to cry wolf if they suspected anyone was trying to do them down, inventors of the small print, masters of the escape clause. But this was clearly something different again. It must have been a no-expense-spared operation, far removed from anything he'd ever had to deal with in the Sûreté.

'It would be interesting to hear your story. I promise it will go no further.'

Giampiero poured himself another coffee. 'There was money at stake. Big money. It was not the first claim Eva had made on the group. Hopefully it will be the last. Insurance companies do not like being taken for a ride and they have very long memories.'

'How many were there, then?' ventured Monsieur Pamplemousse. 'Claims, I mean.'

'This would have been the fourth, if you count the first, legitimate one; each larger than the one before. This time it wasn't so much a claim as a "misappropriation of funds", but it would have amounted to the same thing in the end.' Giampiero sipped his coffee, then added some sugar.

'Eva G. 92-62-92. Height 172 centimetres. Weight 40.82 kilos. Caucasian blonde. Swedish. Born Saltsjöbaden—a small town outside Stockholm, of respectable middle-class parents. Small scar above left

178

ear from an early skiing accident. Birthmark behind right upper thigh.'

The facts were reeled off from memory in the way most men might have talked of their cars.

'At fifteen she went to stay with a rich uncle in Berlin who promised to complete her education. His idea of completing it was to jump into bed with her the first night she arrived. Ten minutes later her hatred of men was born. Two years later she got her revenge by marrying him. Two years after that he got his revenge. He died, but the money he had promised her in his will went instead to a Home for Destitute Women, with a rider saying that he hoped she would benefit in the fullness of time. Her hatred of men was now absolute.

'Suddenly, she found herself alone and without money, so she looked around and soon discovered that the world—especially the international playgrounds of Italy and the South of France—is well blessed with the rich and the elderly and the lonely, many of whom are only too pleased to receive the attentions of the young and the beautiful. It pleases their vanity and they can afford the price. There are many to choose from and, believe me, when Eva set her mind to it she could be very alluring. She could take her pick.'

'I believe you.' Monsieur Pamplemousse thought back to the very first evening. Despite the row he remembered finding it hard to keep his eyes off her. There had been many others in the room who would have been only too pleased to have been the object of her attentions. Supposing it had been her making a play for him and not Madame Sophie? What then?

'Her second husband she met in Cannes. He, poor

179

devil, fell off his yacht shortly after marrying her, but not before he'd taken out a heavy insurance in her favour.

'The inquest returned an open verdict. A little too much to drink. A dark night. A slippery gang-plank. No one saw it happen. The company paid up, but at the same time they put a little red star on her file.

'When, a few years later, her third husband met an untimely end—this time in a road accident—a head-on collision with a lorry on a mountain road in Tuscany, the file was left out.

'Eva had made her second big mistake in choosing another company within the same group so soon after her first claim. Her first mistake was in getting more greedy, but having tasted the good life she found it impossible to give up.

'Again, through lack of evidence, the insurance company had to pay up in the end, but it was noted that soon after she collected the money large sums were withdrawn from her account and certain payments were made to persons unknown. The money was "laundered" as they say, and by a very roundabout route ended up not far from where it started. Other people began to get interested. The tax authorities. Interpol.

'So, plans were laid, and that was where I came on the scene. The first accident was set up, then the second. The right amount of publicity was generated and after a suitable interval an introduction arranged.'

'How did you know she would fall for it? You couldn't have been sure.'

Giampiero smiled. 'Greed is a great motivator. By

then Eva was getting a bit fed up with the kind of life she was leading. It isn't all that much fun playing nursemaid to geriatric millionaires. She jumped at the chance of a younger man. In a way, I quite enjoyed playing the part of the helpless *ingénu* who has suddenly acquired undreamed of wealth and doesn't know how to handle it. As a student of human nature you must agree that given the sum involved the probability of its succeeding was pretty high.

'Soon after we were married I began to make it grow sour. I developed a mean streak which Eva didn't like at all.'

Monsieur Pamplemousse tried to picture the scene. 'Weren't you afraid you might go the same way as the others?'

Giampiero laughed. 'I took out some insurance policies of my own. First, I absolutely refused to change my will in her favour. Then, on the excuse that no company would offer me cover with my record, I made certain that I was of more use to her alive than dead.

'After that I began sowing ideas into her head. Other possible ways of screwing me for the money. Moving in the circles she did she had accumulated certain contacts. Connections with the fringe of the Mafia, people who would do anything provided the price was right.'

Monsieur Pamplemousse signalled for some more coffee. His own had gone cold. 'And the price?'

'They would keep half the money extorted from me. The rest would find its way back to her. After that she would disappear out of my life.

181

'It looked all too easy in the beginning. The head was meant as a preliminary salvo; a warning of what was to come. It was a reasonable replica of my own. It ought to have been—I happen to know the man who made it; he is one of the best. The arrangement was that at the appointed time I would be sitting at that particular table—by the entrance. The people carrying out the operation were far removed from those who organised it and had never seen me. Afterwards there would have been a note demanding money. A large sum.

'You can imagine her reaction when she was refused the table. Eva was not used to her requests being refused.

'She always got what she wanted. When she discovered that you had actually ordered the same dish— not all that surprising in view of the fact that it is a speciality—she was almost beside herself with rage.

'What was even worse from her point of view was that the people carrying out the task had by then got it fixed in their minds that you were the right target. Hence the second warning up on the hill the following morning. By then she was beginning to panic. She needed to contact them but didn't know how. She needed time to put matters right and time was the one thing she didn't have. That was when she tried to get you out of the way for a while by sawing through your balcony rail. One way and another you were a bit of a problem all round—from our point of view as well as hers. The local police had to be warned from on high not to be too interested.'

Monsieur Pamplemousse mulled this matter over in

his mind. He wondered what would have happened if he'd agreed to take another table that first night. Perhaps that was what life was all about; choosing the right table—or the wrong one—whichever way one looked at it.

'What I still don't understand,' he said at last, 'is why I didn't receive any demand notes. What went wrong?'

Giampiero smiled again. 'They were addressed to me. I have them still. I tried to warn you to be on your guard, beyond that . . .'

It was said in exactly the same tone of voice as had been used for the rest of the story. Monsieur Pamplemousse felt a chill as he realised how narrow his escape had been.

How could anyone be so matter-of-fact about someone else's life? Then he shrugged. Every man to his job. There was a time when he might well have acted in the same way.

'I still find it incredible that you should carry off the charade of the false hands for so long and get away with it.'

'Any more incredible than making people believe you have two false legs? I must say I believed that myself for a while. I felt very sorry for you.'

Giampiero had an answer to everything.

'Besides, people tend to turn away from the abnormal. They don't want to embarrass you. As far as Eva was concerned it was never an *affaire d'amour*. She was only too pleased to leave the *consommation* of our *mariage* until later. Sex was not her prime motivation. And although she didn't know it, the marriage wasn't for real anyway. The "priest" was from Interpol—the best man and all the other guests were from the office.'

Again there was a silence as Monsieur Pamplemousse digested the facts. He glanced around the square. The *boules* game was already under way. The window in the outfitter's was in place. He looked up towards the mountains and thought of Doucette. Perhaps he would buy her a gazebo when they got back to Paris. He could stand it on their roof garden. Except that the sun would never be that strong. She would probably demand an electric fire. That would mean running a lead up. It was typical that she should take to it in such a bizarre way. Typical, also, that she had put the fear of God into her captors. They probably still didn't know what had hit them. He hoped she was all right up there.

'I shouldn't worry.' Giampiero broke into his thoughts. 'They won't come back.'

'Shouldn't you be chasing after them?'

Giampiero shrugged. 'That is for others to do. I have finished my part. Besides, the Mafia in my country are very predictable. The moment the heat is on a link in the chain will be broken.' He made a brief throat-cutting motion. 'Someone along the line will quietly . . . disappear. We will never reach back to those that matter. The ones at the top.

'As for Eva . . . I would not like to be in her shoes at the present moment.

'Consider the facts. She made a deal. A deal involving a great deal of money. As soon as she heard about the shooting in the hospice yesterday she left, but they will catch up with her, make no mistake.

'They have one great advantage. They know who

she is, but she does not know them. One evening, wherever she is, there will be a knock at the door.

'And when they catch up with her they will not let her out of their sight, not until the insurance money is paid out. And when they discover, as they will do in the fullness of time, that the money doesn't exist, they will not be pleased.

'I think we shall not hear of Eva again for a long time to come—if ever.'

Once again, the matter–of–fact tone in which it was said contrasted strangely with the life going on around them. They would go their separate ways and the ripples would die away. Working for *Le Guide*, where the biggest crime was a misprint, had its compensations.

He stood up. 'Thank you. Perhaps we shall meet again one day.'

Giampero held out his hand. 'Perhaps. It is a small world.'

'It is like my insurance on Madame Pamplemousse,' said Monsieur Pamplemousse meaningly. 'That, too, is small.'

Giampiero smiled. 'Ah, but have you ever enquired as to Madame Pamplemousse's insurance on *your* life? That is a much more pertinent matter.'

'*Bonne chance* to you, too!'

'*Ciaou!*'

The exchange was automatic but without rancour.

Monsieur Pamplemousse left and made his way back into the hotel. For a moment he toyed with the idea of going back up to his room, but there was no point. His luggage was packed, a note left for Doucette.

His goodbyes had already been said to Madame Sophie. There had been a strangely muted meeting in her room the previous evening before dinner. He'd had no wish for a repeat performance of the activities earlier in the week now that Doucette was there. But he needn't have worried—Madame Sophie had her own set of rules. It was a question of territories.

She had been all sweetness and light. She quite understood about Madame Pamplemousse and wished her well. She was lucky to have such a fine husband.

It was as if nothing had happened between them. But her farewell kiss had lingered in his mind and like a schoolboy he hadn't washed before going down to dinner.

That same evening when he and Doucette arrived back in their room there was a fresh bouquet of flowers awaiting them. Doucette had attributed it to him and he hadn't denied it for fear of sparking off a whole train of questions. For a while it had been like a honeymoon all over again. But the moment had been short-lived. There had been complaints about the missing balcony rail—someone might have got killed—disapproving sniffs arising out of the smell of stale smoke which still hung about the furnishings, implying that he'd taken up the 'habit' again; and a rather nasty scene about having to share the room with Pommes Frites.

Pommes Frites had been at his most unco-operative. When he didn't want to be moved his weight seemed to grow four-fold, as did his snores. The ones he'd given vent to that night had been among the worst Monsieur Pamplemousse had ever known; like a herd of cows suffering the after effects of a particularly bacchanalian New Year's Eve party.

Things were soon back to normal and breakfast had been taken in monastic silence. Shortly afterwards Madame Pamplemousse had left for the gazebo.

Monsieur Pamplemousse glanced into the kitchen. Auguste was supervising the removal of some plastic bags of ice cubes from a work top. He must be about to make some pastry. As he caught sight of Monsieur Pamplemousse his face lit up and he waved to him to come in.

Motioning Pommes Frites to stay where he was, Monsieur Pamplemousse entered the holy of holies.

'Forgive me.' Auguste was already hard at work, up to his wrists in flour. 'It is a large wedding and there is no one so hungry as those being given a free meal. Most of the guests will have been "saving themselves".'

Monsieur Pamplemousse watched, wondering what the secret was. Why didn't his pastry turn out like Auguste's? Why didn't Doucette's for that matter? Why didn't most people's?

'The secret?' Auguste laughed. 'There is no secret. A cold surface to work on. The pastry mix and the butter must be of exactly the same consistency. If the butter is too hard it will not roll out properly—it will go into lumps. If it is too soft it will spread. That is all. That and these . . .' He held up his finger tips. 'A lot of hard work with these.'

Perhaps, thought Monsieur Pamplemousse. But how many bothered? Life was too short for most people. Therein lay the difference between those who were just content to make pastry and those who set their sights on higher things, like a third Stock Pot.

He said his goodbyes.

'*L'année prochaine?*' Auguste looked at him enquiringly.

'*L'année prochaine.*' Something inside him made him add, '*Bonne chance,*' in a tone of voice which he hoped embraced all that had happened during his stay.

Auguste smiled. 'Life goes on. If you are a thinker, then it makes you laugh; if you "feel" then it becomes a tragedy. Me?' He lifted up the dough with both hands. 'Me, I am happy with my pastry!'

His luggage was waiting for him in the hall. He paid his bill and asked for Madame Pamplemousse's to be sent on.

Madame Sophie was still busy in the dining room. There had been another delivery from the *fleuriste*. She blew him a kiss with her eyes.

'*L'année prochaine?*'

'*Oui, l'année prochaine.*' He'd keep his door double-locked next time. Or would he? Perhaps it would not be necessary.

The chambermaid carried his bags for him through to the back of the hotel where his car was parked. Her nose was held high in a permanent sniff. The bare patch of lawn marking the spot where the gazebo had been stood out like a sore thumb. He opened the car boot and felt in his pocket for some change while the maid bent over to put the bags in. Even her backside looked disapproving.

Suddenly, the sight of her skirts riding up over her buttocks proved irresistible. He did something he had never done before. He reached over and gave her a pinch. Her behind felt hard and unyielding.

The effect was instantaneous, if not entirely satisfactory; the sting from her hand extremely painful. The only consolation was that he'd saved himself ten francs. Pommes Frites obviously didn't know quite what to make of it all as he clambered in on the passenger's side and made himself comfortable.

The engine started immediately. He must change his battery more often.

As he backed the car to turn out of the hotel he realised someone was watching him from the shadows. Inevitably it was Inspector Banyuls. He must have witnessed the whole episode.

Inspector Banyuls undoubtedly had witnessed it. As Monsieur Pamplemousse came to a halt by the gate he leaned through the window.

'Incredible!' His breath was stale as though he hadn't slept for several nights. 'Tell me, how do you do it? A man of your age.'

Monsieur Pamplemousse thought for a moment and then, remembering something, reached for a small phial on the parcel shelf. He removed the top and shook a dozen or so pills into the inspector's hand. 'Take three or four of these before you go to bed tonight. You'll find they will work wonders.'

Inspector Banyuls was too surprised to refuse. He stammered his thanks as the car moved off. 'You are more than kind. I won't forget.'

'No, I'm sure you won't!' Feeling an unwinking gaze emanating from the passenger side, Monsieur Pamplemousse shifted uneasily in his seat. He wondered if he'd been over-generous. They *were* Pommes Frites' pills, after all. Travelling about played havoc with one's 'systems' and they were really kept for emergency use in case of constipation. Touch wood, he'd only had to use them once. In Le Touquet. As he remembered it, half a tablet had been more than sufficient. Inspector Banyuls was due for another sleepless night.

He took a last look round the square. As they drove past the office of the P.T.T. he wondered how long it would be before his parcel reached Paris.

It would have been nice to have stayed for lunch, but with a wedding breakfast going on the service would have been stretched. Besides, he had to make Rouen by Sunday. Ideally, that meant Clermont Ferrand by nightfall. If he went over the top by the Route Napoleon it would take longer than cutting across to Orange and the *autoroute*—it always did. But the weather was good, the sky blue and clear. It was an ideal day. He hadn't known it quite so good before. Sometimes he'd gone that way and once up the mountains he could have been anywhere. When the cloud was low it was a waste of time.

A little way out of town he pulled into a small lay-by—a pimple on the side of the road which had been hacked into the hillside.

He looked back down towards St. Castille, nestling snugly in the valley. Through his binoculars he could see the square. Cars were beginning to arrive at the hotel. He glanced at his watch. Twelve thirty. The pace would be quickening imperceptibly. Felix would be at his place making sure all was well. Sophie would be welcoming the guests. Conversation would have stopped for the time being in the kitchen.

He wondered what his verdict should be on La Langoustine. Was it ready for a third Stock Pot? Was *Auguste* ready for it? Without a shadow of a doubt he should retain his second. But there were other considerations. Undoubtedly a third would change the lives of the Douards. Perhaps that was what Sophie needed. Another challenge. They would have to take on more staff. Prices would rise accordingly. The clientele would change. It was something he, personally, would regret, but he must not allow that aspect to colour his judgment.

One thing he knew for sure, Pommes Frites was ready for his lunch. Pommes Frites wasn't all that keen on views—especially when he was hungry. As far as Pommes Frites was concerned, once you'd seen one valley, you'd seen the lot. He was getting restive.

Monsieur Pamplemousse made a mark in his notebook. He'd reached a decision. Now it was up to others. To the directeur of *Le Guide*.

He felt in the compartment beside the steering wheel and took out a small jar. It was time Pommes Frites had some vaseline rubbed on his nose. The hot weather had made it very dry. That, and all the sniffing he'd had to do over the past few days. It was something bloodhounds suffered from.

His ministrations completed, Monsieur Pamplemousse started the engine again. He would drive on a little way and look for a picnic spot. He was glad they'd decided on a picnic. Pommes Frites liked picnics and it was just the day for one.

Fastening Pommes Frites' seat belt again he pulled out into the road and took a last quick look across to the other side of the valley, towards the hills where the gazebo lay . . . it sounded like the opening words to an English song he'd once heard. How did it go? . . . Over the hills where the gazebo lay . . .

As they rounded a corner and began the steep climb he tried it out, adding a few 'toots' from the car horn for good measure.

'. . . over the hills, where the gazebo lay . . . toot! toot!
And my Doucette sits knitting all day . . . toot! toot!
Oooooooooh, over the hills . . . toot! toot!
Where seldom is heard,
A discouraging word,
For her *mari* is far, far away . . . toot! toot!'

Pommes Frites wagged his tail. He liked it when his master started to sing—especially when he sounded the horn at the same time for no apparent reason. It showed that all was well with the world and that the next meal wasn't very far away.

No dog could possibly ask for more.

Monsieur Pamplemousse and the Secret Mission

1

DINNER WITH THE DIRECTOR

'Pamplemousse, I have to tell you, and I say this not simply in my capacity as your commander-in-chief, Director of *Le Guide*, the greatest gastronomic publication in all France, but also, I trust, as a friend and confidant; we are, at this very moment, sitting on a *bombe à retardement*. A *bombe* which could, moreover, explode at any moment.'

Having delivered himself at long last of a matter that had clearly been exercising his mind for most of the evening, the Director sat back in his chair with a force which, had his words been taken literally, might well have triggered off the mechanism and blown them both to Kingdom Come. As it was he took advantage of the finding of a piece of white cotton on the lapel of his dinner jacket in order to study the effect his pronouncement had made on his audience of one.

He eyed Monsieur Pamplemousse with some concern. Normally Monsieur Pamplemousse managed to retain an air of unruffled calm no matter what the situation. It was a habit he had acquired during his years working as a detective for the Paris Sûreté, when to show the slightest spark of emotion would have been taken by others as a sign of weakness. But for once he appeared to have lost this valuable faculty. His

5

features were contorted out of all recognition and he seemed to be fighting to avoid losing control of himself altogether before finally disappearing under the dining-room table.

The Director jumped to his feet. 'Are you unwell, Aristide? I assure you, it was not my intention to cause alarm. I merely . . .'

Monsieur Pamplemousse struggled back into a sitting position, regaining his composure in an instant. The mask slipped back into place as if it had never left his face.

'Forgive me, Monsieur.' He mopped his brow with a napkin. 'I don't know what came over me.'

The fact of the matter was he'd been searching under the table for his right shoe. It had become detached from its appropriate foot earlier in the evening under circumstances best left unexplained to his host, and he'd been taking advantage of the other's preoccupation with his problems in the hope of solving one of his own.

The Director looked relieved. 'I feel you may have been overworking lately, Pamplemousse. Too much work and no play. Perhaps,' he added meaningly, 'a rest of some kind might be in order? A spell in some quiet, out of the way place for a while.'

He reached across to an occasional table and lifted the lid of a small satinwood-lined silver cigar box. 'Can I tempt you?'

'Thank you, Monsieur, but no.' Monsieur Pamplemousse picked up his glass and passed it gently to and fro just below his nose, swirling the remains of the wine as he did so, savouring the aroma with the accustomed ease of one to whom such an action was as natural as the breathing in of the air around him. It was a noble wine, a wine of great breeding; a Chambertin, Clos de Bèze, '59. He wondered if the Director made a habit of drinking such classic wines with his meals or whether he wanted some favour that only he, Pamplemousse, could provide. Suspecting the latter, he decided to pay more attention to what was being said.

'It is necessary that I protect my olfactory nerves, Monsieur,' he added primly. 'Nerves which, like my taste buds, are on duty day and night in the service of *Le Guide*; selecting and savouring, accepting and rejecting . . .'

'Yes, yes, Pamplemousse . . .' The Director snipped the end off his Corona with a gesture of impatience. 'I am fully aware of your dedication to duty and of your total incorruptibility. Those qualities are, if I may say so, two of the main reasons why I invited you and Madame Pamplemousse to dine with us tonight.'

The implication that perhaps they were the only two reasons was not lost on Monsieur Pamplemousse, but he accepted the underlying rebuke without rancour. Had he been totally honest there was nothing he would have liked better than to round off the meal with a cigar; especially one of a more modest nature than his host had chosen. In his experience large cigars tended to lose their appeal halfway through, when they either went out or the end became too soggy for comfort. A slim panatella would have been ideal. He felt his mouth begin to water at the thought. However, with his annual increment due in a little less than a month there was no harm in sacrificing the pleasure to be derived from inhaling smoke in exchange for a few bonus points.

'Apart from which,' he added, 'Madame Pamplemousse does not like the smell of tobacco fumes in my clothes.'

'Ah!' The Director's voice held a wealth of understanding. 'Wives, Pamplemousse! Wives!' He paused before applying the flame of a match to his cigar. 'Would Madame Pamplemousse rather *I* didn't?'

'Of course not, Monsieur.' Monsieur Pamplemousse refrained from embarking on a tedious explanation of his wife's ability to distinguish between smoke which came about through self-indulgence and smoke which was acquired second-hand. The former attracted a sniff full of accusation, the latter a snort which merely expressed disgust.

Instead he sat back, wishing his host would get on with the business in hand rather than continue to beat about the bush. That there was something on his mind was clear. Equally, it must be a matter too delicate to be discussed in the office. The Director didn't normally invite members of his staff, however valued, to his home. That it was something he did not wish to talk about in the presence of either his own wife or Doucette, was equally apparent. Several times during the meal there had been a gap in the conversation; sometimes an uneasily long gap, but each time it had been neatly plugged by an abrupt change of subject, rather as if the Director, like the chairman of a television chat show, had armed himself with a list of topics to cover every eventuality.

8

Talk over the fish soufflé – a delightfully airy concoction containing a *poisson* he didn't immediately recognise – had been devoted to the future of the E.E.C. The *gigot d'agneau*, done in the English manner with roast potatoes, peas and mint jelly, had come and gone over a discourse ranging from the price of eggs to the iniquities of the tax collector. The fact that the dish had been accompanied by a strange yellow substance, like a kind of thick pancake, had gone unremarked – and in the case of Madame Pamplemousse, who had a naturally suspicious nature, uneaten. It had been overshadowed by talk of the history of clocks and the invention of the fusee mechanism of regulation by means of a conical pulley wheel, a subject on which the Director was something of an expert.

The cheese and the sweet – a totally entrancing syllabub, again done in the English way using sherry rather than white wine, had triggered off a long monologue from the Director about his early days on the Paris Bourse.

At the end of the meal, the *petits fours* reduced to less than half their original number, the coffee cups drained, the Director, with an almost audible note of relief in his voice, drew breath long enough to suggest that perhaps Madame Pamplemousse would like a tour of the house. Madame Pamplemousse had been only too pleased. Madame Pamplemousse, in fact, could hardly wait. She had been on the edge of her seat ever since they arrived.

It was the kind of house that many people dream of, but relatively few set foot in, let alone achieve. Situated on the edge of a small forest, it was less than thirty kilometres from Paris, yet it could have been a million miles away. Mullioned windows looked out on to gardens of a neatness which could only have been brought about by the constant attention of many hands over the centuries; not a blade of grass was out of place, not a flower or a rose ever shed its petals unnoticed. He was glad he had parked his car with its exhaust pipe facing away from the shrubbery.

Beyond the gardens lay orchards and fields in which corn grew and sheep could be seen grazing peacefully within the boundary walls, their concentration undisturbed by any sound other than those made by passing birds en route for sunnier climes or bees going about their endless work. In its day it must have been even more remote and self-contained, well able to live off its own fat.

It was a tranquil scene, as unlike his own flat in the eighteenth arrondissement of Paris as it was possible to imagine. Doucette would be in her element; so, for that matter, would Pommes Frites, who'd taken advantage of the moment to go off on his own voyage of exploration. He'd seemed in rather a hurry and Monsieur Pamplemousse hoped he was behaving himself. Habits acquired in the streets of Montmartre, where every tree and every lamp-post received its full quota of attention, would not go down well in such gracious surroundings. Alarm bells would sound.

Alone at last, he sat back awaiting the moment of truth, but the Director was not to be hurried. Putting off the evil moment yet again, he reached for a bell push.

10

'I'm sure you won't say "no" to an Armagnac, Aristide. I have some of your favourite – a '28 Réserve d'Artagnon.'

Not for the first time Monsieur Pamplemousse found himself marvelling at the other's knowledge and attention to detail. Such thoughtfulness! Nineteen twenty-eight – the year of his birth. Beneath the somewhat aloof exterior there was an incisive mind at work – cataloguing information, sorting and storing it for future use as and when required. Unless . . . He stiffened; unless the Director had had his file out for some reason!

His thoughts were broken into by a knock on the door.

'*Entrez*!'

Monsieur Pamplemousse glanced up. Had a butler entered bearing balloon glasses and bottle on a silver salver he would not have been unduly surprised. An elderly retainer, perhaps, kept on in the family despite his advancing years, because that was the way it had always been and because his wife, an apple-cheeked octogenarian from Picardy, would not be parted from her stove. That would account for a certain Englishness in the meal.

What he didn't expect to see framed in the doorway was a figure of such loveliness and roundness and juxtapositioning of roundnesses, each vying one with the other for pride of place, it momentarily took his breath away and nearly caused him to slip back under the table again.

'Ah, Elsie,' the Director turned in his chair. 'A glass of the Réserve d'Artagnon for our guest. I think

11

perhaps I will join him with a cognac; the Grande Champagne.'

Monsieur Pamplemousse watched in a dream as the apparition wiggled its way to a marble-topped side cabinet on the far side of the room and bent down to open one of the lower doors.

He closed his eyes and then opened them again, allowing the figure to swim into view and place two large glasses on the table in front of him, before clasping the bottle to her bosom in order to withdraw the cork.

'Say when.' The voice came as a surprise. Somehow it didn't go with the body.

Half expecting one of the three musketeers depicted on the label to wink back at him, he focused his gaze on to two large round eyes of a blueness that beggared description. Lowering his gaze slightly in an effort to escape them he found himself peering into a valley of such lushness and depth it only served to emphasise the delights of mentally scaling the mountainous slopes on either side to reach their all too visible cardinal points. A voice which he barely recognised as his own and which seemed to come from somewhere far away, tardily repeated the word 'when'.

'Thank you, Elsie. That was an excellent meal. I'm sure Monsieur Pamplemousse will agree, won't you, Aristide?'

Monsieur Pamplemousse cleared his throat. 'Stock Pot material,' he said, not to be outdone in gallantry. The lamb had been a trifle overdone for his taste, the merest soupçon, but that was a minor criticism. Had he been on duty reporting on the meal for *Le Guide*, he would most certainly have recommended the chef for a Stock Pot.

'Forgive my asking, but the cake which accompanied the lamb . . .'

'Koik!' Elsie's eyes narrowed as she fixed him with a withering look. 'That's not koik. That's Yorkshire puddin', innit.'

'Ah!' Monsieur Pamplemousse sank back into his chair feeling suitably ashamed of himself, his copybook blotted. So that was the famous pudding from Yorkshire he had heard so much about. It had been a memorable experience, an eye-opener. He looked at her with new respect. 'Is it one of your recipes?'

''course.'

'Perhaps,' he ventured, oblivious to a disapproving grunt on his right, 'perhaps you could show me how to make it one day? With Monsieur le Directeur's approval, of course.'

Elsie gave a giggle as she crossed to the door. 'Saucebox!' She jerked a thumb in the direction of his host. 'You're worse than what 'e is and that's saying something. See you later,' she added meaningly.

The Director shifted uneasily in the silence which followed Elsie's departure.

'Nothing in this life is wholly perfect, Pamplemousse,' he said at last. 'A nice girl, but she has a strange way of expressing herself. I imagine it has something to do with the difference in the English education system.'

Monsieur Pamplemousse looked thoughtful. There were times when he wondered about the Director.

His thoughts were read and analysed in an instant.

'She also suffers a great deal from *mal de tête*. You wouldn't think so to look at her, but I have never known a girl so given to headaches.'

Monsieur Pamplemousse cupped the glass of Armagnac in his hands. It was dark with age. The fumes were powerful and heady. There was a velvety fire to it which would cling to the side of the glass for many days to come.

'*C'est la vie*, Monsieur!'

'The trouble is I took her in to oblige a friend. She is learning the language and she came over to do her practicals – there was some kind of domestic trouble – it's all rather embarrassing. I engaged her out of sheer kindness, hoping she would help the children with their English, but it hasn't worked out. They say they have difficulty in understanding her. Rapport is low. She will have to go, of course. My wife does not approve.'

'Wives, Monsieur,' sighed Monsieur Pamplemousse. 'Wives!'

He could hardly blame her. It was difficult to imagine Doucette allowing him to be alone in the kitchen with Elsie for five minutes, let alone accept her as part of the ménage. Wherever she went there would be trouble with the distaff side.

'What particularly grieves me is that in the meantime I have discovered she is possessed of a hidden talent. A God-given gift – and at its highest level, Pamplemousse, it *is* a God-given gift – she cooks like an angel; an angel from heaven, without help, without recourse to recipe books . . .'

Monsieur Pamplemousse nearly choked on his

Armagnac. 'You mean . . . she cooked the meal this evening? Not just the pudding from Yorkshire, but the *entire* meal?'

The Director nodded.

'Including these exquisite *petits fours*?'

'*Especially* the *petits fours*. "Afters", she calls them. They are one of her specialities. That and a dish called "Spotted Dick". She has a great predilection for Spotted Dick.

'I tell you, Pamplemousse, her departure will cause me untold grief. Such talent should not be let go to waste, but unless I find someone to take her in soon I fear the worst. She has only to meet the wrong person, someone less scrupulous than you or I, and poof!' The Director left the rest to the imagination. 'With a figure like that the pressures must be enormous. Even some kind of temporary shelter would be better than nothing.'

Monsieur Pamplemousse felt his mind racing on ahead of him. Things were beginning to fall into place. The reason for the unexpected invitation to dinner. What was it the Director had said earlier? *We* are sitting on a time bomb, Pamplemousse. And what of the strange incident during the meal? The cause of his losing a shoe.

It had happened soon after the entrée. Having decided that the oak, splat-back chairs had been chosen more with an eye to matching the Louis XV refectory table than to their comfort, which was minimal, he had taken advantage of a momentary lull between courses to stretch out his right leg which was in great danger of going to sleep. Almost immediately he wished he hadn't for it encountered another leg, apparently doing the same thing. At first he thought it was an accident and would have apologised to the owner of its opposite number had the Director not once again been in full flight.

A moment later he'd felt a soft but undeniably persistent pressure on the top of his shoe. Then, seconds later, after a half-hearted attempt at withdrawal, there had been another even more persistent squeeze; a sortie from the opposite side of the table from which retreat was impossible. Then came the mounting of the shoe by a toe, a toe which had wriggled its way upward and over the tongue towards his ankle. Soon afterwards it had been joined by a second toe and within moments, so great was the onslaught, so totally irresistible, it began to feel as though there were many more than two toes at work; a whole regiment of toes in fact, gripping and caressing, squeezing and embracing.

A quick glance at Doucette had assured him that all was well. True, she was wearing her pained expression, but that was not unusual. Her attention appeared to be centred wholly on her host.

So, too, was that of the Director's wife. He had to marvel at the duplicity of women. No one would have thought from the rapt expression on her face that her mind was on anything other than her husband, and that other things were going on, or as matters turned out coming off, under cover of the table. In a matter of moments his shoe had parted company with his foot, pushed to one side in order to facilitate an exploratory reconnaissance of his lower calf.

Clearly there were undercurrents at work in the

Director's household. Undreamed of depths yet to be plumbed.

Suddenly, he came back to earth with a bump, aware of a silence. A question had been posed; an answer was awaited.

'We have only a small flat, Monsieur,' he began, 'and Madame Pamplemousse is not, I fear, the most understanding of persons when it comes to such matters. Besides, there is Pommes Frites to be considered. He is somewhat set in his ways. I doubt if he will take kindly to moving out of the spare room . . .'

He tried to picture Doucette sharing her kitchen with Elsie, but try as he might he couldn't bring it into any kind of focus.

'Pamplemousse,' the Director had assumed his slow, ponderous voice; the one he reserved for children and idiots. 'I am not asking you to share your flat with anyone. That is not at all what I have in mind. Besides, I doubt if anything short of an earthquake will move Tante Louise.'

Monsieur Pamplemousse felt a certain dizziness. He wondered if he had heard aright. Perhaps the Armagnac was a mistake; he should have said 'when' earlier.

'You doubt if anything short of an earthquake will move Tante Louise, Monsieur?' he repeated, playing for time.

'Does the name St. Georges-sur-Lie mean anything to you, Pamplemousse?'

'St. Georges-sur-Lie? Is it not somewhere in the Loire region? Not far from Saumur?'

Why did the words ring a faint but persistent bell in the back of his mind? He had a feeling he'd heard the

17

name mentioned only recently. Someone in the office had been talking about it.

He closed his eyes, glad to be on safe ground again. The Loire, cradle of French literature and cuisine. The Loire, where they spoke the purest French. He had come to know it relatively late in life. In his younger days he had avoided the area because of the picture it conjured up; all those coachloads of tourists with their cameras. The loss had been his.

'I see *asperges* pickers at work in the fields; *champignons* grown in caves that were hollowed out in the cliffs along the river bank in the days when the great Châteaux were being built; I see walnuts and honey, *pâté* from Chartres, *rillettes* and *rillons* made from pigs raised in Angers . . .'

Getting into his stride now that he was on his own territory, confident that his recollections couldn't fail to be a plus when it came to increment time, Monsieur Pamplemousse gave full rein to his imagination. 'I see freshwater fish too; perch and barbel, poached and served with *beurre blanc; matelotes* made with eel caught in the Loire itself; I see *tarte tatin* and pastry shells made of *pâte sucrée* – a layer of pastry cream flavoured with liqueur, then filled with apricots or peaches, ripe and freshly picked, the colour of a maiden's blush, still warm with the sun's rays and decorated with almonds . . .'

He paused for a moment as the memory of an almond-filled tart he'd bought one Sunday morning after Mass in Pitheriens came flooding back.

'There is a small restaurant in Azay-le-Rideau where they serve a most delicious *Gigot de Poulette au pot au feu*. It goes well with the *Bourgueil* of the region. Michelin have given them a star; perhaps it deserves another visit. A reappraisal. I would be happy . . .'

'Forget all that, Pamplemousse.' The Director's un-feeling voice cut across his musings like a hot knife through butter. 'Close your eyes again and consider instead a small hotel in St. Georges-sur-Lie. An hotel where they serve pastry so hard it would tax the in-genuity of a woodpecker. *Bœuf* so overdone it would bring a gleam to the eye of a cobbler awaiting delivery of his next consignment of leather, and *Îles flottantes* so heavy they make a mockery of the very name as they sink to the bottom of the dish.'

The Director's words had the desired effect. He remembered now where he had heard the name. One of his colleagues – Duval from Lyons – had been reminiscing and had described how he'd broken a tooth while staying there. It had given rise to much mirth at the time. Madame Grante in Accounts had had to retire to the *Dames*.

'Does it have a mention in Michelin?'

'Nothing. Not even a red rocking chair, although God knows you couldn't find a quieter spot.'

'Gault Millau?'

'They gave it a black toque two years ago and then promptly dropped it. It hasn't appeared since.'

'And no others?'

'There was a brief mention in a guide published by one of the English motoring organisations. I believe they awarded it five stars. But even they seem to have had second thoughts.

'Strictly speaking it should be Bernard's territory

19

this year, but as you know he is not available for the time being.'

'How is Bernard, Monsieur? It was a bit of a shock.'

'Still waters, Pamplemousse. Still waters.' The Director reached for the cognac. 'He is tending his roses in Mortagne-au-Perche awaiting trial. He denies everything, of course, but I understand his wife has left him. It is all most unfortunate. Rather like your affair with those chorus girls, only not on such a grand scale. I am having to pull strings.' He seemed anxious to change the subject.

Monsieur Pamplemousse stirred uneasily in his chair. He always felt worried when the Director brought up the matter of his early retirement from the Sûreté. It was usually a prelude to some kind of demand; a reminder that but for *Le Guide* he, too, might be tending his roses.

'Perhaps, Monsieur,' he began, 'a visit from your good self would put an end to speculation . . .'

The Director gave a shudder. For some reason the words seemed to have struck home.

'That, Pamplemousse, is the very last thing that must happen.'

'Forgive me, Monsieur, but given all the facts as you have related them to me, I cannot see why . . .'

The Director put a finger to his lips. 'Walls, Pamplemousse, walls!' Crossing swiftly to the door he opened it and peered outside to make sure no one was listening, then turned back into the room. In the time it took him to complete the operation he seemed to have aged considerably, like a man possessed of a great weight on his shoulders.

'The Hôtel du Paradis in St. Georges-sur-Lie,' he said gloomily, 'is owned by my wife's aunt Louise.

'It is a problem beside which the one with Elsie is but a pin prick, a mere drop in the ocean, a passing cloud in the weather map of life.

'As a child I remember some terrible experiences at the hands of her mother with whom I used to go and stay – she was a family friend. She smoked a great deal, which was unusual for a lady in those days, and she had a habit of bathing me with a cigarette in her mouth. The ash used to fall all over me.'

Monsieur Pamplemousse tried to picture the Director sitting in his bath covered in ash and failed miserably.

'Now her daughter, Louise, has inherited the hotel and wishes it to be included in the pages of *Le Guide*. I have told her, the Guide does not work that way, but she refuses to understand.'

Monsieur Pamplemousse considered the matter for a moment or two. 'If that is the only problem,' he said slowly, 'would it not be possible to stretch a point for once? You say that in the past views have been divided. Clearly, there is room for manoeuvre . . .'

'Never!' The word came like a pistol shot.

Monsieur Pamplemousse felt his increment in jeopardy as the Director fixed him with a gimlet stare. '*Le Guide* is like the rock of Gibraltar; immovable, incorruptible. It has always been so and while I am in charge that is how it will remain.'

'I am sorry, Monsieur. I was only trying to be of help.'

'I understand, Aristide. It is good of you. I apologise.' The Director put a hand to his brow. 'But you must understand, *Le Guide* is my life. Suppose we "stretch a point" as you suggest and the connection is discovered. Think what a field day the press would have. The reputation so painstakingly built up over the years and nurtured and cared for, would be gone for ever. The climb upwards can be long and arduous, the fall a matter of seconds.'

'But with respect, Monsieur. She is, after all, your wife's aunt.'

'When things go wrong, Aristide, she is *my* aunt. I cannot afford to take the risk. Remember, too, if *Le Guide* falls, we all fall.'

If the Director had substituted the word 'France' for 'we' the effect could hardly have been more dramatic.

Monsieur Pamplemousse fell silent and allowed his gaze to drift out of the window. He was just in time to see his right shoe go past. Or rather, to be strictly accurate, he saw Pommes Frites go past carrying it in his mouth. *Merde!* He bounded to the window and to his horror watched both disappear into the shrubbery at the side of the long driveway. Pommes Frites not only looked as if he was enjoying himself, he wore the confident air of a dog about to bury his favourite bone in a place where no one else would ever find it.

The Director glared at him impatiently as he hobbled back to his seat. 'What *is* the matter with you this evening, Pamplemousse? Are you having trouble with your foot? You seem to be walking in a very strange way all of a sudden.'

'It is nothing, Monsieur. An old war wound.' It

wasn't a total untruth. He had once injured his foot doing rifle drill, bringing the butt down with considerable force on his big toe instead of on the parade ground. It still ached from time to time during inclement weather.

The Director looked suitably chastened. He cleared his throat in lieu of an apology.

'I was about to say, Aristide, it isn't simply a question of *Le Guide*. That in itself would be bad enough, but there is my position in local government to be considered. It is only a minor appointment, but the office carries with it certain advantages. Next year I may be Mayor. One whiff of scandal, and poof! You understand?'

Monsieur Pamplemousse understood all too well. A man in Monsieur le Directeur's position thrived on power. In the end it became a *raison d'être*.

'I am being assailed on all sides, Pamplemousse. Here at home. In the office. The only real peace I have is when I journey between the two and even then the car telephone is always ringing. Yield to Tante Louise and my way of life is in jeopardy. Refuse and it will be made a misery. Either way the outlook is dark.

'Elsie is one problem, but in the end it will go away; Tante Louise is another matter entirely. When you meet her you will find that in most respects she is a lovely lady; thoughtful and gentle, kind to animals . . . but take my word for it, Pamplemousse, when the female of the species looks you straight in the eye and says "I am only a poor helpless woman, all on my own with no one to turn to for advice and I don't understand these things," watch out!'

'When *I* meet her, Monsieur?' Monsieur Pample-mousse felt his heart sink. He sensed trouble ahead.

The Director drained his glass. 'Pamplemousse, I want you to leave for St. Georges-sur-Lie tomorrow morning. I want you to go there, reconnoitre, make notes and afterwards translate those notes into action. Either the Hôtel du Paradis must be raised above its present abysmal level so that it can be considered for future inclusion in *Le Guide* – and there your expertise will be invaluable – or Tante Louise must be brought to her senses, in which case you will need to draw on your well-known powers of persuasion.

'Take as much time as you like; two weeks . . . three . . . but remember from this moment on you will be on your own. There must be no communication with Headquarters. While you are away your flag will be removed from the map in the Operations Room. You will be visiting a sick aunt in the country; a white lie, but in the circumstances a justifiable one. Tante Louise is undoubtedly sick – no one could be such a diabolical cook and remain in good health. Also, you will be in the country.

'We will meet again on the occasion of your annual interview. I trust you will be the bearer of good news.

'Remember, Pamplemousse, the three A's; *Action, Accord* and *Anonymat*. No one outside these four walls must know what is happening.'

Having delivered himself of an address which would have brought a glint of approval to the eyes of General de Gaulle himself had he been alive to hear it, the Director hesitated for a moment as if about to enlarge on the subject. Then, hearing the sound of voices approaching in the corridor outside, he hastily changed his mind.

'Remember Bernard,' he added hurriedly. 'Remember Bernard, and don't let it happen to you. We cannot afford to lose *two* good men in one year.'

'Two?' Monsieur Pamplemousse raised his eyebrows enquiringly. 'I really do not see . . .'

The Director put a finger to his lips. '*Anonymat*, Pamplemousse,' he hissed as the footsteps stopped outside the door. 'Above all, *anonymat*.'

2
A FRUITFUL JOURNEY

The journey home was not the happiest in living memory. Whereas a larger, faster car might have coped, the *deux chevaux* was not at its best. The brief given by Monsieur Boulanger to his team of designers when they set about building the first Citroën 2CV was to produce a vehicle for all seasons and all occasions; status and speed were to have low priority. More important was the ability to carry a farmer and his basket of eggs across a ploughed field on a Saturday, allowing him to arrive at market with his wares uncracked, yet have sufficient room to enable him to don his hat and best suit the day after in order to transport his entire family to church. Above all, it had to be cheap and reliable; cheap to buy, cheap to run, and requiring the minimum of attention.

Doubtless all the possible permutations such a wide brief encompassed kept Monsieur Boulanger's minions awake for many a night as they added an inch or two here, or mentally removed a superfluous nut and bolt there in a search for a solution which in the end turned out to be both eccentric and ageless.

What none of them probably included in their calculations, bearing in mind that the computer had yet to

26

be invented and in those days one had to draw the line somewhere, was the possibility of their brainchild being driven by a man wearing only one shoe and with the back seat occupied, not by a basket of eggs, but by a large bloodhound. A bloodhound moreover, who wasn't in the best of moods and who steadfastly refused to co-operate by leaning with the bends, as would most normal passengers, but on the contrary made driving as difficult as possible by putting all his weight very firmly in the opposite direction whenever they tried to negotiate a corner.

Had Monsieur Boulanger envisaged such a possibility he might have extended his original brief, instructing his designers to add a non-slip pad to the accelerator pedal and to modify the otherwise admirable suspension, perhaps even adding a reinforced hand-strap for the benefit of those passengers who, like Madame Pamplemousse, were of a nervous disposition.

As it was the occupants sat, or rolled about, in complete and utter silence, each busy with their own thoughts. Madame Pamplemousse, her eyes tightly closed, was in a world of her own. Monsieur Pamplemousse, in the few moments when he was able to relax, kept going over the evening's conversation, trying to recall if he had at any time acceded to the Director's request.

The Director had clearly assumed his answer would be in the affirmative – it had been a command rather than a request – but he couldn't remember a point where he'd actually agreed. Certainly the word '*oui*' had never passed his lips.

One way and another it had been a strange evening, what with Elsie and then the business with the Director's wife. It needed thinking about.

Pommes Frites' silence was due to the fact that he was in a bit of a huff; a huff which wasn't improved by having to travel in the back of the car. He much preferred sitting in the front alongside his master, even if it did mean wearing a seat belt. At least in the front you could see where you were going rather than where you had been, and you weren't subjected to other indignities.

He stared gloomily out of the rear window at the following traffic, treating the waving and flashing of lights from other late-night revellers with the contempt they deserved. There were times when the behaviour of human beings was totally beyond his comprehension. The same people who would pass him by on the street without so much as a second glance went berserk if they happened to catch sight of him looking out of the back window of Monsieur Pamplemousse's car, pointing at him and nudging each other as if they had never seen a dog before.

As they joined the *Périphérique* at Porte de St. Cloud and entered the tunnel under the Bois de Boulogne, Monsieur Pamplemousse came to a decision. He would make an appointment with the Director first thing in the morning and reject the whole idea. It might not go down too well; his annual increment would be put in jeopardy and the kitchen needed redecorating, but that was too bad. He could hear little warning bells in the back of his mind, bells which all his past experience told him one ignored at one's peril.

The matter decided, the road ahead wide and clear, he settled back in a more relaxed mood.

'You are being very quiet tonight, Doucette,' he ventured, glancing across at his wife. 'Is anything the matter?'

Madame Pamplemousse opened her eyes for a moment and then allowed her hand to rest on his. 'I was thinking. Do you still find me attractive, Aristide?'

Taken aback by this unexpected remark, Monsieur Pamplemousse played for time. 'Of course I do, *chérie*. What a strange question. Why do you ask?'

He received a shy look in return. 'It's just that . . . if you do, I suppose others must too. Earlier this evening I felt someone playing with my foot. It must have been the Director because at the time you were leaning across to pass the wine. I was quite taken aback. I didn't know which way to look.'

Narrowly missing a lorry-load of vegetables on its way to Rungis, Monsieur Pamplemousse changed lanes and negotiated the exit at Porte Dauphine with a sense of outrage. To think, all the time he'd been listening to the Director's ramblings, treating his words like pearls of wisdom, giving them his undivided attention, he was being cuckolded under the table! It only served to confirm his decision. He would definitely *not* be going to St. Georges-sur-Lie. For two pins he would telephone him that very night and tell him so.

Doucette's next words came like a bucket of ice-cold water.

'I think he must have given *you* ideas, Aristide.

29

Perhaps he even made you a little jealous. I saw you reaching out with your foot – and then I felt it too. You haven't behaved as you did this evening since we first went out together. Do you remember that little café we used to visit together in the rue de Sèvres? We were having an aperitif on the pavement one evening. It was *my* shoe then and the waiter kicked it flying. A number thirty-nine *autobus* ran over it and you had to buy me a new pair.'

Monsieur Pamplemousse felt his heart miss a beat. Shooting a set of *tricolores* still at red, he entered the Place des Ternes rather quicker than he had intended. Madame Pamplemousse hastily withdrew her hand as he fought to regain control of the car.

'I'm sorry, Aristide. That was my fault. I should not disturb you while you are driving.'

'That's all right, Couscous.' Monsieur Pamplemousse tried to keep the note of panic from his voice.

There was a stirring in the back seat. Ever alive to his master's moods, Pommes Frites was beginning to take an interest in things at long last, but for the time being it went unnoticed.

Even the most thick-skinned of animals would have sensed that all was not well, and Pommes Frites was no slouch when it came to following the drift of a conversation. It was an art he'd first acquired on his initial training course with the Paris police, and one which he'd managed to perfect during travels with his master when they'd been thrown into each other's company for many long hours at a time.

His vocabulary was small, depending on certain

key words, but given those key words he was able to build up a fairly comprehensive and accurate picture of what was going on around him.

The key word in the present situation was undoubtedly 'shoe'. The word 'shoe' had definitely made him prick up his ears. It reminded him of the game he'd invented that evening; the ultimate rejection of which was yet another cause of his present mood.

It had been a good game while it lasted; one which had started out full of promise and which the other participants had given every sign of enjoying as well.

Like many an invention it wasn't entirely original – its human equivalent had many names, but basically it involved two players putting alternate hands one on top of the other as fast as they could while singing 'Pat-a-cake, pat-a-cake, baker's man . . .'

Pommes Frites' was a simplified version for five players and took place under the table without the benefit of musical accompaniment. In the beginning it had consisted simply of his putting his paw down firmly on top of his master's shoe in order to relieve the boredom of what seemed like an interminable meal going on above his head. The results, however, had exceeded his wildest expectations; Monsieur Pamplemousse's foot responded with enthusiasm. Flushed with success, he'd tried putting his paw on other toes within range and in no time at all there were feet and shoes and legs everywhere. However, like all good things the game had eventually come to an end. Much to his disappointment, instead of the others following him out into the garden in hot pursuit of his master's shoe, as he had assumed they would, the front door slammed behind him and he found himself locked out.

Pommes Frites didn't normally suffer from pangs of remorse, still less from guilt complexes; the analyst's basket was not for him. However, looking back on things he couldn't help but feel that taking the shoe in the first place had been a mistake, burying it in a fit of pique a cardinal error. Somehow or other he felt responsible for his master's present mood and for the difficulties he was obviously encountering.

Adding it all up, putting two and two together, taking everything into account, all things considered, in Pommes Frites' humble opinion Monsieur Pamplemousse would be well advised to leave town as soon as possible, if not before, and with that thought uppermost in his mind he turned and faced the front, directing all his attention towards the back of his master's head.

Monsieur Pamplemousse, as it happened, was rapidly approaching a point where he would have needed very little encouragement to leave town.

No wonder the Director's wife had given him an odd look when they said their goodbyes. Emboldened by the Armagnac and by what he'd taken to be her advances over dinner, he had prolonged his embrace rather more than he would normally have done, pressing into her hand at the very last moment a small *billet doux*: 'Your toes reveal what your eyes conceal.'

His heart sank as he remembered the words. He wondered if she would show it to the Director. She might even be reading it to him at that very moment. On the other hand, her response had not been entirely negative. A trifle cold at first, perhaps, but he'd put that down to the presence of her husband. There had been a more positive reaction at the very last moment. A kind of hesitating reappraisal of the situation, ending in a quick hug.

Either way it was not good news. It put an entirely different complexion on things.

'I'm not the only one who is being quiet, Aristide,' said Madame Pamplemousse as the lights of the Place de Clichy came into view. 'Are you worried about something?'

'Monsieur le Directeur has made me an offer.' Monsieur Pamplemousse made a snap decision as they turned a corner, crossed over the south-east tip of the Cimetière de Montmartre, and entered the relative gloom of the rue Caulaincourt. 'I may take him up on it. It will mean leaving tomorrow, but with my increment coming up . . .' He left the rest to Doucette's imagination.

Pommes Frites, settling down as best he could in the back of the car, heaved a sigh of relief.

'At least it will save us the problem of wondering whether we should ask them back or not.' Madame Pamplemousse sounded relieved too. The Director's house had been so grand, the thought of entertaining them was already beginning to bother her, especially with the kitchen still to be done. She was unsure where to place the Director. Their table was too small to put him all that far away.

Monsieur Pamplemousse read and understood her

thoughts. It was a very feminine reaction. He took her left hand in his again. She gave it a quick squeeze.

'Will you be away for long?'

He shrugged. It was hard to say. In this instance there was no knowing. But it had always been that way. Working for *Le Guide* was no different in that respect from his days with the police. You set out on a project not knowing when you might return. On the other hand he liked it that way. So too, he suspected, did Doucette. It enabled her to 'get on with things'.

'I shall get on with things while you are away.'

'I'll send you a postcard.'

He always did. Usually a picture of the hotel where he was staying. There would be a cross marking his room. His whole life was contained between the covers of a postcard album.

'I'd better go out early and buy some things so that you can have a picnic.'

Pommes Frites pricked up his ears again. It was another of his 'key' words. Pommes Frites liked picnics. Before they arrived home he picked up one or two more; St. Georges-sur-Lie to name but a few. He wondered vaguely what it would be like there; if he would have to share his master's room or whether he would be allowed to sleep outside. Sleeping outside was nice and the nights were still warm.

He was still wondering next morning as Monsieur Pamplemousse packed the car ready for the journey. He was pleased to see his inflatable kennel being loaded into the boot. It was a good sign.

As they drove up the ramp and out of the garage, Monsieur Pamplemousse pushed his hand through the lift-up window and waved, in case Doucette was on the balcony to see them go.

The *boulangerie* on the corner was crowded; the butcher was arranging his window display. A black couple leaned out of a first floor window in the hotel opposite. A street cleaner on his *Caninette* was already out riding along the pavement looking for evidence of careless *chiens*. Pommes Frites gazed at him non-committally.

Water gushed up out of the gutters and ran down the hill, guided on its way by the traditional mounds of rolled up carpet or sacking. Monsieur Pamplemousse followed its course as they headed towards *Le Guide*'s offices in the seventh arrondissement. By the sound of it they were likely to be away for a couple of weeks or more and there was some tidying up to do before he left. Besides, he must prepare a story for his colleagues, even though it went against the grain; even more so when he encountered sympathetic cluckings from the other early arrivals.

'Too bad.'

'Hope she's soon better.'

'Take care.'

A sleepy Operations Manager noted down the details and removed his flag from the map, putting it away in a drawer marked '*en suspens*'.

After he left the office, for no better reason than the fact that he encountered a traffic hold-up near the southern approaches to the *Périphérique*, Monsieur Pamplemousse doubled back down the rue Dantzig and immediately found himself caught up in a one-way system which took him further west than he had intended.

As he drove down the rue Dantzig he caught a glimpse of the *Ruche*, the old wine pavilion shaped like a bee-hive which had been left over from the 1900 Paris Exhibition and later turned into artists' studios. In its time it had housed Modigliani, Chagall and Léger, replacing the Bateau-Lavoir in Montmartre as a centre for inspiration. The sight of it caused him to make another snap decision, a minor change at the time, but one which was to have a profound effect on the days to come. Heading towards the *Périphérique* again, he turned right instead of left at the junction with the Boulevard Lefebvre.

The reason was simple. It was a nice day. The sun was shining. Why not take the pretty route out of Paris? He would go via Monet's old house at Giverny and picnic somewhere on the banks of the Seine. Perhaps near Nettle Island where Monet himself had loved to go. It would be a way of killing two birds with one stone. He'd been wanting to get on with an article he was preparing for *L'Escargot, Le Guide*'s staff magazine. It was on the subject of food in books and paintings, and like all such things it was taking longer than intended. There were diversions and side-tracks. For a start it had meant re-reading the whole of Zola with his descriptions of gargantuan meals born out of knowing what it was like to starve, living off sparrows in a Paris garret.

Truthfully, he was also in no great hurry to reach his destination. The more he thought about it in the cold light of day the less he liked the idea. It was a formidable task and he had a nasty feeling in the back of his mind that the Director hadn't come quite clean. Any diversion would be welcome if it put off the evil moment of his arrival.

Taking the Porte de Passy exit, they were soon in Bougival, whose soft light and river mists had been immortalised by Renoir and Manet and other painters over the years. Unlike Argenteuil, it still retained much of its old-world charm. He began to feel better. There were two good restaurants in Bougival. It was time they were reported on again. Perhaps, when he got back, he could entertain the Director and his wife there. It would be a way out of Doucette's problem.

Medan came and went. Medan, where Zola had lived and entertained before the Dreyfus case when he wrote *J'Accuse* and had to flee to England, ending up in a dreadful hotel where he wrote of biting on an unexpected clove in a cake. He wished he had a tenth of Zola's ability to recall tastes and smells. Not that it would have helped much in his work for *Le Guide* where everything, including smells, had to conform to a common standard, one person's writing indistinguishable from another's.

It was all very well the Director telling him he had to do something about improving the hotel. Hotels didn't improve overnight. There was more to it than that. It took time. Years of hard work. On the other hand, there must be *something* there; some spark which needed catching. Gault Millau seldom made mistakes, although clearly they had had second thoughts.

At Vernon he turned off for Giverny. They had

made good time. The car park was nearly empty, the coaches had yet to arrive. The house with its walls made pink by grinding brick dust into the plaster was as he remembered it; the garden which in its heyday had kept six men at work was in full bloom.

He wandered down to the wistaria–clad Japanese bridge by the lily ponds, trying to picture the heavily bearded yet slightly dandyish figure of Monet, rising early in order to study the sunrise before embarking on one of his huge breakfasts of sausages and eggs, followed by toast and marmalade. Food, not art, would have been the subject under discussion. Monet loved good food, simple food he called it. *Asperges* from Argenteuil, truffles from Périgord, *cèpes* from his own cellar, brought up and cooked in the oven, wines from the Loire or from Burgundy, roast duck – its wings removed at the table and sent back for regrilling in a seasoning of pepper, salt and nutmeg as a special treat.

Elsie would have liked it. They would have got on well together. She might even have coped with the old man in his more irascible moods, when things weren't going right and he made a bonfire of his work. She would probably have put her foot down over his monastic timetable. Lunch at eleven o'clock sharp; at this time of the year set out on a table beneath the linden trees. He looked at his own watch. It was barely eleven–thirty. Perhaps he would follow Monet's example and have an early lunch too. Already his taste buds were beginning to throb. The thought transmitted itself to Pommes Frites who wagged his tail in agreement.

A few minutes later they were on their way again, looking for a suitable spot.

Doucette had excelled herself with the picnic. Spiced beef, *pâté campagne*, smoked cod's roe, chicken and ham pie, salad in a separate container, a crisp *ficelle*, sorbet in a freezing jar, *tarte aux pommes, fromage*, a bottle of Pommard and another of Badoit. The small picnic table he always carried in the boot was soon filled; the tablecloth hidden beneath all the goodies. A sunshade in position, Monsieur Pamplemousse unclipped one of the car seats, put it carefully into place, removed his tie, tucked a large serviette into the top of his shirt, and took a firm grasp of his knife and fork as he prepared to do battle.

Perhaps he should play *pieds* under the table more often. It was very rare he was given such a treat. There was even a bone for Pommes Frites. The thought crossed his mind that perhaps Doucette wanted him out of the way; maybe she had taken the Director's advances seriously. He dismissed the idea. Much more likely she had a guilty conscience. Besides, the Director had Elsie to contend with.

He wondered if the Director's wife would answer his note. Luckily Doucette never opened his mail. All the same, the thought made him feel hot under the collar.

Mopping his brow with the serviette, he helped himself to some more pie, cutting off an equal portion for Pommes Frites. It disappeared before his own was halfway to his mouth.

The Seine had a purplish sheen to it in the September sunshine; the Pommard was a real treat. A single vineyard. He made a mental note to call in the next time he was down that way and replenish his stocks. It would make a nice diversion.

The thought triggered off another. Why not call in and see Bernard on the way to St. Georges-sur-Lie? Helping himself to a wedge of *Saint-Paulin*, he went to the car for his map. Mortagne-au-Perche wouldn't be too far out of his way. *En route* to Bernard he could stop off at a garden centre and buy him a rose. Perhaps a 'Maiden's Blush'. He would appreciate the joke.

Afterwards he could go via Illiers-Combray where Marcel Proust had spent childhood holidays with his Tante Léonie, dipping spoonfuls of madeleine crumbs into her lime tea.

As he cleared away the picnic things, Monsieur Pamplemousse tried to recall the exact details of Bernard's case. He'd been away in Alsace at the time and so had missed out on all the juicy bits. By the time he got back to the office there were other things to talk about.

What was it the Director had said? Remember Bernard. Don't let it happen to you. Don't let *what* happen? Once again, he had a nasty feeling the Director was being less than frank. There were areas of a decided greyness.

It took a while to find Bernard's house. Mortagne, high up above the surrounding countryside, was busily provincial. He stopped in the main street to ask the way. The first two people professed not to know; the third was so bubbling over with excitement, mistaking him for a journalist, he had a job to get away and through-traffic behind ground to a halt, hooting impatiently.

As the Director had surmised, Bernard was tending his roses, dead-heading a bed of *Gloire de Dijon*, looking for outward-facing buds like a man with time on his hands.

'Coaches used to stop and admire these,' he said gloomily, after they had exchanged greetings. 'They still come, but mostly to stare at me.'

Monsieur Pamplemousse opened the boot of his car and produced his gift. He rather regretted his choice now. Bernard seemed to have taken things hard. He decided not to make too much of it.

'I'm not sure of the name. It is pink with white towards the edges. It dates back to before 1738. The man at the nursery said it should grow well.'

Bernard brightened. 'You know, it's kind of you to call. I often think of you. In a way our two cases are very much alike. I mean, the way you were found hanging about in the toilets at the Follies without any clothes.'

'I was not hanging about,' said Monsieur Pamplemousse stiffly. 'I was merely taking refuge. I had no clothes because they had been taken from me at gun point. The whole thing was a frame-up. A plot to discredit me.'

'I really meant that in the end it was your word against theirs,' Bernard broke in defensively. 'If I remember rightly they never did find your assailant.' He led the way towards the house and pointed to a table and some chairs set out under a tree. 'Make yourself comfortable. I'll fetch something to drink.'

He reappeared a moment later carrying a tray. Monsieur Pamplemousse watched while he poured out a Kir. The Cassis bore the Chapel label. Bernard must have bought it on his travels. He'd had it once before, home-made, rich and fruity, made to the highest standards. He felt honoured at being given such a treat. The wine was a Sancerre; the bottle glistening with beads of cold on its outside.

'What happened?' he asked, trying to jog the other's memory before the conversation took a turn. 'I was away at the time.'

Bernard gazed gloomily at his glass and then took a copious draught. 'I still don't really know. I mean I don't know what came over me. It was during that hot spell we had earlier in the year. That didn't help. I'd had a large lunch. That didn't help either. I started to feel rather strange soon after I set off and after I'd driven about sixty or seventy kilometres it got so that I could hardly stand it.'

'What sort of strange?'

'Well, that's just it. Nothing like it has ever happened to me before . . . at least, not in the same way. I mean . . . sort of . . .'

Monsieur Pamplemousse watched in surprise as Bernard started shrugging his shoulders and winking, whilst at the same time emitting a series of shrill whistling noises.

'You mean . . . you felt like *une coucherie*? A little diversion?'

Bernard blushed. 'You can say that again. I tell you, I don't usually go in for that sort of thing, but if *une fille de plaisir* had come along at that moment I don't know what I would have done. Well, I do . . . I was beginning to feel quite desperate. More than that . . .'

'More?' Monsieur Pamplemousse raised his eyebrows enquiringly.

Bernard blushed again and then mopped his brow. He poured out another Kir. 'I felt as though I could have taken on all comers, if you'll pardon the expression. I felt like the prize stallion at the Cadre Noir. Unfortunately, I was miles from anywhere. At least, I thought I was miles from anywhere.'

Monsieur Pamplemousse found himself hoping Bernard had a good lawyer. If he found himself in the dock up against a prosecuting counsel who meant business he wouldn't stand a chance.

'So what happened then?'

'I parked by the side of the road and went into a wood meaning to try and sleep it off. I'd put it down to too much drink. I was in such a state by then I sort of – well, it sounds a bit silly talking about it across a table like this – but I got lost. I must have been going round and round in circles. That was when I heard all these voices.'

'Voices?' Monsieur Pamplemousse reached for the bottle. His throat felt unaccountably dry. 'What sort of voices?'

'Girls' voices. I'd parked near a school. A convent, actually, which makes it sound even worse. You know what convent girls are supposed to be like. They were on some sort of ramble. I bumped into them in a clearing and . . .'

'And?'

'They say I started behaving in a funny kind of way. Like . . . beckoning to them . . .'

'Beckoning?'

43

Bernard nodded. 'I can actually remember doing it in a hazy sort of way. First of all some big blonde sixth-former came over.' He paused in order to emit another series of whistles. 'I think she must have been in charge. Then the others followed.'

'Beckoning doesn't sound a very major crime,' said Monsieur Pamplemousse thoughtfully. 'I don't see what all the fuss is about. A good lawyer . . .'

'It depends,' said Bernard, slowly and carefully, 'on what you beckon with. What's annoying is that I'm sure most of them weren't really bothered. They seemed to be enjoying it – the big blonde one especially – she started to undo her blouse. Then one of the juniors began to cry. Now they've all ganged up on me. It's thirty against one – I don't stand a chance. Besides, one of them had a camera. Blown up and in colour it won't look good in court. The Mother Superior definitely has it in for me.'

Monsieur Pamplemousse stayed to finish the bottle of wine and then at a suitable moment took his leave. The visit had done little to raise his spirits; rather the reverse. As he drove off Bernard was busy removing his new rose from its container. From all he'd said he would have plenty of time to nurture it during the coming months. No wonder the Director had talked about having to pull strings.

At Illiers-Combray he stopped as a matter of course at 4 rue du Docteur-Proust. Like Monet, Proust had enjoyed what might be called 'simple food'. *Sole meunière* had been one of his favourites. Scrambled eggs another. He wondered if he had followed

44

Escoffier's advice and speared a clove of garlic with the fork before making them.

On the door there was a sign: 'Hours open 14.15–17.00. Next tour 16.00'. He looked at his watch. Just too late.

In the square opposite the church with its forbidding interior, there was a shop selling madeleines, shell-shaped as they always had been after the shells pilgrims to Santiago-de-Compostela had worn in their hats. He toyed with the idea of buying some, but his mind was on other things. It was like starting off a case in the old days. He needed to put himself in the right mood. Sometimes that took days, during which time he knew he wasn't always good to live with.

Pommes Frites, dozing off his lunch in the car, opened one eye sleepily as Monsieur Pamplemousse climbed back in.

Abandoning all thoughts of his article for the time being, Monsieur Pamplemousse put his foot hard down for the rest of the journey. The article could wait. Proust had died in 1922, Monet in 1926 – two years before he himself had been born. Zola in 1902. His current problem was of the present and suddenly he was anxious to get to grips with it. If he arrived at St. Georges-sur-Lie in good time he would be able to take Pommes Frites for a pre-dinner stroll round the village so that they could get the feel of it.

After Illiers he drove through kilometre after kilometre of open hedgeless farmland between flower-decorated villages with only the occasional black-faced sheep – the Bleu de Maine of the area – to watch him pass. The very monotony gave him time to think. No wonder the area had a high suicide rate. The warning bells were growing louder; more to do with things that hadn't been said rather than those which had. Gradually the scenery became more wooded again. Here and there a thatched cottage dotted the landscape and the road wound past half-hidden *boires* – hollow dried-up areas the Loire would flood later in the year.

St. Georges was on him almost before he realised it. First a farm building with a faded Dubonnet advertisement painted on the side, then another with an equally faded sign: 'Hôtel du Paradis 200 m.'

As he turned into a square he found himself facing the hotel itself. Stone steps, grey and time-worn, led up to an oak door open to the street. At first floor level there was a long balcony. To the right there was a small garden with climbing roses against the wall and a few tables and chairs set out under a yew tree; doubtless in its time it had watched over many a wedding party or christening celebration. Nailed to its trunk was a notice: PARKING. Below it an arrow pointed towards the back of the hotel.

Driving through the square he spotted one of the new automatic Sanisettes which were already commonplace in Paris. It had been placed not far from the hotel dining-room, its entrance door discreetly facing the other way. Not discreetly enough apparently, for someone had already sprayed the word NON in large black letters on the outside.

Reflecting that the invention of the aerosol was a mixed blessing, he looked around. Peace reigned supreme. There was hardly a soul about. Window boxes filled with begonias and periwinkles adorned the window ledges of houses to his left, geraniums and nasturtiums overflowed on to the cobblestones. To the right there was a sprinkling of shops; a *boucherie*, a *droguerie* – its brooms and plastic bowls spilling out over the narrow pavement, a *bureau de tabac* and a small *pharmacie*, all dozing in the afternoon sun.

In a side street leading down to the right of the hotel there was a grocery store and next to that on a corner, the *boulangerie*; beyond that a cluster of farm buildings and a line of weeping willows showing where the river must be, then open country again.

As he turned into the hotel car park he felt rather than saw a movement in the far corner near a row of stables, as if someone had dodged out of sight.

There was one other car; a Renault 14 with a 75 Paris number plate. As he drew up behind it he noticed its windows were covered in steam. Either someone was boiling a kettle inside, which seemed unlikely, or else ... even as the thought entered his mind a hand reached up and rubbed a patch clear on the back window. A moment later a woman's head appeared in the hole. Her face was flushed, her hair awry, her lipstick smudged. She looked as though she had been pulled through a hedge backwards, pulled through for a reason which was not hard to fathom.

She looked somewhat taken aback as she focused her gaze on to Monsieur Pamplemousse not more than a couple of metres away; even more so when she caught sight of Pommes Frites staring unblinkingly from the passenger seat.

Monsieur Pamplemousse raised his hat and then backed politely away, parking as far as he could from the other car. His mind was racing. Once again the Director's parting words came back to him, only this time more clearly. Something clicked in his mind. The warning bells were now much louder.

Signalling Pommes Frites to follow him he made his way out of the car park towards a telephone kiosk he'd noticed on a corner near the square. As they passed a lane at the side of the *boulangerie* he saw the doors were open; no doubt to let the heat from the ovens out. A blue Renault van was parked nearby. He nodded to a bearded man in white overalls who was watching him from the doorway, but it wasn't acknowledged. Instead the man turned and went inside.

He dialled his office number. 'Véronique . . . Pamplemousse here. Give me Monsieur le Directeur, please.'

There was a pause. A long pause. He got ready for the encounter to come.

'I'm sorry, Monsieur Pamplemousse. Monsieur le Directeur says to tell you he left early.' The voice at the other end sounded aggrieved on his behalf. It was the voice of one who did not take kindly to repeating so palpable a falsehood to someone she knew. He decided not to make an issue of it and compound her embarrassment.

'Never mind. Do you have Bernard's telephone number?'

There was another pause. Shorter this time. 'He has changed his number. It is now ex-directory.'

'It is most important.'

'Do you have a pencil?'

He wrote it down and murmured his thanks.

'How is your aunt, Monsieur Pamplemousse?'

'It is hard to say at this moment in time. I am reserving judgment.'

'If there is anything else I can do for you . . .' He repeated his thanks and then hung up.

Bernard sounded slightly out of breath. Doubtless he was still in the garden.

'I will not keep you. I have just one question to ask. It is to do with your misfortune. Tell me where you had lunch that day.'

The reply confirmed his worst suspicions. The meal he'd eaten in St. Georges-sur-Lie had obviously left a deep impression on Bernard.

'It was one of the worst I can remember. A little place not far from Saumur. The chief asked me to call in there, God knows why . . .'

Monsieur Pamplemousse allowed the voice to drone on, but his mind was hardly on the conversation as he stared out at the toilet on the other side of the square. For two pins, if he'd had an aerosol he would have added the Director's name to its concrete façade. How could anyone be so two-faced, so . . . so . . . Words failed him.

'Thank you, Bernard . . . you too . . .'

He paused as a thought struck him. 'Take care – and Bernard, I cannot promise, but if it is at all possible, if all goes well, you understand – I may be able to help you with your problem. I will be in touch. *Au revoir*. I must go now. I have another call to make.'

He stood for a moment lost in thought, then he picked up the phone and inserted another coin in the box.

'It's me again . . . Pamplemousse. There *is* something else you can do for me. Several things, in fact.'

If Véronique was surprised to hear his voice again she didn't register it; his list of requirements drew no comment.

'I will do my best, Monsieur Pamplemousse.'

'Can you address them to me care of *Poste Restante*, Tours, and mark them urgent.'

'*Oui*, Monsieur Pamplemousse.'

'When I get back, Véronique, I will give you a large tin of *rillettes*. It will, if I have my way, be made not from the pigs of Angers, but from Monsieur le Directeur's own flesh and bones.'

Replacing the receiver before the other had time to reply, he came out into the sunshine again and gazed up at the Hôtel du Paradis.

Still waters indeed! Deep, dark, muddy, blacker than black waters more like it; waters thick with mire. No wonder Michelin hadn't seen fit to award the hotel a red rocking chair; by the sound of it a red mattress would have been more to the point.

Pommes Frites followed the direction of his master's gaze, taking in the ivy covered walls and the dining-room to the left of the entrance, its tables already set for dinner. He knew a good hotel when he saw one. There would be steaks; rich, succulent steaks, red and oozing with juice; liver, and bones – lots of fresh, juicy bones to gnaw. He couldn't wait to get at them.

Together they made their way towards the front door, each busy with his own thoughts. Their steps reflected their mood. Pommes Frites' were jaunty and full of anticipation. Monsieur Pamplemousse's, on the other hand, were grim and purposeful; they were the steps of a man with a mission; a man who might not as yet know quite where that mission would take him but, come what may, no one was going to stop him completing it. The saving of Bernard was rapidly taking precedence over the saving of the Hôtel du Paradis.

3

DINNER FOR TWO

Breathing heavily after his exertions with a towel, Monsieur Pamplemousse paused and gazed disbelievingly at a *bidet* which stood below and slightly forward of the washbasin in his bathroom. A mirror above the basin reflected Pommes Frites peering round the open door leading to the bedroom. He, too, was registering disbelief. Disbelief tinged with growing concern was written large all over his face as he watched his master slide the *bidet* out on its rails and remove, one by one, and in the reverse order in which they had been carefully placed ready for dinner, underpants, a shirt, trousers and a bedraggled pair of socks. Pommes Frites did not wag his tail. He sensed it was not a tail-wagging occasion.

Also reflected in the glass was the mirror image of the obligatory card on the back of the bathroom door giving the number of the room and the price, *par nuit, par personne*, together with a list of the various facilities it included. In this case the *chambre* was *numéro un*, and apart from a *grand lit* and a *balcon*, it included a *salle de bains* containing a *bain*, a *lavabo* and a *bidet*. *Petit déjeuner* was twenty francs extra; *chiens* fifteen.

The Hôtel du Paradis boasted four other bedrooms offering between them a choice of *lavabo* and *bidet*, *douche* and *lavabo*, *W.C.* and *bidet*, or just a *douche* and *bidet*. But in none of them was it possible to enjoy all five facilities at the same time.

In the end, so great had been his desire for a long and relaxing bath after the journey, Monsieur Pample-mousse had chosen *numéro un*, above the dining-room and facing the square. It had seemed well worth the extra twenty francs a night and if the worst came to the worst he could always make use of the automatic toilet in the square outside. Now he was beginning to regret his choice.

Not only was the room, with its hideously unfor-gettable flowered wallpaper, one of the most depres-singly uncomfortable he had encountered in a long time, filled with dust-ridden sporting trophies and furnished with bizarre examples of bygone carpentry handed down from another era, the plumbing in the *salle de bains* had to be seen to be believed.

Undecided looking pipes emerged from the un-likeliest of places and hovered before setting off in various unexpected directions. Some were sawn-off and plugged; others disappeared into yet more holes in the wall never to reappear again. The one thing they all had in common was the fact that they had been installed by someone possessed of an unswerving belief in the adage that the shortest distance between two points was a straight line; which gave rise to an effect not unlike that of the engine-room of an early submarine; cramped and dangerous. Taking a bath had not been an enjoyable experience. The only saving grace was a heater in the middle of the wall. Operated by a cord switch, it had been installed with a blind disregard for the laws of safety, probably by the same hand responsible for the plumbing, but its warm glow offered a welcome contrast to the rapidly cooling water which emerged from the tap marked CHAUD.

All of which wouldn't have been so bad, but when he went to clean his teeth in the washbasin, scalding hot water from an entirely different system gushed forth from a tap marked FROID and made his bristles go soggy with surprise.

But the unkindest cut of all happened when he emptied the basin and discovered that for some strange reason the waste pipe went via the *bidet*. The one bright spot was that he hadn't been sitting on it at the time. Getting his clothes wet was bad enough, but clothes could be dried and ironed. He shuddered to think of the suffering that might have been caused to his bare and sensitive flesh had it been in the path of the same water that had practically melted the handle of his toothbrush.

What particularly grieved him was the fact that the trousers were his special working ones; the pair with a secret compartment in the right leg – a modification of Madame Pamplemousse's which enabled him to conceal his notebook beneath the folds of a table-cloth while making out his reports. Thankfully the notebook itself was still on the bed where he'd left it. He had a feeling he would be making good use of it before his stay was out.

Dressed once again in the clothes he'd worn for the journey, he crossed and opened the French windows leading to the balcony. The square was deserted; the few shops closed for the day. Below him and a little to one side stood the Sanisette. Its concrete façade looked slightly out of place alongside the other buildings, but no doubt in time it would become an accepted part of the scene.

Through a gap in the houses on the far side of the square he could see fields of *asperges*, through another gap some goats. Beyond that fields of fading sunflowers rose majestically towards the clear September sky, their huge yellow heads bowed down under the weight of it all. The sight reminded him that he had work to do. Apart from their health-giving properties, sunflower seeds were thought by some to have aphrodisiac powers, probably on account of the impression they gave of drinking in the sun's rays; an association of ideas. Perhaps . . . perhaps even now someone in the village was stirring a cauldron ready for the evening meal.

Almost immediately he dismissed the idea. Deep down he had a feeling that the cause of Bernard's fall from grace would be nothing quite as obvious; an accident rather than a deliberate act. His meeting with the Director's aunt had been necessarily brief – a quick exchange of pleasantries while he'd been checking in, but his first impression had been of someone almost transparently honest, and he believed in first impressions. Instinct told him that whatever had happened to Bernard was not of her making.

Turning back into the room he nearly tripped over Pommes Frites who lay with his chin between his paws gazing lugubriously at the head of a lion-skin rug on the floor at the foot of the bed. There must at one time have been a taxidermist of note in the area. In Tours several years before he'd come across a stuffed elephant which had belonged to Barnum and Bailey's circus, and in the same city he'd once stayed at an hotel where there was a stuffed lion standing in a make-believe jungle by the lift shaft. He'd even come across the odd stuffed horse standing around in fields during his travels.

Whoever it was had been kept well supplied by Tante Louise's forebears. Animals or heads of animals stood or peered down from walls on all sides as they left the room, silently following their progress as they made their way down the stairs.

An air of gloom enveloped them as they descended to the ground floor. Monsieur Pamplemousse was not a devotee of the art of the taxidermist. On the whole stuffed animals made him feel depressed. It was a feeling that was clearly endorsed by Pommes Frites, who glanced uneasily at a large brown bear who stood expectantly holding a tray marked POSTE behind the reception desk. Pommes Frites liked other creatures to react. You knew where you were with creatures that reacted.

Monsieur Pamplemousse's spirits sank still further as they entered the dining-room. There were about twenty tables; some seventy places in all, but only one was occupied, and that by a young couple who looked as if they were there for the peace and quiet rather than the food.

He looked around and was about to take his seat near the window and as far away from the others as possible, when the door leading to the kitchen swung open.

'*Vous avez une réservation*?' The voice went with its

owner, a large, well-preserved madame of uncertain age who bustled forward clutching a menu with the air of one used to being in command. Monsieur Pamplemousse had met her counterpart a thousand times before, in bars, bistros and tiny restaurants the length and breadth of France. She would be a widow, married once to a man who had died in a war. Whatever the time they were always of a previous age, just as they had been in Napoleon's time. *Formidable* was the only word to describe them.

'No, Madame,' he began. 'I –'

'In that case, Monsieur . . .' Her words were punctuated by a thud as a plastic *RÉSERVÉE* notice was grasped and plonked down very firmly in the centre of the table by a hand which continued on its way in one sweeping movement towards another table near the couple in the corner.

Monsieur Pamplemousse braced himself. If it was to be a battle of wills then it was one which needed to be won early on in his stay rather than later. He had no wish to be seated next to the only other occupants of an otherwise empty room, simply to save someone else's feet.

He pointed in turn to a compromise position on the other side of the window. 'I would prefer that one.'

The pause was only fractional; the flicker in the eyes that met and held his was one of respect rather than disapproval. As was so often the case, challenge was the best form of defence.

Pommes Frites, confident of the outcome of the argument, brought it to a conclusion by settling himself under the table, awaiting his master's choice. He hoped it would be something he could get his teeth into. Something meaty. A large steak, perhaps – or some *carré d'agneau*. Something that would allow for a reasonable division. Experience told him he would not have to put up with any newfangled cooking – all slivers of underdone meat with bits of fruit on top and brightly coloured vegetables. Pommes Frites was not a devotee of *nouvelle cuisine*.

Experience told Monsieur Pamplemousse as he ran his eye down the *carte* that neither of them was in for a gastronomic treat. It was handwritten in purple ink – often a good sign, but in this case in letters so faded they had obviously been penned many months before. He looked in vain for an additional list of dishes of the day. No piece of paper fell out from between the pages when he held up the folder and shook it. There wasn't even a dish that the chef – or, as he suspected, the Director's aunt, had marked with an asterisk as being particularly recommended; a speciality of the house.

He glanced around the room at the empty tables, each with its quota of napkins folded hog's-head style on top of the waiting plates, surrounded by sets of rather sad-looking cutlery. The enormity of the task in front of him suddenly sank home. On the one hand there was his brief to put forward or even to implement suggestions as to how to bring about improvements in the restaurant. On the other hand there was the problem of discovering what dish or combination of dishes had caused Bernard to disgrace himself after his visit.

He ran his eye down the menu, considering the options. There were many foods credited with the power to increase sexual desires, most of them he'd covered in an article for *L'Escargot*. Others promoted 'staying power'. He'd once read that in India men rubbed garlic ointment on their vital parts in moments of need. A sobering thought which momentarily put him off the *potage aioli*. Besides, Bernard's 'staying power' under what might be called 'field conditions' had hardly been put to the test. Perhaps it was something he had drunk? Perhaps some brandy, egg-yolk and cinnamon concoction had triggered it off? Again, that would have been a deliberate act totally out of character with the Bernard he knew. Looking at the row of bottles behind a small bar near the entrance to the dining-room he could see a selection of various marques of cognac and a sprinkling of Armagnacs, but there wasn't even a bottle of advocaat and he doubted very much if the hotel was into serving any kind of 'concoction'. It would be a bottle of cognac plonked on the table along with a glass and a 'help yourself'. The request for an egg to go with it would have been greeted by a sniff. He shuddered to think what would happen if you asked for cinnamon as well.

Tia Maria was supposed to heat the blood, but that, too, was absent and it would have needed a great many glasses to induce in Bernard the kind of blood heat that would have caused him to behave as he had.

On the other hand, perhaps unwittingly he'd stumbled on a selection of dishes which against all the odds had combined to produce an unprecedented effect; like someone discovering a system to beat the bank at Monte Carlo. He resolved to put his theory to the test. There was no time like the present and he was hardly likely to lose control of his emotions with the waitress.

Moules were nowhere on the *carte*, fish with ginger was obviously an unheard of concept, frogs' legs were conspicuous by their absence.

In the end mentally, and without any great feeling of optimism, he settled on artichoke – once sold in the streets of Paris because of its 'heating qualities', cow's liver – something the Romans had set great faith in, drying it in order to grind up as part of a love potion – and *tourte au lapin* with spinach and potato. With luck, being in the Loire Valley the pie would be made with prunes as well. Prunes figured largely in local recipes, and in the old days they had been served in brothels to stimulate the customers and promote a brisk turn around in the trade. As for potato; no less an authority than William Shakespeare had pointed out its aphrodisiac qualities in *The Merry Wives of Windsor*. If none of that had any effect he might end up with *ananas; ananas* with sugar piled high on top, followed by an Armagnac.

Feeling pleased that his research had borne fruit, Monsieur Pamplemousse sat back and wondered what Bernard's choice had been. Had it been the forty franc menu with the rabbit pie, or the forty-five one with liver? Perhaps he had done as he was now doing, gone the whole hog and eaten *à la carte*. He wished now he'd thought to telephone and ask, but it was too late; the Madame was already advancing towards him at a brisk pace, pencil and pad poised for action. With only two other customers and the prospect of an early night she would not take kindly to any delay.

'*Vous avez choisi, Monsieur?*' She flicked open the pad.

His choice went without comment until he asked for *pommes frites* with the *lapin*.

'*Non, Monsieur.*'

'*Non?*'

'*Non. Pommes vapeur.*' Again their eyes met. Again there was a feeling of a battle to be fought. He wondered whether *frites* were not available – too much trouble, or whether his choice had simply met with disapproval. Hearing his name mentioned, Pommes Frites poked his head out enquiringly. For the sake of peace Monsieur Pamplemousse decided on a tactical withdrawal.

He nodded his agreement. '*Pommes vapeur.*' She was probably right. Gastronomically speaking it was a better combination. *Frites* would soak up the rich juices from the pie and lose their crispness. It had really been a concession to a 'certain other' not a million miles away. Pommes Frites was not keen on *vapeur*, he liked his namesake best, often eating large quantities. Looking rather put-out, he disappeared under the table again.

His capitulation was rewarded by a slight thawing out. 'I would not recommend the *pommes frites*, Monsieur.' It was said with feeling born of past experience. '*Terminé?*' Without waiting for a reply, the *carte de table* was exchanged for a basket of bread and the *carte des vins*.

Monsieur Pamplemousse gazed at both with an equal lack of enthusiasm. The bread looked like a poor imitation of the Poilâne wheat loaves presently fashionable in Paris. Long-lasting and delicious when baked by Poilâne, but from the tired look of the slices he'd been given they must have long ago outlived their life expectancy. Why, in heaven's name, did they serve it when there was a perfectly good *boulangerie* not a stone's throw away?

He opened the *carte des vins* and as he did so his spirits rose slightly. Not unexpectedly, it was the usual commercially available booklet, sectionalised and decorated with anonymous men operating ancient presses. The pages had been inscribed by someone using the same purple ink as had been used for the *carte de table*. What was surprising was the fact that although none of the entries had been accorded a vintage there were some very familiar names; mouth-watering names. The Bordeaux section in particular sported some highly respected representatives of the 1855 classification.

He hesitated, trying to decide whether to choose a local wine as he'd intended or something more exotic. Again, he found himself wondering about Bernard. Had he opted for a half carafe of the house wine, included in the price of the menu, or had he indulged himself? If the Kir they'd had that afternoon was anything to go by, he suspected the latter.

His choice of a Ducru Beaucaillou met with a total lack of response. The bottle when it arrived was covered in dust. He reached forward and felt it quickly while the waitress searched under her apron for a corkscrew. It was cold from the cellar. Catching her eye he withdrew his hand again, waiting while she opened it. He half expected her to pass the cork under her nose and then pour it without comment, but in the event he detected a hint of grudging approval in her perfunctory sniff.

Swirling the wine round in the glass he looked at it against the white cloth. The colour was surprisingly rich. It was rich to the nose as well, with a cedary bouquet. It had a feeling of depth and age which over-rode the coldness to the lips. He decided to take his meal at as leisurely a pace as possible so that it would have time to open up.

As he put the glass down again he caught sight of the year on the label. It was a '66. He could hardly believe his good fortune.

'This is the wine which is on the list?'

The waitress craned her neck, taking in both the list and the label. '*Oui*. There is something wrong?'

Monsieur Pamplemousse made a non-committal gesture. He had done his duty. If the hotel wished to offer wine at give-away prices that was their business. He had no wish to query his good fortune any more for fear it would go away.

'*Terminé?*' As the wine list disappeared from under his nose in a manner which brooked no further argu-ment he resolved to make a closer study of it at the earliest opportunity. Who knew what other goodies were contained within its pages? Left on his own again he held the cork below the folds of the table cloth. An approving sniff greeted its appearance. Pommes Frites liked red Bordeaux. It always gave him an appetite. Sometimes he was allowed the dregs in his water bowl. He especially liked the crunchy bits. In his opinion the more crunchy bits there were the better the wine.

As if to underline the change in their fortunes, the setting sun, which had been half-hidden behind a building, cast a shaft of evening brightness across the table. It carried on across the room, illuminating the flushed faces of the couple in the corner. There was a flurry of movement and for a moment or two Monsieur Pamplemousse gazed at them, wondering if perhaps they were falling victims to Bernard's disease. He decided not. It was merely young love. All the same, it might be worth keeping an eye on their choice of food.

Throwing caution to the wind, he withdrew his notebook from a side pocket and began to write, slowly and methodically awarding points here, taking away others there, totting up the pluses and the minuses since their arrival.

Looked at from any direction his deliberations made sorry reading. Mathematically it could have been reduced to a series of figures which grew less and less equal the more the meal progressed.

The arrival of the rabbit pie reminded him of the Director's words. 'Pastry, Pamplemousse, that would tax the ingenuity of a woodpecker.' If the noise coming from under the table was anything to go by, even Pommes Frites was having trouble masticating it. He reached down and gave him an encouraging pat. He wished now he'd insisted on *frites* after all. The rich juices he'd pictured savouring were non-existent. It was a meal of unbelievable awfulness. Had there been less at stake he would have sent a message to the kitchen congratulating the Director's aunt on her effrontery. Several times during the course of the evening Pommes Frites looked out from under the table-cloth as if he could hardly believe his eyes let alone his taste buds.

Halfway through the sweet course Monsieur Pamplemousse reached for his tablets. Dyspepsia was an occupational hazard and although he was blessed with a moderately good digestive system, there were limits to its powers of endurance. He slipped a second one under the table. Pommes Frites crunched it gratefully.

'*Terminé?*'

'*Oui.*' There was nothing more to be said. He contemplated Madame Terminé through half-closed eyes, wondering if his meal had brought about any great change. Sadly it had not. It was possible that beneath her tightly corsetted exterior there beat a heart of gold, but if so neither food nor wine had made it any easier to detect. She flicked the table with her napkin.

'*Café?*'

'*Non.*' Coffee after such a meal might only compound the problem of going to sleep. 'Do you have a *tisane?*'

'Here or in the *salon?*' The emphasis on the last word was such that any suggestion of a choice was clearly window-dressing. He wondered what the reaction would be if he insisted on taking it at his table. Not wishing to be relegated to the cheerless room he'd seen on first entering the hotel, he decided on another approach.

'I'll take it up to my room.'

As they left the dining-room the young couple in the corner were already receiving their marching orders in the form of a folded bill on a plate. The restaurant of

65

the Hôtel du Paradis was definitely being terminéed for the night.

On the way to the stairs he hesitated, torn between going straight up to his room or going out of the back entrance to the hotel in order to inflate Pommes Frites' kennel for the night. He had just decided in favour of carrying on up the stairs – the kennel could wait until they took their post-prandial stroll – when he caught sight of the Director's aunt through an open doorway at the end of the passage. Dressed in a long white apron, she looked rather more tired and fraught than he remembered from his arrival earlier in the evening.

Partly on an impulse and partly out of curiosity he made his way towards the kitchen. Almost immediately he regretted the decision. His appearance prompted the inevitable question which he should have foreseen.

'Did I enjoy my meal?' He played for time before answering. Natural politeness towards a member of the opposite sex suggested a non-committal answer. His training with *Le Guide* forbade anything other than a non-committal answer. But his taste buds and his digestive juices, not to mention his reason for being there told him it was necessary to be cruel in order to be kind.

'With the greatest respect, and since you have asked, I cannot remember when I had a worse meal!'

Her jaw dropped and for a moment he thought she was going to cry.

'I'm sorry to put it quite so bluntly, but I would not be doing you a favour if I did otherwise. The artichoke was undercooked – I had to tug the leaves away from the heart. It was also discoloured. If you are going to prepare it days ahead then it should have had a slice of lemon tied to it to prevent that happening. And it is not sufficient just to put it on a plate; it should have been served with melted butter or with hollandaise.

'As for the *lapin* – dying of old age is one thing, encasing it within pastry so hard it could have served as a funeral casket is another matter again. And when you keep *pommes vapeur* hot you should cover them with a cloth. In that way you will absorb any excess moisture and they will arrive at the table dry and floury instead of sodden as the ones were tonight.

'Even the pineapple had not been treated with respect. Clearly it had spent over-long in a refrigerator – upright at that. It should have been kept at room temperature on its side in a paper bag and turned regularly. Keep a pineapple upright and all the flavour disappears. Also it should be cut downwards with the grain – not across.'

Madame Louise gazed at him curiously as she digested the information. 'You speak knowledgeably,' she ventured at last. 'Justine told me you were making notes over your meal. Are you in the same business?'

Realising that in giving vent to his indignation he might have gone too far, Monsieur Pamplemousse interrupted her hastily.

'I am interested, that is all. I was making notes for a book I am writing. It is set here, in the Loire Valley. Your Madame Terminé would do better if she attended to the needs of your customers rather than their actions – which are none of her business.'

Turning to remove a kettle from the stove, Madame Louise gave a laugh. It transformed her features.

Monsieur Pamplemousse felt his bad temper evaporate. As it did so there came a sudden feeling of guilt and a desire to help. She reached up for a tin. 'Justine would not be pleased if she heard you call her that.'

'It is true,' said Monsieur Pamplemousse defensively. 'She would be more at home in a station buffet making sure everyone caught the last train.'

The Director's aunt gave a wry smile as she added water to the cup. 'All the same, I do not know what I would do without her. Doing the cooking is bad enough. Finding the food to fit the menu is worse. Sometimes I have to go as far as Tours.'

'If you'll forgive my saying so,' broke in Monsieur Pamplemousse, 'that is quite the wrong way to go about things. You should always make the menu fit the food.' How many times had he heard chefs utter those very words? You went to the market early and bought well, then you returned and wrote the menu around the food.

'If you buy the best of ingredients you can never really fail. It is more than half the battle. You may end up with something you hadn't intended, but it won't be an out and out disaster.'

Well, hardly ever, he added under his breath. There were always exceptions to every rule.

Brushing a strand of hair from her eyes, Madame Louise looked up at him. 'That is a man talking. Men are always so full of confidence. It is hard for a woman when she is on her own with no one to turn to.'

As he took the tray from her Monsieur Pamplemousse was reminded once again of the Director's words.

'I understand. I'm sorry if I sounded a little abrupt just now, but you did ask.'

'You were quite right to tell me. Perhaps if more people did that, life would be easier. Do you have any more complaints?'

'Since you ask, there is a little matter of the plumbing in my room. There appears to be a problem with the waste pipe from the hand basin. It connects with the *bidet*. I'm afraid I had an accident earlier this evening. If you have an iron I could borrow I would be grateful.'

As he made his way up the stairs Monsieur Pamplemousse felt himself being watched. Glancing back down he saw that the Director's aunt had come out of the kitchen and was busying herself at the reception desk. Catching his eye she waved good night.

'Watch it, Pamplemousse,' he thought. 'Watch it.'

The bed in his room had been made up for the night. The sheets and counterpane turned back. A softer pillow replaced the round, hard sausage that had been there when he first arrived. It had been fluffed up to make it more comfortable and inviting.

He put the *tisane* down on the floor beside the only armchair and crossed to the French windows. The doors were ajar behind drawn curtains, but the shutters were closed, making the room feel airless despite the cooling down after the heat of the day. He decided to open them for a while, at least until it was time to put Pommes Frites to bed.

Outside all was quiet; the shops and houses mostly shuttered like his own room. In the time it had taken to reach the upper floor via the kitchen dusk had fallen.

Apart from the lights of the hotel, the only illumination came from the Sanisette below.

He glanced down at it and as he did so he gave a start. Something very odd appeared to be happening to the roof. At first he thought it was a cat and then he decided it was the wrong shape; it was much too tall and slender, more like a rolled umbrella. It looked like – it couldn't possibly be, of course, but it looked as if a long loaf of bread was sticking out.

Even as he watched, it rose higher in the air and began waving to and fro like a short-sighted elephant reaching up with its trunk for some out of reach delicacy.

Turning back into the room he made a dive for his working case. A moment later he was back on the balcony again, focusing his binoculars in the direction of the toilet. Issued by *Le Guide* to its staff so that they could furnish reports on the scenery while on their travels, they were normally set at infinity, but at last the object he'd been searching for swam into view.

He'd been right; it *was* a loaf of bread. To be precise, a *baguette*. A *baguette* which, at the very moment of coming into sharp focus, disappeared from view again into the depths of the Sanisette. For a moment or two he held the glasses in position, wondering if the wine at dinner had been more potent than he'd bargained for, or whether he was experiencing the first symptoms of a response to his gastronomic experiments, a blurring of his senses, but he knew what he'd seen.

Pommes Frites eyed his master sleepily as he leaped over the lion's head and dashed past him for the second time in as many minutes. Normally he would have been only too pleased to join in the fun; it would have been an automatic reaction. Give him someone or some*thing* going at speed and he was after it like a shot – the faster it went the more he liked it. But like his master, Pommes Frites was beginning to feel the after-effects of the meal. He decided that for the time being at least he would remain on the alert, ready to follow on behind at a moment's notice if required, but until that moment he would attend to his own needs. He had other, more pressing matters on his mind.

Outside in the square Monsieur Pamplemousse gazed in growing frustration at an illuminated orange sign on the side of the toilet. It bore the word OCCUPÉ.

He banged on the stainless steel door with his fist. '*Ouvrez la porte!*'

The silence was unbroken and absolute. He tried again. At least whoever was in there couldn't get away. Somewhere behind him he heard a shutter being opened and a light came on from an upper window.

Reaching into his trouser pocket he found a one franc coin and tried inserting it in the slot, but the machine refused it immediately.

He studied the instructions on the side. A time limit of fifteen minutes was imposed. After that the door opened automatically. Given the fact that the present occupant must have been inside for at least five minutes, possibly more, he shouldn't have long to wait.

For a moment he was tempted to call up for Pommes Frites, then he decided against it. He'd made enough noise already. He didn't want to waken the whole village.

71

Almost immediately he received proof that he'd made the right decision. There was a click and a soft whirring noise as the half-round door began to slide open.

To his surprise a figure dressed from head to foot in black appeared in the opening.

'*Pardon*, Madame.' Automatically, as he stood back a little to give her room, he went to raise his hat before realising he wasn't wearing one. Bent double, a shopping basket clasped behind her back, she sidled past without answering.

He hesitated, wondering whether or not to challenge her, but with what and on what grounds? Perhaps the toilet was in great demand that night?

Determined to get to the bottom of the matter he decided to try his luck with the franc again. Once more it was refused. This time doubtless because the machine was going through its cleansing cycle. Thank goodness he hadn't been taken short. He bent down to re-read the instructions and as he did so there was a sudden flurry of movement from behind. Before he had time to react something heavy struck him a vicious blow on the back of the head. Over and above the jarring sensation in his brain, he was aware of the sound of running feet, and then, as he clawed at the empty air in a vain effort to stop himself from toppling forward, everything went black.

4

POMMES FRITES AT LARGE

The rest of that night passed in a series of fits and starts, a montage of events and impressions which came and went, merging with each other like the opening of an old newsreel. He vaguely remembered coming round and finding himself lying on the cobblestones outside the toilet. They had felt surprisingly damp until he realised it was his own blood. Somehow or other he'd managed to stagger back to the hotel where he must have passed out again, for the next thing he could recall was finding himself sitting up in bed with a jacket round his shoulders.

He remembered being irritated by all the questions everyone kept throwing at him; looking in vain for Pommes Frites, then for his binoculars. He'd been very worried about his binoculars. They were Leitz Trinovids belonging to *Le Guide*. Madame Grante in Accounts would not be pleased if he reported them missing. He'd had trouble enough when he'd lost the cap on the 50mm lens of his camera. With the kind of wild logic given only to those who have to deal with other people's expenses, she had demanded double payment. One for the cap he'd lost, a second for its replacement. In the end he'd bought a new one himself to avoid any further argument.

After that he must have dropped off to sleep; a drugged, dream-filled sleep from which he struggled awake every now and then to the sound of dogs howling. Once or twice he thought he recognised Pommes Frites' bark amongst them, but each time he fell back into instant dreams; dreams which were mostly to do with being chased by people armed with huge loaves of bread, bread which always turned out to be made of stone like ancient clubs.

When he finally woke the sun was high in the sky. He lay where he was for a while, allowing his mind to grapple as best it could with the facts at its disposal; the strange surroundings, the events of the night before and the reason for his being there; then he looked at his watch. It was nearly eleven thirty. He'd slept for well over twelve hours. Such a thing hadn't happened in years.

The shutters over the balcony doors must have been left open from the previous night, for the sunlight illuminated the room with a translucent glow through the thin curtains.

Climbing out of bed he crossed the room and pulled them apart. The sudden shock of the sun straight in his eyes caused him to wince. In the square below a woman with a shopping basket who was about to enter the *boucherie* nudged her companion and pointed up at him. The other woman put a hand to her mouth and said something, then they both laughed.

Turning back into the room he looked at his reflection in a tall mirror next to a chest of drawers and realised for the first time that he was completely naked. His head was bandaged and he needed a shave.

On his way to the bathroom he saw with relief that his binoculars were lying on top of the leather case. His clothes were neatly folded over the chair, his jacket carefully draped over a hanger suspended from the wardrobe door handle, otherwise everything was as he'd left it when he came up from dinner the night before.

Ten minutes later he was lying in the bath, the water almost up to his chin. He wished he'd thought to bring some bath salts with him. The room was devoid of any of the free gifts one had almost come to expect; a sachet of *bain moussant* would have gone down well at that moment. Apart from anything else the surface of the bath had a rough feel to it, the result of years of scouring with coarse powders. He wondered idly if it was the very same bath the Director had suffered in as a child. It was hard to picture a tiny Director covered in cigarette ash.

The thought together with the chilly water made him get out sooner than he might have done, and fifteen minutes later, shaved and freshly groomed, he made his way downstairs, but not before making the surprising discovery that the rest of his clothes – the ones that had received the soaking in the *bidet*, had been pressed and put away in the wardrobe. The shirt was carefully arranged with a piece of pink tissue paper between the folds. The trousers were hanging from a rail.

When he reached the hall he found the Director's aunt talking to an elderly man carrying a black bag. Even without a stethoscope round his neck he looked every inch the country doctor.

They both seemed surprised to see him.

'Shouldn't you still be in bed?' Madame Louise reached for a chair.

Monsieur Pamplemousse held up his hand in polite refusal. 'I am perfectly all right, thank you.'

'Nevertheless . . .' The doctor motioned him to sit. 'It is as well to be on the safe side. Last night you were anything but all right.' Taking an instrument from his case he lifted Monsieur Pamplemousse's eyelids, first the left and then the right, peering at them closely with the aid of a spotlight. 'You have no difficulty in focusing? No loss of vision?'

Monsieur Pamplemousse went to shake his head and then thought better of it. Doctors were like dentists, they asked you questions under circumstances when it was difficult to reply.

'No vomiting?'

'Not that I am aware of.'

'Good. There are no signs of concussion. They would have appeared by now.' The doctor stood back. 'You've had a lucky escape.'

'What happened?' Madame Louise looked at him anxiously. 'We had a shock when you came back after your walk. Were you attacked?'

'Poof!' Monsieur Pamplemousse brushed the question to one side, trying to make light of it. 'It was nothing. A slight accident. I went to use the Sanisette and I must have tripped and fallen awkwardly.' For the time being he had no wish to discuss the matter with anyone until he'd marshalled his thoughts, least of all with the doctor or Madame Louise.

'I feel it is all my fault.' The Director's aunt sounded

weary, as if the whole thing was yet another nail in her coffin. 'I should have warned you about the toilet on your floor. The door is always jamming shut. I keep telling Armand to fix it. There is another on the floor above. As for that monstrosity outside in the square, it has been a source of trouble ever since it was erected. No good will come of it.'

'You had breadcrumbs in your wound!' said the doctor accusingly. He made it sound like a major crime; an act of self-degradation. 'If it was some kind of attack then the police must be informed.'

Monsieur Pamplemousse decided it was time to change the subject. 'I have very little memory of what happened. All I recall is waking up in bed, but how I got there is another matter.'

'You have this lady to thank,' broke in the doctor.

'And Justine. I couldn't have managed you by myself. Getting you up the stairs was hard enough, but then lifting you on to the bed and undressing you.' Madame Louise blushed. 'We couldn't find your pyjamas.'

'They were under my pillow,' said Monsieur Pamplemousse. Somehow the thought of being undressed by Madame Terminé aroused mixed feelings. He was glad he hadn't known about it at the time.

'Oh! But . . .' She looked as if she was about to say something and then changed her mind. 'You must be hungry. You haven't had any breakfast. Let me cook you something. An omelette perhaps?' She turned to the doctor. 'An omelette *fines herbes* wouldn't hurt would it, Docteur Cornot?'

The doctor closed his bag. 'On the contrary.'

Monsieur Pamplemousse's heart sank. He didn't want to hurt Madame Louise's feelings, particularly after all she had done for him, but he had a clear mental picture of what any omelette cooked by her would be like. To begin with the eggs would be over-beaten so that they would start off too liquid, then it would be over-cooked; hard in the centre and not *baveuse*. The herbs would have been added to the mixture before-hand, not whilst it was cooking, so that little bits would have stuck to the pan and much of the flavour lost.

A thought struck him. 'Do you have any large potatoes?'

'Yes, but . . .'

'Put two in the oven to bake. There is a recipe I know. *Oeufs à la Toupinel*.' His mouth began to water. It was a long time since he'd eaten it. It was not something one normally encountered in restaurants.

'In the meantime I must go and look for Pommes Frites. While I am gone you could perhaps prepare me a sauce Mornay if that isn't too much trouble. I forgot to inflate Pommes Frites' kennel last night. If he's been out all night without shelter he will not be pleased.'

The doctor held out his hand as he made to leave. 'On the contrary, Monsieur, if your dog is a large bloodhound, and I assume that is the one since he is a stranger to the village, then the last time I saw him he was looking very pleased with himself indeed. Some-what worn out, but undoubtedly pleased.'

'Pleased?' Monsieur Pamplemousse repeated the word nervously. 'Why? What has happened?'

Madame Louise caught the doctor's eye. 'I'm afraid

Pommes Frites is in disgrace. We have had to put him in the stables out of harm's way awaiting the arrival of the *vétérinaire*.'

'The *vétérinaire?*' Monsieur Pamplemousse felt his heart miss a beat. 'Where is he? I must go to him at once.'

Doctor Cornot picked up his bag. 'There is nothing wrong with him. At least nothing that a good night's sleep won't cure. Although that is not to say it will stay that way. There are those in the village who would wish to see him *coupé*.'

'*Coupé*? Pommes Frites *coupé*?' Monsieur Pample-mousse's voice was a mixture of surprise and indignation.

'Last night while you were asleep he went on the rampage. Hardly a *chienne* escaped his attentions. I hesitate to bandy numbers about, but it must reach double figures at the final count. I am not saying that in the final analysis all were unwilling, but as far as I can make out they were hardly given the choice.'

'*Merde!*' Monsieur Pamplemousse's thoughts raced ahead as the doctor's voice droned on. Clearly Pommes Frites had had an attack of the Bernards. A bad one by the sound of it. But why? To the best of his knowledge they had eaten precisely the same thing. Perhaps it was a question of quantity? On reflection, out of purely selfish motives he had been more than generous with the *tourte au lapin*. But that would have been more likely to bring on an attack of indigestion rather than the other. Perhaps it was a matter of certain ingredients affecting only certain metabolisms. What was sauce for the goose was an aphrodisiac to the gander. He resolved to have a quiet word with the *vétérinaire* to see if he could recall any similar happenings in the past. In view of the amount of custom Pommes Frites must have generated for him he could hardly refuse to give an opinion.

'I will go and put the potatoes in the oven.' Madame Louise turned to leave.

'Thank you. And please . . .' He suddenly felt embarrassed at criticising everything she did, but there were certain things that needed to be said. 'Would it be possible to have some *proper* bread with it?'

There was a moment's hesitation. 'I will send out for some.'

'Don't worry. I will go.' He sensed a sudden constraint and realised that for some reason he was treading on dangerous ground. In any case it gave him an excuse to visit the *boulangerie*. One way and another it was getting high on his agenda.

As he said goodbye to the doctor and stepped outside the hotel a woman with a red setter on a lead waved at him from the other side of the square. Monsieur Pamplemousse quickened his pace. The dog appeared unwilling to go anywhere near the hotel and the woman had to drag it along the pavement, so that he reached the *boulangerie* before her. For a moment or two he thought she was going to follow him inside.

'*Une ficelle, s'il vous plaît.*' A *baguette* would really be too painful a reminder.

While the girl was reaching up for his bread he cast an eye over the window display, hovering between a *tarte aux pommes* and a *tarte aux fraises*. Through the glass he could see a small crowd beginning to collect outside.

Word must have travelled fast. He ordered two *tartes aux pommes*.

'Is Monsieur in?'

'*Non*, Monsieur.' The girl wrapped the *tartes* quickly but expertly into a pyramid shaped parcel, as if they were a Christmas present. 'He has finished his second baking. Besides, today is Wednesday.'

It was said without offence but the inference that he should have known these things was unmistakable.

Thanking her, Monsieur Pamplemousse paid for his purchases, collected the change, then took a deep breath as he turned towards the door and braced himself for the onslaught to come.

'*Assassin!*'

'*J'accuse!*'

'Poofs' and cries and counter-cries greeted his exit from the shop.

'*Treize! Treize chiennes* in one night.' A man with a golden labrador pushed his way to the front. 'It is *répugnant*. He is a menace to society. He should be *coupé*.'

'And his owner with him!' shrieked a woman who looked as if she couldn't wait to carry out her threat personally.

Monsieur Pamplemousse drew back and held up his hand. 'I protest!' he exclaimed. 'What right have you to say such things? It could well be a case of mistaken identity. How dare you make accusations based on *évidence circonstancielle*.' Privately the thought crossed his mind that thirteen was an unlucky number. Perhaps Pommes Frites had run out of targets.

'*Évidence circonstancielle! Évidence circonstancielle!*' The man looked for a moment as if he was about to have a fit.

'In the dark,' said Monsieur Pamplemousse mildly, 'one dog is very like another.'

'In the dark, Monsieur, *oui!*' The man reached into an inside pocket and withdrew a photograph which he held up and waved triumphantly for all to see. 'But by flashlight, *non!* There is nothing *circonstancielle* about that one's *membre*. *Substantiel* would be the word, and for the use to which he is putting it!'

A murmur of approval went round the group.

'May I see that?' Monsieur Pamplemousse reached out and took the picture from the man. As he looked at it his heart sank. The clarity of the polaroid image was such that it would have brought tears of joy to the eyes of its inventor, Doctor Land. On the reverse side of the coin it would have caused even the most skilled of defence lawyers to furrow his brow in dismay had he been unfortunate enough to undertake the case of Pommes Frites versus The Rest.

The legs which supported him to such good purpose in the picture would not have kept him upright for more than a second in a court of law. Even a plea of diminished responsibility would have been thrown out on an instant. It was very clear that Pommes Frites knew exactly where he stood with his responsibilities and what he was doing with them. Had he been one for singing, he would undoubtedly have been giving voice to the words of the Hallelujah Chorus.

Monsieur Pamplemousse was suddenly and irresistibly reminded of a remark he'd once heard attributed to that famous English man of the theatre, Noel

Coward. It had been made when he'd encountered a similar situation while taking a small godson out for a walk in the country.

'The one below has lost his sight,' he'd explained, in one of his flashes of instant wit. 'And the one on top is pushing him all the way to a home for the blind.'

'It is no laughing matter, Monsieur.' The man snatched his photograph back.

'On the contrary,' said Monsieur Pamplemousse firmly. 'In my opinion most things are a laughing matter when looked at in a certain light. The gift of laughter is what raises man above the beasts in the fields. When did you last see a cow laugh? Or a sheep?

'As for Pommes Frites,' he assumed his most conciliatory manner, 'you are absolutely right. He must not be allowed to go unpunished. Were he able to write I would insist on letters of apology all round. To seek pleasure in life is one thing. To obtain it at the expense of others and without their permission is totally inexcusable.'

Taking advantage of the sudden change of atmosphere brought about by his audience having the rug withdrawn from under their very feet, Monsieur Pamplemousse set about beating a hasty retreat before they had time to reply.

'Do not be too hard on him, Monsieur,' a voice called after him as he pushed his way through the crowd.

When he reached the stable at the back of the hotel car park he found Pommes Frites fast asleep in some straw. He might not have received the gift of laughter, but if the seraphic smile on his face was anything to go by it would have been an unnecessary embellishment.

He toyed with the idea of raising his voice in rebuke for the benefit of the others, then thought better of it. That would have been an unnecessary gilding of the lily. He had no wish to tread on Pommes Frites' dreams. Clearly they were giving him much pleasure.

Closing the stable door carefully so as not to disturb him, he made his way towards the back entrance of the hotel. On his way past a second stable he heard a rasping sound and glancing inside saw someone bent over a bench filing the end of a piece of copper piping clamped in a vice. It was the same person he'd seen dodging out of the way when he'd first arrived. Perhaps he had come to do the plumbing in his room. Just outside the back door to the hotel an old woman sat on a stool, a bucket by her side, head bent, hard at work peeling some vegetables. Like the plumber she offered no response to his greeting. For a moment the thought crossed his mind that perhaps she was the one who had come out of the toilet the night before. He dismissed the idea as quickly as it came. She was much too frail. Whoever had attacked him wielded a fairly hefty punch. What used to be known in the force as a bunch of *cinqs*.

Upstairs in his room again he put the binoculars back in the velvet-lined compartment of the case and then locked it. Although there was nothing in there to connect him with *Le Guide*, there was no point in taking chances. He hesitated for a moment or two over his notebook and then slipped it into the secret compartment of the trousers hanging in the wardrobe before making his way back downstairs.

Entering the kitchen he nearly bumped into Madame Terminé who was bustling in the opposite direction carrying a pile of dirty laundry. He held the door open for her. Did his eyes deceive him or was she regarding him in a new light? There was a kind of intimacy in her glance which he hadn't noticed the night before. Already, although he had only been at the hotel for one night he could sense a change; a feeling of tendrils reaching out and taking root. In normal circumstances it would have been a clear signal to move on. Familiarity was not encouraged by *Le Guide*. Familiarity could cloud the judgment.

The Director's aunt was busy by the stove. She, too, looked up and seemed to greet him as an old friend rather than as a client. She was wearing a freshly starched white apron and her hair was noticeably tidier than he remembered it earlier that morning. He judged she was perhaps ten years younger than himself. Perhaps in her mid forties. At times she looked much older.

'Are you sure these potatoes are what you want? It doesn't seem a very good way to start the day – especially after what happened.'

'On the contrary.' Monsieur Pamplemousse looked round the kitchen as he spoke, taking it all in; the *batterie de cuisine* above the long cupboard between the stove and the window – a row of burnished copper pans hanging up, and close to them an array of knives of all shapes and sizes. Beyond that again a selection of *marmites* and casseroles, some old and richly worked, others new and hardly used. Fish kettles and enamelled iron *terrines* completed the picture. Whatever else she lacked, Tante Louise certainly wasn't short of equipment. He suddenly realised he was starting to think of her as 'Tante' rather than plain 'Madame'.

He glanced down at the stove. It looked clean and serviceable if a trifle large for the amount of work it was called on to do. High above it some early eighteenth-century potholders hung from a large beam. They, too, looked clean and dust-free without the greasy surface one might have expected.

'On the contrary,' he repeated. 'The potato is much maligned. Can you think of another vegetable with so many virtues? The potato goes well with everything. It is never assertive. Full of goodness, but never boring. It can be boiled and baked and sliced and fried. Above all, although it is with us the whole year round you never get tired of it.

'Besides, what I am about to prepare is not just a potato. It is a dish fit for a king. I shall need some butter and cream, nutmeg, ham – preferably lean, and it will need to be finely minced. Breadcrumbs and Parmesan cheese. Then I shall need some eggs for poaching.'

While he was talking he reached up and took a *couteau d'office* from the rack on the wall, feeling its blade as he did so. It was a Sabatier, five inches of high quality carbon steel, but it was blunt, sadly and undeniably blunt. Not only that but it was badly stained. Cutting into the potato would transmit an unwholesome taste.

'Do you have any lemon?'

While he was cleaning the blade he felt Tante Louise

watching him. 'You seem very at home in a kitchen. You must do a lot of cooking.'

He sought for a suitable answer. It was true to say he felt at home in a kitchen. His time with *Le Guide* had not been wasted. He'd lost count of the number of hours spent watching others at work; marvelling at the expert way they dealt with even the most mundane of tasks. In the right hands even the chopping of a carrot became a work of art. But as for cooking itself; Doucette usually frowned on his excursions into a kitchen which was common property most of the time but became *hers* whenever he used it. Like the Director's aunt, ownership changed according to circumstances. Accusations of using up every pot and pan within sight were rife and not without reason. In the kitchen he became the *gros bonnet*; the big hat, the boss of all he surveyed.

He gave a non-committal shrug, wondering how best to broach the subject of sharpening the knife without causing offence. But in the event he needn't have worried. Tante Louise was only too willing to acknowledge her inadequacies.

Reading his thoughts as he looked around she opened a drawer and handed him a steel. 'Why is it sharpening knives is always considered man's work. I have Madame Camille's son, but he is more of a problem than a help. I wouldn't trust him with them.'

Monsieur Pamplemousse supposed she must be talking of the man he'd seen earlier. Come to think of it, there was a family likeness. 'Have you never thought of getting married?'

For some reason the Director's aunt coloured up.

She crossed to the oven and opened the door. 'The potatoes are ready.'

'In that case,' Monsieur Pamplemousse took the hint, 'perhaps you would be kind enough to prepare two poached eggs.'

Removing the potatoes from their rack, he grasped the newly sharpened knife and cut a hole in the top of each. Scooping out two-thirds of the inside of each potato with a spoon, he began mashing it in a bowl along with the butter and cream, adding salt to taste and then a pinch of nutmeg.

Replacing the mixture in the potatoes, he left a cavity in the top of each into which he poured a teaspoonful of the Mornay sauce and another of the freshly minced ham.

'Eggs, please. Now some more of the Mornay.'

'Breadcrumbs . . . grated Parmesan . . .' He felt like a surgeon carrying out a delicate operation. 'Can you put the rest of the butter in a saucepan to melt?'

Adding a few drops of the melted butter he placed the potatoes carefully on to a heatproof dish and put them back into the oven to brown.

'Ça va.' He wiped his hands on a cloth, realising he should have worn an apron. It was just like home. At home he always forgot an apron until it was too late. He looked at her shyly. 'Since I seem to have made free with your kitchen, perhaps you would like to join me? We could share a bottle of Vouvray. It will go well. Unless . . .' he decided to leave the ball in her court. 'Unless you are too busy?'

'There is no one else for lunch. That would be very kind. I will ask Justine to fetch the wine.'

While she was gone he quickly opened the oven door again, breathing a sigh of relief at what he saw. Despite his air of confidence it was many years since he'd last cooked *œufs à la Toupinel*. The result was eminently satisfactory, exactly as he remembered it; golden brown and sizzling in its juices. He hoped it would live up to its looks. In the end it was always the simplest dishes that were the best. He'd once conducted a survey among the great chefs, the ones who'd been awarded three Stock Pots, to see what they ate when everyone else had gone home, and they all said the same.

He loaded up a tray and carried it proudly into the dining-room, almost regretting for a moment that it was empty. It deserved an audience. Even Madame Terminé would have been better than nothing; or Pommes Frites. He wondered what Elsie would have thought of his efforts. Somehow he felt they would have met with approval. Pommes Frites would certainly have got up to have a closer look. For a moment he toyed with the idea of fetching him in, but decided against it. If there was any left over he would take it out for him afterwards. Apart from anything else he wasn't sure if Pommes Frites would totally approve of his little *tête-à-tête*; jealousy might creep in, although given the events of the previous night he could hardly kick up too much fuss. All the same, it was better to be safe than sorry.

A table had been laid for two just inside the door, as far away from the window as possible. The bread, freshly sliced, was in a basket in the middle alongside an empty flower vase. No doubt the Director's aunt didn't want the whole world to know she was lunching with one of the guests; with the *only* guest in the hotel.

Tante Louise made a grimace at the other tables as she entered carrying a wine bucket with an already opened bottle clinking against the ice inside. 'It will be different later in the week – I hope. Friday is the day of the annual *Foire à la Ferraille et aux Jambons* and the village will be *en fête*. There will be a parade and lunch outside in the garden so that everyone can watch. I hope you will still be here.'

The Iron and Ham Fair apart, Monsieur Pample-mousse felt sure he would still be there. The way things were going the Fair would have come and gone long before he'd even begun sorting things out.

He broke off a piece of bread and popped it into his mouth while he was serving. It had the characteristic, slightly sour taste of a genuine *pain au levain*. The inside was airy and cream coloured, slightly chewy. The village baker must be one of a sadly dying breed who cared enough for his art to use a chunk of dough from the previous day's baking as a starter, rather than do it the easy way with yeast. He probably used stone-ground flour as well. No wonder the shop was often crowded.

The Vouvray was a contrast in taste; fruity and yet bone dry, with an underlying firmness which came from the Chinon grapes. Overall there was an acidity suggesting a year which lacked sun. It should have been drunk and not kept. Compared with the wine he'd been served the night before it was disappointing. A glance at the label confirmed his suspicions.

'I know what you are thinking. I'm afraid I know

nothing of wine.' Tante Louise took the glass he had just poured. 'I have to rely on the judgment of others. I inherited the cellar from my father, and he inherited it from his father before him, but I'm afraid neither of them passed on their taste buds when they died. They both spent most of their time abroad and when they came home they always made up for lost time, squandering what was left of the family fortune – if it ever existed. Grandma swore it did, but no one ever found it.'

The words were said without any trace of bitterness, but Monsieur Pamplemousse pricked up his ears, adding a visit to the cellars to his growing list of things to do at the earliest opportunity. It sounded intriguing.

Photographs of an imposing, moustachioed figure – presumably the grandfather – adorned the walls wherever you looked. He seemed to be for ever posing against a tropical backcloth with a glass in one hand and an outsize rifle in the other, his right foot placed firmly on whatever animal had been unfortunate enough to cross his path. Size had clearly been no passport to mercy; large and small, all were doomed to an untimely death. No wonder the local taxidermist had flourished. He wondered how they'd all been transported home. Come to that, how he'd managed to travel with such an enormous cellar. Had the Chablis been served at jungle temperature? And had the champagne exploded after all the shaking about? Or had there been hordes of native bearers weighed down by some gigantic ice box?

He suddenly realised Tante Louise was talking.

'I hope you don't mind my asking?'

'Of course not.' He wondered what he'd let himself in for. 'I shall be only too happy.'

'It seems a strange thing to ask of a guest and you must say if it interferes with your writing, but perhaps it may give you some ideas.'

Monsieur Pamplemousse gave a start. He'd forgotten about his 'writing'.

'Once this week is over things will settle down again.'

'Yes. Er, what would you like me to do?' He put on his thoughtful look, the one he assumed when he was weighing pros and cons.

'Just to be there and offer advice really. I wouldn't expect you to do any manual work, but the more time goes by the more I realise there are so many things I don't know about. I want so much to succeed. The Hôtel du Paradis has been in the family for generations. To lose it now would be like breaking faith with all those who have gone before. Mama, Papa, Grandmère . . . that's her picture on the wall.'

Monsieur Pamplemousse followed the direction of her gaze and dwelt on a gilt-framed picture hanging on the wall beside the bar. He'd noticed it without paying a great deal of attention over dinner the night before. He saw what Tante Louise meant. Grand-mère did not look the sort of person one would wish to break faith with; not if one believed in an afterlife and possible recriminations. Even in repose there was a firm line to the jaw and an upward tilt to the head which denoted strength of purpose. With Grandpa away on safari for months on end she'd probably had plenty of time to develop it.

'Sometimes everything seems to be going well and then, for no reason at all, it comes to nothing. We have been in guides and out of them again. I do not understand the reason. I have a niece who is married to someone very important in Paris – an old family friend in fact. I have written to him several times, but he is always too busy. He sends messages to say he is in conference.' Monsieur Pamplemousse knew the feeling. 'Once, a little while ago, there were some men from Paris. They arrived one night in a large, black American car and made offers. When I refused they threatened.'

'What sort of offers?'

Madame Louise blushed. 'Offers I would not wish to repeat.'

'And then?'

'I put something in their soup. They never came back.'

Monsieur Pamplemousse wiped his plate carefully with some bread and then speared the last remaining crust of the potato with his fork. It was the best part, crisp and earthy to the taste, wearing its goodness on its sleeve. Despite her slightly helpless manner, Tante Louise had obviously inherited some of her Grand-mère's toughness. She would be a force to be reckoned with. Yet again, he was reminded of the Director's words.

'If those men come again,' he said, 'tell them Pamplemousse sends his regards.'

Before there was time to reply he rose to his feet, removed the serviette from his collar and dabbed at his lips. 'Now I must leave you. I have to go into Tours.

Thank you for the meal. Although I say it myself, a King could not have eaten better.'

'And I feel like a Queen. It was delicious.'

He paused at the door, a twinkle in his eye. 'If I am to be your consort, may I offer some advice?

'For a *village fleuri* – a *village* moreover which is about to be *en fête*, your rooms are singularly lacking in colour. Flowers are like women; they are not born to blush unseen.'

Conscious that his step was a little lighter than usual, Monsieur Pamplemousse made his way towards the front door, then changed his mind and headed towards the back entrance. He may have emerged the victor in his encounter with the local inhabitants earlier that morning, but there was no sense in tempting fate.

The old woman he'd seen in the yard outside was no longer there. She must have finished her chores. The paving had been washed down, the table scrubbed. Two bowls and a bucket were placed neatly on a shelf, ready for the next day.

After the shade of the dining-room the sunshine was dazzling. He glanced in at the first stable. The door was still open but the old woman's son was no longer there. As he neared the second stable his pace quickened. Pommes Frites would be awake by now, wagging his tail with pleasure at seeing him. He wished now he'd managed to save some of the lunch for him. The previous night's activities would have whetted his appetite. If his total score bore any relation to it he must be starving. It would be no use pretending he hadn't had any lunch. Pommes Frites' sense of smell was too good for that. In any case he knew from past experience it would be impossible to look him straight in the eye without registering guilt.

Taking a deep breath, Monsieur Pamplemousse paused in the doorway so that he could take full advantage of standing with his back to the light, preparing himself for the onslaught of the fifty or so kilograms of welcome he expected to receive.

But if to expect nothing is to be blessed, then conversely Monsieur Pamplemousse's chances of entering the Pearly Gates at that moment would have received a severe jolt; the whistle that had formed on his lips died away as, like Tweedledum and Tweedledee before him, answer came there none. The normally ubiquitous Pommes Frites was conspicuous by his absence.

Idiotically, he almost found himself looking for some kind of note. Reaching down he felt a compressed patch in the middle of the pile of straw. It was cold to the touch. Tucked away inside it lay a half-eaten bone.

Whatever had caused Pommes Frites' absence must have happened some while ago and been of an unexpected nature. It took a lot to part Pommes Frites from a bone once he'd got his teeth into it. To abandon one altogether pointed to something very pressing indeed.

Perhaps he'd had another of his uncontrollable urges. Worse still, perhaps he was stuck with them. Like some kind of migraine they would keep coming back without warning. His heart sank at the thought. Doucette would not take kindly to the idea, nor would the eighteenth arrondissement.

Feeling deflated and suddenly very much alone,

Monsieur Pamplemousse glanced towards the entrance to the car park, noted with relief that the street outside was deserted, and then made his way slowly towards his car. It was time he set out for Tours. No doubt all would be revealed in due course. It usually was with Pommes Frites, and it was no good being impatient.

Pressing the starter he put the 2CV into gear, let in the clutch and began moving off. Almost immediately he became aware that something was amiss. There was a lack of response and the steering felt sluggish. It took a matter of seconds to absorb the facts, marshal them into some kind of logical order and reach a solution. He drew up by the side of the road.

Climbing out again he did a circuit of the car, gazing at the wheels with a mixture of mounting anger and frustration. '*Sapristi!*' Intended to run with a pressure of 1.4 kilograms per square centimetre at the front and 1.8 at the rear, all four Michelin X tyres were as flat as the proverbial *crêpe*.

He looked around for help, but St. Georges-sur-Lie was closed for lunch. The *boulangerie* on the other side of the road was shut, its blinds drawn to keep out the sun. The van which was normally parked at the side was nowhere to be seen.

Faced with such a situation, lesser men might well have resorted to violence of one form or another, kicking the wheels, attacking the bonnet with their bare fists, or even bursting into uncontrollable tears.

Monsieur Pamplemousse did none of these things. Calmly and methodically he removed the keys from the dashboard, selected the second one on the ring, and after unlocking the boot, withdrew a large metal cylinder, little realising as he did so that he was setting in train a series of events which later that same week would save him from a particularly shocking and unpleasant demise.

5

SWINGS AND ROUNDABOUTS

Fifteen minutes later, tyres inflated, hands and nails freshly scrubbed following a visit to his room, camera equipment on the back seat in case he came across a particularly rewarding view – one that would merit a *jacinthe* or a pair of binoculars in *Le Guide* – Monsieur Pamplemousse set off in the direction of Tours, joining the N152 near Langeais so as to hug the north bank of the Loire. Chameleon-like, its luminous colours reflected the mood of its surroundings and the sky above as it sparkled its way towards Saumur. Watched over by sand martins diving to catch the occasional fly as it wound its way lazily in and out of the dozens of golden sandbanks exposed by the low water, it was still a river to respect. It might have seen grander days but it was a river of sudden whirlpools and currents. You took it for granted at your peril. The occasional tree root sticking up out of the water acted as a reminder that in winter, when heavy rain fell over the Massif Central, it could become a raging torrent in a matter of hours, with anything up to six thousand cubic metres of water heading westwards towards Brittany and the Atlantic Ocean every second of the day.

As he slotted himself into the stream of traffic heading east Monsieur Pamplemousse reflected, not for the first time, on the wisdom of a belt and braces approach to life he'd acquired through his years in the Paris police.

Tubeless tyres were undoubtedly a great invention – until they went down, when blowing them up with a foot pump was an impossibility. All the same, the carrying of a cylinder of compressed air was a needless extravagance in many people's eyes. Madame Grante's, for example. How often in the course of a lifetime did one have need of it? Nevertheless, without it he would still be sitting outside the Hôtel du Paradis waiting for a garage mechanic to turn up.

For the time being at least he preferred to gloss over the fact that the prime reason for carrying a cylinder was so that he could blow up Pommes Frites' inflatable kennel when he went to bed at night. Doing it by mouth was hard on the lungs; worse than blowing up a packet of balloons at Christmas. Pommes Frites' kennel was a large one – king size. He wouldn't be best pleased if he knew his cylinder was empty.

It seemed strange driving along by himself. It was the kind of outing Pommes Frites would have enjoyed, and Monsieur Pamplemousse found himself keeping a weather eye open for likely spots where they might have stopped while he took photographs and Pommes Frites had a run. On the other hand Pommes Frites would probably have ignored the danger signs and gone in for a swim. That would not have been a good idea. Some of the invitingly white sandbanks – the *sables mouvants* – could be death traps.

One thing was certain. If Pommes Frites had gone in for a dip the heat inside the car would have dried him off in no time at all. Monsieur Pamplemousse felt tempted to roll back the roof and then thought better of it. In his present condition the hot sun on his head would not be a good idea.

One way and another there was a lot to think about. Paris suddenly seemed an age away. It was hard to believe that it was only three days since he'd sat listening to the Director pouring out his tale of woe, and watched Elsie pour out the Armagnac. He wondered if she was still surviving or whether she had moved on. Elsie would probably survive wherever she went. She was one of nature's survivors. He could have done with her help at the hotel, for already a plan was beginning to form in the back of his mind. It was a plan which he knew would tax his culinary powers to their limit, for he was only too well aware that his job for *Le Guide* was merely that of a critic. More often than not it was a case of the legless trying to teach an athlete how to run. No one ever erected a statue to a critic, still less a food inspector.

Buildings came into view, followed by a road junction. Turning right at the Place Choiseul he joined the line of north–south traffic crossing the river by way of the Pont Wilson and entered the rue Nationale. Another day, another time, he might have turned left and booked a table at Barrier just up the hill, the coolness of the courtyard with its fountains would have been a welcome relief.

Spring and late autumn were the best times to visit Tours. Now the atmosphere was humid; a combination of the freak weather and a lack of air brought about by its existence in an alluvial hollow. To the left lay the old city, ahead and to the right the vast area rebuilt after the war. It was hard to believe, sitting in a near-stationary traffic jam on a hot, cloudless day, that nine thousand inhabitants had died during the first bombardment and later during the liberation. Twelve hectares of the city razed to the ground. Hard to believe too that Balzac had once praised the street where he was born as being 'so wide no one ever cried "make way"'.

The thing about aphrodisiacs, one of the points he remembered trying to bring out in his article, was that in many cases success or failure lay in the minds of those who used them, just as some people set out to get drunk and achieved their objective rather quicker than those who were determined to stay sober. To some extent it was psychosomatic – an association of ideas, moonlight helped, moonlight, roses and the right words.

Joining the queue to turn right into the Boulevard Heurteloup, he found a parking space opposite the P.T.T. and climbed out. As he went to cross the road a small blue van suddenly appeared as if from nowhere, missing him by a hair's breadth. The driver seemed to be looking for a parking space too, and it was with an uncharitable feeling of pleasure at having commandeered the last one that he eventually reached the other side and made his way into the building.

A large and satisfactorily fat official-looking beige envelope awaited him. On the back was the familiar logo of *Le Guide*; two *escargots* rampant. He was glad he'd taken the precaution of having it sent *poste restante*.

The Director's aunt would have put two and two together and made five in no time at all.

It wasn't until he was on the outskirts of Tours again, heading westwards along the D7 on the south side of the Cher, that he remembered the cylinder of compressed air. He'd meant to replace it while he was there. He glanced in his mirror to see if there was any possibility of doing an about turn and decided against it. There was a long string of traffic nose to tail, a large Peugeot – all jutting-out mirrors and periscopes, towing an outsize caravan, a lorry laden with sand, two more cars, and . . . he snatched another quick look and was just in time to see a small blue van nudge its way out on to the crown of the road in an attempt to see if the way ahead was clear for overtaking. It disappeared again. The driver had evidently decided it wasn't.

Monsieur Pamplemousse looked around. To the left lay the first of the great mushroom caves of the region, carved out of the soft Tufa rock; to the right, beyond a line of poplars, the Cher. The nearest bridge would be at Langeais, soon after it joined the Loire. He decided to play it by ear, seizing the first opportunity that presented itself.

It came sooner than he expected. At Villandry, a car in front slowed momentarily to avoid a pedestrian crossing the road outside the great Château which dominated the area. Anticipating a gap in the traffic coming the other way, he took his left foot away from the brake pedal and pulled hard on the hand-brake, turning the steering-wheel at the same time. The car spun round. It was a trick he'd learnt while on attachment to the Mobile Squad. It looked more spectacular than it actually was. He'd tried it out once before in the Ardèche. Pommes Frites, who'd been asleep in the passenger seat at the time, hadn't spoken to him for days afterwards. The 2CV rocked as he brought it to a halt in a space between two trees, then it sank back on to its suspension with an almost audible sigh of relief. Horns blared and a succession of irate drivers made gestures at him through their open windows; he could almost hear the 'poofs' which went with the shaking of arched wrists and the thumping of foreheads. Children's faces pressed against rear windows stared back at him as they disappeared from view. The lorry driver, a Gauloise clamped tightly between his lips, tapped his forehead and gave him a pitying look as he drove past. He probably thought the bandage was the result of a previous attempt to do an about turn. Behind them all came the van. It must have been one of millions and yet there was something disquietingly familiar about it. The driver was looking away from him. He relaxed as it went on its way. It was probably nothing, a coincidence . . . and yet . . .

The gravelled area outside the Château was crowded with sightseers. The café on the far side looked as if it was about to burst at the seams. Between each gap in the trees on his side of the road there were parked cars as far as the eye could see. Once again he'd been extraordinarily lucky in finding a space.

Grabbing his camera case and the envelope, Monsieur Pamplemousse locked the car and waited for a gap in the traffic, hoping to reach the entrance before a coachload of American tourists.

If Pommes Frites had been with him he probably wouldn't have bothered. More than likely *chiens* would be *interdits*. As he remembered them, the gardens were a dog's paradise; a wondrous sixteenth-century maze of three hundred year old lime trees and boxwood hedges intermingled with flowers and vegetables and criss-crossing paths forming a mathematically precise and harmonious whole which was quite unique. Above it all stood an ornamental lake feeding innumerable fountains and streams which in turn led to a moat surrounding the Château itself. The sound of so much water would have played havoc with Pommes Frites' staying powers. The temptation to leave his mark would have been as irresistible as it would have been unpopular.

Once inside, he found an unoccupied arbour near one of the fountains and settled himself down. The contents of the envelope was even better than he'd hoped for. The Director's secretary had done her stuff. In an accompanying letter she listed the contents.

1. Copy of *L'Escargot*. September issue. (I had to obtain this from Madame Pamplemousse as the file copies were missing and there are no back numbers.)
2. Note from Madame Pamplemousse (attached to magazine).
3. Letter marked '*Privé et personnel*'.
4. *Fotocopie* of entry in Monsieur Duval's diary as requested.
5. Some extra P189's as requested.

He tore open the envelope containing the note from Doucette. It was brief and to the point.

'I hope you want this for the article on page three and *not* the one on page eleven. D.'

It sounded as though the euphoria of their evening out had already worn off. He opened the magazine in order to refresh his memory. The first article, coincidentally, was A JOURNEY THROUGH THE LOIRE VALLEY by *L'excursioniste*. That would be Guilot from Dijon. He had a weight problem and was always going on long hiking holidays, coming back worse than when he'd set out. Most of the article was devoted to Savonnières and its soapwort – still used in preference to modern soaps for cleaning old tapestries. It was followed by a long list of eating places.

The second article was his own. APHRODISIACS: DO THEY WORK OR IS IT ALL IN THE MIND? by A. Pamplemousse. It was longer than he remembered it.

He resolved to send Doucette a postcard. A picture of the Loire Valley. Perhaps he would get one while he was still at Villandry. It would make a change from the usual one of whatever hotel he was staying at and there probably wasn't one of the Hôtel du Paradis anyway.

Putting the magazine aside for future study, he scanned the photostat. It was of a handwritten entry. The background was dark, presumably because the ink had faded and the copy had needed more exposure. The writing was neat and scholarly, as befitted the Founder of *Le Guide*; an ascetic figure whose portrait adorned the wall of the Director's office, viewing all who entered with a stern eye, especially at annual interview time. He looked at the date – August 30th, 1899 – a year before the Michelin Guide had been born. History recalled that in those days the Founder did most of his journeyings by boneshaker, an early Michaux. It was incredible to think that he might have travelled all the way from Paris on such a machine. No wonder he had a fanatical glint in his eye. His obsession with *Le Guide* must have been quite frightening, particularly as circulation would have been strictly limited in those days.

He began to read: 'Friday night. Days still hot – but nights getting cooler. Hotel crowded. My room overlooks the square. It is comfortable although the plumbing leaves a lot to be desired.' Some things never changed. 'However, it delivers an adequate supply of scalding hot water of a brownish colour.' Perhaps they did. 'Unfortunately there is a *pissoir* below my window. Neither the sight nor smell can be deemed pleasant.' That, at least, was one thing which had improved. 'Tonight I dined off *huîtres, deux douzaines, truite saumonée berchoux* . . .' He racked his brains. That must have meant it was stuffed with pike forcemeat. The salmon had probably been caught somewhere in the Loire estuary, pink from gorging itself on prawns. '*Lapin aux pruneaux* and *tarte bourdaloue*.' That would have been apricots in millefeuille pastry. 'The *lapin* was over-salt, promoting a strong thirst. Otherwise excellent. A repeat of the previous night. Wine . . .' He went on to list some local names.

Monsieur Pamplemousse closed his eyes for a moment as he tried to picture the scene. They might even have sat at the same table. The Founder would have wanted to be near the window so that he could keep an eye on what was going on outside. He wondered if there had been a Madame Terminé in those days, whisking his plate away before he'd had time to wipe it clean with his bread. More than likely. There had been Madame Terminés all through history.

As for Monsieur Hippolyte Duval himself, he marvelled at his stamina. Two dozen oysters, followed by salmon trout, rabbit, and apricots in pastry – no doubt he'd eaten an equally large lunch that same day, and yet in his portrait he looked the picture of health, as slender as a bean pole. Perhaps it was all the cycling he did. Monsieur Pamplemousse wondered for a moment if he ought to invest in a bicycle and then rejected the idea. Pommes Frites would not take kindly to following on behind.

He glanced down at the sheet of paper and as he did so his senses quickened. He read the words again.

'I wonder if tonight I shall taste once more the ambrosial delights of the Elysian fields, or was it all a dream?' Something else had been added and then scratched out, making it unreadable.

The following entry, a part of which had been included at the bottom of the page, simply said: 'On to Saumur where I visited the stables of the *École de Cavalerie*. Must return to Paris soon!' There was no mention of what might or might not have happened the two previous nights. No hint of remorse or of hope for the future.

When he'd said 'a repeat of the previous night' did he mean he'd actually eaten exactly the same meal, or was there some hidden meaning? Were the Elysian fields similar to the ones Bernard had discovered, albeit behind the hotel and *sans* the schoolgirls, or was it simply a flight of fancy brought on by a good meal and all the wine. From what little he knew of *Le Guide*'s Founder, he wasn't given to flights of fancy.

The entry put a whole new complexion on things. It could be that the latest happenings were simply a matter of history repeating itself. In which case he must look for a deeper reason. Perhaps there was something in the water? If that was so, why didn't the whole village run amok?

One thing was for sure: the hotel had been vastly more popular in those days with Tante Louise's Grand-mère in charge than it was now.

He picked up the envelope marked '*Privé et personnel*'. It was creamy in colour; the handmade paper rough to the touch. Even without opening it he knew whom it was from. The writing was a mixture of styles – on the one hand heavy and sensual, with blotched and corrugated strokes, and yet with very definite repeated loops in the letters 'o' and 'd' indicating deceit. There was no indication as to whether it had been sent to his home address first or had gone straight to the office. Whichever way, if he was the Director he would watch out.

'*Cher ange gardien.*' He wondered how long it had taken her to think that one up. How much time had been spent weighing up the pros and cons of what to call him; rejecting the over-familiarity of Aristide and the formality of Monsieur; trying to find the right phrase. '*Ange gardien*' – he liked it. He wouldn't at all mind being her guardian angel, playing eternal footsies under a table in some heavenly garden. He'd never been called a guardian angel before.

'Please forgive my writing to you but I feel you are

the only one to whom I can turn. Please, *please*, can you do something about Elsie? Henri is besotted with her. He has even taken to singing "Rule Britannia" in his bath, and if we have any more of that dreadful pudding I shall scream. Please can you help? It will make me *very* happy. Chantal.'

From a personal point of view it was a thoroughly non-committal note. Although there were a number of lines between which messages might have been read, he searched in vain. There was no hint that she had read his own note. Perhaps that was as well. Perhaps it would never, ever be mentioned. One day it would be found tucked away in a box and people would wonder. At least he hadn't signed it. He consoled himself with the thought that she wouldn't have written at all if she hadn't felt some kind of rapport.

He stood up. Trying to read between lines would get him nowhere. There was work to be done. Time for a quick wander and a few photographs for *Le Guide*'s reference department while he was there.

He looked around for a suitable vantage point and decided to climb some steps leading up to the second level where a herb garden was laid out. Even there his 24mm wide-angle lens failed to take in all he wanted. He backed along a path overlooking the main garden, trying to frame a picture with the pergola on one side and the Château on the other. It really needed a helicopter to do it justice. He shifted his position slightly, trying to maintain the verticals and at the same time bring an overhanging branch into shot for foreground interest. As he checked focus on the split image in the centre of the picture his pulse quickened. Towards the middle of the gardens, near where he had been sitting a few minutes before, was a familiar figure.

Slowly and deliberately he lowered the camera and crouched down behind the balustrade. Undoing his bag he took out the narrow angle lens, clipped a tele-extender to it, and changed over from the wide angle. At something like forty metres the nine degree angle of view should give him what he wanted. Switching the exposure to a two hundred and fiftieth of a second to counteract any camera shake, he set the exposure mode to automatic aperture and using the end pillar as a support, stood up, focusing as he went. For a moment he had difficulty in finding what he was looking for then it swam smoothly into view. He realised where he had seen the man before and why he hadn't im-mediately recognised him. People outside their normal environment and wearing different clothes always took longer to place, even allowing for the beard. Without his white hat he looked just like anyone else. It was the hands that gave it away. The one shielding his eyes from the sun as he scanned the gardens was large and purposeful; a hand made large by the work he did – the constant kneading of dough. It also explained the blue van. It must be the same blue van he'd seen parked near the side entrance to the *boulangerie* the day he'd arrived.

He pressed a button on the base of the camera, allowing the motorwinder to take over while he con-centrated on holding the figure in the centre of the frame. Luck was with him. If he'd asked his subject to provide him with a variety of poses he couldn't have been more helpful. Back view, side, fully frontal; the camera clicked inexorably on, recording them all.

The next moment he had gone. Monsieur Pample-mousse lowered the camera, but the baker was nowhere to be seen. It was probably of no consequence anyway. There was no reason why he shouldn't spend his day off as he chose. On the other hand, the Châteaux of the Loire Valley were for tourists, not for the people who lived in the area and saw them every day of their lives.

He began dismantling his equipment, replacing the standard lens, changing the film. If Pommes Frites had been there he would have sent him off to investigate. Pommes Frites liked nothing better than a good chase. He wondered what he was doing. Even more impor-tant, where he was doing it.

As it happened, Pommes Frites was at that moment having similar thoughts, only in reverse. Pommes Frites was wondering what had happened to Monsieur Pamplemousse. He had several important matters he wanted to convey to him. How he was going to com-municate them was another matter again, but given the fact that his master was nowhere to be seen the problem didn't really arise.

Having noted the fact that his car wasn't there either, Pommes Frites put two and two together and decided to retire to the stable for the time being where he could finish his bone and bring himself up to date with his thoughts.

There were some, Philistines all, who might have jibbed at the idea of comparing Pommes Frites' brain with a computer, but those who knew him well would have seen the parallels at once.

Admittedly, size for size, there was no comparison. Pommes Frites had rather a large head; a micro-chip

111

would have been but a flea on its surface. Nevertheless, both worked on similar principles, that of reducing everything to a series of questions to which the answer was either 'yes' or 'no'. If the answer to a question was 'yes' it was allowed through. If the answer happened to be in the negative then no amount of knocking, or protestation, or crawling, or appeals to better nature, or name-dropping would allow it through to the next compartment. Pommes Frites had a lot of compartments in his brain and some doors opened more easily to the touch than others, but in the end, as with his man-made counterpart, it was all a matter of correct programming.

That morning, the big programmer in the sky who looked after Pommes Frites' thought processes, had fed him with a great deal of information, all of which had to be absorbed and digested and mulled over before any sort of logical print-out could be obtained, hence the bone.

Given a sudden fall in the electricity supply even the most sophisticated of computers had a habit of printing gobbledygook; lack of bones produced a similar effect in Pommes Frites.

Trails was the subject under analysis. Trails, their origins, destinations and meanings. Pommes Frites had followed quite a few trails that morning. Upstairs and downstairs, in and out of buildings, round and about the village; trails of various kinds, strong ones and faint ones – trails that criss-crossed and merged. There was one trail in particular, reminiscent of a scent he'd picked up outside the Sanisette the night of his master's accident, that was giving him considerable food for thought. There were certain aspects of it which didn't for the moment make sense, and were therefore causing a blockage *en route* as it were, giving rise in turn to a not inconsiderable piling-up of other, lesser pieces of information, each of which had to await its turn in the queue.

Pommes Frites swallowed the remains of the bone, gave a deep sigh, lowered his problem-filled head carefully between his paws and closed his eyes. In his experience brains, like computers, often worked best when they were left to get on with the job.

Some twenty or so kilometres away, in Saumur, Monsieur Pamplemousse was also having to wait. In his case it was outside a high-speed film processors near the Place de la Bilange. It was a kind of limbo. Unlike Monsieur Duval, *Le Guide*'s Founder, he had no wish to visit the one-time Cavalry School, now the National School of Equitation. If all the posters were anything to go by they were probably getting ready for the annual Equitation Fortnight. Anyway, horses frightened him – he much preferred a wheel at all four corners. For the same reason the Museum of the Horse lacked appeal. The mushroom museum a little way out of town would have been more in his line, but there was hardly time. In the end he decided to go for a wander in the market.

On a sudden impulse he stopped by a *poissonerie* and bought some oysters; four dozen. There was no sense in doing things in a half-hearted way. In Roman times they would have eaten that many with their aperitifs. Casanova was reputed to have eaten fifty or more every evening with his punch. He began to wish he'd ordered more.

Fired with enthusiasm he called in at another shop on his way back to the film processors and bought five kilos of *pruneaux*. If they worked at all it would be enough to inflame a whole regiment.

His enthusiasm for the project in hand lasted as far as the other side of the Loire when he remembered Pommes Frites. Pommes Frites hadn't eaten any oysters. Neither for that matter had Bernard. They wouldn't have been available in August. In Paris, maybe, but highly unlikely in St. Georges, where they would be more conservative about the lack of an 'r' in the month.

Seeing a telephone box, he pulled in at the side of the road. It was time he phoned Bernard.

'What did I eat?' There was a long pause. 'Nothing special. It was a hot day. I was more thirsty than anything. I had a *salade frisée*. That made it worse. The bacon was much too salt. Then I had a grossly overdone *entrecôte*, with some abysmal *frites* and some more salad, followed by a dreadful *tarte aux pruneaux* . . . hello . . . are you there?'

'I'm sorry. I was thinking.' Monsieur Pamplemousse came back to earth. 'I am working on a theory that it was something you ate. The *pruneaux*, perhaps.'

There was a snort from the other end. 'If you laid prunes all the way from here to St. Georges–sur–Lie and I ate every one of them it would not account for what happened that day.' Bernard sounded aggrieved at being reminded of it all.

'*Courage, mon ami.*'

'That's all very well. *Courage* doesn't pay the bills. My reserves are diminishing rapidly. Already I am having to drink my '75s.'

Monsieur Pamplemousse felt at a loss for words. Bernard was a Bordeaux man, something of a connoisseur. His background was the wine trade and he had connections. If he was drinking his '75s he must be at a low ebb. A thought struck him.

'What did you drink that day?'

'It's funny you should ask. Do you know . . .' Bernard's voice perked up. He'd obviously struck a chord. 'I ordered a half bottle of St. Emilion and when it came – you won't believe this – it turned out to be a Figeac. Beautiful it was too; I remember making notes at the time; soft and velvety and big with it. Much too good for the food and nowhere near the price it should have been. If you ask me they don't know what they're sitting on and most of the people who go there wouldn't know a Mouton-Rothschild from a Roussillon even if the label looked them straight in the eye.'

'Anything else?'

'No. I don't like having too much wine at lunch time. It makes me sleepy. Besides, I didn't get much chance to look at the list. It got whipped away from me by some battle-axe of a female.'

Monsieur Pamplemousse smiled to himself. He wondered what Madame Terminé would think if she heard herself referred to that way.

'I must go now. *Au revoir.*'

'*Au revoir*. And thanks for calling.'

Bernard sounded much more cheerful than when he'd

first picked up the phone. Monsieur Pamplemousse wished he could say the same. He felt like a drowning man clutching at straws. Instinct told him that his theory had to be right. Experience told him that finding the answer would mean a lot of hard work. A lot of hard work and a good deal of luck. But luck was something you had to recognise and use when it came your way. Lots of people had their share but failed to capitalise on it.

He put his foot hard down on the accelerator, anxious now to be back. It was almost five o'clock and if he was to put his plan into action in time for the Fair he would need to deliver the shopping with all possible speed. He would also need to be up early the next day. That evening he would have to study his article more fully and refresh his memory. He would need to make out a detailed chart.

Not far from St. Georges-sur-Lie he overtook a long line of caravans and lorries; a travelling circus-cum-fair from Bordeaux. Dark-skinned children watched impassively as he overtook them. The drivers neither helped nor impeded his progress, absolving themselves of all responsibility.

During his absence preparations for the holiday had already got under way in the village. The tricolor hung limply from a pole which had been erected in the centre of the square, bunting joining it to some of the surrounding balconies. Tables and chairs had been set out in the garden of the hotel, ready for the influx of visitors. A white van was parked nearby and a man in blue overalls was attaching some loudspeakers to a branch of the yew tree.

As he turned into the hotel car park he took a quick

glance to the right. The blue van was parked in its usual place, although the baker was nowhere to be seen, which perhaps wasn't surprising. He was probably keeping out of the way. He wondered what he would think of the photographs.

To his great relief Pommes Frites was there to greet him, bounding out from the stable, tail wagging, full of the joy of living and of seeing his master again. Quite recovered from his previous night's adventure, he watched the boot being unloaded with interest, then led the way excitedly towards the hotel, dashing here, there and everywhere, investigating and sniffing, looking in the stable adjoining his own and drawing a blank, standing up with his paws on the window sill, peering into the kitchen.

Tante Louise saw him and waved back.

'I have a favour to ask.' Monsieur Pamplemousse handed over his pile of shopping, wondering if in bringing his own food he would cause offence. 'The prunes are to go with the *lapin*. It seemed to me yesterday that if I were to criticise it at all it would be for lack of prunes.'

He needn't have worried. The Director's aunt seemed only too pleased. She followed him into the hall and stood at the foot of the stairs as Pommes Frites, nose to the carpet, hurried on ahead.

Monsieur Pamplemousse took his key from her. 'I have been thinking about tomorrow . . .' he said. 'I have some ideas.'

'That's very kind.' For a moment it looked as if she was about to add something, then she changed her mind.

Sensing her embarrassment, Monsieur Pample-mousse came to the rescue. 'I have in mind a *menu gastronomique*,' he said grandly. 'A *menu gastronomique surprise*. If you will allow me the use of your kitchen then together we will prepare a meal fit for the President.'

With a confidence that he was far from feeling, he climbed the stairs and made his way along the landing towards his room. Pommes Frites was waiting for him, scratching the bottom of the door, his excitement unabated. Monsieur Pamplemousse looked at him. There were signs, unmistakable signs.

He reached down. '*Qu'est-ce que c'est*? What are you trying to tell me?'

Pommes Frites lowered himself down on to his stomach and looked up soulfully. It was the kind of expression which implied that although in many res-pects the world was a wonderful place, certain aspects of it left a lot to be desired. In short, he had warning messages to convey which meant that all was not well.

Monsieur Pamplemousse slipped the key into the lock, turned it as gently as possible and pushed the door open. The inside of the room was dark, the shutters closed to shield it from the hot sun. Pommes Frites stood up very slowly, remaining still for a fraction of a second while he took stock of the situation, then he relaxed and led the way in.

Following on behind, Monsieur Pamplemousse crossed to the window, unhooked the shutters and threw them open, flooding the room with light. As he did so there was a crackling sound from just below the balcony. It was followed almost immediately by a

118

bellowing amplified voice not far off the threshold of pain, then a raucous burst of music. His heart sank as the noise from the loudspeaker echoed round the square. Sleep would not come easily the following night. No doubt there would be dancing into the early hours.

As he turned back into the room he caught sight of some flowers; a bowl of dahlias standing on a table near the other window. He suddenly felt guilty at having made the suggestion. It couldn't be easy running an hotel almost single-handed, and with the level of custom he'd seen so far money must be tight. Perhaps the problem was self-solving. Perhaps if the Director could hold out long enough his aunt would have to close the hotel anyway.

Aware that Pommes Frites was watching his every movement, he opened the drawers of the dressing table. Nothing appeared to have been disturbed. Pommes Frites didn't even bother to put on his 'you're getting warm' expression; it was all a bit of a let-down. Instead he was wearing his long-suffering, impassive look.

He paused at the spot where he had left his case, the one belonging to *Le Guide*. Pommes Frites began to show more interest. Monsieur Pamplemousse picked it up and examined it more closely. Someone had been at one of the locks. There was a small, barely discernible scratch across the bottom of it. He could have sworn it hadn't been there earlier on when he'd taken the camera out.

Reaching for his keys he opened it and quickly ran through the contents. Leitz Trinovid glasses; the special compartment for the Leica R4 and its associated lenses and filters. Beneath the removable tray was the compartment with all the other equipment; the folding stove and various items of cutlery and cooking equipment for use in an emergency. The report forms were intact inside the lid compartment.

He snapped it shut again. Whoever had tried to open the case had failed. It was a tribute to Monsieur Hippolyte Duval and the high standards he had laid down in the very beginning. If a job was worth doing at all it was worth doing well.

He turned his attention to the wardrobe. As he did so he felt a sudden movement behind him. Turning quickly he was in time to catch Pommes Frites rising to his feet. Tail wagging, a look of approval on his face, he came over to join his master. The signs were clear; he was getting warm at last.

Opening the wardrobe door, he riffled through his pile of shirts and other clothing, then reached out for the single clothes-hanger, feeling as he did so for a tell-tale bulge, knowing at the same time that he would be looking in vain.

His worst fears were realised. The trousers hung limply in his hand, the right side bereft not only of a leg to go inside it, but of any extra weight whatsoever. His notebook, his precious notebook, was no longer there.

Sensing that something was expected of him, Pommes Frites responded. Lifting up his head, he closed his eyes and let out a loud howl. It was a howl which said it all. Monsieur Pamplemousse couldn't have put it better even if he'd tried.

6

ALARMS AND EXCURSIONS

Grasping an oyster shell firmly in his left hand, Monsieur Pamplemousse speared the contents neatly with a fork and twisted it away from its housing, holding it up to the light with the air of a gastronome bent on extracting the last milligram of gustatory pleasure out of the task in hand.

Privately he was wishing he hadn't bought quite so many. He couldn't think what had possessed him. Four dozen! Thirty-seven down and eleven to go. He couldn't remember the last time he'd eaten more than a dozen. Two dozen was the most he'd ever consumed at one time.

Pommes Frites, curled up beneath the table, was being no help whatsoever. He was pointedly ignoring the whole thing, although in fairness even if he had been ready and willing to lend a paw Monsieur Pample-mousse would have thought twice about letting him. For some reason best known to himself, Pommes Frites tended to chew oysters – unlike chunks of meat, biscuits and many other items of food, which often went down so fast they barely touched the side of his throat. In chewing them he usually managed to get the odd valve stuck between his teeth which resulted in a lot of noisy lip-smacking for upwards of several hours afterwards.

He toyed with the idea of slipping some into his napkin while dabbing at his mouth, but decided against it. Madame Terminé was hovering by the bar keeping a purposeful eye on his progress. Nearer still a couple with their heads bent close together were watching his every mouthful with a look of awe. It was too risky.

It was a shame really. There it was, sitting on the end of his fork, a survivor of a family of perhaps one hundred million offspring, the result of a chance encounter by its mother with some floating sperm, left to its own devices at an early age, enjoying its one and only brief period of freedom until the vagaries of the currents off the Brittany coast had caused it to land eventually on one of the white tiles at Locmariaquer where it had spent its childhood until it became old enough and fat enough to be moved elsewhere, to Riec-sur-Belon perhaps, where it had passed the next five years or so, pumping water through itself at an inexorable rate of one litre per hour every hour of its life, surviving attacks on its person by crabs and star-fish, and on its already thick and heavy shell by the boring-sponge and the dog-whelk, fighting for the right to its share of food against the rival claims of barnacles, worms and mussels, and for what? To end up unwanted on the end of a fork in St. Georges-sur-Lie! It seemed a gross miscarriage of justice; an unfair return for so much hardship and labour.

He opened his mouth and popped it in, savouring the taste of the sea as it slid down, helped on its way by a cool draught of Muscadet. It was the least he could do in the circumstances.

He wondered for a moment about its sex life. Oysters were reputed to change sex many times; their mating habits were haphazard in the extreme. What, if it ever felt the need, which by all accounts was doubtful, would an oyster use as an aphrodisiac?

The thought produced another. Apart from a feeling of fullness, unwelcome at such an early stage in the meal which, to say the least, was extravagantly conceived, what other effect were the oysters having on him? He gazed across the room at the figure hovering behind the bar. Was it his imagination or was her gaze a soupçon more thoughtful than he remembered it? Did not her eyes appear a little darker, her lips a deeper shade of red? Had not thirty-seven, no, thirty-eight oysters made her breasts appear to rise and fall a little faster as if trying to escape whatever man-made device it was that held them in place? No one could deny that she was well endowed. Nature had not been unkind.

The answer came swiftly. Glancing impatiently at her watch, she was practically on top of him before he had time to gather himself together. Her acceleration from a standing start was impressive.

'*Terminé?*'

'*Non, merci.*' He managed to reach the dish a fraction of a second before her. Picking up a piece of quartered lemon he squeezed it over the remaining oysters before she had time to whisk them away. He must not weaken now.

As if to punish him the salmon trout came on a cold plate, the *lapin aux pruneaux* on an even colder one. It must have been put in the fridge. He found himself reaching automatically for his notebook and then remembered it was no longer there. The thought depressed him.

The arrival of the main course caused a stirring beneath the table cloth, a reminder that Pommes Frites preferred flesh to fish; fish was for cats. As far as Monsieur Pamplemousse was concerned he was more than welcome to his share.

The *tarte* was even worse than he'd feared. To use the word *millefeuille* was a debasement of a language rich in other words which might have been used to describe the pastry. In a pâtisserie contest it would have been a non-starter. *Unefeuille* would have been a better description. *Unefeuille* which had set rock hard and stuck to the plate. Manfully he struggled on.

'Would you like a *tisane*?' With probably the nearest she'd ever come to registering any kind of emotion other than impatience that evening, Madame Terminé removed the plate and ran a portable cleaner briskly over the cloth. He hoped the crumbs wouldn't jam up the works. There were rather a lot of them. She skirted with practised ease round a lump of cream. 'I could bring it to your room.'

Monsieur Pamplemousse considered both the suggestion and the manner in which it had been made. Was it his imagination working overtime again or was there some deeper meaning in the words. Looked at in a certain light it sounded more like an invitation than a suggestion. *Tisane* and Madame Terminé. The one a sop to the indigestion he felt coming on, the other a definite additive. It could be fatal.

'*Un café, s'il vous plaît*. Here, at the table.'

Unmistakably he had blotted his copy book. Serving

124

coffee at table was not what was uppermost in Madame Terminé's mind at that moment. He glanced round the room. The couple had gone. The only other occupants, a man and a woman in the far corner, were nearing the end of their meal. He'd seen them arrive in a BMW bearing an Orléans registration. He was elderly, florid and overdressed. She was young and plump with a perpetual pout. What his old mother would have classed as 'no better than she should be'. If the amount of champagne they had drunk that night was anything to go by her headache on the way home would be perfectly genuine. Perhaps her escort had heard rumours about the hotel too.

The coffee arrived. It was strong and hot and acrid. He broke a lump of sugar in half and stirred it in, holding the spoon upright for a while to take away the heat. He was anxious for something, anything to take away the taste of the pastry.

It had not been a good meal. Apart from the oysters, which had been as near as possible in their natural state anyway, it had been a thoroughly bad meal. The wine was a different matter. The wine would have been accorded a mention in any guide book. For content, although not for presentation. Presentation was not something the Hôtel du Paradis would ever be noted for. The Bonnes Mares had been delivered and opened without any showing of the label. Madame Terminé had passed the cork briefly past the end of her nose as usual and that was that. Woe betide any man who queried her findings. All the same, had he been there for *Le Guide* he would certainly have made a recommendation for the award of a Tasting Cup, possibly two.

He glanced out into the square. Although he couldn't see it, the moon must be full, for it was almost like daylight. The loudspeaker van had long since disappeared. The Sanisette glowed in a state of readiness. The only other lights came from the *pharmacie* window and what looked like a police car parked outside. Perhaps it was some kind of an emergency. A nudge from below reminded him of his obligations. It was time for a stroll. Undeniably a good idea, but there was a world of difference between thought and execution. He was having difficulty enough rising from the table let alone walking anywhere. Had Madame Terminé's implied offer been genuine and had he taken her up on it the encounter would have been disappointing in the extreme. She would probably have got impatient and cried '*terminé*' before he'd got his trousers even halfway off. As an exercise the meal was a dismal failure. Perhaps Monsieur Duval had gone for a spin in the moonlight afterwards on his bicycle and in so doing had set the various elements in motion so that they merged one with the other to produce a potent and active whole.

As he made his way slowly down the steps of the hotel Monsieur Pamplemousse had to admit to himself that there was very little possibility of that happening in his case. He couldn't remember when he'd last felt so bloated. He now knew what a goose, force-fed to enlarge its liver, must feel like – every day of its life. Slowly he made his way down one side of the square. Pommes Frites would have to make do with one circuit that night, but then one circuit to Pommes Frites was worth more than ten of anyone else's. Nose to the ground he ran hither and thither, pausing every now and then to leave his mark, stopping occasionally to register something more important than the rest. Who knew what plans he was hatching? His nose was working so much overtime it would need more than its weekly dose of vaseline at this rate.

As he drew near the police car a figure detached itself from the shadowy side. '*Bonsoir*, Monsieur Pamplemousse.'

'*Bonsoir*.' He tried to keep the note of surprise from his voice.

'We heard you were staying in the village.' The remark came matter-of-factly as if it was the most natural thing in the world. Perhaps the information had come from the card he'd filled in when he registered. He didn't think anyone bothered to read them any more, unless there was a very good reason.

He nodded towards the *pharmacie*. 'Trouble?'

The man nodded. 'A break-in. A store-room at the back. It must have happened earlier today but it was only discovered this evening.'

'Did they take much?'

'A few drugs. The usual.' There was a shrug and a brief smile. 'Not a case for the Sûreté.'

'*C'est la vie*.' He returned the shrug. It was the kind of thing that was common enough in Paris, but sad to encounter it in a small village in the Loire. The world was not improving.

'Monsieur has had an accident?'

Monsieur Pamplemousse gave a start, then remembered his bandage. No wonder the young couple in the restaurant had been talking about him.

127

'It is nothing. It looks much worse than it really is.'

'All the same, Monsieur should be careful.'

Responding automatically to the other's salute, he went on his way, wondering if the remark had been merely a pleasantry or whether it had contained some kind of warning. What with one thing and another St. Georges-sur-Lie was beginning to reveal as many undercurrents and *tourbillons* as the Loire itself.

His feeling of unease lasted all the way back to the hotel. There he paused for a moment at the bottom of the steps, tossing a mental coin, wondering whether or not he would be able to summon up enough breath to inflate Pommes Frites' kennel. He decided against it. In his present condition it would not be a good idea. More than ever he wished he'd remembered to renew the cylinder of compressed air while he was in Tours. His room was hot enough as it was without risking Pommes Frites waking up in the night and climbing on to his bed. Once there he was like a dead weight. On the other hand, another night in the straw might not be a good idea either. Straw harboured insects.

In the end Pommes Frites decided matters for him by bounding on ahead up the steps. It was only too clear where his preferences lay.

As they entered the hotel he heard the sound of an argument coming from the entrance to the dining-room. The man from Orléans was complaining about his meal. From the look on his companion's face he would not be receiving value for money in return for his investment that particular evening. Not even Joan of Arc on her way to the stake could have worn a more heavily martyred expression, nor have had

128

her mind more obviously set on a policy of non-co-operation.

Taking his key from the rack behind the reception desk he caught Tante Louise's eye and gave a sympathetic palm-down shake of his right hand. He would not make a good patron. Confronted with such clients he would be hard put to keep his temper, even if their complaints were justified. That would have made him crosser still. There was nothing worse than arguing a case when you knew you were in the wrong.

Opening the door to his room, he reached round the corner and switched on the light. The bed cover had been turned back and his pyjamas laid out with the arms crossed as if in a position of repose.

He glanced into the bathroom. In his absence a large jar of bath crystals had been placed on a small table. He began to feel even more guilty at the way he was taking over things.

He checked the drawers to make sure they were as he'd left them. The single hair he'd left at the side of each was still in place, the tiny mound of talc on top of the wardrobe door hadn't shifted. Nothing had been touched.

Doing his own round of inspection, Pommes Frites looked considerably less confident. His computer was hard at work again, absorbing the evidence afforded by his nose, sifting and sorting it. The more he sniffed the less happy he became. There was a great deal to think about. His pending tray was full to overflowing. He was glad now that he'd insisted on accompanying his master. The adjoining room received his special attention. Several times he went inside and stood with his paws on the edge of the bath peering in like a cat on the edge of a goldfish bowl.

Had Monsieur Pamplemousse been in a more receptive state of mind he would have recognised the signs and perhaps done something about them. As it was, his only ambition was to get undressed and climb into bed. Sleep was the order of the day, or to be pedantic, the night. A drowsiness triggered off by all the wine he had drunk was beginning to take over. Aided and abetted by far too much food, it was enveloping him like a cloud. Work would have to come later, or to be pedantic again, much earlier. First thing in the morning. There was so much to do, so much to read. There were lists to be prepared. In his mind's eye he'd pictured his room as the nerve centre of the whole operation. The walls covered in charts . . .

In the square outside there was the sound of a car door slamming, then a second door. An engine started up, revved impatiently into life by the driver. There was a squeal of protesting tyres as the clutch was let in much too quickly, then a roar and more screeching as the car disappeared into the night.

It would be an unhappy drive back to Orléans. No stopping *en route* to admire the Loire or any of its many tributaries by moonlight.

Monsieur Pamplemousse lay back and closed his eyes, allowing his mind to drift, wondering what the Director's wife might be like as a travelling companion, or Elsie . . . or Madame Terminé. Madame Terminé would have had a job getting into the 2CV. There would be no room for hanky-panky.

A few moments later the sound of heavy breathing

filled the room. Not to be outdone, Pommes Frites lay down and curled himself up on the lion-skin rug at the foot of the bed, resting his chin on his paws in a way which would enable him to keep a watchful eye on both his master and the door. If he was going to do guard duty he might as well do it in reasonable comfort.

How long he slept was – and Monsieur Pample-mousse would have been the first to admit the fact – a matter of academic importance beside the reason for his waking. Beside the reason for his waking it was of as little moment as the loss of a grain of sand might be to the Sahara Desert.

The reason was simple enough; it was a clear case of cause and effect. The cause: a chemical reaction brought on by the juxtaposition of oysters and bread and salmon trout and sauces and rabbit and prunes and pastry and wine and apricots and cream and coffee and other embellishments and condiments too numerous to mention. Confined for too long and tiring of each other's company, they were now trying to make good their escape by the quickest route possible. Had he paused to consider the matter, Monsieur Pamplemousse might well have laid the blame fairly and squarely on the subversive activities of the oyster and the prune, but pausing to consider anything other than the rumbling demands of his stomach was not uppermost in his mind at that particular moment. All his senses were concentrated on one objective, and one objective only; the relief of Monsieur Pamplemousse.

Cursing his lack of foresight in not taking a room with a toilet in the first place, fulminating on the idiocy of having a lion's head rug in the middle of the room as he tripped over it and nearly went headlong, apologising with a singular lack of conviction to Pommes Frites as he trod on him, he wrenched open the door and made his way along the corridor, balancing as he went the opposing needs of haste and the inadvisability of disturbing still more an already seriously upset status quo.

As he reached the door at the end and tried unsuccessfully to open it, Tante Louise's words in the hall that morning came back to him. It was followed by a feeling of panic. '*Merde!*' He racked his brains in an effort to remember the alternatives he'd been offered the day he arrived. Was the room next to his the one with the hand basin and W.C., or was it *numéro trois*? And if it wasn't either of those then which one could it be? It was a mathematical problem with complications of a complexity he had neither the time nor the inclination to solve.

Seeing a narrow flight of stairs to his right he made a bound for them. Tante Louise had said there was another toilet on the floor above. Logically, the door that faced him as he reached the top of the stairs and turned the corner would be the one he wanted. But logic and plumbing at the Hôtel du Paradis did not go hand in hand.

As the door swung open he clutched at his pyjama trousers, fumbling to do up the cord again as he skidded to a halt. Madame Terminé looked shorter than he remembered her. Perhaps it was the absence of shoes. Her feet and ankles were slim like a young girl's. Her thighs, silhouetted against the light from a small table lamp, were firm and white. Standing with one hand resting on the knob of a brass bedstead, her long hair loose and hanging down her back, her breasts large and firm, the nipples as prominent as if they were fresh from a dip in a mountain stream, she looked for all the world like a Botticelli come to life.

How long they stayed looking at each other he knew not. It seemed like an eternity, but it could only have been for a second or two. Surprise gave way to other emotions. She moved as if about to say something, but before she had time to open her mouth he spared her blushes.

'*Pardon*, Monsieur.' He gave a slight bow. '*Excusez-moi*.'

He was not a moment too soon. Conscious that he'd punctuated his attempt at gallantry in a loud and most ungentlemanly way; at one and the same time a full stop, an exclamation mark, and a long drawn-out series of dots – a signal that it would be unwise to linger, he raced back down the stairs again, hoping she wouldn't take it as a true expression of his feelings.

Pommes Frites gave him a jaundiced look through bloodshot eyes as his master dashed into the room and then disappeared again clutching a franc in his hand. He decided to stay where he was for the time being. Many things were possible, but being in two places at the same time was not one of them.

As decisions went it might not have altered the course of events; events that those who believed in such things would have said were predestined anyway from the moment Monsieur Pamplemousse got into his car in the eighteenth arrondissement and set course for St. Georges-sur-Lie, but it did lose Pommes Frites a ringside seat at their actual fulfilment.

Having lost several seconds fathoming out the security arrangements which protected the occupants of the Hôtel du Paradis from the outside world – no less than three very stiff bolts and a chain, followed by several more seconds grovelling around the cobble-stoned square in search of his franc which he'd dropped in his haste, Monsieur Pamplemousse arrived outside the Sanisette.

Thankfully, though not surprisingly, the light was at green, indicating that it was unoccupied and ready for use.

Breathing heavily and with a trembling hand, he inserted his coin in the slot of the electronic cash-box located beside the list of instructions and waited impatiently for the quarter-circle stainless steel suspended door to slide open on its base guide. One of the more infuriating things about living in an in-creasingly computerised world was that man had to wait for machine, and machines refused to be hurried. It was just the same with the garage beneath his block of flats in Paris. Instead of just driving in you had to break a beam of light and wait while an arm which barred your way was lifted. It usually took up to ten seconds. An eternity if you were late home and in a hurry.

Had there been anyone abroad at that time of night they might well have paused, and having paused won-dered what kind of dance Monsieur Pamplemousse was performing. Was it a Gavotte or the Boston Two-Step? Or even the jive? Perhaps a combination of all three, with some jungle rhythms thrown in for good measure as he thumped unavailingly and impotently on a door made silent by a core of fibreglass wool sound–deadening material.

At last there was a whirr of machinery from somewhere inside. Having examined Monsieur Pamplemousse's franc and not found it wanting, the coin analyser sent it on its way and issued instructions to admit him. At the same time two fluorescent tubes mounted above the laminated glass base of the sky-dome were switched on, along with an air heater in the technical area at the rear, an extractor fan in the roof, and the sound play–back system.

Unmoved by the speed at which Monsieur Pamplemousse entered the public area, the door closed again in its own good time, two air jacks securing it in a locked position. Outside, an orange light came on illuminating the word '*occupé*', whilst in the technical area the heater, having ascertained that the ambient temperature was within the permitted tolerance either side of 19°C as laid down in the handbook, switched itself off.

Having no need for either coat-hook or handbag-hanger, ignoring the hand–basin with its automatic soap and presence–operated warm water dispenser, indifferent to the many and varied items of electronic gadgetry at work on his behalf, Monsieur Pamplemousse sank gratefully into place, offering up as he did so a prayer of thanks.

Given the fact that they were the last coherent words he was to utter for some while to come it was perhaps as well that he addressed them heavenwards. At least it gave him the benefit of having made early contact with the forces of good on high, rather than with their opposite number below, directly connected as the latter were with the Sanisette by means of an enamelled cast-iron drain trap in the base.

Even the least mechanically minded of occupants would have detected a change in the normal pattern of events as a clunking and grinding began somewhere towards the rear.

Monsieur Pamplemousse clutched frantically at the bowl as he felt it begin to tilt, slowly and inexorably turning him head over heels in a backwards direction to the sound of the Grand March from *Aida*. Jamming him doubled-up and powerless to move in the opening behind, it exposed him to the depredations of a high-speed revolving brush, a brush which sought out corners and probed where no man had probed before. The final indignity was provided by a centrifugal pump which completed the cycle by unleashing a spray containing a mixture of water, disinfectants, detergents, germ killers and, for good measure, a bio-degradable anti-fungus agent.

To say that his whole life flashed before him while all this was happening would have been an exaggeration. Forty seconds, however long it may seem at the time, was nothing for one who had led such a long and adventurous life. To say that Monsieur Pamplemousse spent the time marvelling at the way so much equipment had been packed into such a small space would have been as far from the truth as it would have been to say that he emerged a happier, cleaner man than when he went in. Cleaner, yes. Not since he'd been a babe in arms had he felt quite so cleaned and scrubbed and disinfected. But happier, no.

As he tottered back across the square for the second night running, Monsieur Pamplemousse couldn't remember ever having felt quite so unhappy in his life.

He let himself in to the hotel and crawled up the stairs with but one thing in mind; an overpowering desire to sink as quickly as possible into a very deep bath.

Pommes Frites' look of surprise at his master's appearance changed to one of consternation and alarm when he saw what he had in mind. Jumping to his feet, he began racing round the room like a thing possessed, rolling his eyes as if in the grip of some kind of fever. Then, seeing it was getting him nowhere, he suddenly stopped dead in his tracks and for the second time that day let out a howl, only this time it was a howl of warning rather than sympathy; a cry of anguish not just from the heart but from his very soul. It was the kind of howl that would have caused any members of the Baskerville family, had they been staying at the Hôtel du Paradis, to sit up and take immediate notice before pulling the blankets over their heads in an effort to shut out the noise.

But for the time being at least Monsieur Pamplemousse was too far gone to care. Battered and bruised, smarting all over, still hardly sure whether he was coming or going, standing on his head or his heels, he felt as though he had been passed through a *lavage automatique* backwards. At least in a car wash they posted signs, telling you to retract your aerial and warning of possible damage to badges, wing mirrors and other protruding accessories. Some of his accessories felt as if they had been damaged beyond repair.

Turning off the hot tap he sprinkled the crystals into the bath and then clambered in, sinking slowly back until the water was lapping his chin. Oblivious to all but its soothing effect, luxuriating in its new-found softness, unable to summon the energy to reach up and turn on the heater, he closed his eyes and relaxed.

Pommes Frites eyed his master mournfully for a moment or so, and then he, too, lay back on his rug. He'd done his best. No one could say he hadn't done his best. What happened now was in the lap of the Gods. Far stronger forces than his were needed to cope with a master whose indifference to his fate, whose inability to cope with even the simplest of messages, whose sublime disregard not only for his own safety but for the feelings of others were of such proportions they were almost beyond belief.

7

NONE BUT THE BRAVE DESERVE THE FAIR

'I am sorry, Monsieur, such a thing is not possible. In any case we cannot accept complaints from the general public. It is necessary to go through the proper channels.'

Monsieur Pamplemousse took a deep breath, counted up to ten, and with commendable restraint, began again.

'Monsieur, I have been through so many channels this morning it makes the Loire look as placid as an *enfants*' paddling pool on a hot day. I have been on to the *Mairie*, and there I have spoken to the *Service de la Santé*, the *Chef de la Salubrité Publique*, the section dealing with the *environnement*, and the man whose job it is to judge the suitability of candidates for the *village fleuri* competitions. All of them have assured me that it is not their responsibility. They none of them wish to know. I have now been in this telephone kiosk for over half an hour getting absolutely nowhere while contributing to its upkeep to the tune of so many francs I have long ago lost count of them, and it is very, very hot. I am speaking to you as a last resort. If I do not get a satisfactory reply I shall catch the next train to Paris where I shall take great pleasure in squeezing one from you, drop by drop. When I have done that I shall make use of my many contacts with the press to make sure that before I call in and see my *Député* while *en route* for my lawyer, the affair which you treat so lightly receives maximum publicity.'

Taking advantage of the momentary silence, Monsieur Pamplemousse poked his head outside the booth and mopped his brow. All around the square stalls and tables were being set up. They had been arriving since dawn, along with battered vans full of junk and delivery vehicles laden with hams and sausages. Smoke rose from a mobile *crêperie* and he caught the pungent whiff of cooking oil from a hot-dog stand. To say that it was hot inside the telephone booth was the understatement of the year. It felt like an oven, draining reserves of both strength and temper. It was always the same; one contained oneself up to a certain point and then let rip on some poor, unsuspecting individual who happened to be in the wrong place at the wrong time.

'With the greatest respect, Monsieur . . .' the voice was more conciliatory, as he knew it would be. The press had its uses. 'Innumerable precautions have been taken to ensure that such an accident cannot possibly occur. On entering the toilet an infra-red beam detects your presence. Then there is an electronic detector with not one, but two sensitivities. First of all it ascertains if your weight is more than 4 kg, then it checks to make sure that it is more than 25 kg. This happens whether you are standing or sitting. Only when it is happy does the detector allow the door to be closed. On leaving, the door closes and locks automatically, then no less than *three* independent mechanical, electrical and pneumatic systems come into operation to make absolutely certain there is no longer anyone present. Only then, and I repeat, *only* then can the cleaning cycle begin. The floor and the toilet bowl tilt back to be received by the technical area . . .'

Monsieur Pamplemousse fed another five franc coin into the machine. He could see that in no way was it going to be a quick conversation.

'Monsieur,' he began, 'I yield to no one in my admiration for your product. I have acquired an intimate knowledge of its working parts. I know exactly what happens when the cleaning cycle begins. I have, as you put it, "been received" and I bear the scars to prove it. I can see that it is clearly a scientific achievement of the first magnitude. It has raised what is, after all, one of man's most basic and universal and necessary functions to the level of space travel. No doubt the day will come when one of these devices will be sent up on a rocket and landed on the moon for the benefit of any passing astronauts, regardless of race, colour, creed or sex, who happen to be taken short. However in the meantime, last night, here in St. Georges-sur-Lie . . .'

'Pardon, Monsieur, did you say St. Georges-sur-Lie?'

'I did.'

'Aahaaah!' The voice at the other end sounded relieved, as if that one single fact explained everything. 'We have had a certain amount of trouble at St. Georges-sur-Lie.'

'Trouble? What sort of trouble?'

'Sabotage, Monsieur. Sabotage of the very worst kind. Vandalism is one thing. The units are designed to cope with that. They are constructed in architectural grade concrete with a fluted exterior design to prevent unauthorised bill-posting, the internal surfaces are protected by anti-stick paint, the metal parts sand-blasted, metallised and painted. Also, as part of the service, there is a periodical pressurised steam cleaning . . .'

Monsieur Pamplemousse suppressed a sigh and fed in his last five franc coin. Better not to interrupt the flow. It might cause further delays. A girl in a red and gold uniform went past carrying an instrument case. Heads turned, for she was wearing tights and the shortest of skirts, her bottom encapsulated in the briefest of snow-white pants. He wondered idly how old she was. She looked in her early twenties but was probably about fifteen. No doubt she was taking part in the Grand Parade that afternoon. There was a poster on the wall opposite advertising the appearance of a local drum and fife band, led by Miss Sparkling Saumur. He turned his attention back to the phone.

'. . . it was like it right from the beginning. One expects a certain amount of opposition. People are resistant to change. Even in the world of *aménagements sanitaires* there are those who would stand in the way of progress – they prefer the cracked porcelain bowl they know to one made of cast aluminium, enamelled to the highest standards. Others object to paying for something which nature requires them to do at regular intervals whether they like it or not. But this is different. Wires have been cut. Sand has been injected into the mechanism of the door leading to the technical area – we have had to change the lock three times. The sound tape has been tampered with – the music erased and replaced by a voice uttering threats and warnings to anyone using the services. The skydome has been interfered with . . .'

'Who would do such a thing?'

'Poof! That, Monsieur, is anyone's guess. You may well ask. There is no accounting for some people's behaviour. In my profession I could tell you some tales. These units are expensive and they require a minimum number of operational cycles each day to make them viable. This one has been standing idle for over six months.'

'I mean, what sort of qualifications would he need?'

'A knowledge of electricity. The ability to find his way round a circuit diagram. It is not difficult. Common sense – or the lack of it. We will look into the matter immediately, of course . . . although several of our engineers have refused to go there any more.'

Monsieur Pamplemousse saw the remains of his time ticking away on the meter. 'I must go. Thank you for your help.'

'*Enchanté*, Monsieur. Thank you for being so patient and understanding. It cannot have been a pleasant experience. And, Monsieur . . .'

'*Oui?*'

'I trust such a thing will never happen to you again, but should you be so unfortunate, should the impossible occur, you will find there is a telephone installed in the technical area . . .' There was a click and the line went dead. It saved Monsieur Pamplemousse the trouble of explaining that the part of him nearest the technical area had not been the one he normally used for conversing with, although at the time it would have been more than capable of giving vent to his feelings. He replaced the receiver and left the kiosk, momentarily lost in thought as he gazed at the back of the hotel.

Apart from the old woman still eternally peeling vegetables near the back door to the kitchen area, there was no one in sight. He'd been up even earlier than her that morning. It was a good thing he had too, for the car park was now full to capacity and his own car was totally hemmed in. He would never have got to the market.

Pommes Frites was nowhere in sight; he was probably still upstairs, keeping a low profile and catching up on lost sleep. One way and another he must have foregone quite a few hours over the past two nights. Perhaps, dog-like, he was instinctively following the doctor's advice: a darkened room and plenty of water. Monsieur Pamplemousse made a mental note to make sure his bowl got filled up; in the prevailing weather he probably had need of it.

There was a small queue outside the *boulangerie*, but no sign of the owner. He was probably snatching some sleep before his second baking. He'd already been hard at work that morning when Monsieur Pamplemousse went past; smoke rising from the wood-fired oven.

The old woman picked up a bowl and went into the kitchen. Taking advantage of her absence he slipped through the car park, in and out of the cars, and took a quick look inside the stable next to the one Pommes Frites had occupied. It was empty. At the far end, under a window, there was a work bench with a vice, and to one side of it a board with a selection of tools fixed to the wall; a file or two, several screwdrivers of various sizes, some pliers. The bench had been brushed down. A drawer beneath it was fastened by a padlock. It looked very workmanlike, neat and tidy.

Catching sight of something light-coloured on the darkened surface of the floor, he bent down and picked it up. It was a small piece of crust from a loaf. Under the bench was a wire hair grip.

Hearing the sound of voices, he slipped both into his wallet and hurried outside. Pausing for a moment by his car, he pretended to check the wheels before leaving the car park.

Resisting the temptation to buy an old typewriter on the first stall he came to, he hovered over a pair of kitchen scales at the next, wondering if he should get them for Doucette. He had no use whatsoever for the first – it would be sheer self-indulgence; the second would be too late for her birthday, too soon for Christmas, and presents in between were usually regarded with suspicion. He settled instead for a pocket corkscrew. It had the name of a *négociant* from Burgundy engraved on the side and must have been a give-away at some time.

The finding of the crumb had set him thinking. The hair pin too. There was probably a simple explanation for both, and yet . . .

He continued on his circuit, past displays of clothes, past tables clearly belonging to professional antique dealers from neighbouring towns – their owners organised and impassively getting on with their knitting or reading a paper, past other tables littered with open cardboard boxes and trays full of oddments and bric-à-brac; hinges, locks, old keys, cotton-reels – the more useless the item the more hopeful the owner. He stopped by a stall selling old postcards and riffled through them. There might even be one of the hotel. He wondered if Doucette had kept all his cards over the years. If she had there would be enough for her to open a stall of her own by now.

Glancing towards the front of the hotel he saw Tante Louise standing on a pair of steps hitching a row of coloured lights to a branch of the tree. Below her Madame Terminé was bustling to and fro laying the tables for *déjeuner*. He hobbled over towards them, conscious of a certain stiffness setting in.

'May I help?'

Tante Louise looked down. '*Non, merci*. I know where they go. Armand should be doing it. He knows about these things – but he has disappeared.'

Madame Terminé gave a loud sniff as she went past, glancing skywards. He had a feeling that part of her reaction was meant for him; a reproof for what hadn't happened the night before. Hell hath no fury like a woman scorned. He hoped it wouldn't affect her work that day. A lot depended on Madame Terminé's ability to stick to the seating plan he'd drawn up.

'What did she mean by that?'

'Justine? Oh, nothing. It's simply that Armand is a little strange sometimes. It is always worse when the moon is full.' He held the steps while she came down. 'It is very sad. He could have been many things, but no one wants to employ him any more. I only do so because of family ties. He is the son of old Madame

Camille who you've seen outside, and if she went I don't know where I'd be. Her mother worked for my grandfather, but as for her husband . . . who knows? There was a lot of family inter-marrying in those days and sometimes it backfired. Armand is harmless enough, but he mixes with strange people.' She picked up the cable. 'I think she is also a little put out over your helping so much in the kitchen.'

Monsieur Pamplemousse looked even more thoughtful as he climbed the stairs to his room. It was like doing a jigsaw. You did the edges first and then started on the middle. Suddenly, from being on the point of writing to the manufacturers complaining that there must be pieces missing, they came to light and a picture began to take shape.

As he'd suspected, Pommes Frites was fast asleep, effectively blocking the doorway to the bathroom. For some reason best known to himself, Pommes Frites had become obsessed with the bathroom. He opened one eye and watched while his master pottered around the bedroom, picking up a piece of paper here, consulting a chart there.

The fact of the matter was, with zero hour approaching Monsieur Pamplemousse was anxious to set the wheels in motion. He looked at his watch for what seemed like the hundredth time that morning. It was barely twelve o'clock. Hard to believe that he'd been up and about and working for close on eight hours. Hard to believe in one sense, easy in another. He suddenly felt inordinately tired as he lay back on the bed and closed his eyes while he took stock of the situation. The idea of serving a *menu surprise gastronomique* had been something of an inspiration; the planning and the execution had taken it out of him. At least it had cured him for the time being of the ambition he'd once had, and still had from time to time, of one day retiring and opening his own small hotel. Like many such ambitions the dream was better than the realisation, but without such dreams what would life be all about? Working for *Le Guide* was probably as good a compromise as any.

All now depended on Madame Terminé following his instructions to the letter; serving the right dishes to the right tables according to a pre-determined plan so that he could note the effect if any, putting ticks in little boxes. He opened his eyes again and picked up one of the charts. Monsieur le Directeur would have been proud of him. He wondered if anyone since Roman times had organised a menu with so many aphrodisiac variations and possibilities. Bernard would appreciate it. It might even jog his memory. There must be something he'd forgotten.

The apéritif had been his first stroke of genius; the *potage noisette* his second. In one fell swoop he would eliminate many possibilities. He went over the ingredients of both again in his mind, making sure nothing had been forgotten.

The apéritif he'd prepared early that morning, boiling it up first before leaving it in the refrigerator to cool. Red Bourgueil from Touraine, cinnamon – he wondered if perhaps he'd been a little over-generous with the cinnamon, almost two large spoonfuls had gone in – ginger, vanilla, honey, cloves. It should set their red corpuscles going, getting them in the right mood for the *potage*: pounded almonds mixed with the yolks of hard-boiled eggs and chicken stock, then more honey. The cream was a bit of a problem. Strictly speaking he should have mixed it in while he was making it, but according to the researches he'd done while writing his article, the appearance of a bowl of cream on the table was often a great attraction to the female of the species. Ideally, too, he should have added a few pine kernels, perhaps even standing some cones on end; one opposite each place setting. The more phallic symbols there were around the better. Symbols and symbolism ran right through the literature of aphrodisiacs and played almost as large a part as did the ingredients themselves. What was interesting, and what none of his researches had ever told him for sure, was whether, like hypnotism, you could only persuade people to do things they had a deep desire to do anyway, never the other way round.

In the end timing had been one of the chief factors which eliminated many possibilities; timing and availability coupled with intent and the danger involved. The latter had included all the drugs with known side-effects, like mescaline, cannabis, Spanish fly and ginseng, which in any case was too slow-acting to have been the cause of Bernard's problem. For similar reasons he rejected avocado laced with nutmeg – awarded special mention in his article because it was one of the least dangerous. Its preparation required time, implying malice aforethought, and when it acted it was reputed to be a case of lighting the blue touch paper and retiring immediately. Cucumber stuffed with truffles was too exotic.

Whatever it was it had to be as anonymous and taken for granted as the arrival of the *facteur* with the morning mail, as accepted a part of the daily scene in the Founder's time as it was today, innocuous on the surface and yet powerful and long lasting. The length of the fuse was less important than staying power. Bernard must have driven for more than an hour before he finally succumbed; Pommes Frites' staying powers the other night were not open to question.

Uncooked celery stalks – if stories were to be believed – fulfilled most of the requirements. Rich in methaqualone, they were highly prized in some northern countries like Greenland and Norway. Rabbits thrived on them. But it would be unusual to find them eaten raw in large quantities in the English fashion. They would be much more likely to find their way into a salad or be cooked in some way.

It was a problem and no mistake.

Getting up from the bed, he went out on to the balcony. By leaning over the rail he was able to see along to the garden. Already there was a sprinkling of early arrivals. One man was holding his apéritif up to the light, discussing the contents of the glass with his companion. Draining it, he signalled to Madame Terminé for a refill. That was something he hadn't bargained for. He wondered if he'd made enough. More than ever he regretted the loss of his notebook. With its neatly ruled and divided pages it was ideal for keeping records under cover of the table cloth.

Slightly to his relief, Pommes Frites ignored an invitation to accompany him downstairs. He would have his work cut out keeping track of things as it was without any other distraction. Apart from which, after last night's meal it wouldn't do Pommes Frites any harm to go without for a day.

By the time he arrived in the garden more than half the tables were occupied and Madame Terminé was waving some new arrivals in, uttering cries of '*avancez*', whipping the serviette off the table and into their laps as they sat down. His own table, arranged towards the back of the garden close to some steps leading down to the cellars, had the double advantage of being in the shade and yet affording a view through a gap in the others so that he would be able to see the parade when it took place.

Putting his Leica and a writing pad on a chair beside him he settled down and looked around. To his right a party of four were already into their soup, rewarding his efforts with a great deal of lip-smacking and comments and wiping of bowls with their bread. He wondered what they would say if they knew why he'd made it. To his right a local was protesting about there being a fixed menu with no choice – demanding that he be told in advance so that he could choose his wine. He received short shrift from Madame Terminé. Madame Terminé was, in fact, in her element. He could see now how she had acquired her brusque manner; it must have been ingrained in her from the days when the Hôtel du Paradis was always full. With over forty people to serve there was no time for pleasantries; the pace never slackened for a moment. His own apéritif was poured in passing without a drop being spilled nor a hint of anything other than exactly the right measure.

Not too little, not too much. His '*merci*' was registered and acknowledged with the barest of nods.

Some more girls went past, walking self-consciously and awkwardly on their high heels, aware that they were being watched by all the people at table and taking comfort in the safety of numbers. They were a motley selection, some barely into their teens, others twice their age. Bottoms of various shapes, sizes and denominations, pert or full, tight or wobbly, turned and faced the hotel as they made their way across the square. Most of them would probably automatically pull their skirts down over their knees if they caught you looking at them in a restaurant or an *autobus*, and yet there they were, as bold as brass, generously displaying thighs and bosoms for all the world to see, their faces lobster red from the combined effects of over-tight uniforms, the hot sun and the comments from the crowd.

'Poor things.' Tante Louise joined him for a moment. 'Fancy having to wear those uniforms in this heat. I must give them something to drink.'

She disappeared into the hotel again and a few minutes later came out with a jug and a pile of paper cups. He watched as she followed after them like a mother hen.

On the far side of the square he recognised the gendarme he'd spoken to the previous evening, on traffic duty now, directing cars away from the area where the band would be performing. People were already starting to form small groups in front of the stalls on either side. Despite the heat, the hot-dog stand was doing a roaring trade.

Above the sound of the Fair, which had been building up all the morning – the steady rumble of a roundabout and the cracking of rifle fire – he could hear a staccato roar like the high-pitched buzzing of a swarm of angry bees. It came from a tarmac area just beyond the fairground where later that afternoon there would be miniature car racing. It was the latest craze; radio-controlled toy cars treated with all the solemnity of the real thing. Marshals with their flags. Pit stops. Mechanics in overalls wielding tiny screwdrivers and bottles of benzine, and all the usual hangers-on. From the tree above his head the loudspeaker crackled into life as someone blew into a microphone, then it went quiet again.

Madame Terminé bustled past with the first of the entrées. He made a quick note on his pad. Table four was getting a selection of open tartlets; eels, *moules*, *asperges*, accompanied by spinach; table seven was getting frogs' legs, brains, *jambon* with *ananas* and turnip. It was hard to picture turnip being an aphrodisiac. On the other hand Scotsmen ate it with their haggis. They probably had need of it, wearing kilts in all the cold weather they had to endure.

He had never made so much pastry in his life before. One thing was certain; it couldn't be any worse than the stuff they normally served, and it had the merit of making everything easier to organise beforehand.

The Director's aunt came back across the square. Above the other sounds could now be heard the banging of drums and the trilling of fifes. Refreshed, the band was tuning up in readiness for its big moment.

She paused on her way past and put the jug down on

his table. 'There's a tiny drop left in case you get thirsty.'

Monsieur Pamplemousse thanked her and picked up his camera, checking as he did so that he'd set it to shutter priority and with a speed fast enough to accommodate the marchers when they appeared. He'd opted for the 45–90 mm Angenieux zoom; a new toy he was trying out on behalf of *Le Guide*. He ran through it. The colour would be slightly warmer than a normal Leitz optic, but at its widest he was able to get a bit of foreground interest with an overhanging branch framing the top of the tree and tables to either side; at its narrowest it was tight enough to be able to get some reasonable groupings on the band when it arrived.

He made another quick note. Table three had just taken delivery of an artichoke tart, kidneys and cream and *foie de veau*; they were looking slightly enviously at the table next to them who were deeply into *escargots*, *ris de veau* and hare. He decided to keep an eye on them in case they tried to do a swop. That would not be good for his records.

He took a quick glance around. Everything seemed to be normal. It was a scene that was probably being repeated all over France wherever the sun was shining. The tables were full; the conversation animated.

The only abnormal note being struck at that moment, or to be strictly accurate a succession of abnormal notes, came from somewhere beyond the square as the band, having embarked on an arrangement for drums and fifes of 'The Entrance of the Gladiators', set off on its journey.

154

As the sound drew near, Monsieur Pamplemousse raised his camera, zoomed in and focused on a vertical rod supporting a canvas hood on one of the stalls in line with the centre of the square, then zoomed out again in readiness for the big moment.

He wasn't a second too soon. Intended to be played as a quick-step, the march was being performed in double quick time. Whether the band was trying to keep up with Miss Sparkling Saumur, or whether Miss Saumur was trying to keep one step ahead of the band, was a moot point, but they entered the square at a pace neither the composer, Julius Fusic, nor the organisers of the Fête had ever anticipated. With a rippling motion not unlike that of a giant tidal wave building up and then pausing before making a final plunge at the end of its travels, they came to a shuffling halt facing the Hôtel du Paradis several bars ahead of the final notes.

Monsieur Pamplemousse zoomed in on the leader, trying to hold her image steady in the viewfinder as she bobbed up and down, marking time as if treading the very grapes she had been chosen to represent. *Merde!* It still wasn't tight enough for what he wanted. Quickly he changed to a narrow angle lens – the one he'd used at Villandry. Fortunately it still had the two-times multiplier attached. He pulled the jug nearer and rested the camera on top to steady it.

At nine degrees Miss Sparkling Saumur looked rather frightening. Sparkling was not the word he would have used. Miss Fixed-Intensity would have been more apt. Mouth working, hair billowing out behind her, knuckles white through gripping her baton, she seemed to be in the throes of forces beyond her control. Beads of sweat which had collected on her brow formed a tiny rivulet and ran down her cheek. It clung for a moment to her upper lip, then a tongue, long and red and moist, emerged to lick it away, slowly and deliberately performing a full circle as if in anticipation of more to come.

He started the motor drive. With luck it would make a good cover picture for the magazine; a change from the usual landscape or hotel. If only she would stay still for a second. Pressing the rubber cup against his eye he tried hard to hold focus as she filled the frame, first with the whole of her head, then so close he had to sacrifice the top of her forehead in order to avoid cutting off her chin. Her eyes, blue and shining with a kind of intense inner light, seemed to be staring straight into his. He would get Trigaux in the Art Department to process the film for him. It was the kind of thing he revelled in, squeezing the utmost out of a negative. Now he'd lost the chin. Taking his head away from the viewfinder he suddenly realised to his horror that she was heading straight towards him. Not only that but the rest of the band were following hard on her heels, pushing and shoving, their sheets of music falling unheeded to the ground. The drums had taken on a strange rhythmic beat, the few fifes left playing had become shriller, more insistent.

He jumped to his feet and looked around for somewhere to go, but the wall behind him was too high, the tree was without any kind of foothold. On either side his way was barred by the other tables and beyond those to his left he was hemmed in by the crowd in the square. Gazing heavenwards in desperation he had a brief glimpse of Pommes Frites standing on the balcony, looking down in wonder at the sight below, and then they were on him, shrieking, pulling, grasping, clutching, tearing at his clothes like beings possessed of insatiable thirsts and unquenchable desires of a kind no man had hitherto dared name let alone attempt to gratify.

Pommes Frites' eyes grew rounder and rounder as he watched his master disappear down the steps leading to the cellars, lost beneath a heaving mass of arms and brown legs, discarded red and gold uniforms, white knickers, brassières, heaving bosoms and tangled hair. It was a scene of such complexity that had Dante been making preliminary notes for his Inferno he would have undoubtedly put them to one side fearing that the critics of the day might have accused him of being over-fanciful.

Pommes Frites turned and hurried back into the room. Pausing briefly at the door, he grasped the handle firmly in his mouth and turned his head. A moment later it swung open. It was a trick he'd learned on his induction course with the Paris police; one which had earned him bonus points at the time, and then later that same year applause from the crowd when he'd demonstrated it at the annual police Open Day.

Over the years he'd had occasion to try it out more than once in the course of duty, but he had a feeling that never before had it been used on a matter of quite such urgency and importance.

8

THE DARK AND THE LIGHT

Doctor Cornot clicked open his pen and began to write. 'You are a very fortunate man, Monsieur.'

Monsieur Pamplemousse sat up in bed and glared at him. 'I am *not* fortunate,' he bellowed. 'I am most unfortunate! In the space of three days I have been hit over the head, upended in a Sanisette, and now I have been ravaged by a gang of female musicians. Do you call that fortunate?'

The Doctor tore a piece of paper from his pad. 'I suggest you apply this to the affected parts three times a day. The swelling may persist for a while and there is a certain amount of soreness, which is not surprising in the circumstances. But nothing is irreparably damaged. No bones are broken.'

'*Bones*!' repeated Monsieur Pamplemousse bitterly. 'I should be so lucky!'

'You are not the only one to suffer,' the doctor continued unsympathetically. 'I have hardly slept since yesterday. Half the members of the drum and fife band are still under heavy sedation. Madame Lorris, their trainer, is in an intensive care unit at Tours and likely to remain there for some while. I fear for her sanity. She had only just recovered from an unhappy experience earlier in the year when she heard voices uttering threats in the Sanisette. Others – the ones who were unlucky enough to be bringing up the rear and so received the full brunt of Pommes Frites' rescue bid – will be unable to sit down for a week. As for Miss Sparkling Saumur, there is talk of her being deposed. I do not care for some of these modern expressions, but to say that she got her *culottes* in a twist would have been all too apt had she still been wearing them . . .'

Monsieur Pamplemousse gave a shudder and held up his hand. 'Stop! I do not wish to be reminded.'

Doctor Cornot picked up his bag and then paused and gazed at him curiously. 'In a sense it is none of my business. My business is to attend to the sick and in that respect one may say that since your arrival in this village business has never been better. I turn a blind eye to many things I see in passing. If I didn't . . .' he gave a shrug. 'But in this instance I must confess to a certain curiosity. What *did* you give them?'

'*I* gave them nothing,' said Monsieur Pamplemousse firmly.

'Well, someone did. And whatever it was it had exceptional power. Its effects were fairly instant and long lasting. Poor little Hortense is in a dreadful state. She cannot stop moaning and her mother has had to tie her to the bedstead and lock the door. Admittedly she has always been advanced for her age and has been suffering the consequences of late, but . . .'

A thought struck Monsieur Pamplemousse. 'Have there been other "happenings" in the past?'

'Not with Hortense. Her problems are more imaginary than practical. She reads too many magazines and they put ideas into her head. But there have been rumours of "goings-on" from time to time. Not on such a grand scale as yesterday and none that have involved me directly.'

'For example?'

'Stories of people – couples usually – often from outside the area – the locals do not patronise the hotel very much these days, but couples who have come to dine and then, for some reason or other, lost all control of themselves. Sometimes even before they have been able to reach the safety of their cars. There was a case only a few months ago. The police had to be called . . . buckets of water were thrown in Reception. One of the gendarmes got badly bitten when he tried to separate them.'

Monsieur Pamplemousse recalled the couple he'd seen the day of his arrival; two who *had* made the car park. 'Do you have any theories?'

Doctor Cornot gave another shrug. 'Nothing in this world happens without a good reason. From all that I have heard it had nothing to do with alcohol. According to a colleague who attended them they were well below the limit which would have prevented them from driving. They were running a temperature and their pupils were severely dilated, but otherwise there was no trace of their being under the influence of any kind of narcotic. In any case, they were not the type; the girl was a perfectly respectable member of society – a librarian. He was a watch repairer from Chartres. Neither had been involved in anything of the kind before. Ergo, they must have been exposed to something abnormal.'

'Would you be prepared to stand up in court and give evidence?'

'Believing something to be true is one thing. Proving it is quite another matter. To answer your question – no. Anyway, in your case it will not be necessary. After all, you were the one who was attacked.'

'I am really asking on behalf of a friend. A friend who also had a strange experience after dining here. His case comes up soon.'

'In that case, Monsieur, I would look back into history. I would visit the offices of the local newspapers and go through their files for the turn of the century. Consult records. Search for previous happenings. Dig out all the evidence I could find. Then I would advise your friend to get himself a good lawyer.'

'You are saying?'

'I am saying that this hotel has a curious history. My father, whose practice I inherited, used to relate stories of similar occurrences. They had been told to him by his father before him. There was a time when the Hôtel du Paradis enjoyed quite a reputation in these parts. That is how it got its name. Once upon a time it was simply called the Hôtel du Centre. Then, on the death of Madame Louise's grandfather it all stopped; as suddenly as it had begun. It is only recently – within the past few months – that it has started again.'

Monsieur Pamplemousse lay back and closed his eyes, mentally picturing a photograph on the stairs which showed Tante Louise's grandfather clutching a bottle of claret as he stood with one foot on a rhinoceros carcass. He had a roguish twinkle in his eye and a satisfied air. Come to think of it in most of the pictures there had been one or two native girls hovering in the background. Naked, nubile and with an undeniably

161

contented expression on their faces. It was not beyond the bounds of possibility that on one of his many expeditions to Africa he had stumbled across some secret formula, some witchdoctor's brew, that he'd managed to keep to himself. No wonder he kept making return trips.

'Supposing,' he began, 'supposing there does exist some thing or some combination of things, that triggers off this behaviour? A catalyst of great power and intensity. And suppose someone were to discover the secret, what then?'

'I would say that someone would need to tread very carefully,' said the doctor, 'for he would be in possession of knowledge which many men would stop at nothing to own. Such knowledge in the wrong hands could be an easy source of great wealth and power. It is the kind of knowledge men have been seeking all through history. On the surface the begetter of much pleasure, but in practice, as you know only too well, also the cause of much pain, discomfort and misery.

'It did not escape my notice, Monsieur, that just now when you listed your current misfortunes you mentioned that you were hit on the head the night you arrived. It did not surprise me unduly, for the wound was not really consistent with your story of having tripped and fallen over. Nor did you seem over-anxious to report the matter to the police. In passing I asked myself why. Since we live in an area where such attacks are rare, and since robbery was not the motive, the only reason I could think of was that you had accidentally stumbled on something you shouldn't have and that someone was saying very forcibly "Keep off!

Do not interfere in matters which are not your concern." '

At that moment the telephone by the side of the bed rang shrilly. Monsieur Pamplemousse lifted the receiver. '*Un moment.*' He held his hand over the mouthpiece. 'Thank you, Docteur. You have given me much food for thought. If I may, I would like to continue this discussion later. It is possible I will have something more tangible to talk about by then.'

Doctor Cornot nodded. 'If that is so, then congratulations. It will be a pleasure. I will come and see you again tomorrow. In the meantime, *au revoir*. Fortunately this time you will *have* to stay in your room otherwise I would add "take care".'

Monsieur Pamplemousse digested the last remark without fully understanding it and then, as the door closed, put the receiver to his ear again. It was Tante Louise.

'There is a long distance call for you. I said you were not to be disturbed but whoever it is insists on speaking to you. I'm afraid it is a bad line. It is hard to understand what he is saying. Would you like me to ask him to call again later?'

'*Non. Merci.*' Monsieur Pamplemousse winced as he reached behind to plump up his pillow and make himself more comfortable. It felt as though every bone and muscle in his body was aching. As soon as he was through with his caller he would ring down and ask someone to take his prescription round to the *pharmacie* for him.

Pommes Frites stirred and looked at him sympathetically over the end of the bed. It was an 'I know exactly how you must be feeling, we're all boys together' look. Had the giving of winks been part of his repertoire of tricks, Pommes Frites would undoubtedly have given his master an extra large one at that moment. Not that Monsieur Pamplemousse was in a particularly receptive mood for such pleasantries. Breathing heavily, he glared at the end of the receiver.

'Who is that?

'*Pardon*?' he repeated. 'I cannot understand a word you are saying.'

Banging the earpiece with his free hand, he tried again. 'Monsieur, I do not know who you are or what you want of me, but I have enough things on my mind at present without having to deal with illiterate idiots. You sound as though you have a handkerchief stuffed down your mouthpiece. If you cannot talk to me properly then . . .'

'Pamplemousse, I *am* talking with a handkerchief down my mouthpiece. I am doing so because I do not wish my voice to be recognised. Now, please let me say what I have to say.'

'*Pardon*, Monsieur le Directeur.' Monsieur Pamplemousse found himself automatically sitting to attention. 'Forgive me, I did not realise . . . you may speak freely. There is no fear of our being overheard.'

'I trust you are right, Pamplemousse. Things are in a sorry state. What was the last thing I said to you?'

Monsieur Pamplemousse racked his brains. He disliked conundrums at the best of times, but clearly the Director expected an answer. '*Au revoir*?' he ventured.

A noise like an explosion came from the other end.

Monsieur Pamplemousse tried again. '*Bonne nuit*?'

'No, Pamplemousse.' The Director appeared to be having trouble in controlling his patience. 'I was referring to the three A's: *Action, Accord* and *Anonymat*, but above all, and correct me if I am wrong, Pamplemousse, above all we agreed on *Anonymat*.'

'That is true, Monsieur, but . . .'

'Since you have been at St. Georges-sur-Lie, *Action* appears to be negligible, *Accord* as far as I am concerned is non-existent. As for *Anonymat* – all France knows of your goings-on. It is headline news. Pommes Frites was on breakfast television this morning.'

'Pommes Frites, Monsieur? But that is not possible. He is here with me now. I could reach out of bed and pat him . . .'

'Bed!' thundered the voice at the other end. '*Bed!* Do you realise what time it is?'

Monsieur Pamplemousse groped for his watch. 'But, Monsieur, I still do not understand . . .'

'Have you looked outside you hotel recently, Pamplemousse? Your *balcon* is being watched by millions. Ever since Pommes Frites was seen peering through a gap in them, the colour of your curtains has been discussed and analysed and photographed. I'm told they have achieved the highest ratings since the World Cup. No doubt by courtesy of satellite, Pommes Frites and your curtains were also seen by millions in San Francisco and Peking as well. Do you call that *Anonymat?*'

'*Excusez-moi*, Monsieur. *Un moment.*' Letting go of the receiver and regardless of his condition, Monsieur Pamplemousse jumped out of bed and rushed to the window, pulling the curtains to one side as he went.

Almost as quickly he dropped them again. Clutching the window frame for support, he took a moment to regain his composure before trying again, this time through a much smaller gap.

But if he'd been hoping that like a mirage the view would have disappeared he was doomed to disappointment. Overnight a great change had come over the square. Gone were all the stalls and vans which had arrived for the fête. Their place had been taken by other vehicles, making it appear, if anything, even more crowded. In front of his room, pointing straight towards him from the top of some scaffolding, was a television camera. Even as he watched a red light came on and the operator pressed his face to the viewfinder as he took a firm grip of the panning handle. On the ground below another man wearing headphones was supervising while a man disgorged a small mountain of other equipment; two more cameras, tripods and lights. Cables snaked their way across the cobblestones towards a mobile control room. Men in jeans and checked shirts and girls with clip-boards added to the bustle. A mobile canteen had replaced the hot-dog stand. On the roof of the Sanisette, surrounded by empty beer cans, a man crouched holding a Nikon camera with an ultra-long-focus lens. By his side stood a battery of other lenses.

In the centre of the square, watched by a small knot of interested spectators, he recognised Miss Sparkling Saumur being interviewed in front of a second television camera. In direct contrast to her uniform for the parade, she was soberly dressed in a long black skirt, a white blouse done up to her neck and low-heeled shoes. Taking a handkerchief from her bag, she dabbed at her eyes as she turned to point with her other hand in the direction of the cellar steps. The floor manager stopped her for a moment, gave her a comforting pat, and then asked her to do it again using her other hand. Something to do with the light no doubt. A make-up girl stepped forward and dabbed at her forehead. The producer was obviously squeezing the most out of the situation.

Very slowly Monsieur Pamplemousse made his way back to his bed, climbed in and picked up the receiver again. He had to admit that *anonymat* was not the word he would have used to describe the scene outside.

'I'm glad you agree with me for once, Pamplemousse. At least we have achieved some *accord*. I tell you, the press this morning does not make pleasant reading. It is like Bernard all over again only this time it is even worse. Do you know how many?'

'I was not in a position to make an accurate count, Monsieur.'

'Over forty.' The Director sounded gloomy. 'The youngest was six years old, the oldest was seventy-three. All victims of your uncontrollable lust.'

'With respect, Monsieur. It was not they who were the victims, it was I.'

'That is not what the journals are saying, nor the television.'

'I have the scars to prove it, Monsieur. I can get a certificate from the doctor.'

'I do not wish to hear about them, Pamplemousse. And who is Madame Toulemonde?'

167

Monsieur Pamplemousse racked his brains. The Director was in one of his darting moods.

'She is selling her story to *Ici Paris*. They are advertising it already under their "coming attractions". Soon the presses will be turning.' There was a rustle of paper. 'Blonde, thirty-nine year old Madame Justine Toulemonde. "How I Fought Like a Tigress to Retain My Honour." She says she was attacked by you in her room two nights ago. You were like a man possessed. It was only her training with the Resistance Movement that saved her.'

'A complete and utter fabrication, Monsieur. If I was possessed of anything it was an urgent desire to visit the toilet. I had a bad attack of the *douleurs*. If she was attacked in her room she must have kept her eyes closed for it was not I.'

'She says you have a mole on your left knee. Do you have a mole on your left knee, Pamplemousse? I can easily check with your P.27.'

'*Oui*, Monsieur, but I can explain. She must have seen it the first night I was here, when she was undressing me. I had been hit on the head by a *baguette* . . .'

Monsieur Pamplemousse held the receiver away from his head as a spluttering sound came from the earpiece. Pommes Frites watched sympathetically as his master gazed towards the ceiling waiting for the noise to subside.

'That, Pamplemousse, is the most unlikely story I have ever heard. I knew there would be a woman at the bottom of it. I said to Chantal only last night, mark my words, always with Pamplemousse there is a woman at the bottom of things. *Cherchez la femme*.'

'What did your wife say, Monsieur?' asked Monsieur Pamplemousse uneasily.

'Never trust a man with loose shoes.' The Director sounded puzzled. 'I can't think what she meant.'

'There is no reading the female mind, Monsieur. Women are beautiful creatures. They have qualities which in many ways make them superior to men, but I sometimes feel that when the good Lord created them he must have reached a point when he sat back, wondering if he had not been a little over-generous with his gifts, that perhaps enough was enough. It was at that point he must have decided to take away their sense of logic in order to help balance the scales. It makes them say strange things at times.

'As for Madame Toulemonde, if she is as inaccurate with her forthcoming revelations as she is with her present pronouncements, then we have nothing to fear. She is neither a natural blonde – that I can state categorically – nor will she ever see thirty-nine again – a fact which does not require the use of an electronic calculator to verify. If she received her training in the Resistance Movement then even at *forty*-nine she would have needed to attend unarmed combat lessons in her pram.'

Taking advantage of the momentary silence at the other end, Monsieur Pamplemousse pressed home his advantage. 'How are things *chez vous*, Monsieur?' he ventured. 'How is the young English *mademoiselle*? What was her name? Elsie?'

From the even longer silence that followed he knew he had scored a direct hit. A direct hit and a diversionary move at one and the same time.

'*Chez nous*, things are not good, Pamplemousse. *Chez nous*, I would say things have never been worse. There have been ultimatums. Zero hour is approaching fast. What with that and Bernard, now this, I am beginning to wonder where it will all end.'

'I am glad you rang, Monsieur,' said Monsieur Pamplemousse with a confidence he was far from feeling. 'Despite all you may have read and heard, I have not been idle. Progress is being made. I do not wish to go into details at present, but I hope soon to be in a position to render a full report.'

'I hope so, Aristide. I hope so.' The Director's voice sounded full of gloom. 'If they are not then we will need to add a further "A" to our list. "A" for *Adieu*. In the meantime I will give you another.'

'Monsieur?'

'*Allure. À toute allure*. There is no time to be lost.'

Monsieur Pamplemousse replaced the receiver on its cradle and lay back for a moment. Talking to the Director had left him feeling quite exhausted. It often did. It was like playing squash with at least six opponents. Balls came at you from all directions. One moment reaching a high, then next moment down in the depths.

He climbed out of bed again and crossed to the window. As he made a tiny gap in the curtains and peered through he saw the red light come on over the lens of the camera opposite his window. Someone in the control room must be glued to the monitors. The technicians were probably on permanent standby, waiting to record any and every movement.

Making his way to the door, he opened it and

tip-toed across the landing. He could hear voices below and as he peered over the bannisters he caught a glimpse of two men sitting on the bottom stair. One of them had a camera slung round his neck.

Back in his room he slipped the bolt and then slumped into the armchair. It was all very well for the Director to say make all possible speed, but how? He couldn't have been more heavily guarded if he'd been incarcerated in a top security prison. No doubt the back stairs were being watched as well. It was like being in a state of siege. For a moment he toyed with the idea of adopting some kind of disguise. The chances were they didn't know what he looked like – apart from a general description, and from past experience he knew how widely they could vary. Clearly they didn't have his name. The Director would have made a point of it if they did. Tante Louise must have hidden the register. He was tempted to telephone down and ask her to come up. She might have some ideas. Then he abandoned the thought. She was probably being watched as closely as he was, her every conversation listened to. Gun mikes would be trained on his window.

He wished he could reach outside and close the shutters. The heat was really getting intolerable. Although there was a stillness in the air, his pyjamas felt wringing wet; his bed looked uninvitingly dishevelled.

Stretched out on the rug, Pommes Frites resembled a late-night reveller who'd abandoned all hope of getting home and decided to doss down on his astrakhan coat instead. He envied him his ability to shut out the world, letting its problems take care of themselves. The biggest crisis in his dreams was probably a drama called 'The Great Bone Robbery'.

Glancing round the room, he saw that someone had rescued his camera and bag of equipment. From where he was sitting it looked remarkably undamaged; a tribute to Leica. Perhaps when it was all over he would write to them. If Hasselblad could make capital out of their cameras being sent to the moon . . . His note pad was missing, but he'd hardly managed to write anything on it anyway.

He closed his eyes. There was no chance whatsoever of getting any sleep. He had far too much on his mind. But the rest would do him good. What was needed was some kind of diversion. A distraction of major importance. One which lasted long enough to take everyone's mind off the job in hand so that he could make good his escape. One which . . .

It was dark when Monsieur Pamplemousse came to again. Forcing himself awake he climbed unsteadily to his feet, nearly tripped over the recumbent form of Pommes Frites, and made his way to the bedside table. Strange, but it was still only six o'clock by his watch. He crossed to the window and slowly parted the curtains. The sun was hidden behind a layer of haze. In the sky above there were banks of cumulus cloud. No red light came from the camera. Its operator was slumped over a book, his headphones round his neck. The scene in the square was less animated than it had been earlier. Boredom had set it. Now would be the time for action. Later on they would be on the alert again, expecting something to happen. Lights had been rigged up facing the hotel. They were probably ready to be switched on at a moment's notice.

As he turned away from the window Pommes Frites rose slowly to his feet. It was a ritual awakening, performed in a time-honoured manner. First there was the stretching of the back legs, the lifting of the rump in the air, then came the stretching of the forelegs, outwards as far as they would go, usually followed by a rippling motion which started at the rear and made its way slowly but inexorably towards the front as muscles were brought back to life. Last of all came the pushing forward and slight raising of the head, coupled with the closing of the eyes; a prelude to a yawning return to normality.

On this particular occasion Pommes Frites' head made momentary contact with its opposite number attached to the rug below, giving an effect in the darkened room not unlike a mirror image in a pool, and as it did so Monsieur Pamplemousse suddenly had one of his blinding flashes of inspiration.

It was a notion which was at once ridiculous and bizarre, eccentric and outlandish, and yet of such simplicity he had the feeling it might just work. It had to work. He would make it work. In all the accounts he had ever read of great escapes through the ages the common factor, the connecting link which ran through them all was the element of surprise. Surprise was the one great weapon the escapee possessed. *Ennui* and the fading light were on his side.

Never one to allow the iron to grow cool once it was in his hand, Monsieur Pamplemousse reached for his suitcase, his issue one from *Le Guide*. Removing the tray which normally carried his camera equipment, then the second which accommodated the emergency cooking apparatus – its contents a miracle of the folding-metal worker's art, he reached into a compartment at the very bottom and withdrew a small leather sachet.

Pommes Frites watched with interest as Monsieur Pamplemousse laid the contents out in a neat row on the floor in front of him; a selection of needles, a hank of thread, a thimble, a tape measure and a pair of folding scissors. Undoubtedly his master was up to something – he recognised the signs, and the enthusiasm, determination and speed with which ideas were being translated into action communicated itself. He wagged his tail. Pommes Frites liked a bit of activity every now and then. He'd enjoyed a very good sleep, several very good sleeps in fact, now he was more than ready for action, and although cutting up his bed was not exactly what he would have chosen had he been asked to fill in a questionnaire, he was quite prepared to go along with whatever his master had in mind.

Despite the heat, ever anxious to please, he didn't raise any objection when Monsieur Pamplemousse wrapped the lion skin round his body, and he happily lay back with his paws in the air while it was sewn into place. Nor did he demur unduly when the head was pulled over his own. Admittedly it made it hard to see where he was going and his growls took on a hollow, roaring sound, but if that was what was wanted, then so be it. Walking wasn't easy; it was more a matter of progressing round the room in a series of leaps and

174

bounds. However, this seemed to please his master out of all proportion to the effort it took. He basked momentarily in the words of praise and the encouraging pats his activities evoked.

'*Bonne chance*.' With his master's words ringing in his ears he hurried out on to the landing. In the past he had tended to look down on dogs who wore any kind of clothes. There were quite a few of them about in Paris, not so much in the area where he lived, but he came across them occasionally while on excursions further afield. Dogs in coats, sometimes even in plastic boots and hats. He always treated them with the contempt he felt they deserved; not even worthy of a passing sniff. But suddenly, as he made his way down the stairs, he discovered the change the wearing of any kind of uniform brings about. It was a whole new world. The effect he had on others was electrifying. As he ambled out into the square in a kind of sideways lope people scattered right, left and centre. Women screamed. Men shouted. Somewhere a whistle blew. He broke into a trot, uttering growls of delight. It was all very satisfying. Quite the most enjoyable thing he'd done for a long time.

Upstairs in his room Monsieur Pamplemousse watched Pommes Frites disappear into the gathering gloom with an air of equal satisfaction. He let go of the curtains. Now he must quickly translate deeds into action on his own behalf. It wouldn't be long before the makeshift disguise was penetrated. There wasn't a moment to be lost. Dressing with all possible speed, he grabbed his case and made for the door, pulling himself up just in time as it began to open.

The back view of Tante Louise came into view. She was carrying a tray on which reposed a large jug and a glass.

'I've brought this for you,' she announced. 'It's iced *tisane*. I made far too much yesterday for the girls in the parade and it seems a shame to waste it.'

9

THE STORM BREAKS

In 1856, following a violent storm during the Crimean War which badly damaged the French fleet sheltering in the Black Sea outside Balaclava, Napoleon III charged Monsieur Antoine Lavoisier, a celebrated chemist of the time, to devise a system of weather forecasting which would ensure that such a thing never happened again.

Thus began a series of developments which some hundred and thirty years later led Monsieur Albert Forêt, an amateur weather enthusiast who lived in St. Georges–sur–Lie, to open the door of a slatted white-painted box set exactly two metres above the lawn in his back garden and note that the indicator on a mercury barometer within showed an alarming fall in pressure.

Even as he entered the new reading on a pad, a gust of wind funnelled through the gap between his house and the garage, raising clouds of dust from the driveway on the far side. Simultaneously, a device inside his greenhouse closed the windows automatically.

All of which indicated that an enormous quantity of air was being sucked upwards to a great height, leaving behind a vacuum which, by the laws of nature, had to be filled.

Monsieur Forêt closed the door to his box, made

sure the greenhouse was properly fastened, then hurried indoors calling out instructions to his wife to secure all the shutters while he telephoned a friend in the next village who owned a vineyard.

Half a kilometre or so away, Monsieur Pample-mousse took a quick glance out of the Hôtel du Paradis at the now deserted square and then looked up at the sky. The cumulus clouds which had begun to develop earlier had come together, forming one vast towering mass of cumulo-nimbus, the top layer of which had already taken on the ominous shape of an anvil.

'I think we are in for a storm,' he called.

Tante Louise shivered as she led the way down some stairs between the entrance to the dining-room and the kitchen. 'I hope not. I hate thunder. It always makes me feel as if something awful is about to happen.'

'In that case,' said Monsieur Pamplemousse comfortingly, 'the cellar is probably the best place to be.' As he spoke he wondered where Pommes Frites had got to. Perhaps success had gone to his head and even now he was sidling along a bank of the Lie suffering delusions of grandeur, King of the Jungle and all he surveyed. He hoped not. Pommes Frites didn't like thunder either. At home in Paris he usually hid in a cupboard. Hiding in a doorway in St. Georges-sur-Lie would be bad for his image.

As it happened, he needn't have worried, for Pommes Frites wasn't very far away. His mission completed, he was lying just inside the hotel stable with his nose to the ground watching some ants scurrying to and fro, their pace almost twice its normal rate as they sought urgent shelter.

After a lot of thought, he had reached the conclusion that not only was biggest not necessarily always best, but that he'd had quite enough of being dressed up for one day. Just outside the village he'd met a man with a gun. Fortunately shock had affected the other's aim, but it had been a nasty moment. It was also extremely hot inside the skin and he couldn't wait to be rid of it.

All that apart, Pommes Frites had another matter on his mind. Soon after his encounter with the farmer he'd stopped to relieve himself in a most unregal manner through a convenient hole in the skin, and while passing the time by sniffing the ground under the tree of his choice he'd come across a scent which he knew only too well and which meant only one thing – trouble. The trail had led him back to the hotel and there it had petered out, largely because of the difficulty he was experiencing through having a wad of stuffing between the end of his nose and the ground.

For the time being he had decided to stay put, give trail-following a rest, watch points, and await developments.

Some ten thousand metres above Pommes Frites' olfactory organ, in an area where the temperature was well below zero, the newly elevated air mass had started to cool rapidly and condense, while coincidentally, a mere five or six metres below him, Monsieur Pample-mousse, having adjusted to an ambient cellar temperature of 13°C, stood contemplating the contents of a small hessian bag.

As if savouring the bouquet of an old and classic wine, he passed it gently to and fro beneath the end of his nose. It was a cocktail of smells. He could detect thyme, rosemary, mint, verbena . . . a hint of lime, but over all there was a scent which was at once strong, heady, aromatic, woody, elusive. It was like hearing a piece of music which had a dominant theme one couldn't quite place. He loosened a drawstring at the top of the bag, rubbed the contents between forefinger and thumb, then sniffed again. The over-riding smell was now even more pronounced. It seemed to come from some pieces of darkish brown bark, dry and curly like old pencil shavings.

'How long have you had this?'

'It's been there ever since Grandpa's day. He used to bring it back from Africa. Mama said he had an arrangement with one of the tribes, but I think they're extinct now.'

Monsieur Pamplemousse couldn't help but wonder if they had worn themselves out. There were worse ways of becoming extinct. Pommes Frites could vouch for that. He must have drunk well that first night. No wonder he'd been in a bad way.

'And it hasn't been used all that time?'

'No, it's been lying there wrapped in tinfoil and sealed with wax. Grandpa didn't come back from one of his expeditions. They say he was eaten by a crocodile. Grand-mère died a little later of a broken heart and after that things were never quite the same. Mama closed the restaurant for a while and by the time she eventually re-opened *tisane* had gone out of fashion. It's only recently become popular again. It seemed a pity to waste it and in Grand-mère's time it was very much in demand.'

'I bet it was!' thought Monsieur Pamplemousse.

Perhaps the news had spread as far as Paris and that was why the Founder, Monsieur Hippolyte Duval, had journeyed so far on his bicycle. Perhaps, like Bernard, he'd been an innocent victim of his thirst. In his diary he'd mentioned the *lapin* being over-salty.

'We . . . *you* must have it analysed.'

'Analysed? Why?' The Director's aunt looked genuinely surprised. 'There's nothing wrong with it is there? Besides, there's hardly any left. Only a couple of bags.'

'All the more reason.' He looked round the cellar, wondering what his next move should be. Tell the Director? Keep it a secret? Try and find an analyst first? One of his old colleagues in the Sûreté should be able to help, or at least give him an introduction to the right person. Instinctively he knew he was holding in his hands part of the fortune Tante Louise's *Grand-mère* had spoken about so often and yet so vaguely. Perhaps in the end she'd wanted the secret to die with her. Perhaps her joy of life had died with her husband. Somehow, he felt the *tisane* had always been used to give pleasure rather than for any financial gain.

'It's a mess.' Tante Louise misunderstood the look on his face. 'I keep telling myself to get down here and sort it all out but somehow there's never time. I wouldn't really know where to start. I leave it all to Armand.'

He could see what she meant. In their time the racks lining the walls must have held several tens of thousands of bottles, all in neat and orderly rows, numbered and labelled, entered in a book. Now they were in a state of disarray, covered in cobwebs, old wine mixed with new. He put the bag of *tisane* back on a shelf with the other one and took out a few bottles of wine at random. 1950s were mixed with 60s and 70s. Dotted here and there were some older vintages. No wonder one took pot luck in the restaurant. He came across a dust-covered Château Latour '28; its label still intact. Despite being near the river the cellar must be good and dry. He gazed at it reverentially. It was probably still at its peak – the '28s had needed all that time to come round. Further along he came across a single bottle of Mouton '29 sandwiched in amongst some bottles of Beaujolais. Someone was still doing the buying, but what a waste to put them away without rhyme or reason. He shuddered to think of all the delights that must have been drunk unregarded and unlauded.

'Would you care to see Grandpa's original cellar?' Tante Louise pointed to a door at the far end, barely visible in the light from an unshaded, but blackened bulb. 'That's where he kept what he always called his *vins du meilleur*.' She reached up to a crevice high in one of the walls and took out a large iron key. As the door swung open Monsieur Pamplemousse caught his breath. For a brief moment he felt something approaching the awe those who first entered the tombs of the ancient Egyptians must have experienced: awe, coupled with an enormous sense of privilege.

There were precedents, of course. From time to time old cellars were discovered; collections of wine came to light. There was the Dr. Barolet sale of Burgundies in the late sixties. That had really been the start of the high-powdered auctions which were now commonplace. Then there were the great English collections; ancient families who'd come to realise they owned more wine than they would ever drink in their lifetime. But this was something different and personal. Never in his wildest dreams had he pictured it happening to him. With the utmost care he lifted a bottle from its rack; an 1870 Lafite – possibly the greatest vintage before Phylloxera took its toll.

The first flash of lightning entered the cellar through a glass porthole let into a wall of the outer room. It went unheeded by Monsieur Pamplemousse as he held the bottle up for inspection. Full of tannin, the wine would have taken fifty years or more to become drinkable. It was the product of a more leisurely age. Such an investment in time and patience would be unthinkable nowadays, preoccupied as growers were with stainless steel vats, quality control, and quick returns on money invested.

An explosive crack like rapidly falling masonry sounded overhead as the violent expansion of hot air caused by the lightning manifested itself in a shock wave.

Feeling Tante Louise's hand on his arm he put the bottle gently and carefully back in its place. To drop it would be an unthinkable crime. 'Don't worry. We shall be safe down here.'

To his surprise she reached across in front of him and turned out the light, then pulled the door half shut. 'Ssh! Listen.'

Straining his ears he caught a faint sound from the other end of the cellar. Someone was trying the door at the bottom of the steps leading from the garden; the same steps down which he'd fled the day before. After a brief pause there was another rattle, louder this time, then a thump as whoever was on the other side put their full weight against it, producing a splintering sound.

'Who can it be? I got Justine to nail it up last night. The lock was broken.'

Monsieur Pamplemousse squeezed in front of her and peered through the gap into the outer cellar. As the door gave way a second flash of lightning, even more vivid in the darkness than the first, momentarily silhouetted a figure in the opening. The face was in shadow, but the outline was all too familiar; indelibly imprinted on his mind ever since he'd encountered it the night he'd arrived. There was the same shopping bag, but this time with a *baguette* sticking out of the top.

Another roll of thunder and with it the sound of rain, sudden and almost tropical in its intensity, muffled the exclamation of surprise from beside him. He gave Tante Louise's arm a warning squeeze and drew her back with him, freezing her into silence a fraction of a second before the light in the other room came on. But he needn't have worried – the intruder had other things on her mind. Going straight to the shelf where he'd left the *tisane*, she took the two containers from the shelf and slipped them into her bag. Whoever it was, she must have reached the same inevitable conclusion as he had.

It was all over in a matter of seconds. The next instant there was a rustle of skirts, the light went out and there was a creak from the outer door as it swung shut again.

'But . . .'

'Wait here.' Monsieur Pamplemousse let go of Tante Louise's arm, switched on the light, and hurried towards the outer door. Halfway along the cellar there was another flash of lightning. The crash of thunder which followed was almost instantaneous, but in the short space of time between the two he heard a familiar and welcome bark from somewhere outside. Pommes Frites was on hand and doing his stuff. Taking the steps two at a time he emerged into the garden and then paused as he absorbed the strange picture that presented itself.

On a bright sunny day Pommes Frites would have presented a fearsome sight; in the middle of the storm he looked positively awesome. The first clap of thunder had nearly made him jump out of his own skin – the second had caused him to split the outer lion's skin in several places, leaving it as tattered as his nerves. With the rain-sodden mane half off his head, pieces of bedraggled fur hanging in shreds and not one, but two tails, he looked like some strange creature created by a latter-day Frankenstein.

Brandishing the *baguette* in one hand in an effort to keep Pommes Frites at bay, feeling in her bag as she went, his quarry backed towards the Sanisette.

Almost at the same moment as she reached it things began to happen in the sky immediately overhead. Negatively charged super-cooled ice crystals and positively charged water droplets, falling at different speeds, were building up a vast potential difference; a difference which in turn produced a gigantic discharge of electricity between sky and ground, heating the air in its path to a temperature five times greater than that on the surface of the sun.

The initial strike path of the flash led straight to the Sanisette, justifying as it landed on its target the designer's foresight in providing an earth return for the protection of anyone unfortunate enough to be taken short in the middle of just such a storm. At the very last moment part of the jagged flash seemed to change its mind and break away in order to complete its journey by another route. A route which took it via the figure trying desperately to unlock the door.

Observers from windows overlooking the square said afterwards, and Monsieur Pamplemousse had no reason to disagree with them, that the *baguette* seemed to glow momentarily before the body was thrown violently to the ground.

Oblivious to the intensity of the rain and hail he hurried towards it, but even as he did so he knew it was a futile gesture; a reflex action born out of a hopeless inability to think of anything else to do. The body lay forlorn and twisted where it had landed. Beside it the charred shopping bag had burst, its contents disintegrating rapidly in the torrent of water which flowed in all directions.

Reaching down Monsieur Pamplemousse turned the figure gingerly towards him, wondering as he did so if he, too, might receive a shock by the very act of touching it.

The right hand was holding a bunch of keys, the left was clutching the remains of what had once been a brass periscope to which pieces of bread from a hollowed-out *baguette* still clung.

The body in its long black dress looked like that of an old woman, but the face was that of Armand.

*　　　*　　　*

'Why on earth didn't you tell me?'

'About Armand? You didn't ask.'

Monsieur Pamplemousse gazed at Tante Louise. She was right, of course. Undeniably right. He hadn't asked and he should have done. When someone registers at an hotel you can't really expect the owner to say, 'Yes, of course you may stay, but I have to tell you that the man who does the odd jobs is a little strange – especially when there is a full moon. He has a habit of dressing up in women's clothes, but it has always been that way and as everyone in the village knows, we don't talk about it any more.' On the other hand it would have helped. He certainly wouldn't have taken all those photographs of the *boulanger* if he'd known.

'He kept himself to himself. As far as I know he never did anyone any harm. He was a very simple person.'

Instinctively Monsieur Pamplemousse found himself running his hand over the back of his head. Hitting someone with a brass periscope disguised as a *baguette* didn't sound like the action of a simple person. He could still feel the bump.

'I still do not understand how he could have behaved like that.' Tante Louise sounded betrayed, as well she might.

Monsieur Pamplemousse shrugged. All his years in the Sûreté had done little to further his understanding of what made some people behave the way they did; rather the reverse. In his experience a person with a lot at stake and protecting his territory was capable of anything. Desperate situations begat desperate actions. Betrayal of the one person who had befriended him would have been of small concern to Armand.

'There is no such thing as a simple person. In Armand's case who knows what went on in his mind while he was working away at his bench. No doubt his old mother kept him here because she thought he would be safe from temptation, but being without temptation doesn't necessarily cure the disease – in some cases it makes it fester and grow.

'I suspect you will find that the visitors you had from Paris that time – the ones who made you an "offer" – didn't go away totally empty handed. They didn't sound the sort who would. They would have tried a different tack. Armand would have come to their notice through a local contact, perhaps even from some establishment in Paris he'd written to over the years who'd kept his name "on file". Your visitors probably made him an offer too – but one he couldn't refuse.'

'What sort of an offer?' Tante Louise looked confused. 'He never wanted for anything.'

Monsieur Pamplemousse shrugged again. The preliminary medical report had confirmed his suspicions. Armand had been deeply into drugs; probably brought on initially by the kind of twilight life he'd been forced to lead, and the people he'd associated with in consequence. No doubt in the beginning Tante Louise's visitors had asked for nothing more than a day to day report on the comings and goings at the hotel – who had eaten what and the effect it had had on them. Hardly an onerous task in return for a regular supply of what had probably become almost a necessity in Armand's life. It was easy to picture the attraction such an offer would have had for him. No doubt they even provided plans of the Sanisette.

It was when his masters became impatient at the lack of progress that the trouble would have started; the cutting off of supplies would have triggered off a series of desperate measures of which breaking into the *pharmacie* would have been but one. There was no doubt in his mind that Armand had been responsible.

His own arrival on the scene could only have added to Armand's feeling of panic, but he decided not to say anything about that to Tante Louise for the moment for fear of further questioning.

'It is best forgotten about. Anyway, there are more important things. There is the future to think of.' As he spoke he allowed his gaze to wander round the office. It was the first time he had been in there. On top of a bureau in one corner he noticed yet another picture of Tante Louise's grandfather, taken when he was much younger, the game more modest. He was standing outside the hotel holding aloft a brace of pheasants. Alongside him was a well-built, fair-haired girl, wearing a beautifully serene and yet slightly provocative smile. She looked full of the joy of life, like a ripe peach, lusty and full of juice.

'That was Grand-mère. It was taken soon after they got married. She was on the stage in Paris – a dancer in a cabaret, but she gave it all up to come and live here.'

Lucky grand-père! There would have been great celebrations when he arrived back from the big city with his capture. They must have had many friends

189

visiting them in those days; even more when rumours of the *tisane* began to spread.

Standing nearby was another, more recent photograph. Black and white instead of sepia. The subject looked very familiar. It was the eyes more than anything. The eyes and the hands.

'That's Jean. He owns the *boulangerie* opposite.' Tante Louise blushed as she caught his look. 'It was taken before he grew his beard.'

'If you ask me,' said Monsieur Pamplemousse, 'that is someone else who also behaves strangely. There was a time when I suspected him of being up to no good.'

'Jean? He wouldn't hurt a fly. His only problem is jealousy. He is always on at me to marry him and when I say "no" he gets very gloomy. The quality of his bread goes down. You won't believe this but once, when someone was staying here and he suspected their motives, he let down all their tyres. There was a terrible scene.'

Monsieur Pamplemousse tried his best to look surprised. 'Why don't you marry him? It would seem an ideal arrangement and it would make life easier for your guests. It might also improve the cooking. Cooking for love is a sure recipe for success.'

The blush deepened. 'Jealousy is one thing, but I couldn't marry a man with a beard.'

Monsieur Pamplemousse looked at his watch. It was almost ten o'clock. The day before, after the ambulance and the police and everyone else had been and gone he'd retired to his room and slept as he couldn't remember ever having slept before, deeply and solidly and satisfyingly. Now he felt refreshed and hungry.

'Could you conquer your dislike of beards long enough to order me some croissants and a brioche or two?' he enquired. 'I'll be down in about thirty minutes.'

Apart from food, a bath was what he needed most of all. Considering his insistence on having a room with a bath he'd made precious little use of it since he'd arrived. Now he would make up for it. A good, deep, long bath, followed by a leisurely breakfast. Fresh orange juice, rolls, coffee, croissants, brioche, *confiture* . . . as he stood up he caught sight of his reflection in a mirror . . . and a shave. The face poking out of the top of the dressing gown definitely needed a shave.

'I'll see if I can find Justine. I think she is avoiding me – and with good reason. She knows my feelings about people who try to sell "their story" to the newspapers. I have told her – if she does then we are finished.'

'I couldn't marry a man with a beard.' Monsieur Pamplemousse repeated the words to himself as he slowly climbed the stairs to his room, and as he did so he gave an inward sigh of compassion for all the people in the world who were prepared to sacrifice years of possible happiness because they lacked the ability to discuss even the simplest facts of life. It was all a matter of communication.

Tante Louise was more than ready to take up the cudgels on behalf of someone else whose privacy she thought was being invaded, but she couldn't do it on her own behalf for fear of being thought rude, a violator of another's privacy herself. He'd been about to offer her a more up-to-date photograph. He had thirty very good likenesses, but unfortunately all with beards. It would have been rubbing salt into the wound.

As for the *boulanger* himself – whoever said no man is an island was talking nonsense. All men were islands; some allowed in more tourists than others.

Pommes Frites jumped to his feet as Monsieur Pamplemousse entered the room. Fully recovered from his ordeal in the storm, he wagged his tail with pleasure as he followed his master across to the balcony.

Outside the clearing up operations were well under way. Shopkeepers were putting sodden mats on the pavement to dry, washing floors and wringing their mops as if trying to squeeze out the memory of both the storm and its solitary casualty. A van was parked alongside the Sanisette and two men were poring over a circuit diagram, scratching their heads as they tried to restore it to working order. Others were dismantling the scaffolding tower, coiling up camera cables into neat figures of eight as they went. The rest of the media seemed to have disappeared. Put to flight by Pommes Frites, routed by the storm, they were probably miles away by now, devoting their minds and talents to other things. There was nothing so dead as yesterday's story.

The sky had cleared and the sun was shining, but the temperature had gone down. In the fields opposite the goats were drying out, their beards damp-looking and tousled. Like the sunflowers surrounding them they were battered but unbowed. He wondered idly what they were thinking about as they munched their way through the morning. It was hard to tell with goats; unlike Pommes Frites, who from his behaviour had sensed that it was nearly time to move on.

Pommes Frites, in fact, was beginning to show distinct signs of being difficult again. The moment he heard the bath water running he started scratching on the outer door, looking imploringly over his shoulder, as if willing his master to take him out for a walk instead. Monsieur Pamplemousse pretended not to notice. Turning to face the bathroom mirror, he studiously attended to the lathering of his face.

As he pulled his jaw to one side to assist the passage of the blade a long drawn out howl came from the other room. Pommes Frites was bringing his big guns into action. Well, two could play at that game. The second lathering was accompanied by 'O Sole Mio'. Their voices blended well. The bathroom added a certain mellifluousness to the notes as they echoed round the walls. It was quite pleasing. Perhaps they should team up. He could see the posters. Pamplemousse and his singing dog, Pommes Frites – in concert!

Pommes Frites clearly didn't agree. He peered round the bathroom door hardly able to believe his ears. Had he been less busy on the task in hand Monsieur Pamplemousse might well have noticed that he was wearing the doleful expression of one steeling himself for the performance of a distasteful task. It was the kind of expression a dentist might don as he uttered the classic phrase 'This is going to hurt me more than it hurts you', knowing full well that the reverse was true.

Turning off the bath tap, Monsieur Pamplemousse reached down and tested the temperature of the water. It was even more tepid than usual. No doubt the rapid cooling of the ground by the deluge of rain and hail had something to do with it. The boiler was probably working overtime trying to catch up.

As he rose to his feet again he became aware that Pommes Frites was regarding him in a very odd way indeed. If he hadn't known him better he might well have been forgiven for thinking that he was poised for some kind of attack. There was something about the way he was standing, back legs splayed slightly apart, body tensed and drawn back, arched like a tightly coiled spring awaiting the moment of release. He dismissed the thought instantly as being unworthy between friends. If the truth be known Pommes Frites was probably doing nothing more than limbering up, practising one of his well known leaps in case he had need of it.

Bending over, he reached across the bath for the cord switch which operated the wall heater. As he did so the unbelievable happened. Unable to contain himself a moment longer, Pommes Frites gave a warning growl and then launched himself forward, sinking his teeth as he did so into the nearest available object. And as he dug his feet in and tugged, the sound of growls and tearing cloth combined with a roar of surprise and indignation in a way which made their previous efforts at a duet pale into insignificance, drowning as it did so the splash of something heavy landing in the water, the flash that accompanied it, the hiss of escaping steam which rose a split second afterwards, and the sound of running feet as someone entered the room.

10

A MOMENT OF TRUTH

'What's up? Is anything the matter?' Tante Louise nearly tripped over Pommes Frites as she entered the bathroom. 'I was on my way back from the *boulangerie* when I heard Pommes Frites howling. Then there were a lot of other sounds as if someone was in pain . . .'

She broke off and put a hand to her mouth. '*Mon Dieu!* It is not possible.'

Monsieur Pamplemousse clambered unsteadily to his feet and then froze as he followed the direction of her gaze. The electric fire lying in the bottom of the bath looked unbelievably sordid and sinister.

His blood ran cold. He might still have been touching the tap, or testing the temperature of the water, or even . . . even operating the cord switch while sitting in the bath as he had done the night of his mishap in the Sanisette. It was no wonder that Pommes Frites had been so agitated. He must have been instinctively aware that something was wrong without actually knowing what it was.

'How could it have happened? Did you slip?'

Monsieur Pamplemousse looked up at the wall above the bath. 'I think it was helped on its way.' The screws had been removed and the wooden plugs in which they'd been embedded prized out slightly so that the fire had rested on their protruding ends, needing only the slightest of tugs to release it. Nails holding cable clips to the ceiling had been carefully removed, the cable itself remaining in place through years of over-painting.

'Armand again?'

He nodded. 'I'm afraid so.'

'He must have been crazy.'

He wondered if the thought made her feel better or worse. It certainly removed from his own mind once and for all any faint feeling of remorse it might have harboured about whether or not he could have acted more quickly the day of the storm.

'Crazy and desperate. Perhaps he mistook me for someone else.' It occurred to him as he spoke that perhaps the notebook filled with cryptic writing in his own special code had made Armand suspicious. That and the locked case. He must have felt that things were closing in around him.

He reached down and patted Pommes Frites. To his credit Pommes Frites responded not with one of his 'I told you so all along' expressions, for which he could have been forgiven, but instead rubbed himself con-tentedly against his master's leg. There was really no need for words. 'Good boy' would have been totally inadequate. The pat on the head said it all; the trust which had been so nearly shattered wholly restored.

As he removed the piece of pyjama material from Pommes Frites' mouth Madame Terminé came into the room.

'Oh, la, la!' She took in the situation at a glance

but passed no other comment. It might have been an observation on the state of the weather. She would probably be the same on Judgment Day.

'If Monsieur would care to remove his *pantalons* I will repair them for him.'

'For you, Madame, I will happily oblige. It may give you material for a further chapter in your memoirs.'

'That was very naughty of you,' said Tante Louise reprovingly as the outer door slammed shut. 'And also unnecessary. Justine has already apologised.'

'Then she can work out her repentance with a needle and thread,' said Monsieur Pamplemousse. Wrapping a towel round his hand, he took hold of the cable, lifted the fire out of the bath and placed it carefully on a shelf away from everything else. The fuse would have blown, but from the look of the wiring there was no sense in taking unnecessary risks.

'And now,' he continued, 'I am about to remove the rest of my clothing so that I can take a bath at long last. I shall be down for breakfast in fifteen minutes.'

As the door closed for the second time he pulled the plug and began helping the dusty water on its way with his hand. Depressingly, when he refilled the bath the temperature of the water started to go up and then rapidly went down again. He was washed and dressed and seated in the dining-room in ten minutes flat.

The croissants were delicious. Warm and light and buttery to the taste. He was halfway through his third when Tante Louise entered carrying a pot of coffee in one hand and his notebook in the other. His spirits rose. Suddenly, without bothering to look out of the window, he knew the sun would be shining.

197

'The maintenance men found it in the Sanisette and brought it to me. It has your name inside. There were other things too – mostly to do with drugs.' The Director's aunt shivered. 'He must have been taking them even as he watched the hotel through that dreadful periscope.'

Monsieur Pamplemousse took the notebook and thumbed through it quickly to make sure it was intact. The writing danced about like the moving images in an old-fashioned flick-a-book.

Tante Louise looked at him curiously. 'The book you are writing . . . food plays a big part? I couldn't help noticing when they gave it to me.'

Monsieur Pamplemousse gave a start. He had forgotten about his book. '*Oui, c'est ça,*' he answered non-committally. 'You could say that.'

Translated into a readable form, the notebook was almost publishable as it stood. One day he might even try. He knew he wouldn't, of course – it would be breaking faith with *Le Guide* – but it was nice to have unfulfilled dreams.

'It is nearly finished?'

'The present chapter is. There are still a few loose ends to tie up. I may do that on the way back to Paris.' Calling in on Bernard would be one such end. He couldn't wait to break the news. Given all the evidence at his disposal Bernard should be home and dry. With luck he wouldn't even have to stand trial.

'It will seem strange without you. So much has happened I can hardly believe you have been here less than a week. I think I may close down for a while. The season is over . . .'

He stared at her. 'Close down? But you can't. Mark my words, your season is only just beginning. The name of the Hôtel du Paradis has been in all the *journaux*. Its precise location has been shown on every television screen in France. People will start to come out of sheer curiosity. They will bring their cameras and they will take photographs of the square and of the cellar steps where only two days ago I was ravaged. They will take pictures of the Sanisette. Then they will almost certainly wish to stay here in the hotel.

'It will be like St. Marc in Brittany, where Monsieur Hulot took his famous holiday. Thirty years later people still go there and ask if they can sleep in "his" room. Human beings get a vicarious pleasure out of reliving these things. You will have to engage a chef, of course. You cannot carry on as you are.'

'A chef! I cannot afford one.'

'Nonsense! You are sitting on a fortune.'

'But that is no longer so. If what you say is true it has been washed away in the storm. By now it will be well on its way to the sea. Anyway,' Tante Louise pulled a face. 'I could not have made money out of Grand-mère's *tisane*. It would not have been right.'

Monsieur Pamplemousse wetted his finger and dabbed at some lumps of crystallised sugar that had fallen from his brioche. 'I am not talking of the *tisane*. I am talking of the wine you showed me. A lot of it is pre-Phylloxera – bottled before the turn of the century. I know someone who would help and advise. Someone you could trust. He owes me a favour.'

That would be another matter to talk over with Bernard. Given his contacts in the trade he was sure to help.

'If you auction only half of it in London or New York it will pay for a new kitchen. You can have the hotel rewired, instal new plumbing and heating. Paint the outside.'

He licked his finger again and wiped it dry with the serviette. 'Grandpa would not be pleased if his precious wine was left so long it became undrinkable. That would be a tragedy – to see such an expenditure of love and care and time turn to vinegar. It would have him turning in his grave.' He nearly said turning in his crocodile, but thought better of it.

'Besides,' he brushed some crumbs from his jacket as he rose from the table, 'as far as a chef is concerned, I know of someone who would be eminently suitable. She cooks like a dream and it is time she branched out. You will be doing many people a favour if you take her on. You will have to watch her puddings from Yorkshire – they will not go well with the *noisettes de porc aux pruneaux*, but I think I can safely say that I have only to give the word and she will be here. Who knows? One day you may have a star in Michelin, a toque in Gault Millau, or even a Stock Pot in *Le Guide!*'

He was whistling as he made his way back up the stairs. It was always pleasant when things worked out for the best. He wanted to telephone the Director straight away to tell him the good news – put in some groundwork before annual increment time, but prudence dictated otherwise. He'd managed to escape too many questions so far.

His pyjama trousers were neatly laid out on the bed, folded for packing this time, not for sleep. On top of them was a small square parcel wrapped in brown paper and tied with string. He decided to open it later. Now that he had set the wheels in motion all he wanted was to get away as quickly as possible.

The Director's aunt was waiting for him behind the desk in the entrance hall as he came down the stairs with Pommes Frites. She had another parcel. This time it was unmistakably bottle shaped.

'It is for you. A present from Grandpa.'

He hardly knew what to say. 'You are very kind. I shall think of you when I drink it.'

'I hope you will come back soon.'

'That would be nice.' Even as he uttered the words he knew he wouldn't be back for some while. One day, perhaps. The integrity of *Le Guide* had to be preserved at all costs. It wouldn't do for Elsie to recognise him. Next time it would be someone else. Perhaps Bernard would pay a return visit.

Goodbyes said, the luggage packed into the boot, he wandered back into the square. There was time for some quick shopping. Pommes Frites' supply of vaseline was running low.

On an impulse, as they entered the *pharmacie*, he took a bubble-packed razor set from a rack just inside the door. 'I would like this gift-wrapped, *s'il vous plaît*,' he announced grandly.

He felt the assistant's eyes following him as they left the shop. By the time they reached the lane at the side of the *boulangerie* she was standing in the shop doorway.

The *boulanger* eyed Monsieur Pamplemousse and

201

Pommes Frites nervously as they appeared at the entrance to his *laboratoire*.

'Pardon, Monsieur.' He pointed to a notice on the door. '*Chiens* are *interdits*.'

Monsieur Pamplemousse inclined his head in acknowledgment. 'We are not stopping.'

He looked around the room. It was always interesting to enter other people's worlds. The doors to the huge ovens at the back were open; the long wooden paddles used for sliding the loaves around so that they would bake evenly were clipped to a rack on a white-tiled wall nearby, their work done for the day. Near the doorway, where the temperature would be coolest, was the croissant area – an enormous slab of shining marble. The floor below was as spotless as the *officine* in the *pharmacie* he'd just left. He could see that Pommes Frites would not be popular if he left a trail of paw prints all over it.

'This is for you. A small parting gift.' He held out the parcel. 'If you take my advice you will use it. If you do not then I can only say that the softness of your brain is equalled only by the hardness of the crust on certain of your *baguettes* and you do not deserve the good fortune that awaits you on your very doorstep.'

Without waiting for a reply he turned and led the way back to the car park behind the hotel. It was a very satisfactory end to his visit. One last good deed. Thankfully his tyres were all intact. It would have been a very ignominious rounding off of things if they hadn't been.

As they drove through the square he waved goodbye to Tante Louise once more and then added another wave as he caught a glimpse of Madame Terminé on the balcony outside his room. He wondered how she would get on with Elsie. They would probably be more than a match for each other. It would be interesting to follow the progress from afar. He narrowly missed hitting a car coming the other way. White faces peered out at him. It was the first of the sightseers. He'd been right.

In the fields outside the village the circus was packing up to leave. He was just in time to miss the first of the huge pantechnicon lorries revving noisily as it tried to haul its load of trailers through the muddied entrance.

It was a pity in a way they were leaving. He felt a little *en fête* himself. It was a long time since he'd done so many good deeds at one and the same time. Tante Louise, the *boulanger* – if he had the nous to follow his advice, the Director, the Director's wife, Elsie, Bernard . . . it was an impressive list. He wouldn't have minded celebrating it with a ride on the merry-go-round. It was years since he'd been on one. Pommes Frites could have had a go on the helter-skelter.

Through a gap in the trees he caught a glimpse of the Lie. It looked dangerously high, but already Sunday-morning fishermen were out looking for eels and perch and pike, perhaps even a trout or two. In the Loire itself the season would end on the last Monday in September, but here it would go on until April. No doubt they had their minds on the evening *matelote* – the thick stew made with wine, mushrooms and cream, and laced with croutons. A sprinkling of waders and terns were watching hopefully from a safe distance.

He passed a notice saying BAL TRAP, then a small forest of acacia. At the side of the road a table had been set up, laden with jars of honey. Vineyards appeared with their inevitable *Dégustation* signs, and between them more fields given over to *asperges*, followed by a wood which seemed to be alive with men carrying guns.

A little further on he stopped in a lay-by near a road junction where a D road crossed the river.

It was the kind of day for a detour. He might even head towards Vendôme on his way to Bernard and continue his researches driving through the countryside where Ronsard had lived amongst the orchards and vineyards, writing love poems which likened the pale skin of his amour with cream cheese, before he eventually died of gout. As he reached past Pommes Frites for the maps he suddenly remembered the parcels on the back seat.

The bottle of wine was beyond his wildest dreams. It was the one he'd taken from the rack in the inner cellar. He resolved to drive more slowly for the rest of the journey. He laid it gently and carefully on the back seat, wondering as he did so who he would share it with. Bernard? It would need to rest for a while after its journey. Perhaps he would save it for a return visit by the Director and his wife; a celebration. Such wine was not meant to be drunk alone. He could hardly believe his good fortune.

The second parcel felt hard and angular. It was a tin. As he tore open the paper he recognised it was the one Tante Louise had kept the *tisane* in. Pommes Frites gave a loud sniff as he prized the lid open, then licked his lips. He remembered both the smell and the taste very well indeed. He had drunk very deeply of both that first night in his master's room when it had been left temptingly on the floor, right under his nose.

Monsieur Pamplemousse held the tin up and savoured the almost overpowering aroma. He would always have good cause to remember it too.

He wondered who had left it for him – Tante Louise or Madame Terminé? If it was the latter, perhaps she was hoping for a return visit. *Tisane* in bed with Madame Terminé; it was quite a thought!

Climbing out of the car, he crossed to the bridge and leant on the parapet while he considered the matter. As a parting gift it must be unique; all that was left in the world. The temptations it offered were enormous. He would lose more than his shoe if he gave some to the Director's wife. One whiff and Elsie would burn her puddings.

He held the tin up to his nose again and wondered about Armand. If Armand had discovered the secret earlier he would still be alive. Perhaps he'd had dreams of escaping from it all. It couldn't have been pleasant spending a lifetime being swept under the carpet; spoken of but rarely spoken to. It was a moment of truth. Perhaps he was holding in his hand the answer to a lot of people's dreams of escape. Deep down, he knew he wasn't doing any such thing – he was simply holding on to a tinful of illusions.

On the other side of the bridge Pommes Frites put his paws on the parapet and peered down at the water as a dark brown patch floated into view, spreading out all the time and growing paler at the edges as it was carried downstream by the strong current. He looked up as Monsieur Pamplemousse joined him. There was no accounting for the way his master behaved at times.

There was a series of plops as first one fish, then another, then a third, rose to the unaccustomed bait.

As they got back into the car Monsieur Pamplemousse wondered if the fishermen further downstream would benefit in the fullness of time. Perhaps there would be a sudden and unaccountable rise in the piscatorial birthrate. He might even read about it in the *journaux*. There would be articles. Expert opinions would be called on, but they would never guess the real truth.

Two kilometres further on they met a road block. There was a caravan – a Mobile Headquarters – at the side of the road. Two gendarmes with walkie-talkies and rifles were standing outside the door chatting. A third gendarme stepped out into the road as he pulled in. He touched his cap as Monsieur Pamplemousse opened the window.

'Pardon, Monsieur. We are stopping all traffic. There is an escaped lion in the area.'

'An escaped lion?' Monsieur Pamplemousse tried to avoid catching Pommes Frites' eye, but he needn't have worried. Pommes Frites was pointedly watching a butterfly hovering over the bonnet.

'Has it come from the circus?' he asked.

'They deny all knowledge. They say they have only one lion and he is too old to bother with escaping.' The gendarme gave a shrug. 'It won't get very far, but it is said to be enormous. There have been two sightings reported already this morning. If Monsieur was thinking of a picnic . . .'

Monsieur Pamplemousse looked at his watch. 'I was heading for Mortagne-au-Perche, but I am late. I may stop *en route* for a meal.'

The gendarme's face brightened. 'In that case, Monsieur, there is somewhere I can recommend.' He reached into his pocket and took out a card. 'It belongs to a cousin of mine . . . he and his wife are just starting up. Be sure to accompany whatever you choose with the *Beignets de Pommes de Terre*. They are a speciality. Made with potatoes and eggs and gruyère cheese – grated, of course.'

'And onions and butter?' Monsieur Pamplemousse felt his mouth begin to water. There was a stirring beside him as Pommes Frites pricked up his ears.

'*Oui*, Monsieur.' The gendarme seemed surprised at the question. 'With a pinch of nutmeg and salt and pepper.' He wrote on the back of the card and then handed it through the window. '*Voilà!* Be sure and show this to them. They will look after you.'

'*Merci*.'

The gendarme bent down and peered into the car. 'That is a fine *chien* you have, Monsieur.'

'Very.'

'*C'est magnifique*.'

'*Oui*.'

'*Un chien par excellence*.'

'*Par excellence*.' Monsieur Pamplemousse revved the engine.

'I am glad to see he is wearing his *ceinture de sécurité*.' The gendarme touched his cap – twice. '*Bon appétit*, Monsieur. And watch out for the lion.'

'*Au revoir*.' Monsieur Pamplemousse let in the clutch. As they moved off he glanced across at Pommes Frites, but he appeared to be studying the landscape on the far side of the road. There were times when Pommes Frites closed his mind to the outside world. It would be interesting to know what went on at such moments. He decided to put it to the test.

'*Une promenade?*'

There was no reaction.

'*Dormir?*

'*Déjeuner?*'

Patience received its due reward. Pommes Frites turned and delivered a withering look. There were, after all, certain priorities in life. Listening to the conversation with the gendarme he'd caught the odd familiar word or two; enough to get the general picture. He'd also noticed his master reach instinctively for that part of his right trouser leg where he kept his notebook hidden; a sure sign that he meant business. There was no need to go on about it.

Suitably abashed, Monsieur Pamplemousse put his foot hard down on the accelerator. He, too, had got the general picture, and really, there was nothing more to be said.

Monsieur Pamplemousse on the Spot

CONTENTS

'OPERATION SOUFFLÉ'

'Pardon, *Monsieur.*'

Monsieur Pamplemousse jumped as a figure in evening dress suddenly materialised at his right elbow. Hastily sliding a large paperback edition of the collected works of Sir Arthur Conan Doyle beneath the folds of a snow-white tablecloth draped over his lap, he pulled himself together and in a split second made the mental leap from the austerity of number 221B Baker Street, London, Angleterre, to the unquestionably less than harsh reality of his opulent surroundings in the dining-room of Les Cinq Parfaits, Haute Savoie, France.

Inclining his head to acknowledge but not necessarily welcome the waiter's presence, he diverted his attention with some reluctance from the adventures of Sherlock Holmes to focus on a single cream-coloured card listing the various delights of the *menu gastronomique*. He was all too aware as he scanned the menu that his every movement was being followed by a third pair of eyes on the other side of a large picture-window to his right and he shifted his chair in an anti-clockwise direction to avoid their unblinking gaze.

Almost immediately, following a barely perceptible signal from the maître d'hôtel, a bevy of under-waiters descended on his table, rearranged the cutlery symmetrically in front of him, rotated the plate so that the Parfait motif was in line, adjusted the vase of flowers slightly, and then drew a dark-green velvet curtain a few inches to its left, blotting out as they did so part of Lac Léman, the misty foothills of the mountains beyond, and an unseemly intruder in the foreground.

Almost as quickly as it had arrived the entourage again melted discreetly into the background, but not before a large, wet, freshly vaselined nose reappeared on the other side of the window and pressed itself firmly against a fresh area of glass.

Monsieur Pamplemousse gave a sigh. Pommes Frites was being more than a little difficult that evening. He shuddered to think what the outside of the window would be like when it caught the rays of the morning sun.

'Pardon, *Monsieur*.' The maître d'hôtel leaned across. 'May I point out a slight change in the menu? The *Soufflé Surprise* is off.'

'The *Soufflé Surprise* is off?' Monsieur Pamplemousse repeated the words slowly, as if he could hardly believe his ears. 'But that is not possible.'

To say that he had ploughed his way through six or seven previous courses with but one end in view, that of tasting the creation for which, above all, Les Cinq Parfaits was famous, would have been a gross misstatement of the facts; an unforgivable calumny. Every course had been sheer perfection; not just a plateau, but one of a series of individual peaks, each a thing of beauty in its own right, offering both satisfaction and a tantalising foretaste of other delights to come. If he stopped right where he was he could hardly complain. It had been a memorable meal. All the same, to take the mountaineering analogy still further, there was only one Everest. To have travelled so far and yet not to have scaled the highest point of all, that which was embodied in the *Soufflé Surprise*, would be a great disappointment.

He was tempted to ask why, if it was off, was he being shown the menu where the two words *Soufflé* and *Surprise* were printed very clearly between *fromage* and *café*. It was rubbing salt into the wound.

He glanced around the crowded restaurant. 'There will be many sorrowful faces in Les Cinq Parfaits tonight.'

'*Oui, Monsieur*.' The waiter clearly shared his unhappiness. 'What have you instead?'

Looking, if possible, even more ill at ease, the waiter waved towards a large trolley heading in their direction.

8

'We have our collection of home-made sorbets. *Monsieur* may have a *panaché* – a selection if he so wishes.'

'But I have already eaten a sorbet,' said Monsieur Pamplemousse testily. 'I had one between the *Omble* and the *Quenelles de veau.*'

And very nice it had been too – a *Granité au vin de Saint Emilion*, made with something rather better than a *vin ordinaire* if he was any judge, a *Grand Cru Classé* to which orange and lemon had been added, the whole garnished with a fresh, white peach inlaid with mint leaves. A palate-cleanser of the very first order. He had awarded it full marks on the pad concealed beneath a fold in his right trouser leg.

'*Fruits de saison?* We have wild *framboises* . . . gathered on the mountainside just before nightfall by girls from the village. They are still warm from their aprons . . .'

'*Fruits de saison?*' Without raising his voice Monsieur Pamplemousse managed to imbue the words with exactly the right amount of scorn.

'A *crème caramel, Monsieur?*' There was the barest hint of desperation in the waiter's voice. 'Made with eggs from our own chickens, fed from the day they were born on nothing but . . .'

'A *crème caramel?*' Aware that he was beginning to sound like an ageing actor milking every line which came his way, Monsieur Pamplemousse decided to try another tack. 'Have you nothing which includes the word *pâtisserie?*'

Even as he posed the question he knew what the answer would be. It explained the absence of many of the customary tit-bits earlier in the meal. An absence which he had noted with a certain amount of relief at the time, fearing the outcome of any battle involving mind over matter.

The waiter leaned over his table in order to remove an imaginary bread crumb. 'I regret, *Monsieur*, the *pâtisserie* is not of a standard this evening that we in Les Cinq Parfaits would feel able to serve to our customers.' He lowered his voice still further. 'As for the *Soufflé Surprise* . . . pouf!' A low whistling sound somehow reminiscent of a hot-air balloon collapsing ignominiously escaped his lips. He looked for a moment as if he were about to say something else and then decided against it, aware that he might already have spoken out of turn and betrayed a position of trust.

Monsieur Pamplemousse decided not to press the man any further. Ordering the *framboises* he sat back in order to consider the matter. Clearly all was not well in the kitchens of Les Cinq Parfaits, and if all was not well then it put him in something of a quandary.

His presence there was only semi-official, a kind of treat on the part of his employers, the publishers of *Le Guide*. It had been arranged by a grateful Director following the success of a mission on his behalf in the Loire valley. Nevertheless, implicit in the visit was an appraisal of the restaurant, an extra opinion concerning a matter which had been exercising the minds of his superiors for some considerable time. Work was never far away when food was on the table.

Just as *Le Guide* was by general consent the doyen of the French gastronomic guides, so Les Cinq Parfaits was considered the greatest of all French restaurants, which in most people's eyes meant the best in all the world.

Set like a jewel in the hills east of Evian and overlooking the lake, its walls were lined with photographs of the high and mighty, the rich and famous, who in their time had made the pilgrimage to its ever open doors. Presidents came and went, royalty rose and fell, but Les Cinq Parfaits seemed set to remain where it was for ever.

In an area devoted to those whose waistlines were sadly in need of reduction, or were beyond redemption, where consequently cuisine was, generally speaking, *basse* rather than *haute*, Les Cinq Parfaits had proved the exception to the rule and had thrived.

For many years possessor of three stars in Michelin, maximum toques in Gault Millau, and one of less than a dozen restaurants in France to enjoy the supreme accolade of three Stock Pots in *Le Guide*, it was an open secret that it was only a matter of time before one of the three rival guides broke ranks and awarded Les Cinq Parfaits an extra distinction of some kind.

Therein lay the rub. Such a break with tradition, were it to backfire, would lay whoever was responsible open to all manner of criticism. On the other hand, to delay, to be second, would be to risk the accusation of being a follower rather than a leader. It was a knotty problem and no mistake.

If three Stock Pots represented perfection, then a fourth would need to stand for something even more absolute. On the showing that evening, one of the cinq Parfaits, either Monsieur Albert, the father, or one of his four sons, Alain, Edouard, Gilbert or Jean-Claude, was failing to live up to the family name.

Monsieur Pamplemousse glanced around the room. Like all restaurants of its class, staff seemed to outnumber the diners. His notes and reference cards upstairs would give him the exact answer, but he judged the capacity to be about sixty *couverts*. All the tables were full, many of them would have been booked weeks if not months ahead; the clientèle was international. Waiters switched from speaking French to German to English and back again with practised ease.

The ceremony of the lifting of the silver salvers was in full swing. No dish arrived in the dining-room uncovered. No matter how many guests were seated round a table, for the waiter to ask who had ordered what was regarded as a cardinal sin, and the lifting of all the covers in unison was a theatrical gesture which never failed to draw the gastronomical equivalent of a round of applause.

At the next table a waiter who had just finished translating the entire menu into perfect German was now performing the same feat in English for another family. From the snatches of conversation he'd overheard when they arrived he gathered the daughter was at a local finishing school. Clearly her parents were not getting value for money.

Beyond them, at a smaller table, a young girl was sitting alone. From her blonde hair and the colour of her skin, and the fact that she seemed to be on nodding terms with the family at the next table, he guessed she must be English too. Probably at the same finishing school as their

11

daughter. She couldn't have been more than eighteen or nineteen.

He wondered what she was doing there. She seemed oddly out of place and ill at ease, rather as if she was waiting for someone who she knew was going to let her down. Irrationally he found himself wanting to go across and ask if he could help in any way, but he resisted for fear his action might be misinterpreted, as it certainly would be by the other diners, if not by the girl herself. People always thought the worst. Once or twice she looked up quickly and caught him watching her, then just as quickly she looked down again, colouring in a becoming manner.

Holmes would have known all about her by now. He would have built up a complete picture in his mind, picking up some detail to do with the way she wore her belt or the cut and style of her dress.

'Borrowed for the evening, my dear Watson. And in a hurry too. You can tell by the way it doesn't quite match her nail-varnish.'

With difficulty he disengaged himself from the scene in order to return to his book. Reading it was really a labour of love; a holiday task he had set himself – a chance to improve his English while at the same time meeting up again with one of his favourite characters.

The stories were as unlike his own experiences in the Paris Sûreté as it was possible to imagine, and yet there was a certain fascination about them that he found irresistible. The particular story he was reading – *The Hound of the Baskervilles* – was a case in point. He had barely reached the second page when Holmes, from a brief examination of a man's walking-stick, had deduced that the owner was a country doctor who had trained at a large London hospital, left when he was little more than a senior student, was still under thirty years of age, amiable, absent-minded, and the possessor of a favourite dog, larger than a terrier and smaller than a mastiff.

Rereading the passage reminded Monsieur Pamplemousse of Pommes Frites. He looked round, but the face was no longer pressed against the window. It didn't need the intellectual powers of a Sherlock Holmes to tell him that his own particular Watson had gone off in a huff, and even though Pommes Frites' exclusion from the meal had not been of his choosing he felt a sudden pricking of his conscience.

The discovery when they arrived at Les Cinq Parfaits that dogs were *interdits* had been a bitter disappointment. The ban had been imposed after a visiting captain of industry had been set upon one evening by a Dobermann Pinscher belonging to a disgruntled shareholder. It was understandable up to a point, but it was like forbidding visitors to the Eiffel Tower because someone had once been caught trying to place a bomb underneath it; hard to accept and impossible to explain to a creature whose powers of reasoning didn't follow such convoluted paths.

Not that the four-legged visitors to Les Cinq Parfaits did badly for themselves. The kennel area behind the main building was a model of its kind, the service was impeccable, with staffing levels scarcely less than in the restaurant itself. The straw was changed twice daily and there was a choice of food which was served from china plates bearing the hotel crest. Had there been paw-operated bell-pushes Monsieur Pamplemousse wouldn't have been surprised. At fifty francs a day, full pension, *service compris*, it was incredibly good value.

All the same, it wasn't like sharing a table, and in the event Pommes Frites had taken the whole thing rather badly, just as Monsieur Pamplemousse had feared.

Pommes Frites had a simplistic approach to life. Black, to him, was black. White was white. The shortest distance between two points was a straight line, and restaurants were for eating in, regardless of race, colour or breed. Rules of entry which showed any form of discrimination were beyond his comprehension.

Equally, Monsieur Pamplemousse had to admit that he missed Pommes Frites' company. Not just the occasional warmth of a head resting on his shoe, or the nuzzling up of a body against his leg, but also his views on the food, often conveyed by the raising of an eyebrow or a discreet wag of his tail.

Pommes Frites had a bloodhound's sensitivity to smells

13

and to taste, a sensitivity sharpened by his early training with the Paris police and honed finer still during travels with his master over the length and breadth of France. Had they but known it, there were many restaurants who owed their placing in *Le Guide* to Pommes Frites' taste-buds, and Monsieur Pamplemousse would have given a great deal to have noted down his reaction to the meal he had just eaten.

He gazed out of the window at the lights of Lausanne, twinkling on the Swiss side of the lake. Somewhere in-between a steamer slowly made its way back to Geneva. He looked at his watch. It was still barely ten o'clock. He had dined early. There would be time for a stroll before retiring to bed. Perhaps he could take Pommes Frites for an extra long walk that night to help make up for things. There were some emergency biscuits in the boot of the car. When they got back he would open the packet as a special treat.

He glanced up again as a waiter came towards him carrying a silver tray bearing not, as he might have expected, a dish containing a mound of wild raspberries, but a plate on which reposed a single light-blue envelope. He frowned, recognising the colour of the hotel stationery. Who could possibly be sending him a note?

As the waiter disappeared again he picked up a knife and slit open the envelope, aware that the party at the next table was watching him curiously. Inside there was a sheet of white telex paper and underneath a duplicate in pink. The message was short and to the point; a single word in fact. The word was ESTRAGON.

To say that Monsieur Pamplemousse blanched visibly as he digested it would have been to cast aspersions both on his ability to conceal his true feelings and on the subdued and subtle lighting conceived by the architect responsible for the interior design of the restaurant. Bearing in mind the sometimes astronomical size of the bills, blanching of any kind was filtered out by rays which purposely emanated from the warmer end of the spectrum.

Nevertheless, he felt a quickening of his pulse as he carefully refolded the message and slipped it between the pages of his book to mark where he had left off. Any further reading was out of the question. Had he been Sherlock Holmes he would probably have reached for his violin in the hope of applying the panacea of music to soothe his racing thoughts. Instead, Monsieur Pamplemousse did the next best thing; he picked up a spoon and fork. More waiters were heading in his direction. It would be a pity to let the efforts of all those village girls with their bulging aprons go to waste.

The *framboises* were beyond reproach. He added a little more cream.

The word ESTRAGON meant only one thing. There must be an emergency of some kind.

It couldn't be anything personal. He'd telephoned Doucette just before dinner. She'd been in the middle of her favourite serial and he'd had to do battle against background music from the television. In any case, if it was something personal surely the telephone would have sufficed.

In all his time with *Le Guide* the use of the emergency codeword had been minimal. The last occasion he could recall had been all of two years ago when Truffert from Normandy had been caught reading a copy of *L'Escargot*, *Le Guide*'s staff magazine, while reporting on a restaurant in Nice. There had been hell to pay. Anonymity was a sacred rule, never to be broken. Heads had rolled.

But then its use had been in reverse; a call to Headquarters from someone in the field. He couldn't recall a time when the word had gone out from Headquarters itself. He wondered if it was a general alarm. Perhaps all over France colleagues were waiting for their *café* as he was and wondering.

The first cup came and went. Declining a second, he rose and made his way towards the door. As he did so he caught the eye of the blonde girl. She blushed and looked down at her plate as if conscious that he'd singled her out for attention.

On his way out he passed two more tables whose occupants were having to make a fresh decision over the last course, just as he had done. They didn't look best pleased either. The maître d'hôtel probably wouldn't thank him if he paused and recommended the *framboises* – even though they were probably the best he'd ever tasted. They would need all their supplies that evening. To have one dish off was bad enough. To run out of a second would be little short of disaster.

In the foyer he looked for a public telephone booth. It wouldn't do to use the telephone in his room and risk being overheard – not until he knew what it was all about. Despite the fact that it was an automatic dial-out system, he had an old-fashioned mistrust of hotel telephones.

He emptied his change on to a shelf, fed some coins into the machine and dialled his office number. It was answered on the first ring.

'Ah, Monsieur Pamplemousse.' It was a voice he didn't recognise. Normally he didn't have much contact with the night shift. '*Monsieur le Directeur* is expecting you. *Un moment.*'

The Director was even quicker off the mark than the switchboard girl. He must have been sitting with his hand permanently on the receiver.

'Pamplemousse? Are you all right? What kept you?'

'I'm afraid the *café* was a little slow in arriving, *Monsieur.*'

'*Café!* There was a noise like a minor explosion at the other end. 'You stopped for *café?*'

'*Oui, Monsieur le Directeur.*' Monsieur Pamplemousse decided he must proceed with care. The tone was not friendly. 'In view of the gravity of your message I felt it wise not to arouse suspicions by leaving my table with too great a haste.'

'Ah!' The response was a mixture of emotions, of incredulity and suspicion giving way, albeit with a certain amount of reluctance, to grudging respect. 'Good thinking, Pamplemousse. Good thinking.'

Monsieur Pamplemousse breathed a sigh of relief. It was often a case of thinking on one's feet with the Director. Like a boxer, you needed constantly to anticipate.

'How was your meal?' From the tone of the other's voice it was clear he regarded the answer as a foregone conclusion. Not for the first time Monsieur Pamplemousse found himself marvelling at the efficiency of *Le Guide*. He wondered how the news from Les Cinq Parfaits had got through so quickly. It was almost uncanny at times. He had a mental picture of the Operations Room; the illuminated wall-map, the large table in the centre of the room with its little flags to represent the Inspectors. The girls with their long sticks moving them around. The shaded lights. The staff talking in hushed voices as the reports came in. However, tonight was no normal night.

'It left a lot to be desired, *Monsieur*. Particularly towards the end.'

'This is a disaster, Aristide. A disaster of the first magnitude.'

'It was not good news, *Monsieur*,' Monsieur Pamplemousse replied carefully, picking his way through the minefield of the Director's mind. 'It was not good news at all. As you can imagine, I had been looking forward to it. Perhaps,' he tried to strike a cheerful note, 'perhaps it only goes to show that nothing in this world can ever be wholly perfect.' Encouraged by the silence at the other end, Monsieur Pamplemousse began to enlarge on this theme. The Director was in an overwrought state. He had probably been working too hard. He needed soothing. 'One *soufflé* doesn't make a summer, *Monsieur*. There will be others.'

There was a long pause. 'Have you been drinking, Pamplemousse?'

'Drinking, *Monsieur*? I had an apéritif before the meal – a Kir – followed by a glass or two of Sancerre with the *Omble*, then a modest Côte Rôtie, a glass of Beaumes-de-Venise with the sweet. I forewent a liqueur . . .'

'Do you know why I sent you a telex?'

'Because of the *Soufflé Surprise, Monsieur*?'

'No, Pamplemousse.' The voice at the other end reminded him suddenly of a dog barking. 'It was *not* because of the *Soufflé Surprise*.' There was another pause, a longer one this time. 'And then again, yes, you are quite right. It *was* because of the *Soufflé Surprise*.'

Monsieur Pamplemousse decided to stay silent. Clearly

he had, albeit unwittingly, scored some kind of point. Bonus points in fact. Throwing caution to the wind he edged the door to the telephone booth open a little with his foot. The heat inside was adding to the confusion in his mind. The Director's voice when he spoke again was tinged with a new respect.

'Your time with the Sûreté was not wasted, Aristide.'

'*Merci, Monsieur*. I like to think not.'

'You have a knack of going straight to the heart of the problem. Clearing a pathway through the jungle. It is indeed fortunate that we chose to send you to Les Cinq Parfaits at this moment in time. Pamplemousse . . .' The Director paused and Monsieur Pamplemousse instinctively braced himself for the next words. 'Pamplemousse, if I were to ask you for your definition of the words "liquid gold", what would it be?'

Feeling himself on safe ground at long last, Monsieur Pamplemousse didn't hesitate. 'It would be a Sauternes, *Monsieur*. A Château d'Yquem. Probably the '45. I am told that the '28 and the '37, although still wonderful, are now sadly past their best. In '45 there was an early harvest . . .'

'Aristide.' There was a hint of pleading in the Director's voice, as if he was trying to convey some kind of message. 'Aristide, I have to tell you that this is a very serious matter. Think again.'

Monsieur Pamplemousse considered the matter for a moment. He wondered if the Director was trying to catch him out. Perhaps he was thinking of a German Eiswein – the capital made out of what in other circumstances, other areas, would have been a disaster; wine made from juice which had been squeezed from grapes frozen on the vine. That could be called liquid gold indeed. He racked his brains as he tried to think of famous years when it had happened.

'Am I getting warm, *Monsieur*?'

'No, Pamplemousse.' There was an audible sigh from the other end. 'You are not getting warm. You are cold. But your temperature at this moment is nothing compared to what it will be if this problem remains unsolved. Then you will be very cold indeed. We shall *all* be very cold.'

'I have heard that the owner of Château d'Yquem holds the '67 in high regard . . .'

'Pamplemousse! Will you please stop talking about wine. It has nothing to do with wine.' Monsieur Pamplemousse fell silent as the Director's voice cut across his musings. He recognised a warning note and like a professional gambler studying the tables he decided to watch play for a while so that he could get the feel of how the numbers were running before making his next move. A moment later the wisdom of his decision was confirmed. The Director was off on another tangent.

'Do you remember the winter of '47, Pamplemousse?'

'It was a very cold winter, *Monsieur*. I was only nineteen and it was my first time away from home. I was in Paris and I remember shivering in my room and wishing I was back in the Auvergne; at least they had wood to burn there. Food was scarce and there was ice on the inside of my bedroom window.'

'There may well be ice on the inside of your bedroom window again next year, Pamplemousse, if you do not act quickly. Quickly and precisely and with the utmost discretion.

'Listen to me and listen carefully. Walls have ears as you well know, and I do not wish to repeat what I have to say.

'In four days' time you will see a red carpet being laid out on the steps of Les Cinq Parfaits, a red carpet which will stretch all the way from the entrance doors to the helicopter landing-pad at the side of the building. It is a red carpet which in its time has felt the tread of a reigning monarch of Grande-Bretagne and more than one President of the French Republic. Latterly its pile has been compressed almost beyond recovery by the weight of a man of such unbelievable wealth it is impossible to describe; a *grosse légume* who by the blessing of Allah has the good fortune to be sitting on one of the richest deposits of oil in the world.

'Each year he visits Les Cinq Parfaits as a guest of France to carry out what one might call a "shopping expedition" and at the same time indulge himself on all that is best and

19

richest and creamiest on the menu. He is particularly partial to the *Soufflé Surprise*.'

Monsieur Pamplemousse decided to take the bull by the horns.

'With respect, *Monsieur*, I understand perfectly all that you are saying. What you are saying is that this V.I.P. – this *grosse légume* as you call him – being a guest of France, a guest of some importance to our future well-being, has to be cosseted and indulged and made to feel at home while he is here. That I understand, even if I do not necessarily approve. What I do not understand is how it affects my own stay at Les Cinq Parfaits.'

'Because, Aristide, you are *not* at this moment staying at Les Cinq Parfaits. You may think you are, but you are not. To all intents and purposes you are staying at Les Quatre Parfaits. They are a Parfait short. One of the brothers – Jean-Claude – the one who is responsible for the *soufflé* in question, has vanished. Vanished without warning and without trace.'

'That is bad news, *Monsieur*, I agree . . . but surely it is a matter for the local police . . .'

'No, Pamplemousse, it is *not* a matter for the local police. The local police must be kept out of it at all costs. There are wheels, Pamplemousse, and within those wheels there are other wheels, and within those wheels there are yet more wheels. They must all be kept oiled. Without the continuing goodwill of this *grosse légume* – and I must tell you that the speed with which he has acquired his untold wealth has not so far been matched by any show of finer feelings towards his fellow man, rather the reverse – oil will be in very short supply. It may well be diverted towards colder climes than ours.'

'But surely, *Monsieur*, if this . . . this person has to go without his *Soufflé Surprise* it is not the end of the world? Surely some other member of the staff could make one? One of the other brothers? Or if not, someone could be brought in. Girardet, perhaps? He is nearby.'

'Aristide, would you have asked Titian to paint a Monet, or Picasso a Renoir? We are dealing with the creation of a genius.'

Monsieur Pamplemousse fell silent. The Director was right, of course. They were dealing with the product of an artist at the very pinnacle of his profession. Such things were beyond duplication.

'Pamplemousse!' The Director's voice broke into his thoughts again. 'When I say it is a serious matter, I mean it is a *very* serious matter. Who knows where it will end up? Each of the brothers is a specialist in his own right. Today there is no *Soufflé Surprise*. Tomorrow it could be the *Omble*. The day after, the *Ris de veau aux salsifis*. It is a matter that is exercising the minds of certain people at the highest levels of government. In particular of a "certain person" whose name I am not at liberty to divulge for reasons of security . . .'

'A certain person,' ventured Monsieur Pamplemousse, determined not to be outdone, 'not a million miles away.'

'No, Pamplemousse.' The Director appeared to be having trouble with his breathing again. 'A "certain person" who happens to be not two feet away from me at this very moment. Furthermore, he wishes to speak to you.'

Despite himself, Monsieur Pamplemousse stiffened as a second voice came over the phone, clear and incisive; a voice he recognised. A voice which until that moment he had only heard over the radio or on television.

'*Oui, Monsieur.*' His own voice, by comparison, sounded far away.

'*Oui, Monsieur.* I understand, *Monsieur.*

'It is a very great honour, *Monsieur.*

'Without question, *Monsieur.*'

'Now do you understand the gravity of the situation, Pamplemousse?' It was the Director again, revitalised, and showing scarcely less authority than the previous speaker. Now the voice was that of a man with a mission. The voice, Monsieur Pamplemousse couldn't help but reflect, of a man who sensed the whiff of a possible decoration somewhere close at hand. An Order of Merit, perhaps, or membership of the *Légion d'Honneur*?

'From now on you will only communicate directly with this office. The telephone will be manned day and night. The codename of your mission will be "Operation *Soufflé*".

I have already spoken to Monsieur Albert Parfait. He has been instructed to render every assistance. If you require anything else, name it and it shall be yours. Otherwise, I suggest we keep conversation to a minimum.'

'*Oui, Monsieur.*'

'And Aristide . . .' The Director's voice softened for a moment. 'If . . . no, not if – *when* our mission has been brought to a successful conclusion, you may order a bottle of Château d'Yquem . . . the '45. I will see matters right with Madame Grante in Accounts. Your P39s will not be delayed. *Au revoir, et bonne chance.*'

'*Au revoir, Monsieur.*'

Monsieur Pamplemousse replaced the receiver and then stood for a few seconds lost in thought. So much for a quiet week at Les Cinq Parfaits. It was a good thing Doucette hadn't come with him as had at first been suggested. She would not have been pleased.

Gathering up the rest of his change, he pushed open the door, glancing around as he did so. He felt as though he had been inside the booth for hours and yet it could only have been a matter of minutes. Inside the restaurant itself the scene was as he had left it, the soft lights, waiters gliding to and fro, a steady hum of conversation. If only they knew what currents were developing around them.

As he crossed the entrance hall the commissionaire looked at him enquiringly and then stepped to one side. The glass doors slid quietly open for him as he drew near.

Outside the air was cool. It had a crisp feel to it; a hint of autumn. Floodlights concealed in a low wall gave a translucent glow to a bed of late-flowering roses. Nearby a fountain changed from red to green. The swimming pool beyond was deserted. Of Pommes Frites there was still no sign.

He took a silent dog-whistle from an inside pocket, placed it to his lips and blew hard several times. The result was most satisfactory. From somewhere behind the hotel pandemonium broke out; a collection of barks and howls and shrieks that would have brought a smile of satisfaction to the face of any members of the local kennel club. The shrill yelps of Papillons and Pekingese mingled with Beagles and Spaniels and did battle with Pomeranians. He recognised an Airedale or two and what sounded like a Labrador, but conspicuous by its absence was the deeper, full-throated baying of a Bloodhound answering his master's call.

It proved several things at one and the same time. The whistle was working – something he had never been totally sure about ever since he'd first bought it. It also proved that, temporarily at least, Pommes Frites was not in residence. Perhaps his huff was deeper than he'd feared, or else he'd gone off for some other reason best known to himself.

Monsieur Pamplemousse gazed gloomily at the shrubbery, hoping it might suddenly part to reveal his friend and mentor, but parting came there none.

With a heavy heart and a sense of foreboding he replaced the whistle in his pocket and, Watsonless, turned to go back inside the restaurant.

2

STRANGER IN THE NIGHT

Leaning heavily on a stick, Albert Parfait rose to his feet, pushed a large, plain bottle full of colourless liquid across his desk, then hovered uneasily as he tried to regain his balance. Unlike the bottle, which was considerably wider at the bottom that it was at the top, weight distribution was not on his side and for a moment or two it looked as though he might topple over backwards into his chair again.

Monsieur Pamplemousse resisted the temptation to go to his aid. Having been born and brought up in the Auvergne, he recognised the independence of one who also came from a mountainous region.

His restraint didn't go unrewarded. At long last Monsieur Parfait relaxed and waved his stick in a triumphant gesture which managed to embrace at one and the same time his visitor, the shadowy figures beyond the darkened glass separating his office from the kitchen, and the bottle on the table in front of him.

'*Encore!*'

Monsieur Pamplemousse obeyed with alacrity. Ordinarily he was not a great lover of *eau-de-vie*. Given the choice he would have preferred an armagnac, but the opportunity to indulge himself with another *Poire William* was not one to be missed. The somewhat depressing telephone conversation with the Director had left him feeling in need of a 'pick-me-up'.

The bottle emitted a satisfactory gurgle as he topped up his glass; the whole pear within remained tantalisingly encapsulated and unreachable. From the absence of any kind of a label he guessed Les Cinq Parfaits must make it themselves. It would be the job of the youngest recruit to slip the empty bottles over the fruit as it began to form in the late spring. Later in the year, when the pear itself was fully grown, someone else would be entrusted with the task of cutting down pear and bottle and adding the brandy. Later still, others like himself would be lucky enough to enjoy the benefit of their labours. There was a logical progression about the whole operation which appealed to his mathematical side. Truly life was not without its compensations. Just when things were looking black something unexpected happened to restore the balance. He was almost beginning to look forward to whatever fate had in store for him.

Settling back in his chair, he felt the warmth of the liquid rise up from within while he waited for his companion to speak again. The flourish of Monsieur Parfait's stick conveyed a generosity of spirit which would have been hard to resist for fear of giving offence.

He glanced around the room. High up on the wall to his right there was a framed sepia photograph. It was the original of smaller, postcard-sized versions he'd seen on sale in the entrance hall, alongside pots of home-made *confiture* and signed copies of the menu; the almost obligatory current symbols of a successful restaurant.

The photograph was of a small group posing in front of a whitewashed stone building. One of the group, the only man in fact, was in a soldier's uniform and from the way the others were dressed it must have been taken during the First World War, in the days when Les Cinq Parfaits had been known simply as Mère Parfait. Above their heads the words CAFÉ RESTAURANT were just visible, whilst to the right of a smallish window, a doorway with a bead curtain was all that separated the dining-room from the outside world.

It was far removed from the present building, which over the years had been extended, added to and improved beyond all recognition. Bead curtains had been exchanged for glass doors which opened and shut automatically at the slightest movement. Pommes Frites had caused chaos on

25

their arrival by activating the invisible rays of the operating mechanism with his tail which was wagging furiously in anticipation of the pleasures hopefully awaited by his opposite end. The smiles in Reception had become fixed rather than welcoming.

Monsieur Parfait read his thoughts. He pointed with his stick to the sepia photograph; in the centre stood an elderly woman with her arms folded. She bore a striking resemblance to him; there was the same dark, Italian-looking skin, the same nose. She was not one to stand any nonsense.

'That was *Grand-mère*. The one in uniform was my father. He was killed only two months later – I hardly knew him. That was my mother, next to him. And that' – he singled out a small figure between the two – 'that was me. There have been many changes since those days.' He gestured towards the kitchen. 'Not the least in there. In my days it was all smoke and steam, heat and shouting. Now, it is more like a hospital. Everything is stainless steel and polished tiles and air-conditioning. There is no longer any need to shout in order to make yourself heard.'

He pointed once again to the bottle on the table. 'In my day I was like that pear; able to see the world outside, but never free to escape into it. I was a prisoner of circumstances.' He spoke without any hint of rancour, and yet Monsieur Pamplemousse couldn't help but wonder if the accompanying shrug implied regret.

Again his thoughts were read. '*Comme ci, comme ça*. You win one, you lose another. Is it better? It has to be. In the old days chefs were looked down on as the lowest of the low. There were exceptions – Carême, Brillat-Savarin, Escoffier – but they were geniuses, on a par with royalty. Many of their lesser brethren deserved to be treated the way they were.

'Nowadays, chefs are like film stars. People ask for their autographs. We have to be diplomats one moment, businessmen the next. We have to know about turnover and profit margins and cash flows. Cooking is only one of the arts we have to master.

'I tell you, inside every chef these days there is an accountant trying to get out. Our own turnover is over ten million francs a year . . . but this year I have already spent nearly a quarter of a million francs on truffles alone. Fifty thousand has gone on flowers, two hundred thousand on laundry. Think of that! If my old grandmother knew I make more profit out of selling a signed copy of the menu than I do out of selling one of Jean-Claude's *soufflés* she would turn in her grave. As for the helicopter landing-pad – she would see that as a sign of the devil.

'*Alors!* One must move with the times. When I was small I spent all my spare moments in the kitchens. I could not have wished for better training. By the time I was fourteen I had done everything. Then I was lucky enough to be apprenticed to Fernand Point at Vienne. It was he who first inspired me to aim for the heights. For him nothing less would do; nothing was so perfect that it couldn't be improved.

'I married. My wife bore me four sons and we were blissfully happy. Then one day . . . pouf! . . . We were involved in a car crash.' He reached down and tapped his leg. 'I was lucky. I suffered nothing worse than this. But my wife was killed outright. Now I had to bring up the children. I was determined they should not only be as good as me, but better. When the time came for them to go out into the world I made sure that they, too, served their apprenticeship with a master.

'We live in an age of specialisation. If I want to buy a house I go to one lawyer. If I want to make sure when I write a cook book that I am infringing no one else's copyright, I go to another. So I sent my first son, Alain, to Barrier, where he learnt humility. It is not possible to have true greatness without a touch of humility. He is now the *saucier*. Edouard went to Bocuse, who was taught as I was, at the hands of Point. Edouard became the *rôtisseur*. Gilbert was taught by Chapel to use his imagination . . . he is now the *poissonnier* . . .'

'And Jean-Claude?'

'Ah! Jean-Claude!' Monsieur Parfait raised his eyes heavenwards. 'In life there is always an exception. Jean-Claude went his own way. He is the odd one out. He inherited his grandmother's stubbornness and, like his

27

mother, he was born with "the gift". In his own way he is a genius, although I would not dream of telling him so – it would not be good for him. His brothers are exceptionally talented, but they have got where they are by dedication and hard work. With Jean-Claude it has always been there. He is a true "one-off" – a genuine creator. Without him we would have our three stars in Michelin, our toques and our Stock Pots . . . but *with* him . . . who knows? His strength is that when our guests are nearing the end of their meal and feel that nothing can surprise them any more, he surpasses all that has gone before.

'One day he will take over – once he has settled down; he has the necessary qualities.

'In many ways eating at a restaurant like Les Cinq Parfaits has to be like going to a concert or reading a great novel. The opening should catch your attention and make you want to carry on. The middle must give you a feeling of inner satisfaction. After that it is necessary to have an ending which not only leaves you feeling it was all worth while, but which makes you long to return.'

'Like the *Soufflé Surprise*?'

'Like the *Soufflé Surprise*. It is, to date, Jean-Claude's greatest creation. Ask him how he does it and he will shrug his shoulders. Pursue the matter, demand to know what secret ingredient he uses, and he will most likely laugh and change the subject. He will say, "Listen, today must be Wednesday. How do I know? Because I can hear children playing in the distance. It is their half-day." It is like asking Beethoven how he composed the Ninth Symphony when all he had in front of him was a piano and a blank sheet of paper.' Albert Parfait tapped his head. 'The "secret ingredient" is all up here.'

Monsieur Pamplemousse found himself reminded of another great restaurant – Pic of Valence. For a long time he had puzzled over the special flavour of their Kir, generously dispensed from a jug. In the end it had turned out to be nothing more complicated than an added dash of Dubonnet. Perhaps Jean-Claude's "secret ingredient" was as simple. He decided to take the plunge.

'It is because of the *soufflé* that I am here. Jean-Claude's *soufflé* – or rather the lack of it – is the cause of worry in certain quarters.'

Monsieur Parfait gave him a long, hard look. 'So I am told. *They* are worried about their *soufflé* – I am worried about my son.'

Monsieur Pamplemousse returned the look in silence. Albert Parfait's manner belied his words. They were not the actions of a worried man. Since they had met, the conversation had ranged far and wide. To say that the subject of the missing Jean-Claude had been skated around was to put it mildly. It was almost as though the other had been trying not to talk about it. If it wasn't such a bizarre notion he would have suspected that for some reason or other Monsieur Parfait had been trying to gain time. But time for what? Being *patron* of Les Cinq Parfaits must have its headaches. By his own account the climb to the top had been long and arduous; but the higher you climb the harder you fall and it was something that could happen overnight. There were precedents.

The only sign of anxiety had been in the initial handshake. It had been firm but unexpectedly moist. And the moisture had come from within rather than without. Like the rest of the building, Albert Parfait's office was kept at an ambient temperature of 20°C.

'If you will forgive my saying so, you do not seem unduly disturbed by the news of your son's disappearance.'

'Sometimes, Monsieur Pamplemousse, appearances are deceptive. Like you, I have spent a lifetime trying to perfect the art of concealing my true feelings.'

Monsieur Pamplemousse accepted the implied rebuke with equanimity. 'You know, of course, why I am here?'

Monsieur Parfait inclined his head. 'I was informed this evening. We are very fortunate. A happy chance of fate.' He relaxed a little. 'Now that we have met I recognise you, of course. I have seen your picture many times in the newspapers. I had thought you were no longer active . . .'

'I am still called on from time to time.' Monsieur Pamplemousse got the remark in quickly before the other had time to enlarge on the cause of his early retirement. It always left him feeling he'd been put at a slight disadvantage. The word 'Follies' seemed to bring out the worst in people; add to it evocative words like 'chorus' and 'girls' and there was no holding them. It was like trying to convince a collector of taxes of the need to research a handbook on refrigeration in the South of France. If he'd been caught *dans le costume d'Adam* in the Himalayas it would have been a nine-day wonder in the *Bombay Times* and then forgotten about. In the dressing-room of the Follies – never.

'We thought at first you were from one of the guides. A man eating on his own at Les Cinq Parfaits is a rare occurrence. When we see him testing a little here . . . savouring a little there . . . choosing a table where he has a good view of all that is going on around him . . . we begin to wonder. Alain thought you were from Michelin, but then we found you had Pirelli tyres on your car, so that was out. Edouard was all for Gault Millau – especially when you called for a second helping of *Omble*. It was the dog that bothered me. It didn't fit. No one from a guide, I reasoned, would bring a dog. Now I understand. He is your . . . assistant?'

Monsieur Pamplemousse nodded. 'We are rarely parted. He has been instrumental in helping me reach some of my most memorable decisions.' In culinary terms it was true; it was hard to picture being without Pommes Frites. He wondered what Albert Parfait would say if he knew their true identity. That would give him cause to perspire.

He'd had no idea he'd been the centre of so much attention. He must be more careful in future. Perhaps at the next quarterly meeting he would put forward the suggestion that all Inspectors should be accompanied by a suitable companion. There might even be a pool of 'suitable companions' for all occasions. That would bring a flush to Madame Grante's cheeks.

'If you need to bring him inside – if there are important trails to follow – please do. I rely on your discretion. It wouldn't do for the other guests to think you are a favoured customer.'

'Rest assured, Monsieur Parfait, neither Pommes Frites

nor I will abuse your trust. As for trails, time alone will tell, but we will try and keep them to a minimum. I gather the local police have not yet been informed?'

'Thankfully, no. We do not want their great boots tramping all over the hotel. It would be bad for the ambience. This way is much better. With luck, no one need ever know.'

Monsieur Pamplemousse forebore to say that without a large measure of good luck everyone would know. It would be in all the *journaux*.

'When did you last see your son?'

'This morning at around eight o'clock. When I returned from the market in Thonon. He said he was planning to visit a supplier up in the mountains. There is a monastery where they make *Fruits du vieux garçon* – the fruits of the confirmed bachelor. The name always appealed to Jean-Claude.'

'He went by car? There have been no reports of an accident . . . a breakdown perhaps?'

'He would have done – it is a long journey, but his car is still in the garage. He must have changed his mind.'

'Then he can't have gone far. Unless he went somewhere by train and got delayed. Where is the nearest station?'

'Evian. I have enquired there. No one has seen him.'

'Can you think of any reason why he would disappear? Anything that would take him away from home without telling anyone?'

Again there was a slight, barely perceptible hesitation. 'What reason could there possibly be?'

He wasn't answering the question, but Monsieur Pamplemousse decided to try another tack. 'He lives on the premises?'

'All my sons do. Alain, Edouard and Gilbert are married and they live in separate houses in the grounds. Jean-Claude and I both have apartments in the main building.'

'And he had no worries?'

'None that I know of. He is not one to talk about his problems anyway. Life for him is for living. He is always bouncing back for more.'

'And it has never happened before?'

'He has his work. He is a professional. He would not wish to let others down.'

'May I see his apartment?'

'If you think it will help.'

'At this stage anything will help.'

'I will have you shown there.' Monsieur Parfait took a firm grasp of his stick and glanced at a clock on his desk. 'If you will forgive me I will leave you to your own devices. In my profession one also has to be something of an actor. There is a performance to be put on every evening, not once, but several times over. The customers will be expecting me to make my rounds.'

'I am told that later this week you have one of your more difficult audiences arriving,' said Monsieur Pamplemousse.

'Please do not remind me.' Albert Parfait made a face. 'It is not a task I relish. Already the advance guard are here. You may have seen their caravans beyond the wood. On Friday it will be the whole entourage. I cannot begin to describe the problems they bring with them. If I tell you that last year some members of the bodyguard were caught trying to roast a whole sheep in one of the chalets it will give you an inkling. Can you imagine – they stay at Les Cinq Parfaits and they want to do their own cooking!'

'It is hard to picture.' He wondered what sort of symbol they might concoct for *Le Guide*. An upside-down lamb on a spit, perhaps – with a red cross superimposed to show that it was *interdit*? Michelin would be in their element.

'Would it not be possible one year to be *complet*?'

Monsieur Parfait took an even tighter grasp of his stick and for a brief moment allowed his true feelings to surface. 'It would be perfectly possible,' he said bitterly. 'It is also very tempting. But if you were to rephrase the question – if you were to ask me "would it be wise?", then almost certainly the answer is no. There would be repercussions. *Entre nous*, it would offend too many people. People who have long memories. There are, shall we say, wheels within wheels.'

Monsieur Pamplemousse pondered the remark before answering. It was the second time that evening the point had been made.

'And they require oiling?'

'There are many things in life which are helped on their way by a little lubrication,' said Monsieur Parfait simply. 'And there are some that would grind to a halt without it. Oil has many uses. It helps make the world go round and it soothes troubled waters. Our own waters would become turbulent indeed if I chose to be difficult. Once upon a time I might have done, but now, if I am honest, I am too old to be bothered. Besides, I have the future of my sons to consider.'

He reached for a bell-push. 'Now, I must attend to work. I wish you – I wish all of us – *bonne chance.*'

Monsieur Pamplemousse drained the glass and then picked up his book and rose to join Parfait at the door. 'I will do my best. I cannot do more.'

'If you require anything – anything at all, please let me know.'

The handshake accompanying the remark was as firm as it had been earlier. It was also perfectly dry. The *moment critique*, if there'd been one, had passed.

There was a knock at the door.

'*Entrez.*' Monsieur Parfait issued his instructions briefly to one of the two coal-black Sudanese bell-boys who normally ministered to the needs of arriving guests, then relaxed his grip on Monsieur Pamplemousse's hand. '*A bientôt.*'

'*A tout à l'heure.*'

As he followed the boy down a long, deeply carpeted corridor lined on either side with bowls of freshly cut flowers and hung with discreetly inoffensive paintings, Monsieur Pamplemousse was conscious of a pair of eyes boring into the back of his head. Under the pretext of blowing his nose, he paused and half-turned. He was just in time to catch Albert Parfait disappearing into his office. Clearly he had other matters to attend to before he began his tour of the dining-room.

Was it his imagination or had there been something furtive about the way he moved? Furtiveness, along with some other element he couldn't quite put his finger on. Alarm, perhaps? Guilt? He filed the episode away in the back of his mind for future reference.

33

Outside, as they made their way along a short path which led past the restaurant towards the residential area in an adjoining building, he was aware of other eyes watching his progress. He wondered which of the diners had set off the alarm. He had an uneasy feeling that someone other than the *patron* of Les Cinq Parfaits had been responsible for passing on the news that Jean-Claude had gone missing. It was almost as if Albert Parfait would rather the fact hadn't been made known. Perhaps the turbulent waters he'd spoken of earlier contained undercurrents not yet revealed; care would have to be taken if he was to avoid getting caught up in them.

The air was heavy with the fragrance of late flowers; the beds on either side of the path were immaculately cared for. He could hear the soft swish, swish of a sprinkler somewhere close at hand. There was a louder splash from the direction of the pool. Someone must have decided to have an after-dinner swim. He hoped that whoever it was hadn't eaten as well as he had. They might never surface again. Turning a corner, he found himself instinctively looking for Pommes Frites.

The bell-boy, trained to anticipate everyone's wishes before they were even voiced, pointed towards a wooded area behind the hotel. 'He may be over there, *Monsieur*. I saw him heading that way earlier this evening.'

Monsieur Pamplemousse grunted. If Pommes Frites had gone 'wooding' there was no knowing when he would be back. Woods held a fatal fascination for Pommes Frites; probably because he spent most of his off-duty hours in Montmartre, where the nearest thing to a wood was the vineyard in rue Saint Vincent.

'He is a nice dog, that one.' The bell-boy's face suddenly split open from ear to ear in a wide smile. Pommes Frites had obviously not been idle; he had acquired a new friend. Pommes Frites was good at acquiring friends in the right places. No doubt he had also made his presence known to the kitchen staff and certain of the waiters as well. The boy's next words confirmed his suspicions.

'He also has a very good appetite. *Pouf! Sapristi!*'

'He can hold his own.'

'He should take care.' The bell-boy pointed towards the woods again. 'That is where the *bicots* are living. They do not like dogs. They are *fouillemerdes*.' Clearly he considered himself a million light years removed from the occupants of a small group of caravans whose rooftops were just visible between a gap in the trees.

Monsieur Pamplemousse looked at him with interest. *Fouillemerdes* was a word he'd only ever heard used to describe people who leafed through books on the stalls along the banks of the Seine in Paris; for this reason the wares were almost always covered in plastic. As they finally stopped by a door and the boy felt for his keys, Monsieur Pamplemousse glanced uneasily towards the woods. Pommes Frites was well able to look after himself, but all the same he resolved to look for him again at the earliest opportunity.

'They come here every year?'

'Every year.' The boy turned his key in the lock. 'As soon as the holidays are over.'

'The same people?'

'They are all the same, *Monsieur*.'

'How long do they stay?'

'A few days. That is all. Long enough.'

Monsieur Pamplemousse considered the reply. He seemed to have struck a no-go area. Long enough for what? he wondered. The smile on the boy's face had disappeared and he seemed suddenly ill at ease.

Monsieur Pamplemousse decided not to press the matter further for the time being. Instead, he tried a shot in the dark. As he pushed open the door he felt inside his wallet and took out a note.

'Thank you for your trouble. I shall be grateful if you would keep an eye on Pommes Frites for me. Make sure no harm comes to him.'

He hoped he hadn't given too much. The boy had the natural dignity of the Sudanese, and he didn't wish to cause offence.

But he needn't have worried. He was rewarded by an even larger display of white teeth. '*Oui, Monsieur*. It will be a pleasure.'

As the door clicked shut, Monsieur Pamplemousse set to work, quickly and professionally. It was quite like old times. He had no idea what he was looking for. He was simply obeying an instinct, fulfilling a need for some kind of action. It had to begin somewhere and he needed to create a picture in his mind of the person he was looking for.

There were three doors, one in each wall. He tried the one on his left. It opened on to a large cupboard. Inside there hung a row of coats and jackets. He looked at the labels; they were predictably expensive – Yves St. Laurent, Pierre Cardin. The shoes laid out neatly on a rack below were equally fashionable; mostly hand-made from Lobb of London. Albert Parfait was right – chefs did indeed enjoy a new status in society. A pair of Rossignol V.A.S. racing skis stood upright in one corner; some ice-skates hung alongside them.

The bathroom was neat and orderly. A Braun Micron de Luxe electric razor was laid out ready for use beside the washbasin. An electric toothbrush, also Braun, was clipped to the dark-blue tiles above it. Everything had its home. A large inset mirrored cabinet contained a selection of sprays and lotions.

The third door opened on to a large living-room, which in turn led into a bedroom. On one side there was a long picture-window. He drew the curtains carefully and then turned on the lights. An open hatch revealed the kitchen area.

The living-room itself was simple, even austere. It was the unlived-in room of a bachelor who spent most of his time either working or out doing other things.

He wondered what Holmes would have made of it. Probably from a few hastily crushed cigarette-ends in an ashtray and signs of pacing to and fro on the carpet, he would have built up a complete picture, astounding Watson and solving the mystery at one and the same time. However, there were no ashtrays and the beige carpet looked as fresh as the day it was first laid.

He drew a blank in the kitchen. It echoed the tidiness of the bathroom. There were more gadgets, a whole battery of them, ready and waiting. Jean-Claude must be a gadget salesman's dream. A Moulinex juicer stood in pieces on the draining-board, its inside stained orange from carrot juice. He wondered whether the owner suffered from bouts of indigestion like himself, or whether he simply like carrots. Probably the latter. The refrigerator was stocked up with bottles of Evian water. Living where he did he could hardly drink anything else.

He went back into the living-room. There was a notable absence of books apart from a row on a shelf above the desk, mostly to do with work and winter sports. The television was Sony; the video beneath it the latest Betamax. Fixed to the wall was a Bang & Olufsen Beosystem 3000; underneath that a rack of L.P.s. Somewhat to his surprise they were mostly big bands: Basie, Ellington, Buddy Rich, with a sprinkling of older groups – Lionel Hampton, Mugsie Spanier, Benny Goodman.

He found himself warming to Jean-Claude. They were on common ground at last. Perhaps one day they would be able to get together and exchange notes. Doucette didn't approve of his taste in music and complained when he had it on too loud. He envied Jean-Claude his freedom to turn up the volume when he felt like it. Big bands needed a big band sound.

There was a disc by Ben Webster and Art Tatum already on the turntable. It was one he hadn't come across before. The remote controller was on a table near the window. Unable to resist the temptation he pressed the switch. The sound of 'All the Things You Are' gave him an instant lift.

He skimmed through the bedroom, feeling under the mattress, briefly checking the cupboard drawers. There was nothing worthy of comment. It was all high-tech monastic. On a table beside the double-bed a matt-black Italian Stilnoro lamp illuminated a Nordmende clock-radio. The alarm was set for six o'clock. There was also a cordless telephone – the kind with the dialling buttons in the handset, and a small pile of magazines – mostly to do with food and drink. They looked untouched. There was also a catalogue from Sports-Schuster of Munich showing the latest in skiing equipment and clothing. Several items were marked. Jean-Claude must have been making plans for the coming winter season. He didn't look like a man with too many problems.

He returned to the living-room and switched on the quartz-halogen lamp on the desk. A larger version of the bedroom lamp, the low voltage bulb produced a brilliant white light. He picked up the blotting pad and held it under the lamp. Jean-Claude was a doodler on the phone. It was covered with black, geometrical shapes, ranging in complexity from mere squares and triangles to complex, ornate patterns – probably depending on the length of the call. Interspersed with the patterns were telephone numbers. He checked with the handset. They were mostly Jean-Claude's own number, but here and there were others. Taking out his notepad, he jotted these down for future reference.

He turned the blotting pad over. Someone – an executive working for Burns, the big American agency – had once told him that the first thing he did when he was left alone in an office belonging to anyone of importance was to look beneath the blotting pad. In a security-conscious age, when more and more code-numbers had to be committed to memory, people sought refuge by inscribing them on the back of their blotting pads. His friend had built up quite a dossier of useful numbers.

There was nothing on the back of Jean-Claude's blotting pad.

He drew a blank with the drawers on his right. The large drawer with its suspended files on the left took a little longer, but was equally unproductive.

He riffled through the books on the shelf above the desk. Nothing fell out.

Just as he was about to give up, he leant on the blotting pad, smoothing the rough paper thoughtfully with his fingers as he tried to make up his mind what to do next. It felt thicker than he would have expected. Towards the middle there were distinct ridges. He lifted the top sheet. Underneath it was a glossy black and white enprint of a blonde girl. It was the product of a fashion-conscious studio; all high-key lighting and with the softness of the subject burnt out. It made her look old beyond her years, but perhaps that was what she had wanted. She looked vaguely familiar and he wondered if he had seen her on television. The picture was unsigned; the back was stamped with the name of a studio in Geneva.

Underneath the photograph there was a thin manila envelope. It was unsealed and to his surprise, when he held it up and shook the contents on to the desk, a selection of words fluttered down. They were of differing type-sizes and faces, each separately stuck to a sheet of dark backing paper. He laid them out in no particular order. They were in English and judging by the texture of the paper had been cut from a *journal* of some kind. Strangely, at least two of the words were misspelt – unless his command of the English language, which wasn't good, was even weaker than he'd thought.

Monsieur Pamplemousse sat staring at the words for some time, shifting them around, trying to make some kind of sense. Then he stood up and tucked them back in the envelope along with the photograph. It was a task better carried out in his own room.

A few moments later he let himself out quietly through the front door. Cloud from the distant mountains had descended while he'd been at work and it was already dark. Concealed coloured lights made patches of shrubs and flowers stand out like tropical islands. The pool was deserted again. From the car-park he could hear voices and the sound of engines being revved. Doors slammed. He looked in through the dining-room windows, wondering if he should confer with Albert Parfait, but the *patron* was nowhere in sight. He decided against searching him out. It could wait for the time being.

He hesitated for a moment or two, wondering whether to take his things back to his room or look for Pommes Frites first. In view of his previous experience with the silent dog-whistle he decided not to risk using it again. All hell might break loose.

The wood behind the hotel was even darker than he'd anticipated and he began to wish he'd fetched a torch from his car. The paved path ended abruptly and gave way to gravel, then became softer still in a carpet of pine-needles. The shadows closed in almost at once, enveloping him like a shroud. Through gaps in the trees he could see occasional flashes of light from the caravans and there was a smell of something indefinably aromatic burning.

He stopped for a moment in order to get his bearings, allowing his eyes to accustom themselves to the darkness. As he did so he became aware of a movement a little way ahead and to his left; a glimpse of something white at head-height, then blackness again.

He called out, but there was no reply. Taking his belongings in his left hand, he moved forward slowly and gently with his right hand outstretched, zig-zagging slightly as he went. He could feel his heart beating a little faster and in spite of the coolness of the night air he felt beads of sweat on his brow.

Suddenly he sensed another movement immediately in front of him and heard a stifled gasp intermingled with heavy breathing and a strange, soft, sucking sound. Easing forward he felt warmth too. The warmth of another human being, accompanied by a sweet, almost overpoweringly sickly smell.

Stretching out his hand he drew in his breath sharply as it encountered something large and round and hard. He moved it to the right and almost immediately found a second mound, similar in shape, one of a matching pair; equally hard and yet at the same time warm and soft to the touch and covered in the softest down. A mound which even as he touched it rotated as if seeking him out, rejecting and accepting at the same time. A mountain of flesh which rose and fell and became soft and moist before culminating in a peak of hardness the like of which he had never before experienced. The whole effect was so earthy, so basic, so primitively sensual, he felt rooted to the spot, unable to believe his senses.

It could only have lasted a second or two. The next moment he found himself clutching at empty air as the person he'd been touching uttered a second strangled cry, brushed past him and was gone.

Caught off-balance and still recovering from the shock

of his encounter, Monsieur Pamplemousse turned and called out. But he was too late.

He started to give chase, but after only a few yards his foot met with something large and unyielding lying directly across his path. He tripped, staggered forward, and in trying to regain his balance toppled over.

As he slowly recovered his wind, Monsieur Pamplemousse opened one eye and peered at the object lying alongside him. Even in his semi-dazed state it had a familiar look about it. Opening his other eye he took a closer look. He needed no light to aid his identification. He knew at once what it was.

Stretched out on a pile of old newspapers, stiff and motionless, cold to the touch, lay the recumbent form of Pommes Frites.

3

A CAUSE FOR CELEBRATION

For a moment or two there was silence as Monsieur Pamplemousse remained where he'd fallen, trying to get his breath back, while at the same time weighing up the pros and cons of applying the kiss of life to Pommes Frites. Finally, having decided to take the plunge, he leaned forward. Desperate situations demanded desperate measures.

Monsieur Pamplemousse yielded to no one in his love for Pommes Frites. Deep down he knew that had the situation been reversed there would have been no hesitation about coming to his aid. Nevertheless, the prospect of mouth-to-mouth resuscitation was not one he relished. Pommes Frites had a generous nature and in return nature had endowed him with lips to match. Even the famous Westmores of Hollywood might have admitted to having met their match had they been called upon to make him up for the part of a canine Scrooge; Max Factor would have had to work overtime.

All that aside, when he finally screwed up his courage and lifted one of Pommes Frites' lips in order to begin work, Monsieur Pamplemousse discovered that it was not only very large and wet, it also had a most peculiar taste: an amalgam of flavours, some relatively fresh, others obviously deeply ingrained. The overall effect was, to say the least, uninviting, and with a view to tempering necessity with expediency, coupled with a desire to get the whole thing over as quickly as possible, he blew rather harder than he'd intended.

The result was electrifying. Pommes Frites leapt to his feet and gave vent to a long-drawn-out shuddering howl.

At least, to be pedantic and strictly for the record, he opened his mouth and emitted a noise which another member of the family *canidae* would have recognised at once for what it was: not so much a howl as a cry of surprise, pain and indignation all rolled into one. It embodied such intensity of feeling that had they been situated higher up the mountains, in the vicinity of Mont Blanc, for example, or Chamonix, it would have caused any St. Bernard who happened to be on night-duty to drop everything and come running with a keg of brandy round its neck at the ready.

Fortunately, only Monsieur Pamplemousse himself was there to hear it, and for a moment he was convinced that he had been a party to, perhaps even the cause of, the early demise of his closest and dearest friend. It was not a happy thought.

For a split second dog and master stared at one another, each busy with his own thoughts. Then Pommes Frites relaxed. To say that he wagged his tail would have been to overstate the case. He made a desultory attempt at wagging. His brain sent a half-hearted message in that direction, but it never reached its destination. Other factors intervened en route; 'road-up' signs proliferated, diversions abounded. Not to put too fine a point on it, Pommes Frites was feeling distinctly under the weather.

It was a simple case of cause and effect. The cause wouldn't have needed a Sherlock Holmes to trace, and the effect was there for all to see – or it would have been had low clouds not been obscuring the moon.

Basically it had to do with the nature of Les Cinq Parfaits. Les Cinq Parfaits was many things to many people; the one claim it could not make was that of being the kind of restaurant where the clients made a habit of wiping their plates clean at the end of each course with large hunks of *baguette*. Bread, home-made, freshly baked, and of unimpeachable quality, was dispensed freely at the start of each meal, but sad to relate most of it remained uneaten.

Sauces, on the whole, were not mopped up. They were either consumed with the aid of the appropriate implement

43

or they were left on the plate, along with much of the food they had been intended to complement. The reason was not because the clientèle were any more polite or well-mannered than in lesser establishments; it was simply that a great many of them were past their best as trenchermen. Age had taken its toll, digestive systems ruined by over-work rendered them incapable of taking full advantage of the pleasures they were now well able to afford, whilst in the case of the wives, sweethearts or mistresses accom-panying them, they were swayed by vanity and the need to keep a watchful eye on waistlines.

The net result was that each day large quantities of rich food which had taken a great deal of time and energy and manpower to grow and to harvest, to transport and then to prepare for the table, found their way back to the kitchens untouched by knife and fork. Once there, such were the standards set by Monsieur Albert Parfait, it was immedi-ately and unceremoniously consigned to a row of waiting swill-bins for onward delivery next day to a local pig farm whose residents had no such problems.

It was one such bin, overflowing with riches, that Pommes Frites, taste-buds inflamed through watching his master's antics on the other side of the dining-room window, his pride seriously injured, his stomach echoing like a drum, stumbled across in his wanderings earlier that evening. It had proved to be a veritable cornucopia of a swill-bin.

Pommes Frites had lost no time in getting down to serious work. The niceties of menu-planning went by the board, the ambience of his surroundings passed unnoticed. Rules for following fish by meat rather than vice versa were disregarded. There was no dilly-dallying between courses. International preferences concerning the priority of cheese over sweet were solved by the simple expedient of eating both together. Coffee was taken ad hoc.

Alphabetically, but otherwise in no particular order, he consumed in a remarkably short space of time: *Andouillette*; *Boeuf* prepared in a variety of ways; *Boudins*, black and white; *Caviar* (white, from the roe of the albino sturgeon); *Coq au Vin* and *Coquilles St. Jacques* followed by *Crêpes*

Suzettes. D'Agneau sur le grill rapidly became *d'Agneau dans le Pommes Frites*, along with *Ecrevisse*; *Estouffade* (cooked in the local manner with red wine, bacon and mushrooms); *Foie gras*; *Fraises*; *Fromages* too numerous to list; *Glaces* in profusion; *Gratinées*; *Homard* – both lukewarm and cold; *Ile flottante*; *Jambon*; *Journaux*; *Knackwurst* (ordered in advance by a guest from Alsace who was celebrating his birthday not wisely but too well); *Lapereau*; *Loup en croûte*; *Mousse au chocolat*; *Noisette de Chevreuil* served with *morilles*; *Oeufs* from many different sources; *Omble*; *Pâté*; *Pâtisseries*; pieces of plastic; *Pigeonneau*; *Pommes*; *Poulet*; *Quenelles Nantua*; *Queues d'écrevisses*; *Ris de veau*; *Rouget*; *Salade* which had once been green but was now a greyish brown; *Sorbets* in a *panaché* to end all *panachés*; *Truffes*; *Truite*; *Ursuline*; *Vacherin*; *Veau Waffelpasteta* (another indulgence of the guest from Alsace, most of which he'd left for fear of not living to celebrate another birthday); *Xavier* soup; *Yaourt* and *Zébrine*.

He was now suffering the after-effects of this gargantuan meal; a meal which would have caused even the great Escoffier, accustomed as he must have been to preparing vast banquets for Kings and Queens and Princes the world over, to turn in his grave and reach for the indigestion tablets.

Presented with a break-down of the contents of Pommes Frites' stomach, no self-respecting vet would have given overmuch for his chances of surviving the night, let alone of making an early recovery; a medical opinion with which the patient would have wholeheartedly concurred.

Pommes Frites couldn't remember ever having felt quite so full before, or so under par. And it was at that moment in time that Monsieur Pamplemousse, concerned by the expression of unrelieved woe on his friend's face, unwittingly administered the unkindest cut of all. Feeling inside his jacket pocket, he produced what in normal circumstances would have been the panacea for all ills, and held the object to Pommes Frites' nose.

The effect was as devastating and immediate as had been his attempt a few moments earlier to administer the kiss of life.

Pommes Frites stared at the bone-shaped biscuit as if he could hardly believe his eyes and then, having lifted up his head and given voice to a howl which was, if possible, even more desolate than the first, tottered round in a barely completed half-circle, gazed up at his master with a look of mute despair, and then collapsed in an untidy heap on the *journal* at his feet.

Unaware of the cause of this strange behaviour, Monsieur Pamplemousse sprang into action. Clearly he couldn't leave Pommes Frites where he was. Equally clearly, Pommes Frites was in no condition to do anything about the matter himself, even if he'd wanted to.

He looked round desperately but unavailingly for help. Room service at Les Cinq Parfaits was impeccable. Pool service could not be faulted. Call for a Kir Royale and it was on the table by your side, ice-cold and with an assortment of nuts and other goodies, before you had time to call for the sunshade to be adjusted. He had a feeling though that wood service, in particular the discreet removal of a large Bloodhound to a place of comfort, might be stretching things a little too far. Bell-pushes for summoning aid were conspicuous by their absence from nearby trees.

It was then that he remembered the wheelbarrow. He'd seen it soon after his visit to Jean-Claude's room. Large, pneumatically tyred, propped against a wall alongside a bale of hay; it would be ideal.

Fetching it took only a minute or two; getting Pommes Frites inside a great deal longer. Pommes Frites was not in one of his most co-operative moods. In fact, quite the reverse. A disinterested spectator, one with no particular axe to grind, could have been forgiven had he or she jumped to the conclusion that Pommes Frites was positively against the whole operation. Not that he showed any active sign of resistance. It was simply that he did nothing to help. Even the vast amount he had eaten that evening didn't account for the fact that he suddenly felt twice his usual fifty kilograms. Limbs which normally propelled him with ease about his daily rounds became weak and useless, unable to support his weight. His head, normally erect and with a certain nobility about it, lolled from side to side,

46

eyes rolling in their sockets, tongue hanging loose, as if he was suffering from some dreadful and incurable mental affliction.

Three times Monsieur Pamplemousse nearly succeeded in his task, and three times when he tried to turn the barrow upright Pommes Frites rolled out the other side, landing heavily on the ground with his paws in the air.

Fourth time lucky, conscious that sartorially speaking he was far from looking his best, Monsieur Pamplemousse set off at long last on the journey back to his room. As he turned a corner leading to the final stretch he heard voices and paused. Doubling back on himself he tried another route which took him past the dining-room again. Adopting a shambling, crab-like movement so that he could keep his back towards the windows, he swallowed his pride and touched the brim of his hat in a suitable servile acknowledgement of the interest his activities were arousing on the other side of the glass before hurrying past as fast as his load would permit.

Reaching the door to his room he uncovered yet another deficiency of Les Cinq Parfaits. In *Le Guide*, alongside an impressive list of symbols showing the various facilities which ranged from pool-side telephones to coin-operated vibro-mattresses (on request), was one which denoted easy access for those who had the misfortune to be confined to a wheelchair. After struggling for several minutes to enter his room, Monsieur Pamplemousse came to the conclusion that any further projects designed to attract canine customers who wished to arrive in a wheelbarrow would have to remain in the pending tray for a while. Structural alterations of a major kind would be needed; doorways would have to be widened, L-shaped corridors straightened out.

His mission completed, Pommes Frites finally and safely parked in the middle of the room, Monsieur Pamplemousse collapsed on to his bed and lay where he'd fallen for some minutes while he contemplated the air-conditioning inlet above his head. At length, duty calling, he reached for the local telephone directory.

There were three *vétérinaires* listed. The first failed to

answer. The second announced by means of a recorded message that he was on holiday. The third call produced in the fullness of time the sleepy voice of someone who didn't sound best pleased at being woken.

Monsieur Pamplemousse looked at his watch. He had totally lost all track of time. The hands showed a little after eleven o'clock.

He listened as patiently as possible while he was given a run-down of the other's problems, followed by a list of priorities in which attending to ailing and unregistered dogs after six o'clock in the evening appeared to enjoy low priority against ministering to any local cows who happened to have acquired inflammation of the udders.

'*Monsieur*,' he said at last. 'I do know about the *vaches d'abondance*. I realise their importance to the local economy. I know that they are gentle, brown and white creatures who enrich our lives immeasurably. I have heard the sound of the bells they wear around their necks. They have often kept me awake at night when I have been staying in the mountains. I know that without them France, indeed the whole world, would be deprived of some of its finest cheeses; the *Gruyères* of *Comté* and *Beaufort*, *Emmental*, the *Tommes de Savoie*, *Reblochon* . . .

'No, *Monsieur*, it will not be possible to bring him in tomorrow morning.' He glanced across the room at Pommes Frites. He hadn't moved. 'From the look of him he will not be going anywhere for some time to come. He has the appearance of one who has eaten a large quantity of plaster of Paris. Plaster of Paris which has now set hard . . .

'He is in a wheelbarrow, here in my room at Les Cinq Parfaits . . .

'I realise you have had a busy day, *Monsieur*. I, too, have had a busy day. I rose at six o'clock this morning. I have driven all the way from Paris and I, too, am very tired. But this is a matter of great importance and the utmost urgency . . .'

Monsieur Pamplemousse broke off in mid-sentence. He stared disbelievingly at the receiver. It was almost beyond belief but the person at the other end had actually hung up on him.

He hesitated for a moment or two, wondering whether to try again and offer a piece of his mind, or to telephone Durelle in Paris. Durelle would be more sympathetic. He also knew about Bloodhounds in general and Pommes Frites in particular. As one-time adviser to the Sûreté (*Division Chiens*) he had known Pommes Frites during his early days with the force and was well used to his ways.

In the end Monsieur Pamplemousse decided against both courses of action. It was late and Pommes Frites' breathing had become more regular. Regular and noisy. If he carried on at the present rate Les Cinq Parfaits would be liable to lose their red rocking-chair in the Michelin guide. He knew the signs. Soon the heavy breathing would turn into snores. Sleep for Monsieur Pamplemousse would become difficult, if not impossible. The way things were going he might be better off finding alternative accommodation for the night.

Several times Pommes Frites opened his mouth and licked his lips as if reliving in his dreams some recent experience of a gastronomic nature. Monsieur Pamplemousse lifted up one of his eyelids and immediately wished he hadn't. The orb which met his gaze was bloodshot rather than hazel and totally devoid of expression. A strong smell of hay had begun to fill the room; hay and damp newsprint. It was not a pleasant combination.

Dropping Pommes Frites' eyelid back into place, he essayed a few desultory tugs at the bedding and then gave it up as a bad job, resolving to leave matters in abeyance until the morning. At least Pommes Frites wasn't getting worse and there was work to be done.

Heaving a deep sigh he crossed to a desk in the corner of the room and drew up a chair. Upending the envelope he had taken from Jean-Claude's room revealed something which had escaped his notice the first time: a small cutting showing a group of skiers posing against a snow-covered mountainside. It must have been the other way up before – on the back he recognised part of a picture showing a stretch of water; it might have been anywhere. He turned the cutting over again. There were five people in the group – all male – two kneeling and three standing behind, arms

49

akimbo. Although as a group they looked blissfully happy, he was left with a strange and irrational feeling of unease. Against the man in the middle of the back row someone had inked in a black cross and a question-mark. He held the cutting up to the light to examine it more closely. Presumably it had either been cut from a glossy magazine, or from some kind of brochure.

Putting it to one side for future reference, he turned his attention to the remaining cuttings. Something about the type-face rang a bell. In fact, he'd seen it quite recently. A loud snore from behind reminded him; a moment's comparison confirmed his suspicions. Bits of identical newsprint were sticking to Pommes Frites. They must have come from the *journal* he'd been lying on in the wood.

The odd thing was that although they looked genuine enough on the surface, many of them didn't make sense. As with the cuttings, words were misspelt, letters transposed. The whole thing was clearly a fake; it couldn't possibly ever have been a part of something seriously offered for sale to the general public. But why? For what purpose? Who would go to all the trouble of printing a mock-up of a *journal* simply to cut out particular words? Presumably they were meant to be put together at some stage to form a message, but why print the words separately to start with – why not print the entire message? And if they *had* gone to all that trouble, why not get it right? It was all so amateurish.

His senses quickened as he felt under Pommes Frites and came across another piece of newsprint from which a single word had been cut out, part of a headline which read RUSSIAN SUBMARINE . . .

A quick search through the pile of cuttings on his desk revealed the missing word: DANGRE. It was neatly pasted on to a sheet of plain paper, but when he held it underneath the gap in the original it fitted exactly.

He sat down again and counted the words. There were seventeen – none were duplicated. Gazing at them he found himself reminded of the time he'd spent in England shortly after the war. In an effort to improve his English he'd become a crossword addict, revelling in the cryptic

50

clues and the anagrams. The present problem was like an anagram, only using words instead of letters.

He set them out in no particular order, just as he had been in the habit of doing with the crossword: OF, ONE, HURRY, MESSEGE, YOUR, DANGRE, MY, NEXT, POLICE, LOVED, IS, NOT, AWAAIT, DO, IN-FORM, LIFE, IN.

Mathematically the number of possible combinations was beyond his ability to calculate. At least with a crossword one could eliminate certain letters by solving other clues, either across or down. He felt a bit like the proverbial monkey sitting at a typewriter trying to prove the theory that if it kept on typing at random for long enough it would eventually come up with the complete works of Shakespeare. That kind of time, however, was not at his disposal; according to the Director he only had until Friday at the latest.

Bringing logic to bear on the problem, he tried another approach – pairing certain words with each other in the hope of reducing the number of variations: IN-FORM with POLICE, LIFE with DANGRE, LOVED with ONE, NEXT with MESSEGE.

He added AWAAIT to NEXT MESSEGE, YOUR to LOVED and ONE.

Suddenly things began to slip into place. He had a complete sentence: AWAAIT NEXT MESSEGE OF YOUR LOVED ONE.

Returning to the first two pairings, he added MY, IS and IN, and it became IN-FORM POLICE MY LIFE IS IN DANGRE, leaving him with HURRY, DO and NOT.

Laying the words out carefully in a long line Monsieur Pamplemousse reread the complete message: IN-FORM POLICE MY LIFE IS IN DANGRE. DO NOT HURRY. AWAAIT NEXT MESSEGE OF YOUR LOVED ONE.

A sense of elation came over him. He felt a sudden need to communicate his success. What was it the Director had said? My office telephone will be manned day and night. Perhaps even now he was sitting at his desk, drumming.

Reaching for the handset, Monsieur Pamplemousse pressed the appropriate button for an outside line and was halfway through dialling when he hesitated. What had he achieved? He'd pieced together a presumably as yet unsent

51

message, albeit in double-quick time, but it hadn't got him any further. Repeated over the telephone it would sound like a non-event. It would trigger off a set of questions to which he had, as yet, no answers. Far better to sleep on the matter and allow his subconscious to do some of the work. Monsieur Pamplemousse was a great believer in the subconscious.

It had, in fact, already been at work. Even while he'd been dialling the office number it had sent out a message reminding him of something else the Director had said; a promise made, and one which he fully intended taking advantage of. The promise of a bottle of the d'Yquem '45 when his mission had reached a satisfactory conclusion.

Deep down, Monsieur Pamplemousse was only too well aware that he had only really begun to scratch the surface of his problem, but scratches could widen into cuts, cuts into fissures, fissures into crevasses. There was no question of failure. Failure was not a word in his vocabulary; consequently it never entered his mind.

The evening had not been entirely without success. He now had things to work on. It was a cause for celebration. As a *digestif* and an aid to peaceful sleep while his subconscious got to work, he could think of nothing better than a glass or two of Sauternes.

He reached for the telephone again and pressed the button marked 'Room Service'. It was more than likely that Les Cinq Parfaits, for all the riches which graced the pages of its wine-list, riches which reached back to long before he was born, would be unable to meet his request. It was asking a lot, but it was worth a try.

'*Monsieur* is fortunate. We have only three bottles left. When they are gone we shall be reduced to the '62s.'

'Bring me two,' said Monsieur Pamplemousse in a sudden mood of recklessness. He would have one to be going on with and keep one for later, depending on the final outcome. It would help make up for a spoilt holiday and the absence of the *Soufflé Surprise* he'd been so looking forward to.

If the man was surprised there was no sign of it in his voice. It might have been the kind of order he received

52

every night of his life. If there was any emotion at all it was one of respect; respect mingled with the faintest hint of regret.

'Perhaps,' said Monsieur Pamplemousse, 'you would care to share a glass with me as a nightcap – a little *boisson prise avant de se coucher*?'

'It would be an honour, *Monsieur*.' He knew from the tone of the man's voice that he had made a friend for life. Wine was a great leveller; a breaker-down of barriers.

The discreet knock on the door came sooner than expected. An assistant *sommelier*, still wearing his green baize apron, his badge of office – the silver *tastevin* – round his neck, entered the room pushing a trolley on which reposed two ice-buckets and two glasses. There was also a plate of wafer-thin biscuits. A palate cleanser.

Having circumnavigated Pommes Frites with scarcely more than a passing glance, he withdrew a bottle from one of the ice-buckets, holding it up with care for Monsieur Pamplemousse's inspection.

Monsieur Pamplemousse assumed a suitably reverent expression, and then watched with approval while the *sommelier* went to work. From the painstaking way in which he removed the lead foil in one piece, pressing it out flat with obvious pleasure, he guessed the man must come from his own area. Only someone from the Auvergne would go to so much trouble over something which to most people would be relatively unimportant. It was strange how different areas produced people who gravitated towards certain jobs. Half the restaurants in Paris were owned or staffed by Auvergnese. If it was a Frenchman behind the wheel of a taxi, rather than an Asian, the chances were he would be from Savoie. He resolved that when the wine was finished he would replace the foil and add the bottle to his collection, a reminder of his time at Les Cinq Parfaits. Something else for Doucette to dust, as she would no doubt tell him.

Cork withdrawn, passed below the nose in an automatic gesture, the *sommelier* ran some pieces of ice round the inside of the glasses, then dried them and began to pour. Against the white of the cloth the wine was amber-gold,

53

tinged with yellow at the rim. It augured well. There was no sign of maderisation.

'*Monsieur*.' The *sommelier* handed him one of the glasses. Taking it by the base, Monsieur Pamplemousse held it up to the light, then down against the cloth, regarding it for a while, tilting it through forty-five degrees so that he could watch the 'legs' form on the inside. Satisfied at long last, he held the glass to his nose and savoured the rich, unmistakable, honeyed smell, powerful and concentrated.

The sweetness hit the tip of his tongue first. The flavour lingered long after the first mouthful, producing an aftertaste full of finesse and breeding.

'It is how gold should taste.'

'It will improve, *Monsieur*. A *soupçon* more of coldness.'

'I have only tasted it once before and that was in company. Never have I had a whole bottle to myself, let alone two. It is too good to drink alone.'

They stood in silence for a while, then the *sommelier* put down his empty glass with a sigh of regret.

'It is too good, *Monsieur*, for many people to drink at all. Unfortunately, in my profession one comes to realise that the best wine does not always go to those who appreciate it most.'

Pausing by the door, the man looked him straight in the eye. 'Thank you again, *Monsieur*, and . . . *bonne chance*.'

Monsieur Pamplemousse pondered the remark over a biscuit. Perhaps he was being over-sensitive, but in the circumstances and considering what time it was, *bonne nuit* might have been more appropriate.

Pouring himself another glass of wine, he made his way into the bathroom. There was nothing more conducive to thought than a lingering hot bath and the notion of one enhanced by a bottle of Château d'Yquem was positively sybaritic.

But the bath produced little or no result other than an uneasy feeling that his presence at the hotel was a matter of some comment; that others knew far more than he did. Well, it wouldn't be the first time. Most of his life he'd had to battle against such things. He would get there in the end.

As he lay luxuriating in the foam from a sachet of liquid bath oil, he turned over in his mind all that had happened that evening. Memories of his strange encounter in the wood came flooding back and multiplied, aided and abetted by the warm water, Badedas and Sauternes. He began to feel strangely disturbed. Perhaps a cold shower would have done him far more good.

The towels were of the finest cotton, satisfyingly large and absorbent; there was a voluminous dressing-gown monogrammed with the hotel's initials to match.

Topping up his glass for the final time, Monsieur Pamplemousse placed the empty bottle on top of the refrigerator, consigned its companion to the compartment on the inside of the door, adjusted the temperature so that it wouldn't become over-chilled, and retired at long last to his bed. With the alarm set for eight o'clock, he fluffed up the pillows and picked up his book. Opening it at the point where he'd left off in the restaurant, he returned to *The Hound of the Baskervilles*. But reading it did not come easily. He found himself going over the same paragraph again and again; Holmes was explaining to Watson a theory he had formed about some knotty problem.

Monsieur Pamplemousse found himself wondering sleepily what the famous detective would have made of his present situation, especially the encounter in the wood. Encounters of an amorous nature didn't figure largely in Holmes' adventures. He would have taken a coldly analytical approach to the whole thing, listing all the possibilities, trying them out on the Doctor for effect.

He glanced down. His own Watson was still fast asleep, twitching every so often in his dreams. He would get no help there for the time being.

Twisting open his Cross pen, he picked up a pad of paper and began to write. For some while he wrote and scratched out and amended and cut and edited and then rewrote again, filling page after page. Not until he was completely satisfied did he lay down his pen and even then he tore up the used sheets and transferred the distillation of his findings to a fresh page before reading it out loud.

'What we are looking for,' he intoned to his captive

audience of one, 'and there cannot be many in this world who fit the description, is an illiterate English female compositor, who stands about 168 centimetres tall, and is possessed of a *balcon* of such largeness and generosity, of such roundness and hardness, that it almost defies belief.'

Ignoring the snore which came from the direction of the wheelbarrow, Monsieur Pamplemousse tore the sheet off the pad and placed it carefully beneath the glass on the bedside table. Well pleased with the result of his evening's work, he turned out the light and closed his eyes.

One thing was for certain: given the opportunity, he would be able to identify them again anywhere, anytime, anyplace. They were indelibly and disturbingly etched on his memory.

He had another flash of inspiration before sleep finally overtook him. He remembered where he'd seen the subject of the photograph before. It was the girl who had been sitting all alone in the restaurant that evening.

4

TAKING THE WATERS

'I am looking, *Monsieur*, for a woman with exceptionally large *doudounes*. Large, firm and of coconut-like hardness. A woman who is not averse to exposing them to the world . . .'

'Aren't we all, Pamplemousse, aren't we all.' The Director sounded tired, as though he had been up all night. 'May I remind you that you are in the Haute-Savoie, not St. Tropez.'

Monsieur Pamplemousse decided to ignore the interruption. 'They belong,' he continued, 'to someone who works, or has worked, in the printing trade. Possibly someone who has a grudge. I am told there is a great deal of redundancy in the industry. Competition from the Orient is severe.'

'Pamplemousse!' The Director's voice cut in again. 'Why is it that whenever you are on a case there is always a woman involved? Sooner or later sex rears its ugly head. Usually it is sooner rather than later.'

'*Cherchez la femme, Monsieur*. It is my experience in life that there is always a woman involved. Man has a great and undying and unquenchable need for woman. It has been so ever since the Garden of Eden. You could say, *Monsieur*, that were I to find this woman I would be well on the way to solving the problem.'

From the silence at the other end he felt that he had scored a point, and from the length of that silence it was not just an outer or a magpie, but a bullseye; a direct hit.

'No, Pamplemousse, *I* would not say that. You are saying it. The choice of words is yours.' There was a note of acerbity in the voice, and yet Monsieur Pamplemousse felt there were also overtones of respect; respect and some other quality he couldn't quite define. A whisker of apprehension perhaps?

'May I ask you something, Aristide?' The Director was clearly about to change his tune.

'*Oui, Monsieur.*'

'It is only a small thing, of little importance I'm sure. But it kept me awake last night wondering.'

'Please ask anything you wish, *Monsieur.*'

'Why were you pushing Pommes Frites about the gardens of Les Cinq Parfaits in a wheelbarrow last night? Has he suffered some kind of injury?'

'Shall we say, *Monsieur*, that he is indisposed.'

'Nothing serious, I trust?'

Monsieur Pamplemousse glanced towards the subject of their conversation. It was hard to say. Pommes Frites hadn't visibly moved from where he'd been deposited some ten or eleven hours previously. Nevertheless there was some improvement; he appeared to be regarding the outside world through at least one half-open, if decidedly lack-lustre eye which could only be interpreted as a step in the right direction. His jowls gave an occasional twitch.

'It is difficult to form an opinion, *Monsieur.*'

'You must seek medical advice.'

'I am about to phone his *vétérinaire* in Paris. It may take time.'

'Time is not on our side, Pamplemousse.' The Director sounded agitated again. 'A "certain person" has been on to me already this morning demanding news of progress. I can hardly repeat what you have just told me. I understand the workings of your mind, Aristide. I respect them. I know that threads have to be picked up and examined and pondered on before you weave them together into some sort of pattern, however bizarre and convoluted. I know that ordinarily this takes time, but I hesitate to pass on the news that the boilers and generators of France depend for their life's blood on a pair of *doudounes*, however large and desirable they may be.'

'*Oui, Monsieur.*'

'Were they . . .' The voice hesitated. 'Were they very exceptional, Aristide? Clearly, they made a deep impression on you.'

'*Formidable, Monsieur. Extraordinaire*. I will describe the situation and the events leading up to it more fully when I make my report.'

'Good. I shall look forward to that moment. We will go through it over a bottle of champagne. Some of your favourite Gosset.' The Director sounded in a better mood. 'Now, I will leave you to your telephoning. Command the *vétérinaire* to fly down to Geneva if necessary. We will arrange for a car to meet him. Tell him it is a matter of supreme national importance. Oil is a valuable commodity. I need hardly stress the fact that other powers are interested. Powers, Aristide, whose climate is such that their needs during the winter months are even greater than our own. Pommes Frites must be restored to the peak of condition as quickly as possible. I have a high regard for his abilities and they must not be impaired.'

Monsieur Pamplemousse murmured his goodbyes and then with a sigh replaced the receiver. He bent down to pat the wheelbarrow's occupant on the stomach. Almost immediately there was a distant rumble; a warning of worse things to come.

Monsieur Pamplemousse hastily drew the curtains and flung open a window. At least one of Pommes Frites' abilities remained unimpaired; in fact, enhanced was more the word. If he stayed where he was storm-cones would need to be hoisted over the barrow; the air-conditioning would be tested to its limits.

He stood for a moment breathing in the fresh autumn air. The distant sound of a ship's siren announced the presence of a paddle-steamer making its morning round of the lake. Waiters in jeans and sweatshirts were busy on the nearby terrace, laying the tables for lunch – holding wine-glasses above a jug of steaming water before giving them a final polish. Laughing and joking amongst themselves, they looked very different to the slightly aloof figures who had attended him the night before. One of them was busy raking a patch of earth where a mark had been left by the wheelbarrow. He waved as he caught sight of Monsieur Pamplemousse.

Monsieur Pamplemousse returned the wave automatically, his mind suddenly on other things. How, for example, had the Director got to hear about the episode with the wheelbarrow quite so speedily? Someone must have been very quick off the mark in complaining. Someone high up in government, perhaps? Either that, or there was some other source of communication. Whichever it was, it left him feeling irritated.

He turned away from the window and contemplated Pommes Frites for a moment. It was not an inspiring sight. Had they been with him at that moment the powers that be in Paris would have had their confidence in the future well-being of France severely shaken.

Monsieur Pamplemousse reached for the telephone and his notebook. There were times when he felt as if he spent half his life on the phone. It was one of the penalties of working in the field. This morning was no exception. He still had all the numbers he'd found on Jean-Claude's pad to go through. In the old days, back at the Sûreté, it would have been delegated to a subordinate.

His friend Durelle, the *vétérinaire*, greeted his request with a certain amount of derision.

'Drop everything? Do you realise, in my waiting-room this morning I have seven dogs, three cats, a parrot, a tortoise, and an old woman with a budgerigar. The budgerigar is eleven years old and will live for another five or six years at least. The old woman merely needs someone to talk to other than a creature who can only say *Bonjour, Bonne nuit* and *Ooh, la, la*!' She comes here every week.'

'It is a matter of national importance.'

'Are you pulling my leg?'

He didn't blame Durelle for asking. Over the years they had played a series of long-running practical jokes on each other. Childish pranks which had seemed enormous fun at the time, but which didn't always stand retelling. Like puns, they were things of the moment. There was the time when, having heard that Durelle had ordered a new suit, he had persuaded the tailor to parcel up an old sack which

60

he'd found lying in a street, one used to divert the flow of water in one of the gutters of Montmartre until it became too old even for that. It had stunk to high heaven. Durelle had passed no comment at the time, but he'd got his own back by giving it to him as a present the following Christmas. It had gone to and fro for several years until Doucette had put her foot down.

'No, I am perfectly serious. You can check with the office. I am staying at Les Cinq Parfaits, by Lac Léman . . .'

'Lucky devil! I wish I could join you. We could do a spot of fishing together.'

'The grass is always greener on the other side of the fence,' said Monsieur Pamplemousse, slightly aggrieved. 'The way things are going I shan't have much time for fishing.'

'Has he been overeating again? I seem to remember it happening once before. That time when you were both in Normandy. Apples stuffed with quail and baked in pastry, was it not? Afterwards Pommes Frites was given the cream bowl to lick and suffered accordingly. It took him several days to recover.'

'*Chiens* are *interdits* in the dining-room at Les Cinq Parfaits,' said Monsieur Pamplemousse defensively. 'Besides, he appears to have lost his appetite completely. He turned up his nose at a biscuit I offered him, one of his favourites which I keep for special occasions. It is always a bad sign.'

'Has he been taking the local water?'

'We are staying near Evian.'

'Ah, then we must look elsewhere. Are his eyes at all bloodshot?'

'Pommes Frites' eyes are often bloodshot,' said Monsieur Pamplemousse reprovingly. 'He is, after all, a Bloodhound.'

'Yes, of course.' Durelle sounded distracted. In the background there was the noise of a dog barking. 'And his nose? Is it dry?'

'It is hard to say. It has recently been greased. I gave it a liberal coating of Vaseline before we left Paris. Enough to last the holiday.'

'Temperature?'

'Again, it is hard to say. He felt very cold to the touch last night, but he'd been lying out in a wood . . .'

'*Un moment.*' There was a pause followed by a heavy clunk as the receiver at the other end was laid down. There were now several dogs barking. It sounded like a fight. He heard a muttered oath, then a door slammed. When Durelle picked up the phone again he was breathing heavily and his words were interspersed with loud sucking noises as though he had been wounded.

'It is a bad morning. I'm truly sorry I cannot be with you.' The remark was made with feeling. 'I assume you have contacted a local vet?'

'They are not enthusiastic,' said Monsieur Pamplemousse. 'Besides, I need someone I can trust.'

'In that case I can only suggest you send me a specimen of his water for analysis.'

'Pommes Frites' water?' Monsieur Pamplemousse repeated the words dubiously.

'A few millilitres will be sufficient. If you put it on the afternoon train I will get my secretary to arrange for its collection at the Gare du Lyon. You shall have my full report first thing tomorrow morning. We will take it from there. In the meantime, if there is any change for the worse do not hesitate to ring me. I will come at once if necessary.'

Monsieur Pamplemousse replaced the receiver and eyed Pommes Frites gloomily. He foresaw difficulties. It was one thing taking a horse to the water; it was another matter entirely getting it to drink. The converse problems in Pommes Frites' case were all too obvious. Although on the surface Pommes Frites' plumbing arrangements left a lot to be desired – so much so that a passing stranger encountering him for the first time on the slopes of Montmartre might well have been forgiven had he classed them somewhere between 'random' and 'uncontrolled' – nevertheless, they were in fact exceedingly complex. Somewhere within the system there was a highly sophisticated computer which, given certain basic pieces of information, such as the time of day, the state of the weather, and the direction in which its owner-operator was heading, could calculate within seconds the number of trees, parked cars and various items of street furniture likely to be encountered en route. Armed with this information, the section which dealt with quantity control then dispensed measured doses with laboratory-like precision according to the total litreage available, the number of objects and their relative importance to each other.

The one thing Pommes Frites' system lacked was any kind of early-warning system for the benefit of others. Short of lying in wait for him behind a tree, carrying out Durelle's request would not be easy.

Reflecting that even Sherlock Holmes might have admitted to being temporarily baffled by the problem, Monsieur Pamplemousse attempted to extract a crumb of comfort from the laden breakfast tray beside his bed.

Holmes had often begun his cases over breakfast. *The Hound of the Baskervilles* was a good example; breakfast consumed straight after an early-morning pipe filled with the previous day's dottle dried on the study mantelpiece. He must have had a constitution of iron.

Strange, the English predilection for a hearty breakfast. Perhaps it had to do with the uncertain climate. Boiled eggs, served in strange pottery containers, often shaped like hollowed-out human heads which grinned at you across the table. Knowing exactly when the eggs would be done to perfection was a mysterious art which was handed down and could not be described accurately in any cook book.

He wondered if a call from the Director would have been permitted to break the morning ritual at number 221B Baker Street. Mrs. Hudson would not have been pleased to see her efforts grow cold. Nothing, not even the sight of a newly severed digit in *The Adventure of the Engineer's Thumb* was ever allowed to put Holmes off his breakfast.

Monsieur Pamplemousse eyed the remains of his *brioche*. It looked most unappetising. Disappointing to start with, now that it had grown cold it was even less enticing. Perhaps it was yet another of Jean-Claude's skills which had not been passed on. Then, again, perhaps he was already conditioned to not expecting things exactly right; his expectations were now tempered by inside knowledge and the early-morning call from his office.

Crumbling the remains of the cake between thumb and forefinger, he debated his priorities; whether to attend to Pommes Frites or continue with his telephone calls. He decided on the latter. The longer he left Pommes Frites the stronger would be the call of nature once he surfaced.

The first number he dialled was engaged, the second was a garage in Evian. He apologised and tried the third number. It was a *cancoillotte* producer in a village higher up the mountains. *Cancoillotte*, made with well-rotted *Metton* cheese warmed over a low heat along with salt water and butter, was a speciality of the area. It was then melted again with white wine and garlic to be served as a fondue on toast or over potatoes. Just the thing after a ski run on a cold winter's day. The thought almost made him feel hungry again.

The fourth number was a flower shop in Evian. Something about the voice at the other end made him decide to try his luck.

'I am telephoning on behalf of Monsieur Parfait. Monsieur Jean-Claude Parfait. There is some confusion about an order.'

The girl sounded puzzled. There was the sound of rustling paper as if she was looking through an order book. 'Do you know when it was made? There is no record. Monsieur Jean-Claude usually calls in on his way back from market. Was it to do with the restaurant? Monsieur Albert always deals with that later in the day. He should be in any moment. I haven't seen Monsieur Jean-Claude for two days . . .'

'I'm sorry. I think I had better check.' Monsieur Pamplemousse made his excuses and hung up. Perhaps his remarks to the Director, made more in his own defence on the spur of the moment than for any other reason, were not so wide of the mark after all. It could still be a case of *cherchez la femme*. Jean-Claude would hardly be buying flowers for himself.

The sixth number was a ski club near Morzine.

He tried the first number again. This time he got the ringing tone. He counted over twenty rings and then a girl's voice answered. '*Bonjour. Vous voulez parler à qui?*'

She sounded breathless. The words were French but the accent was foreign. He guessed it was English; the pitch went down at the end rather than up. Again, instinct told him to prolong the conversation. He plucked a name out of the air.

'Monsieur Duval, *s'il vous plaît*.'

'*Pardon?*'

He repeated the name. 'Monsieur Duval. Monsieur Henri Duval.'

The reply, when it came, was halting and confused, as if the speaker was suddenly out of her depth, struggling in heavy water. He decided to put her out of her misery.

'*Parlez-vous anglais?*'

'Yes. I mean . . . *oui*.' The relief was evident in the way the words came pouring out. 'I don't know anyone by that name. I think you'd better try the other number. This is the communal phone – the one for the pupils. I just happened to be passing.'

While he was listening, Monsieur Pamplemousse removed his pen from an inner pocket and twisted the barrel. 'Do you have the other number? I am afraid I have mislaid it.'

While he was writing there was a stirring from the confines of the wheelbarrow. It was followed by a loud yawn and a smacking of lips. Pommes Frites was showing signs of life at long last.

'And who shall I be speaking to?'

'You'll probably get Madame Schmidt herself. I saw her go towards her room as I was coming up the stairs.'

Thanking the girl for her trouble, he replaced the receiver and then almost immediately regretted his haste. Having established some kind of rapport he should have taken matters a stage further and found out where she was speaking from. The code was from an outside area. He checked with a list in a folder beside his bed. It was somewhere higher up the mountains near Morzine. It was obviously an educational establishment of some kind.

Monsieur Pamplemousse gazed thoughtfully at the telephone for a moment or two, then picked up the receiver and dialled the number the girl had given him.

This time the call was answered almost immediately.

'Institut des Beaux Arbres. Madame Schmidt speaking. Can I help you?'

He decided to take the bull by the horns. '*Bonjour, Madame*. I hope you can. Forgive my troubling you at this early hour, but I am in the area and I am making some enquiries. I am told that it is possible you have some vacancies.'

'The term has already started, *Monsieur*.' The voice sounded hesitant. 'We like our pupils to be here from the beginning, otherwise it sometimes creates difficulties. The school year begins in September.'

'No matter. There is no great urgency. It is a question of planning for the future. I am staying at Les Cinq Parfaits and while I am here I hope to see as many establishments as I can.'

'*Monsieur* should have an easy task then. As far as I know we are the only school in the area. They are nearly all on the Swiss side of the lake.'

'In that case perhaps it would be as well if I came to see you as soon as possible.'

'You have our brochure?'

'I am speaking on behalf of a friend. He is abroad at present and unable to carry out the investigation himself. I promised I would do my best.'

'He is French? Most of our clients are from overseas. Learning the language is an integral part of the course. A French student would find the going very slow.'

'No, *Madame*. He is English. That is also part of the problem and why I am here.'

'I understand, *Monsieur*.' The voice was perceptibly friendlier. 'The second half of this week will be a little difficult . . .'

'How about this afternoon?' Monsieur Pamplemousse assumed his most ingratiating manner. 'I realise it is very short notice, but my friend spoke most highly of your establishment, and with three children to plan for . . .'

This time there was a distinct thaw. 'Let me see . . . I have another appointment at four. Shall we say two thirty? That will allow plenty of time for you to see around the school and to observe our pupils at work.'

'Thank you, *Madame*. I will be with you at two thirty.
A bientôt.'
'*Au revoir, Monsieur.*'

Pommes Frites looked at him enquiringly as he replaced
the receiver. While his master had been engaged on the
telephone he'd been taking stock of the situation, absorbing his new surroundings, weighing up the scene as best he
could, given the fact that his brain was still far from func-
tioning on all of its many cylinders. Not for nothing had he
accompanied Monsieur Pamplemousse on his travels up
and down the autoroutes and byways of France, sharing
his thoughts at the wheel, his many meals, the passenger
seat of his 2CV, and more often than not his hotel room –
even his very bed. Over the years he'd become adept at
reading his master's mind. Lack of vocabulary, at least on
a scale which would have met the minimum requirements
laid down by the Minister of Education for the schools of
France, did not prevent him getting the gist of conversations or sensing which way the wind was blowing. Rather
the reverse. The ability to recognise certain key words
often gave him the edge in that it allowed him to go straight
to the heart of matters at a time when others more skilled in
their use would have been diverted. Instinct told Pommes
Frites that something was going on.

However, coming up with the right answer was one
thing. Co-ordinating the rest of his body to follow suit was
another matter entirely. He tried shifting his position and
then hurriedly froze as the surface beneath him rocked in a
most unseemly manner and his stomach rebelled accordingly.

The plain fact was, Pommes Frites still felt distinctly out
of sorts. Had he been given to writing to the newpapers on
topics of current interest, he would have happily spent the
rest of the morning lying in the wheelbarrow composing a
very bitter letter indeed to the local *journal* on the subject
of hotels who denied canine guests access to their dining-
room and then left their waste-bins not only unattended
but full to overflowing. It was simply asking for trouble.
Religion was not one of Pommes Frites' strong subjects,
but had he been cognisant of the temptations suffered by

Adam in the Garden of Eden, he could have drawn some pretty pointed parallels. Nor would he have sought anonymity by signing himself 'Disgusted, Evian'; he would have come right out with it and given his full name and address. Whether the local *journal* would have risked incurring the wrath of Les Cinq Parfaits by printing it was purely a matter of conjecture; an editorial decision was unlikely to be put to the test. Les Cinq Parfaits was one of the area's major sources of income, a source whose ripples spread far and wide, giving support to innumerable diverse activities and industries, from mushroom-growers to helicopter pilots and the mechanics who serviced their machines, from wine-growers to owners of motor-launches, from chambermaids and dairy farmers to fruit-growers and butchers and suppliers of chlorine for swimming pools. Advertising revenue would have slumped and circulation figures been put in jeopardy.

However, it summed up the kind of mood Pommes Frites was in as he rested his head on the side of the barrow and watched his master busy himself over a matter that was clearly causing him a certain amount of serious thought and which involved emptying the contents of a small leather suitcase on to his bed.

The sight of the suitcase confirmed Pommes Frites' suspicions. Something was very definitely 'going on'.

Designed at the turn of the century by *Le Guide*'s founder, Hippolyte Duval, for use by Inspectors at a time when emergencies of one sort or another were commonplace, it had been carefully added to and improved upon over the years until it had reached a point where practically any eventuality was catered for; even, reflected Monsieur Pamplemousse as he removed the tray of photographic equipment and exposed a lower one containing a selection of culinary items, eventualities which would surely have been undreamed of by the founder or any of his various successors.

Pommes Frites never ceased to be amazed by the contents of Monsieur Pamplemousse's suitcase, but amazement gave way to incredulity as he watched his master take out what looked like a very ordinary flat metal disc. Then, with one flick of his wrist, he changed it into a totally different shape – a shape not unlike a giant version of the ice-cream containers he was sometimes allowed to share, the ones which tasted of biscuit. Had his master produced a string of flags of all nations from his left ear, Pommes Frites could not have been more taken aback, and for the moment at least it took his mind off his own problems.

Nor did his master show signs of resting on his laurels. Having performed one trick to his obvious satisfaction, he looked around the room for another, peering into the bathroom, opening cupboard doors, until suddenly his gaze alighted on a large, empty bottle standing on top of the refrigerator.

Giving a grunt of satisfaction, Monsieur Pamplemousse slipped the cone-shaped article into the neck of the bottle, held both up to the light, then turned to face Pommes Frites, uttering as he did so the words, 'Une promenade?'

Although simple in content and perhaps not in the same class as such immortal phrases as 'Kiss me, Hardy', or 'Not tonight, Josephine', they were, nevertheless, words which would have caused a keen student of such matters to prick up his ears and reach for a notebook, aware that he was privileged to be present at one of those moments destined to become in its own small way one of historical importance.

Blissfully unaware of either the importance of the occasion or the leading part he was about to play, Pommes Frites climbed out of the wheelbarrow and made his way unsteadily towards the door.

Even in his present comatose state he could tell the difference between a suggestion and a command. His early training with the Paris Sûreté stood him in good stead. Suggestions offered a freedom of choice. Commands were meant to be obeyed without question.

Conscious only that duty called, Pommes Frites followed his master out of the side door and into the gardens of Les Cinq Parfaits.

It was some while before they returned to the room and by then both were in sombre mood, each busy with his own thoughts and studiously avoiding the other's gaze.

The telephone was ringing, and while Pommes Frites lay down on a rug by the window, Monsieur Pamplemousse placed the bottle and funnel carefully on the table beside his bed and picked up the receiver. It was a call from Paris.

'Pamplemousse, what *is* going on? It was my intention to leave you to your own devices, but I have been receiving disturbing reports, reports I can scarcely credit. Reports of bestial happenings in the bushes outside the dining-room. There have been complaints from the guests. Some of them were so put off their lunch they demanded their money back. I would like to think that it was a case of mistaken identity, but I fear the description of both participants tallies. I demand an explanation.'

Monsieur Pamplemousse took a deep breath. There were times in his conversations with the Director when it was possible, by the lowering of suitable shutters, to divert the other's voice along the shortest possible route leading to an exit through the opposite ear, but patently it was not one of those occasions. Patently it was an occasion when tops needed to be blown, his authority asserted and parameters established once and for all.

He spoke at length, choosing his words with care; words which were both rounded and yet at the same time pointed. Explicit words which established his feelings with the utmost clarity and precision. Words which left no room for doubt. When he had finished he sat down on the bed and mopped his brow, waiting for the storm to break. Pommes Frites gazed at his master with renewed respect, aware that a stand had been made.

There was a long pause. 'Forgive me, Aristide.' The Director sounded genuinely contrite. 'I am under considerable pressure at this end, you understand. You are in the battle area, subject to bombardment by long-range missiles, but I am also under fire. Weapons are being held to my head. I have hardly slept all night.'

'*Pardon, Monsieur,*' Monsieur Pamplemousse broke in before the Director got too far with his emotional flights of fancy; once started there was often no stopping him. 'With respect, I must be allowed to do things in my own way and at my own pace. I have, I believe, already made considerable progress. Now there are leads to be followed; there is information to be tabulated and considered. However, it appears that there are others staying at Les Cinq Parfaits who know as much about what is going on as I do – possibly more – and who seem to be aware of my every movement. Not only aware,' he added with some heat, 'but only too anxious to report on them with all possible speed. Let these others do the dirty work.'

'That is not possible, Aristide. I cannot tell you why, but take my word for it, that is not possible. There are, as I said at the very beginning, wheels within wheels. Who knows what is what, or, indeed, who is who? If I were to tell you about some of the machinations which have reached my ears over the last two days you would scarcely credit them.'

Monsieur Pamplemousse rested the receiver under his chin and picked up the bottle containing Pommes Frites' sample. He held it up to the light. Château Pommes Frites. A direct comparison with the real thing would rank it immediately as from a poor year; there was a distinct orange tinge. Perhaps a '63? The year of a hard winter followed by a dismal summer, giving rise to poor flowering conditions. But that was only by direct comparison. On its own it would pass muster.

If his chief did but know it, he was preaching to the converted. Monsieur Pamplemousse was only too well aware of things that went on behind the scenes. Lack of communication. Empire building. Parkinson's Law, which ruled that the appointment of two assistants instead of one meant that jobs could be divided up in such a way that no one person knew enough to become a potential threat to those above. Inter-departmental rivalry. Jockeying for power. Corridors which led nowhere except to closed doors. He'd come across many of those in his time. Blank faces. Denials of the very existence of things one knew only too well existed. Sometimes he wondered how governments functioned at all.

Wondering uneasily if he himself was some kind of pawn in the present game, he reached idly for the cork. It was still lying alongside the ice-bucket where it had been left the night before. Dried out by the warmth of the room, it went back into the neck of the bottle easily enough, needing only a slight tap with the ball of his hand to drive it fully home. There was only the smallest of holes to show where it had been penetrated by the corkscrew.

He held the bottle up to the light again and as he did so a wicked thought entered his mind. Durelle was no fool, but given that the original label was still intact, he might get away with it.

'Yes, chief, I am listening.' He felt decidedly more cheerful now. He couldn't wait to put his leg-pull into action. There would need to be a short note to accompany the bottle, of course. Something along the lines of: 'Pommes Frites now on the road to recovery. No need for further action. A small token of my appreciation. Hope you enjoy it. Aristide.'

It was true. Pommes Frites' eyes now had a decided sparkle. He was growing more alive by the minute. The walk and the consequent chase round the garden must have done him good.

Monsieur Pamplemousse slipped the lead foil over the neck and smoothed it into place. The wine waiter had done a good job. He must be a Capricorn like himself, as well as coming from the Auvergne; a perfectionist twice over. It looked as good as new.

'Oui, Monsieur. Rest assured, I will telephone the very moment there is anything to report. Possibly this evening.'

'And Aristide.' The Director hesitated, then swallowed hard. 'Forgive my impatience. It is always worse for those who stay behind. Things get magnified.'

'Of course, Monsieur. Au revoir, Monsieur.'

He opened the refrigerator and stood the bottle in the door-rack alongside its companion. With the capsule in place and in the artificially white light reflected from the interior it was almost indistinguishable from the real thing. If colour were the sole criterion, Pommes Frites would be in line for an award at the annual wine fair in Paris. There would have to be a P.S. to the message, otherwise Durelle would get suspicious. It was too good a gift. 'Have this one on the house. Madame Grante is paying.' That would appeal to his sense of humour too. Madame Grante in Accounts was notorious for watching every franc.

He glanced at his watch. There was hardly sufficient time for lunch in the restaurant. In any case he had no wish to run the gauntlet of those who had spotted their activities in the bushes, and Pommes Frites might not take kindly to eating by himself twice running. Perhaps a snack by the pool would be the answer. He'd seen a cold table laid out there. A little *charcuterie*; some *saucisses de Morteau et de Montbeliard* – cumin-flavoured – a speciality of the region. Some ham from Chamonix – dried in the crisp mountain air. A salad. Then some *Beaufort* or some *Comté*; perhaps a little of each. If they got a move on there might be time for some bilberry tart to follow – or some more raspberries; they wouldn't be around for very much longer.

If he was lucky they might have some sparkling wine from Seyssel – the most northern of the Rhône vineyards and the nearest thing to champagne. A glass or two would set him up for the rest of the day. He could accompany the rest of the meal with some flinty rosé d'Arbois. It would be light enough not to make him feel sleepy or impede his thought processes.

Pommes Frites rose and accompanied him to the door.

Outside, Monsieur Pamplemousse reversed the card on the handle, changing the sign from one showing a girl in a white dress and old-fashioned bonnet asleep under a walnut tree to one of her hard at work with a feather duster. Halfway along the corridor there was a large trolley laden with sheets and towels, bottles of Evian and packets of soap and perfume. From an open doorway he heard the murmur of voices and some suppressed giggles. The room maids must be getting near.

He glanced down at Pommes Frites as they set off. Pommes Frites looked up and wagged his tail. It was a good sign. One good sign, followed almost immediately by a second, for he licked his lips, and if Pommes Frites was licking his lips it could mean only one thing: life was returning to normal.

5

L'INSTITUT DES BEAUX ARBRES

It took Monsieur Pamplemousse rather longer than he'd planned to get within striking distance of the Institut des Beaux Arbres, and even longer to find the entrance, which was half-hidden behind a clump of fir trees.

Reflecting that the Institut was well-named (most of the *arbres* were not only *beaux*, they were *très grands* as well, and badly needed thinning), he pulled in alongside some large wrought-iron gates standing in splendid isolation within a carved stone archway and climbing out of the car he applied his thumb to a bell-push. A disembodied voice emerged from a small grille above the button. He gave his name and almost immediately there was a buzz from the direction of the gate itself as an electric bolt-retainer slid open. There was a click and the loudspeaker was silent, cutting off the apologies he had been about to make for being late. He glanced at his watch. It was almost three o'clock.

Lunch had been a protracted affair. Word must have got around about his extravagance the previous evening, for a second assistant *sommelier* hovered about his table like a solicitous butterfly, the *carte des vins* already open at what he clearly considered to be an appropriately expensive page. At the waiter's suggestion he had weakened and succumbed to a whole bottle of Pouilly-Fumé instead of the half-bottle of rosé he'd had in mind; a Baron de 'L' '82 from the estate of the Ladoucette family in Pouilly-sur-Loire. Totally delicious, it prompted an entry in his notebook as a reminder to repeat the experience at the earliest opportunity – God, Monsieur le Directeur and Madame Grante in Accounts permitting.

The combination of the wine, food from a cold table positively groaning with temptations, coupled with a somewhat protracted but undeniably thorough survey of such *doudounes* as were on public display around the pool that day, left him in the end with the bare minimum of time to rush back to his room, grab the bottle containing Pommes Frites' sample from the door of the fridge and his Leica from the case, before making an equally wild dash for Evian and the nearest *gare*. He'd been in and out before the maid, busy replenishing the stocks of perfume and unguents in the bathroom, even realised what was happening.

The journey to Evian had been slow; the normally quiet lakeside road busier than usual. Lausanne, on the far side of Lac Léman, was shrouded in autumn mist, the hills beyond barely visible. In one village an unlikely-looking, life-sized painted cut-out of a cow eyed him dolefully as he waited his turn in the traffic which had piled up behind a delivery van parked outside an *épicerie*. It looked decidedly less happy than its real-life counterparts in the fields he had passed on the way down, and he could hardly blame it.

After Evian he headed for the D22 and then turned left in the direction of the mountains, taking a road which grew steadily more narrow and winding. Wooden chalets with tightly shuttered windows dotted the hillside. Alongside them stood piles of neatly sawn logs ready for the coming winter. They were all so similar and so like toy musical-boxes that it wouldn't have been surprising to see a giant key on the outside of each one, to wind them up again in the spring.

Gradually the chalets retreated, to be replaced by isolated farms; the road became steeper, the drop more sheer, making it difficult to overtake anything in front – even the occasional cyclists enjoying a last seasonal fling as they pedalled their way laboriously uphill with lowered heads and bulging thighs. Why was it they always seemed to be going uphill rather than down? It looked very painful and unpleasurable, although he had done exactly the same thing when he'd been their age. There was hardly a hill in the Auvergne he hadn't tackled in his youth, and he must have enjoyed it at the time.

Having got well and truly stuck behind a laborious sand-carrying *camion*, Monsieur Pamplemousse took the opportunity to run through in his mind the reasons for making the journey at all. It was really little more than the following up of a hunch; a feeling he couldn't have put into words. But that was how it was; how it had always been. How many times in the past had he not set off on a journey with as little to go on? That was what it was all about. You started with a problem. Then you took all the available facts and you placed them in some kind of order. Perhaps, if the worst came to the worst you put them all into a hat and gave them a good shake. Then you played a hunch.

Holmes would have done the same. Except, of course, he would have carried it through with total conviction and from the comfort of his lodging house. He tried to picture what Holmes might have told Watson before despatching him up the mountainside in a pony and trap.

First, there was the fact that Jean-Claude's disappearance had not been premeditated, of that he was sure. Had it been, he would have taken more with him. All his toiletries seemed to be intact. There was no marked absence of clothes or suitcases.

Secondly, he was well-known in the area. If he had caught a train or an *autobus* anywhere someone would have seen him, assuming Albert Parfait was telling the truth – and apart from a disquieting feeling that for some reason best known to himself he wasn't being entirely frank, he couldn't for the moment see any reason why he should be lying. Jean-Claude's car was still at Les Cinq Parfaits – that was a puzzle. If anything, it pointed to his not having gone very far, or to his having gone with someone else.

Thirdly, there was the strange encounter in the wood. Fourthly, there was the collection of words he'd come across under Jean-Claude's blotter. How or why they fitted into the overall picture he hadn't the remotest idea. That the words formed a blackmail note of some kind was obvious, but how it related to Jean-Claude's disappearance was another matter.

Lastly, there was the picture of the girl he was carrying in his pocket along with the list of telephone numbers. That the girl was the reason for Jean-Claude's visits to the flower shop he had no doubt; that she was a pupil of the Institut des Beaux Arbres seemed more than likely. She was about the right age. She was English. It was the only school in the area.

Hairpin bends, the nearside edge protected by low stone walls or steel safety-barricades – some bent and twisted where previous drivers had tried to negotiate the corners too fast, caused the lorry in front to slow down almost to walking pace. Frustrated, he stopped in a lay-by and consulted his map. The view down to the valley on his right was breathtaking. In a field just below him an old woman was bent double over a mound of freshly dug potatoes. Nearby a man was picking fruit from a tree. The sound of what seemed like a thousand bells, all tuned to a different pitch, floated up from neatly parcelled areas of pastureland as cows and sheep dipped their heads to munch the rich grass. Old white porcelain baths filled with water for the cattle dotted the landscape, bequeathed by owners who had become affluent and exchanged them in the name of progress for brightly coloured suites made of plastic or fibreglass.

As he set off in the car again he fell to wondering if Albert knew of the girl's existence. If so, did he approve? Apart from the question of age, he saw no outward reason for disapproval. If he'd had a son of his own, he would have been more than happy. Come to think of it, if the girl had been his daughter he would have felt equally happy. Or would he? Jean-Claude would be something of a catch. Anyone who married him would have to be fairly special; the life was not an easy one. Nor would Albert wish to see his son diverted from his chosen path – or, more to the point, the one that he had chosen for him. Already his absence had caused unrest, but that was hardly a reason for family jiggery-pokery. Besides, a girl who had been given the added benefit of a spell at a finishing school, versed in the social graces, ought to be ideal.

He tried to picture her again, sitting in the restaurant, an altogether more vulnerable figure than the one in the photograph. Since she had been alone and clearly worried, she was probably as much in the dark as he was. He found himself wanting to help her if it was at all possible.

He began toying with the idea of asking Madame Schmidt outright if he could see the girl. She could hardly refuse. On the other hand, he had probably made it impossible; by a chance word he had burned his boats. Madame Schmidt would hardly believe him now if he came up with a story about being a friend of the family who happened to be in the area.

He saw the sign marking the turn-off for the Institut a moment too late. Reversing the 2CV wasn't easy, especially as Pommes Frites was beginning to show signs of what American astronauts in their quaint jargon called 'stomach awareness', and insisted on sitting bolt upright with a pained expression on his face, looking neither to the right nor to the left, as if the problem was not of his making – which, in fairness, it wasn't.

The road leading up to the school was narrower still. Unusually, Michelin seemed to have ignored its existence, eschewing even the doubtful honour of awarding it a single dotted black line on their map of the area. The only sign, just before the entrance, had been one warning of danger from falling rock.

He opened the gates, drove through, then stopped to get out and close them again. The bolt clicked home. Madame Schmidt obviously took good care of her pupils. To one side there was a passing place large enough to accommodate a whole fleet of limousines. From the gate the road dropped down again towards a hidden valley and then, a few hundred metres further on, he encountered a junction with a bevy of signs pointing in different directions: to the left, the staff quarters and the delivery area; straight on to the recreation area, students' chalets and visitors' carpark. The main building lay to the right.

There were three other cars parked outside the house: a black Mercedes 220 with a Swiss registration, and two Peugeot 505s – one with a local registration and the other bearing a Paris 75 on its number-plate. The one from Paris looked as if it had recently been driven through a heavy rainstorm; the sides were flecked with mud almost to window-height and there were clear patches on the windscreen where the wipers had been used. Whoever had been at the wheel had been in a hurry.

Madame Schmidt was waiting at the door to greet him. She looked as if she were used to people being late. His apologies were brushed aside as of no great consequence.

Pommes Frites didn't look at all put out at being left in the car; rather the reverse. He assumed his 'aloof from it all, see you when I see you' expression as he curled up in the front seat to await further instructions. Nevertheless, as the door to the Institut des Beaux Arbres closed behind his master he sat up and automatically registered a quick movement behind one of the windows, the falling into place of a curtain. Having stored the information in the back of his mind in case it was ever needed, he closed his eyes and went to sleep again.

Inside the house, Monsieur Pamplemousse was also busily committing various items to memory. Not only the restrained but undoubted luxury of the furnishings and the depth of the carpeting, but also Madame Schmidt herself. Madame Schmidt wasn't quite as he'd expected her to be and it was hard to say exactly why. He always felt ill at ease with members of the teaching profession; they tended to talk in statements or to ask questions which demanded answers. But it wasn't just that. Following her across the hall he sensed a contradiction in styles. On the telephone she had sounded nervous and abrupt, whereas listening to her now she seemed much more to be mistress of the situation. Perhaps it was simply a case of being on her home ground, but somehow he felt it was more than that.

He guessed she must be in her middle sixties. It was hard to tell with some people, particularly those who were able to keep up appearances. Elderly and benign, she could have been everyone's 'Tante Marie', had her grey hair not been quite so impeccably coiffeured, her skin so smooth and wrinkle-free. She defied cursory cataloguing. Her silk blouse reflected Paris chic rather than local tastes, which veered towards spa-town sensible. Heavy jewellery adorned fingers that were long and thin and beautifully manicured. He caught a whiff of expensive perfume as she paused to open the door to her study. Fees at the Institut des Beaux Arbres must either be considerable to keep her in the style to which she was clearly accustomed, or she had independent means.

Motioning him towards an armchair in the centre of the room, she handed him a folder before seating herself behind a desk near the window with her back to the light, making a steeple with her hands. He suddenly felt as though he were back at school, about to be grilled regarding a broken window in the greenhouse.

'Your friend will find all he needs to know inside the folder – the practical details, that is. Most of it is contained in the brochure; the rest are application forms, details of the various courses we have to offer, term times, fees and so forth. Also items like insurance and accident indemnity forms.'

'You seem to have thought of everything,' he murmured.

Madame Schmidt inclined her head. 'We have been established for over thirty years.'

Her accent, although hard to fault, was again hard to place. It was almost too impeccable. He had a feeling that she wasn't French born. It was a feeling that was confirmed almost before he had time to open the folder.

'I was born in England. My husband is German-speaking Swiss. Between us we are able to supervise the teaching of most European languages. The majority of our pupils have English as their first language when they arrive. In fact many of them *are* English.'

Monsieur Pamplemousse glanced through the folder and then turned to the brochure. Wide-angle lenses did the Institut des Beaux Arbres more than justice; the house itself certainly looked much grander than in reality. But if the photographs gave a false impression, the curriculum more than made up for the deception. He ran his eyes down the list. *Cuisine – nouvelle* and *haute* (with the opportunity of learning over one hundred and fifty new recipes per term); the mind boggled. Domestic science included engagement and control of domestic staff, ironing, washing-up (by hand and machine) – presumably for those who couldn't afford servants – and car maintenance (overalls supplied). Protocol covered *savoir-vivre*, the art of conversation and the theory and practice of baptisms and children's parties – perhaps for those who hadn't learned to say no in enough languages during the first part of their course. Elegance and deportment were catered for as well as flower arrangement (according to season). There were classes on child psychology, typing, bridge, art and clay modelling. The list seemed endless. He thought of Jean-Claude.

'Any girl who masters all these things will be much sought after.'

'Some of our pupils have married into the best families of Europe,' said Madame Schmidt complacently. 'They are, indeed, much sought after.'

Discarding a leaflet on supplementary cultural trips which included visits to a watch factory in Geneva and the kitchen of a restaurant near Lausanne (no doubt it would be Girardet), Monsieur Pamplemousse picked up another pamphlet dealing with the various sporting facilities available: riding, windsurfing, water-skiing, sailing, climbing, golf, ice-skating, skiing. He suddenly stiffened on turning the page as a familiar picture swam into view: a group of male skiers. He'd last seen it in his room at the hotel when it had fallen out of the envelope belonging to Jean-Claude. Under it was the caption '*Nos professeurs de ski*'.

'You have a permanent staff of ski instructors?' He tried to make the question sound as casual as possible.

'Naturally. In the summer they do other things, of course. But we like to preserve continuity.' Madame Schmidt regarded him across the top of her desk. 'Perhaps, before we set out on a brief tour of the school, *Monsieur* would like to fill in the registration form giving details of your friend's children. You realise there is almost always a long waiting-list so it is necessary that we have some form of selection. It may take time.'

The implication that his friend's children might not measure up to the Institut des Beaux Arbres' requirements was not lost on Monsieur Pamplemousse. Perhaps if he'd been driving something more exotic than a *deux chevaux* the question would not have arisen.

'I think you will find their background is impeccable. References of the highest order will be made available. For the time being, I am not allowed to reveal the name of my friend – for diplomatic reasons, you understand . . .' A barely perceptible reshaping of the steeple warned him that for some reason he had said the wrong thing. 'I mean, of course, in the sense that it would not be right for me to pre-empt any decision on his part without prior consultation.' Madame Schmidt visibly relaxed.

'You say he has *three* daughters? If you care to fill in their Christian names and a few brief details regarding their ages and previous schooling . . . the colour of their hair . . . any special interests . . .'

Monsieur Pamplemousse's heart sank as he felt for his pen. His knowledge of the English educational system was hazy in the extreme, other than the fact that public schools were anything but that implied by the name. The perfidious Albions were past masters at the art of calling a spade by anything rather than its proper name. They had 'stands' for sitting down, and places called 'downs' that were really ups. They had conquered half the world that way before opting out and leaving it in a state of confusion.

Names like Eton and Harrow sprang to mind, but he had a feeling that they were for boys only; it was part of the English habit to segregate the sexes at an early age, a habit that gave rise to problems later on. A colleague had once had a bizarre encounter in Boulogne with a party of girls from a school on the Channel coast; he still talked about it, releasing tantalising details in the canteen from time to time. It was worth a try.

'It is on the south coast of England. Somewhere near Brighton. Where the rock comes from.' That had been part of the story. It had had them all on the edge of their chairs.

'Roedean?' Madame Schmidt sounded impressed.

'Roedean.' He put pen to paper. It was not an easy word to spell. Worse than that place near London. The one they spelt like 'rough' and pronounced like 'cow'. The language was full of pitfalls. He crossed out the first attempt and tried again. It looked even less likely and he felt glad he wasn't applying for a place.

'They are all three at Roedean?'

'My friend is very wealthy.' He racked his brains for some suitable names. It was dreadful how the mind went completely blank at such times. Thinking up names in one's own tongue was bad enough, but English! There had been the landlady's daughter in Torquay where he'd stayed during his visit to England. She'd taught him a lot more than differences in the language. *Entente* between the two countries had never been more *cordiale*. She'd had a friend who'd also been impressively advanced for her years. He decided to try his luck again.

'I don't recall our ever having had an Ada here before,' said Madame Schmidt with a distinct lack of enthusiasm. 'Or a Reet.'

'Simple names are often the best,' said Monsieur Pamplemousse, conscious that his stock was sinking again. 'I have read that in England they are coming back into favour. It has to do with the Royal Family,' he added vaguely.

The thought triggered off another. 'It is, however, Diana who is the prime concern. The other two have a few years to go yet. Diana is barely eighteen and her father is a little worried about her. She is a lovely girl in every way, but I'm afraid her academic qualifications leave a lot to be desired. It is her parents' wish that she continue with her education for a few more years. There are so many temptations for a girl these days, especially those who have the misfortune to look older than they are. Drink . . . drugs . . . sex . . . it is a difficult age.

'Not,' he continued, warming to his subject., 'that she has experienced any of these things . . . yet. They lead a sheltered life at Roedean.'

'She sounds,' said Madame Schmidt thoughtfully, 'just the kind of girl we like to have at the Institut des Beaux Arbres. Do you have a photograph?'

'A photograph?' Carried away by enthusiasm for his subject, emboldened by the after-effects of the wine he'd consumed at lunch, Monsieur Pamplemousse found himself reaching for his wallet. 'But, of course. I always carry one. She is, after all, my god-daughter.'

Brandishing the photograph taken from Jean-Claude's room, he handed it across the table and then sat back to see what happened.

But if Monsieur Pamplemousse was expecting any kind of reaction, he was disappointed. Madame Schmidt held the photograph up to the light and gazed at it intently for several long moments. 'A very pretty girl,' she said, in much the same tone of voice as she might have used to comment on one of her pupil's flower arrangements. 'From all you have told me I am sure we can give the application every consideration.'

Rising to her feet she took the completed form from Monsieur Pamplemousse and then led the way out into the corridor. 'Perhaps you wouldn't mind waiting here.' She motioned towards a chair. 'I shan't keep you more than a moment. If I may, I will have this photograph copied so that it can go with the application. I do think it's so useful to have a clear picture of whoever one is dealing with, don't you?'

Without waiting for a reply, she entered a room on the opposite side of the corridor and closed the door firmly behind her. Almost immediately there came a murmur of voices. First Madame Schmidt's, then male voices. It sounded as though there were at least two others in the room, possibly three. Monsieur Pamplemousse took the opportunity to remove the lens cap from his camera and check that the exposure system was in the correct mode. He cocked the shutter and then listened outside the door for a moment. The voices were much too low to make any sense out of what was being said, but from the tone of the conversation it sounded as though it might go on for a few more minutes at least.

He glanced around. There were three other doors, two further along the corridor, one on either side, and another at the far end. Larger than the others, the third one had a red cross painted on the outside and he guessed it must be the Sanatorium.

He decided to seize the opportunity to do some exploring.

If he met anyone he could always say he was looking for a toilet.

The first door opened into an office. It was empty. A typewriter, its cover neatly in place, sat on an otherwise clear desk near the window. In the far corner was a copying machine. He wondered if the Institut ran to two such machines or whether the photograph had been used as an excuse. The second room turned out to be a library of sorts. It was also empty. Both rooms were dark and neither worth wasting any film on.

The door to the Sanatorium was locked. As he tried the handle he thought he detected a hurried movement on the other side. On an impulse he half-raised his camera, waist-high, finger on the shutter release button, but no one materialised. Just as he was about to try the handle for a second time he heard the sound of a door being closed somewhere behind him. He pressed the button as he turned. If Madame Schmidt registered the fact she showed no sign other than by a quick glance at the camera.

'I think you will find that everything of interest has already been photographed for the brochure, *Monsieur* . . . ?'

You don't know my name, thought Monsieur Pamplemousse, because I didn't give it to you. He decided there was nothing to be gained by concocting a false one. He'd had enough of inventing names for one day. Madame Schmidt would find out soon enough if she really wanted to know.

'Pamplemousse.' He wound the film on. 'Photography is a hobby of mine. I'm afraid I am a compulsive picture-taker. But as you say, it is good to have a clear picture of whoever one is dealing with.'

His reward was an enigmatic smile which was hard to classify; wintry Mona Lisa, perhaps? Madame Schmidt looked pointedly at her watch and then turned to lead the way in the opposite direction.

'If you will forgive me, I think we should begin our tour. There are many things to show you and I have another appointment at four.'

Monsieur Pamplemousse stood his ground. 'It is not possible to see the Sanatorium while I am here? It was one of the areas my friend was particularly anxious I should report on. Diana is a little delicate and when one's child is away from home in a foreign country . . .'

'I'm afraid it is occupied at the moment. A serious skiing accident. The patient must not be disturbed.'

'Is it not a little early for a skiing accident?' persisted Monsieur Pamplemousse.

'Early ones are the very worst.' Madame Schmidt's smile took on another layer of frost. 'People try to run before they can walk. They are over-confident. It is always bad to be over-confident.'

Monsieur Pamplemousse gave up the struggle and followed her down the corridor. 'Do you have many such casualties?'

'All winter sports are dangerous,' said Madame Schmidt. She paused before opening another door. 'Those to do with the mountains most of all. To some the mountains mean white gold – they are a source of power and energy. To others they can mean death. Sadly, we have had our share of bad luck, but these things go in cycles. I think you will find that overall our record stands comparison with many other similar establishments. If people have been telling you otherwise then I suggest you do not listen to them. It does not do to listen to idle gossip.'

Monsieur Pamplemousse looked at her with mild surprise. His remark had been intended merely as a pleasantry, a bridge to get them from one talking point to another, nothing more. What was it the great English playwright, William Shakespeare, had said? 'The lady doth protest too much, methinks.'

'I will take you first to the lecture rooms.' Changing the subject abruptly, Madame Schmidt led the way across a small courtyard towards a more modern brick-built building. 'Here, the girls are taught secretarial work – shorthand and typing – needlework, painting, and various social activities. We also have our language laboratory. New girls spend a great deal of time there during the first few weeks. All our classes are conducted in French and some of them have a good deal of catching up to do. Diana has French?'

'Diana,' said Monsieur Pamplemousse non-committally, 'has a great many languages. Her parents are much travelled.' He followed Madame Schmidt down a long corridor peering at empty rooms through glass panels in the doors. 'Do you have many pupils at any one time?'

'It varies,' said Madame Schmidt, avoiding, as he had, a direct answer. 'We pride ourselves on giving individual attention. Staff sometimes outnumber the pupils.' She stopped by a noticeboard and ran her finger down a chart. 'This afternoon, for example, many of the girls are making the most of the good weather enjoying a run with our Matron and gym mistress, Fräulein Brünnhilde. The rest are either doing revision in their own rooms or they are engaged in a cooking lesson.

'*Regardez!*' She paused by a door near the end of the corridor and looked through the panel. 'I think perhaps it will be as well if we do not disturb them. They are making a cake in honour of our patron's visit and they seem to have reached a delicate stage.'

Monsieur Pamplemousse focused his gaze on a small group of girls in white aprons struggling with an enormous jug of melted chocolate which they were endeavouring to pour over a castle-shaped edifice. Beyond them he could see a line of stoves and racks of kitchen equipment: saucepans and plates, knives and other paraphernalia. It all looked highly organised.

He glanced back at the group round the table, wondering if he might strike lucky and see the girl from the restaurant but she didn't appear to be there.

'It seems to be a very large cake,' he remarked. 'Large and rich.'

'Our patron has a very sweet tooth,' said Madame Schmidt. 'And an insatiable appetite.'

As she spoke they both heard the sound of a dog barking. Monsieur Pamplemousse pricked up his ears. To be more specific, it was the sound of Pommes Frites barking. He sounded cross about something, although not so much cross as put-out or bothered. His voice was distinctly *agitato*.

He turned away from the window. 'Perhaps I shouldn't keep you any longer,' he began. 'If you are busy . . .'

'As you wish, *Monsieur*.' It was hard to tell whether Madame Schmidt was pleased or otherwise. 'As I said earlier, you will find all you wish to know in the brochure. If you have any other questions you can always telephone. No doubt your friend will be in touch when he has had a chance to consider the matter?'

'No doubt.' As they crossed the courtyard again and approached the main building, the barking stopped. Each, for different reasons, noted the fact with relief.

Back inside the hall he paused by the front door. 'I wonder if I might have the photograph of my god-daughter back?'

'Of course. Forgive me. I had forgotten.' She seemed to have slipped back into her 'Tante Marie' role again. 'I won't keep you a moment.'

As Madame Schmidt disappeared from view Monsieur Pamplemousse stepped outside. Pommes Frites was standing on the passenger seat of the *deux chevaux* peering through the windscreen. He seemed pleased to see his master and as soon as the car door was open he leapt out and ran round the outside on a tour of inspection.

'*Qu'est-ce que c'est?*' Monsieur Pamplemousse followed on behind, but could see nothing. Perhaps someone had been having a quiet prowl while his back was turned. They would have had short shrift from Pommes Frites if they'd tried to look inside the car itself.

He glanced around the area. The Peugeot with the Paris registration was no longer there. He focused the Leica and took a few pictures for luck; first the remaining cars, then the main building. He was about to frame up the entrance when Madame Schmidt appeared in the doorway holding his photograph. He caught her registering a moment of disapproval. '*Fromage*' rather than the Anglo-Saxon word 'cheese' formed on her lips.

Pommes Frites, clearly less than happy with the situation, climbed back into the car and sat waiting for his seat-belt to be fastened, making it absolutely clear that as far as he was concerned it was high time they left. Without being able to put his finger on a specific reason, Monsieur Pamplemousse had an uneasy feeling he could be right.

'You are journeying far, Monsieur Pappernick? To Paris, perhaps?'

'The name is Pamplemousse.' He slipped the photograph back into his wallet. 'No, we shall stay in the area for a little while longer. The weather is too good at present not to take advantage of it.'

'You are wise. I am told Paris is very wet.' Madame Schmidt held out her hand. '*Au revoir et bonne chance.*'

'*Au revoir, Madame.*' Monsieur Pamplemousse climbed in alongside Pommes Frites, fastened both seat-belts and closed the door. '*Et merci beaucoup.* I hope I haven't kept you.'

He swung the car round in a circle and changed up into second gear before beginning the long climb towards the main gate. He caught a final glimpse of Madame Schmidt in the driving mirror as she stood watching their progress from the doorway. Suddenly she was joined by someone else – a man, but the road curved sharply to the right and they both disappeared from view.

The gates at the top of the drive were open; perhaps left that way by the driver of the Peugeot. On the basis of never looking a gift horse in the mouth, he took advantage of his good fortune and breasted the top of the slope at speed, with the result that he came out through the other side of the archway rather faster than he had intended.

In retrospect, reliving the moment later that night, he realised fate must have taken a hand in the proceedings; either that or whichever guardian angel with culinary inclinations had been allocated the task of looking after employees of *Le Guide* that afternoon. Had he been travelling any faster he would almost certainly have crashed through the low retaining wall opposite and hurtled down into the valley below – a thought which didn't bear dwelling on; nor could he have avoided mowing down a group of girls in shorts and singlets who were about to turn in to the driveway, straight across his path.

In the event, the car slewed round, missed hitting both wall and runners by a hair's-breadth, rocked, then miraculously righted itself again and rushed onward. He was aware of a number of things happening almost simultaneously. Or rather, he was aware that certain things were *not* happening as they should. Although his right foot was almost pushing the brake pedal through the floor, it had no effect whatsoever. He could hear the sound of girls screaming, and out of the corner of his eye he could see Pommes Frites' seat-belt was being tested to its limit. Then there was a crash as they cannoned into the road sign a little way down the hill and at last came to an abrupt halt.

'*Merde!*' Monsieur Pamplemousse released both safety-belts and together with Pommes Frites climbed out of the car and hurried round the front to view the extent of the damage. It was less than he'd feared; much less than the sound of the crash suggested. Not for nothing had Monsieur Boulanger kept his designers' sights firmly fixed on two of the main requirements he'd laid down – a long life and minimum repairs. The minuscule dent in the front bumper would have brought joy to their hearts, the dent on the offside wing confirmed their policy of separate and replaceable body parts. The road sign had fared much worse. It now stood at a drunken angle, looking as if it had failed to heed its own warning of danger from falling rocks.

'*Monsieur* . . . are you hurt? Such bravery . . . such panache . . . to drive straight into a *signalisation routière*, and without a moment of hesitation.'

A shadow fell across the bumper as Monsieur Pamplemousse bent down to examine it more closely. It was accompanied by the sound of a woman's voice, slightly out of breath.

He turned and looked up, irritated by the interruption. 'It was nothing. It was our good fortune that the sign happened to be there. Had it not been . . .' Monsieur Pamplemousse left the sentence unfinished, partly because there was no need to labour the point, but mostly because he found himself face to face with, indeed almost touching, two very good reasons why at that moment in time the sun's rays were blocked out. Rising and falling as their owner crouched beside him, they loomed into view like the distant peaks of le Dent d'Oche in the background far behind. A distinct feeling of déjà vu swept over him, and for a brief but disturbing second he was sorely tempted to reach up and attempt a renewal of his experience the night before by way of confirmation. But the moment passed. The sight of a group of girls standing a little way back watching his every movement made him think better of it. Instead, he rose to his feet and converted the movement into one of running his hand over his hair, much as he often did when he was caught about to commit some minor traffic misdemeanour.

The woman coloured slightly as she read his thoughts. '*Monsieur* is too modest. We might all have been killed. How can I ever thank you?'

Monsieur Pamplemousse hesitated. 'Perhaps, *Mademoiselle* . . .'

'*Fräulein* . . . Fräulein Brünnhilde. I am in charge of the physical well-being of the girls at the Institut.' She gestured in the direction of the waiting group. 'We were returning from a run. Normally the gates would have been closed. That is why it came as a surprise.'

Following the direction of her hand, Monsieur Pamplemousse's senses quickened yet again. There were perhaps a dozen or more girls and among them he spied the one he'd been looking for. She caught his eye and he thought he detected a faint glint of recognition, a momentary ray of hope. She looked tired and desperately unhappy.

Strengthened in his resolve, he decided to take the plunge. 'Perhaps, Fräulein Brünnhilde, if you really feel in my debt you would join me for dinner tonight? I am staying at Les Cinq Parfaits. It would give me great pleasure.'

'I think that would not be possible. I am also the Matron. Evenings are difficult. Besides, I do not own a car.'

It wasn't a total brush-off. He decided to try again.

'*Déjeuner*, then? We could have it by the pool?' It would be an opportunity to sample the Baron de 'L' again. It would be interesting to see what effect it had on his guest.

She hesitated. 'That, too, would be difficult. Perhaps . . . a picnic?'

'A picnic? Certainly. I will meet you here at twelve.' It was all too easy. Normally he would never have plucked up the courage. He wondered how many opportunities in

91

life were let slip through lack of courage and simple communication.

'13.00 would be better.' She gave a nervous giggle. 'I shall need to play truant.' The words were imbued with a *soupçon* of wickedness. He wondered whether it was intentional or simply lack of command of the language.

'*D'accord*. Tomorrow then.'

'*Auf Wiedersehen!*'

As he waved goodbye, Monsieur Pamplemousse became aware of a restless stirring beside him. Pommes Frites was getting impatient.

Pommes Frites was right, of course, as he so often was. Time was of the essence. There were important matters to investigate. Things needed looking into, or rather under. As Fräulein Brünnhilde and her party disappeared through the gates, Monsieur Pamplemousse got down on his hands and knees and peered under the car. A brief glance confirmed his suspicions.

From a similar position on the other side of the body Pommes Frites gave what looked remarkably like a nod of agreement. He was not a particularly mechanically-minded dog; the intricacies of hydraulically operated braking-systems passed him by. In emergencies he much preferred his own tried and tested arrangement, that of digging two enormous front paws into whatever ground happened to be available at the time. Now the sight of an open pipe dangling beneath the chassis of the car only served to confirm him in his views. It also confirmed his feeling that someone was out to nobble his master, and if that were the case then he not only had a very good idea who was responsible, but when the deed had actually taken place.

6

POMMES FRITES MAKES A DISCOVERY

Monsieur Pamplemousse seated himself in a chair of an open-air bar overlooking the port in Evian, unwrapped a piece of sugar, broke it in two, dropped the smaller of the two halves into a cup of *café noir*, then settled back in order to contemplate the world in general and his own immediate plans in particular.

The world in general consisted at that moment in time of a row of gulls staring back at him from a position of safety on the harbour wall, a small flotilla of sailing boats halfway across the lake towards Lausanne, two couples at nearby tables, some old-age pensioners waiting patiently for the arrival of a little rubber-tyred train which ran to and fro along the promenade, a few lorries on their way to Switzerland, and a sprinkling of late holiday-makers taking the morning air.

It was all very peaceful and ordered, reminding him that soon after his enforced early retirement from the Paris Sûreté, he'd once toyed with the idea of going there to live. All he'd wanted was to escape from it all. But Doucette, after one night of being kept awake by cowbells, had put her foot down and it had remained a pipe-dream. Doucette always woke at the first creak, or so she said, never the second. He'd consoled himself with the thought that for most people happiness lay in dreams of what might have been.

His own immediate plans were another matter and to some extent dependent on what fate and Fräulein

Brünnhilde had in store. Of the two, he felt that fate could prove more reliable and predictable. Fräulein Brünnhilde had a slightly worrying gleam in her eye.

Alongside him stood two large plastic carrier-bags. One contained two bottles of Evian water, a bottle of red Mondeuse, and a long, heavy-duty cardboard postal tube. The other carrier-bag, with a second one inside it for safety's sake, bulged with goodies culled that morning from the *charcuteries*, *traiteurs* and *boulangeries* of Evian. *Saucisses de Morteau et de Montbéliard* rubbed shoulders with pork and cabbage *saucisses de chou*, *gâteau de foies blonds de volaille* pressed against smoked mountain ham sliced from the bone and sachets of thicker ham stuffed with fresh pork meat – *jambonnettes* the like of which he hadn't seen since he'd last visited Mère Montagne's shop in Lamastre, on the other side of the Rhône valley.

The central layer in the bag was made up of a large wedge of *Reblochon* and a generous helping of *Morbier* which he'd been unable to resist; two thin layers of cheese coated with charcoal on their opposing sides before being squeezed into a rich, cake-like ball out of which oozed a thin black line.

A crisp *baguette* poked up through the middle of the bag like an over-fat flagpole, surrounded by other delicacies from the same *boulangère*; *tarte aux myrtilles*, *galette de goumeau* – *brioche* cakes topped with orange flower-water custard, and some freshly baked *biscuits de Savoie*, feather-light and covered with sliced almonds.

Fresh butter, walnuts, a box of *dragées* – the sugar-coated Savoyard almonds – honey and a selection of *confitures* completed his purchases.

He wondered whether he had forgotten anything. It would be a pity if it were a case of *une économie de bouts de chandelle*; what the English called spoiling the ship for a *sou*'s worth of *goudron*.

Picnics always sounded a good idea, but looking at the carrier-bags he had to admit that not for the first time his eyes had proved bigger than his stomach; a state of affairs that could well be remedied in the not too distant future. On the other hand, Fräulein Brünnhilde looked as though she might prove to be a good trencherwoman. Such a generous figure must need a great deal of sustenance.

He wondered what the incumbents of the Crénothérapie on the hill behind him would think if they could see his shopping list. Would it make them turn restlessly on their couches behind the glass windows of the sun terraces as they lay back paying the penalty of overstraining their kidneys?

A few sparrows possessed of a courage handed down over the years and honed by constant sorties on the table-tops of the *café*, hopped on to the top of the carrier-bag and clung within pecking distance of the *baguette*, eyeing it hungrily. They scattered as Pommes Frites lifted his head and gave them a warning stare, only to regroup and return to the attack a moment later. Refusing to be baited for the sake of a crumb, Pommes Frites treated them with the contempt they deserved.

Fräulein Brünnhilde was something of an enigma. That she and the person he'd encountered in the wood on the first night were one and the same, he didn't doubt for a moment. Unless the local waters were good for more than kidney trouble and arthritis, there couldn't be another like her in the area; it would be a grossly unfair distribution of national wealth. But if they were one and the same, why had she been lurking there? And why had she turned tail and run? She didn't look the sort of person who would retreat in the face of danger; rather the reverse. The person he'd met at the school would have been much more likely to have hit him over the head with her *sac*. And how had she got there? By her own admission she didn't own a car.

A boat from Lausanne – the *Général Guisan* – gave a warning blast on its foghorn as it swept through the narrow entrance to the harbour, leaving swans and ducks bobbing aggrievedly in its wake. Docking it immaculately, as he must have done thousands of times before, the captain looked out from his bridge across the rooftop of the booking hall, making sure everything was in its place. There was a loud clang as the gangplank dropped into place and a flurry of movement from the waiting passengers as they queued ready to board. A woman carrying a bag of shopping broke into a trot as the traffic lights changed and she hurried across the road to catch the boat. Seeing her from the bridge, the captain blew his foghorn again, anxious to be on his way.

Monsieur Pamplemousse wondered if he was doing the right thing. It could be a total waste of time; a dead end. He was simply playing a hunch that he would be hard put to justify if it came to the point. He could picture the kind of conversation he might have if the Director got to hear about it, especially if he ever caught a glimpse of Fräulein Brünnhilde. His own experience of the printing trade was fairly limited, but he had to admit that she was not the kind of vision he would have conjured up had he been called on to describe a typical representative.

Monsieur Pamplemousse felt in an inside jacket pocket and took out an envelope containing the pasted-up version of the words he'd put together two nights before. The message was clear enough: IN-FORM POLICE MY LIFE IS IN DANGRE. DO NOT HURRY, AWAAIT NEXT MESSEGE OF YOUR LOVED ONE.

It was a strange message; there was an inconsistency about it which he found bothering. If Jean-Claude had had a premonition that his own life might be in danger, why hadn't he told someone, or simply written the message out himself? Why go to the trouble of making it anonymous by having fake pieces of newsprint made up? They had to be fake; no one could possibly have published them as they were. Then again, why ask for the police to be informed and in the next sentence say 'Do not hurry'? It didn't make sense. And if Jean-Claude hadn't been alarmed on his own account, who could the message have been meant for? The girl? He'd seen her twice now with his own eyes, alive and well and unharmed. She looked worried, that was true, but if she and Jean-Claude were involved in some way then it was likely to be on his account rather than her own. And how did Fräulein Brünnhilde fit into it all?

There was a movement from under the table and Pommes Frites' head appeared. Monsieur Pamplemousse reached down and patted it. The top felt warm from the sun. Normally Pommes Frites would have been content to sit where he was for a while, basking in his master's attention. Pommes Frites liked nothing better than a good stroke. Given the chance he could put up with being stroked for hours at a time, but for reasons best known to himself he shook his head free and as he stood up, applied the end of his nose to the piece of paper on top of the table. He rested it there for a while, the tip quivering as it absorbed such items of olfactory information as there were to be gained; forwarding them on to the appropriate department for analysis and comparison checks before making a final decision; weighing the results against the obvious needs of his master – the depth of the furrows in his brow, the look of preoccupation which always appeared when he had a problem.

The information duly processed to his satisfaction, the print-out deposited in the tray marked ACTION, Pommes Frites turned and made his way slowly but purposefully in the direction of the exit. Pocketing the sheet of paper, Monsieur Pamplemousse picked up his carrier-bags and followed on behind. He knew better than to query his companion and aide-de-camp at such moments. If Pommes Frites had decided there were trails to be followed, then followed they must be.

In the event, he hadn't far to go; it was hardly worth picking up his belongings. Pommes Frites led the way down a short flight of steps on to the pavement below, wisely hurried past some more steps leading down further to a *W.C. public*, then stopped outside a *tabac-journaux* on the corner. Outside there was a rack of *journaux* neatly arranged according to nationality. Ignoring the ubiquitous *Herald-Tribune*, bypassing Allemagne and Italie, he settled on a section devoted to those from Grande-Bretagne. Rejecting both *The Times* and its pink counterpart devoted to financial matters, registering disapproval of both the *Express* and the *Daily Mail*, declining a fifth, testing a sixth and finding it wanting, he placed his paw very firmly on the one of his choice and gazed up at his master.

Monsieur Pamplemousse patted his head, removed

the *journal* from the rack, paid for it in the shop, then made his way back upstairs again and called for another *café*.

He felt a growing excitement as he compared the type-face and the quality of the paper of his purchase with the original. It matched exactly. Running through the rest of the pages quickly it seemed to have the same kind of errors; sometimes it was simply a matter of words omitted or transposed, sometimes whole lines were missing. Once or twice there was an area of complete gibberish. Excitement gave way to confusion.

Paying for his *café* when it arrived, he settled down and considered the matter through half-closed eyes. If the message he had in his hand had been taken from a genuine *journal*, then it put paid to his original theory that the words had been specially printed, which in a sense put him right back where he'd started from. On the other hand, if someone had gone to the trouble of buying an English newspaper, then the message was clearly meant to be read by English eyes. Elementary, my dear Watson, as Holmes would have said.

His own Watson, having done his bit for the time being, had curled up and gone back to sleep in a nearby patch of sunshine.

On the far side of the road, near the traffic lights, there was a squeal of protesting rubber followed by a loud blare from a car horn. A motorist was complaining at being cut-up by a taxi which had pulled in sharply behind another at a rank outside the port building. There was an exchange of gestures, then the lights changed and the aggrieved motorist was forced to give up the contest. The taxi driver, wholly indifferent, climbed out of his cab and joined his colleague on the pavement.

Monsieur Pamplemousse sat up, cursing his stupidity. In pondering the problem of transportation to and from the Institut des Beaux Arbres he'd considered every possibility from *bicyclettes* to lifts thumbed in *voitures* and back again via *tracteurs* and bulldozers. The one method which hadn't crossed his mind was that of hiring a taxi. He drained his cup. He must be getting old.

This time it was his turn to lead the way down the steps. He took them two at a time.

'Do I make many journeys to the Institut des Beaux Arbres?' The first driver looked him straight in the eye. 'I am afraid I do not understand the question, *Monsieur*.'

Monsieur Pamplemousse felt in his wallet, separating a fifty-franc note from some adjacent hundreds.

'What is it you wish to know, *Monsieur*?'

'Do many people make use of your services? Visitors? Staff? Anything you can tell me?'

The man shrugged. 'Most of the staff have their own cars. So do the visitors. Occasionally we get a call from the *gare* if someone arrives by train.'

'How about the girls?'

The two men exchanged glances. 'May we ask why you want to know?' asked the second driver. 'We do not wish to get anyone into trouble.'

Nor would you wish to lose a lucrative business by the sound of it, thought Monsieur Pamplemousse. He decided to press his luck a bit further, hoping they wouldn't ask him for his identification.

'I suggest it will be better in the long run if you tell me the truth.'

The first driver broke the silence. 'Mostly it is girls playing truant. They want to be taken to the disco at Thonon. Sometimes even as far as Geneva. There is a rendezvous point not far from the school. They are young and anxious to enjoy life, you understand? Almost always they go in groups.'

'I understand.' Monsieur Pamplemousse opened his wallet again. Disappointment registered on both faces as he took out the photograph.

'Do you recognise this face? Did she travel with friends or was she alone?'

The two men scanned the photograph uneasily. 'I want to help her. It is possible she may be in trouble.'

'She made the journey often,' said the second man. 'She used to meet a friend here in Evian. They perhaps went for a walk along the front or had a *café* over the road where you had yours.'

'Was the friend Jean-Claude from Les Cinq Parfaits?'

The question went home and gave him match point. Jean-Claude and the girl had been meeting nearly every day, just for short periods in the afternoon when Jean-Claude could leave his work, after *déjeuner* had been served and before it was time to prepare the evening meal. Occasionally she went to the restaurant to eat, but mostly they met in the afternoons. Everyone knew. It was a very happy affair. Jean-Claude always brought her flowers. No, they had never taken Jean-Claude to the school. Anyway, he had his own car, so what would be the point? There were, of course, other drivers, and who knew? It was accompanied by a shrug as if to imply that some people would do anything for money. The information came pouring out. He almost asked for his fifty francs back.

Monsieur would not be taking the matter further? Not that they had ever done any harm. But a fare was a fare and out of season business was slow. They could do with all the work they could get.

Monsieur Pamplemousse drove slowly and carefully back to Les Cinq Parfaits, partly because he was deep in thought, partly because the repair to his braking-system was only temporary and he still had to rely a great deal on the handbrake.

He took a turn off the main driveway and parked near his room. Feeling in need of a stroll in order to collect his scattered thoughts and marshal them into some kind of order, he set off with Pommes Frites along the same path he had taken the first evening. As they drew near the edge of the woods a *gendarme* detached himself from a tree, obviously intending to intercept them. Calling to Pommes Frites, Monsieur Pamplemousse hurriedly retraced his steps. For the time being he didn't want to talk to anyone, least of all the police. They would only ask questions and before that happened he had one or two questions of his own to ask, questions that called for a succession of telephone calls.

Relieved that he hadn't bothered to return his key to Reception that morning, he slipped in through the side entrance.

His first call was to a Mr. Pickering of Burgess Hill in England, and after two wrong numbers, including a house-wife who accused him, not without a trace of hope in her voice, of making obscene telephone calls, he eventually got through.

For some while *Le Guide* had been toying with the idea of following the lead set many years before by their arch rival Michelin, and issuing a guide to restaurants in the British Isles. The failure of Gault Millau, who had also tried out the idea and had then withdrawn to lick their wounds on safer ground, gave them second thoughts. It appeared on preliminary investigation that British restaurants had enormous subdivisions, reflecting both the diverse nature of the population and its eating habits. Unlike France, where the local restaurant was often an extension of the home, a place where the whole family from *grand-mère* to the smallest *enfant* could go for Sunday lunch, and where everything from weddings to christenings was celebrated, eating out was more of a treat, a special occasion, and the menu was constructed accordingly. Classification was difficult.

In all these matters, Mr. Pickering, who had been retained as an adviser on account of his vast and expert knowledge of wine, was a fountain of information, as indeed he was on many other things. Had the guillotine been reintroduced in France, Mr. Pickering would have known the exact weight of blade necessary, the degree of sharpness required, and the height from which it needed to be dropped for a given thickness of neck. Had the Roman penchant for eating dormice been revived in England, Mr. Pickering would have known all about ways of fattening them first on nuts in earthenware jars, how they should be stuffed, and the correct method of cooking them. 'Regulo 5 for fifteen minutes' he would probably have said in tones of unimpeachable authority.

Monsieur Pamplemousse had learned a lot about the British since he'd met Mr. Pickering. He felt sure he would know all there was to know about English *journaux*. In this he was not disappointed. From a brief description of the nature and the type of the cuttings, and with scarcely a moment's hesitation, Mr. Pickering named it at once.

'They have a bad record of industrial disputes. Progress is not easy in the printing world. There is a great deal of unrest within the rank and file regarding the introduction of new machinery. Meanwhile the owners soldier on with the old equipment.'

'You mean . . . it is actually sold like that? The one I have is not just an early edition – an uncorrected one? They are all like it?' Monsieur Pamplemousse tried to keep a rising note of disappointment from his voice.

'It has a circulation of several million. People get very upset on days when it doesn't appear.'

'Several million? *Morbleu!* Do the readers not care for their language?'

'Frankly, no.' Mr. Pickering sounded surprised by the question. 'In a way it makes the news more palatable if you don't entirely understand it. It leaves you with hope for the future. Life would be unbearable if you knew all that was going on.'

'They do not mind the mistakes . . . the misprints?'

'They rather like them really. It makes it more fun to read. Besides, it's been that way for a long time and the British don't really like change. Sometimes they write to the editor about it, but on the whole the mistakes are in the political area – parliamentary reports – things like that. You don't often find them on the sports pages – there would be hell to pay if you did, and *never* in the cross-word.'

Monsieur Pamplemousse felt bemused and quite out of his depth. No wonder Britain wasn't popular with the other members of the Common Market if that was all they cared about politics.

'And if I were looking for a lady compositor?'

Mr. Pickering gave vent to a series of clicks. It sounded as though he was tapping his teeth with a pen. 'Very unlikely. The printing industry is a closed shop – very much a man's world. I can't picture them allowing women in.

'Talking of crosswords, it's funny you should ring. I was

only thinking about you a moment ago. I've got a sort of French clue in front of me right now . . . "A bad-tempered worker gains in the beginning and gets something to eat". Nine letters.'

Monsieur Pamplemousse fell silent. He had enough problems on his mind as it was without adding to them with trivialities.

'I'll put you out of your misery,' said Mr. Pickering cheerfully. 'It's a sort of anagram. Cross means bad-tempered. An ant is a worker. "I" is the first letter of "in". Put the "i" into "cross" and add the "ant" and you get *croissant* – something to eat.'

'I, too, have a sort of anagram,' said Monsieur Pamplemousse, not wishing to be outdone. He removed the pasted-up message from his wallet and read out the words, jumbling them up in no particular order as he did so.

'Don't tell me,' said Mr. Pickering. 'I like puzzles. I'll ring you back when I've got it.'

'I shall be going out again in about half an hour,' said Monsieur Pamplemousse, throwing down the gauntlet.

'Done!' said Mr. Pickering.

The second call was to an ex-colleague in Paris.

'The Institut des Beaux Arbres? What is it you wish to know exactly?'

'Anything,' said Monsieur Pamplemousse. 'If there is nothing, then I wish to know that too. Anything and everything or nothing.'

His third call was to the Director. Almost immediately he wished he hadn't made it, but it was too late to hang up. The voice at the other end sounded ominously brisk.

'Good, Pamplemousse. You have my telex.'

'No, *Monsieur*.'

'You do not have my telex?' The Director sounded piqued. 'But I sent it to you first thing this morning. It *must* have been received. That is the whole point of using a telex machine – the knowledge that a message accepted has, ergo, been received.'

'It may have been received by Reception,' said Monsieur Pamplemousse patiently, 'but I have not, myself, been to Reception. I have been out shopping.'

'You have been out shopping?' The Director repeated the words in the same tones of awe tempered with disbelief that Mrs. Newton might have used when her husband Isaac came in from the garden and announced that he had just discovered gravity.

'I have been making progress, *Monsieur*. The shopping was a necessary part of a plan I am about to put into operation, a plan which . . .'

'Pamplemousse.' The Director's voice cut him off peevishly in midflight. 'Had you been to Reception this morning, and had you picked up the telex message I was at great pains to send, you would have saved yourself a journey and *Le Guide*, I suspect from the tone of your voice, a great deal of expense; expense which in the circumstances I may find hard to justify when it comes to initialling your P39s.'

Pique changed to irony. 'To save you the trouble of going all the way to Reception, I will read you my message. It said, quite simply: CANCEL ORDER FOR *SOUFFLÉ SURPRISE* IMMEDIATELY.'

'Cancel the order for the *Soufflé Surprise*? I do not understand, *Monsieur*.' He understood full well, but he wasn't going to make things easy for the Director.

'It is perfectly simple, Pamplemousse. There is no longer any cause for alarm. Progress has been made. Some of the best chefs in France have been working on the problem. I cannot go into details, of course, but if I were to mention names like Bocuse, Vergé, Guérard, you will understand the importance attached to the matter. The end result is not quite like the real thing – that would be very difficult in the time, but I think I may safely say that it is good enough.'

Monsieur Pamplemousse thought he detected a sound of smacking lips in the background, and murmurs of agreement. It was rubbing salt into the wound.

'But what about Jean-Claude?'

'Jean-Claude?' The Director brushed the name aside airily as if it were of no importance. 'I'm sure he will turn up eventually.'

Monsieur Pamplemousse took the photograph from his wallet once again and propped it against the telephone for moral support. Was it his imagination or did the face looking back at him have a pleading look? Perhaps it was simply that he now had another picture in his mind, an image of the real thing he was able to superimpose on the first, breathing life into it. He came to a decision.

'That is not good enough, *Monsieur*.'

'What? What is that, Pamplemousse?' The Director broke off from a dissertation he'd been about to give on the problems involved in injecting the right amount of *surprise* into a *soufflé*.

'I said, *Monsieur*, that it is not good enough. There are things going on here which I do not understand.'

'There are things going on everywhere that *I* do not understand, Pamplemousse.' The Director came back down to earth again. 'I have to say, quite frankly, that there are things I do not even *wish* to understand. Things I would rather not know about. But that does not mean to say that I feel it my duty to put them to rights. The world is an imperfect place, Aristide. It has always been so and despite everyone's efforts, so it will remain. That is not necessarily a bad thing. Perfection, taken to excess, can be very dull and boring.'

'Do I take it, *Monsieur*, that I no longer have your support in this matter?'

'If you wish to put it that way, Aristide, yes. I have my orders too. Orders, Pamplemousse, which emanate from an authority even higher than the earlier one. To put it crudely I have been told to tell you to lay off. You have been seen visiting the Institut des Beaux Arbres. That was not part of your original brief. Your brief was to find Jean-Claude.'

'It is my opinion, *Monsieur*, that the two are linked.'

'Pamplemousse . . . you have your orders.'

'I am afraid I do not accept them, *Monsieur*.'

There was a violent explosion from the other end. It sounded as though a desk was being thumped. When the noise died away the Director's voice came through loud and clear and in measured tones.

'Pamplemousse, I have to tell you that if you persist in this stubborn attitude, then you will be on your own. You will get no help from anyone. You will be *persona non grata*. Worse still, you may well find your name besmirched in ways which will make your escapade at the Follies seem like a visit to Papa Noël.'

'So be it, *Monsieur*.' Monsieur Pamplemousse hung up before the Director had a chance to say any more. He was about to take the receiver off the hook again when he remembered he was expecting a different call to be returned and changed his mind.

He hadn't long to wait.

The telephone rang three times in quick succession. The first call was from Paris.

'Guillard here. This Institut you asked me about . . . you might have said.'

'Said what?'

'Well, it's pretty hot stuff. No one wants to talk about it and I've already had all sorts of people phoning me back wanting to know why I was asking in the first place.'

'Did you tell them?'

'No. I thought you'd rather I didn't so I concocted a cock and bull story about wanting to know for a friend. I think they bought it.'

'*D'accord*.' Monsieur Pamplemousse knew the feeling.

'Anyway, I eventually got on to someone I know at the Ministry and it seems they have an appalling accident record. *Incroyable*. It is hard to believe. Nine girls over the past two years. The worst was in an avalanche last winter. The instructors managed to get away, but three of the girls were killed. Two went missing soon afterwards in Lac Léman – presumed drowned. Two more disappeared the year before during an outing to Rome. One ran away and was never seen again. Another one fell down a disused mine shaft.'

'And nothing's been heard of any of them since? No bodies have been found?'

'Nothing at all. They all vanished without trace.'

'Thank you.'

'That's all right. Sorry I couldn't be of any more help.'

'You have done very well. I am most grateful.' He was

about to hang up when a thought struck him. 'You don't happen to know the colour of their hair? The ones who disappeared, that is.'

'*Sapristi!*' There was a muttered oath from the other end. 'You will be wanting to know the colour of their nail-varnish next. I'm in enough trouble as it is.'

'*Tant pis*. Never mind.'

He hung up. It had been worth a try. A shot in the dark.

The second call was from England.

'I say . . . you've been busy. I've tried about six times. The line's always engaged.' Mr. Pickering sounded pleased with himself.

'You have thought of something else?'

'No. It's just that I have the answer to that word puzzle you gave me. Didn't take a couple of minutes actually. How's this? HURRY – LIFE OF YOUR LOVED ONE IS IN DANGER. DO NOT INFORM POLICE. AWAIT MY NEXT MESSAGE.

'Hello . . . I say, are you still there?'

'Yes, I am still here.' Monsieur Pamplemousse reached mechanically for his pen. 'Would you mind repeating that?'

Pickering obliged. 'Forgive my asking . . . none of my business . . . but it all sounds very intriguing.'

Monsieur Pamplemousse refused to be drawn. 'It is a little *divertissement*. I will tell you about it one day.'

Mr. Pickering took the hint. '*Au revoir*, Aristide. Take care.'

'*Au revoir*, Monsieur Pickering. And congratulations.'

Leaving Mr. Pickering to his crossword puzzle, Monsieur Pamplemousse replaced the receiver and crossed to the window. He slid it open. Outside on the terrace the waiters were preparing the tables for lunch. Beyond them, near the entrance, there was a parked police car. It was empty. Near the path leading to the wood the *gendarme* had been replaced by two members of the National Guard, automatic weapons slung over their shoulders at the ready.

Mr. Pickering's rearrangement of the words put a totally different complexion on things. It very definitely turned the message into one which was designed for someone else to send or to be sent on someone else's behalf. Someone already missing, or someone about to go missing?

Turning away from the window he idly picked up his camera from the desk where he'd left it the night before and cocked it ready for the next shot. He had a feeling he might be needing it. The rewind crank didn't move. Either there was slack in the film, which was strange in view of the fact that he was already halfway through a reel, or . . . he cocked the shutter again, then a third time. Still there was no movement. He flipped the back open. The camera chamber was empty.

In the waste-bin below the table he found a roll of film. It had been completely pulled out of the cassette. The Department of Dirty Tricks had been at it again.

The telephone rang for the third time. Blissfully unaware that he had chosen an unfortunate moment, the Director launched into an apology.

'Aristide, I'm glad I caught you. I'm sorry if I lost my temper a moment ago.'

'We all lose our temper from time to time, *Monsieur*. I am about to lose mine.'

'I'm afraid I was not feeling myself, Aristide. A touch of the *furibards*. Too much *soufflé*, you understand? We have been up all night, tasting, tasting, tasting. Also, I was not alone.'

'I understand perfectly, *Monsieur*. While you have been sitting in your office eating *Soufflé Surprise*, others have been busy entering my room – removing film from my camera. While you were enjoying your gastronomic excursions, others were busy sawing through the main pipeline of the hydraulic brakes of my car.'

'What is that?' The Director grasped the nettle with both hands. 'This is terrible, Aristide. Had something happened to you – and to Pommes Frites – I would never have forgiven myself. Thank heaven you discovered it in time.'

'We did *not* discover it in time, *Monsieur*. Pommes Frites and I are lucky to be alive. Had it not been for a road sign which got in the way . . .'

'A road sign? You collided with a road sign? Is there much damage?'

'A new bumper, perhaps. Possibly a new wing. Fortunately with the 2CV it is only a matter of replacement. That is one of its many virtues.'

The Director made a clicking noise. 'This is bad news, Aristide. Very bad news indeed. As you well know, it is the policy of *Le Guide* to require all staff to make use of the standard issue of *voiture*. It is why I visit the Paris Motor Show every year. A special dispensation was granted in your case provided no unnecessary and untoward expense was incurred. Madame Grante will not be pleased. It may be necessary to review the whole situation in the light of what you have just told me.'

Monsieur Pamplemousse took a deep breath. '*Baiser* Madame Grante!'

There was a moment's silence while the Director digested the remark. 'An interesting thought, Aristide.' His voice sounded milder, almost affectionate. 'Not one that appeals to me, I must admit. Sooner you than me. Apart from anything else, who knows what hidden passions you might release. Passions kept in check over the years by constant scanning of P39s.'

'One moment, *Monsieur*.' From outside, beyond the trees, came the sound of a helicopter approaching fast. Fast and low. The noise made it difficult to hear what the Director was saying.

Monsieur Pamplemousse crossed to the window, cupping the telephone receiver under his chin as he did so. The two National Guardsmen were in a state of alert, their machine-guns at the ready as they watched the sky in an area beyond the pool where the tops of the trees were already waving in the down-draught from the plane. The waiters had all stopped work and were watching too. The two coloured boys from Reception hurried past pulling a trolley on which reposed a large roll of carpet. Monsieur Pamplemousse slid the window shut. The director was still talking.

'I cannot persuade you to change your mind?'

'No, *Monsieur*.'

'I sometimes wish I had your sense of right and wrong, Pamplemousse. It is an enviable trait.'

'*Comme ci, comme ça, Monsieur*. Sometimes it is a blessing, at other times it is a curse.'

'Pamplemousse . . .'

'*Oui, Monsieur?*'

'I do not know what you have in mind, and perhaps it is better that I do not ask. Also, I should not be telling you this – it is supposed to be secret – but the "shopping expedition" of a "certain person" has been brought forward for security reasons. He is due to arrive at Les Cinq Parfaits today.'

'I think, *Monsieur*, he is arriving at this very moment.'

'*Alors!*' The Director sounded depressed. 'In that case, Aristide, I can only wish you *bonne chance*.'

'*Merci, Monsieur.*'

As he hung up, Monsieur Pamplemousse glanced at his watch. It was just after twelve thirty. If he was to be on time for his meeting with Fräulein Brünnhilde he would need to leave at once.

He crossed to the fridge and opened the door. The room maid had obviously completed her rounds, for the rack of apéritifs and mineral waters had been restocked, but the bottle of champagne he'd ordered was nowhere to be seen. Worse still, the second bottle of Château d'Yquem seemed to have vanished.

'*Merde!*' He was about to close the door again in disgust when he paused and looked in the freezer compartment. A bottle bearing the Gosset label lay on top of the ice-tray awaiting his pleasure, but there was still no sign of the d'Yquem. It must have been put somewhere for safe-keeping – such riches demanded special treatment. Lifting the champagne carefully out of the compartment he examined the bottle. He could hardly grumble, since he'd asked for it to be as cold as possible, but it was now so cold that the outside was white with ice. He glanced at the freezer control – it had been turned to maximum. He would need to treat the champagne with respect; in its present state it could be lethal.

Closing the door of the fridge, he took the cardboard tube out of its carrier-bag and slid the bottle gently inside it. It fitted as snugly as if it had been made to measure.

Seeing his master reach for the other carrier-bag, Pommes Frites leapt to his feet. Pommes Frites liked picnics and one way and another he had a lot of eating to catch up on. That apart, Monsieur Pamplemousse's mood communicated itself to him in no uncertain manner. Second only to food, Pommes Frites enjoyed nothing better than a spot of action. He licked his lips. All his senses told him that with a little bit of luck he could be enjoying both before he was very much older.

7

THE PICNIC

The journey to Les Beaux Arbres took Monsieur Pample-mousse even longer than it had on the first occasion, mostly because of the state of his car. With its 150,000-kilometre service long overdue and the pads on the cable-operated front-wheel brakes now even more badly in need of replacement following the sabotage of the main system, he had no wish to stop on a steep part of the hill. If they once started rolling backwards there was no know-ing where they would end up. He could hardly hope for another convenient road sign to get in their way, and the bottom of the valley looked too far away for comfort.

Fräulein Brünnhilde was waiting for them behind some bushes. She was dressed in a brightly coloured, trans-parently thin cotton skirt, topped rather disappointingly by a tee-shirt bearing a map of North America. Her blonde hair was tightly coiffeured into a neat but forbidding bun. Paradoxically, she was carrying what appeared to be a groundsheet under her arm.

'It is for the picnic,' she announced as she climbed into the passenger seat.

Monsieur Pamplemousse eyed it uneasily as he helped her on with the seat-belt, adjusting it from N.P.F. (*Normale Pommes Frites*) to a more suitable size – somewhere at the higher end of the scale.

Apart from any untoward implications which might or might not go with the sharing of a groundsheet, he would have much preferred making use of the folding table and chairs which he kept permanently in the boot. In his experi-ence even the lushest of pastureland grew inordinately hard in a matter of moments. That apart, the more inviting it looked the higher the animal population; he'd once seen some incredible figure quoted for just one square metre of earth.

Pommes Frites had even stronger views on the subject of picnics and he gazed disapprovingly at the offending object as it landed on the seat beside him. It was bad enough being relegated to the back of the car without having half of it taken up by what he considered to be highly unnecessary luggage, and he registered his disapproval in no uncertain fashion by breathing heavily down the back of his master's neck. In a matter of moments there was a satisfactory wet patch on the shirt collar.

They had only gone a little way when Fräulein Brünnhilde gave a sudden wriggle. 'I will take shelter while we pass the school gates,' she announced, disappearing below the level of the dashboard with a total disregard as to whether or not her skirt would follow suit. Monsieur Pample-mousse felt a dryness in his throat as he glanced down. Patently it had decided against the idea of accompanying its owner.

Viewed from close quarters, Fräulein Brünnhilde seemed to have grown in stature; the word Amazonian would not be amiss in describing her. The material of her tee-shirt was strained far beyond the limits which might reasonably have been specified by even the most generous of garment manufacturers. From his vantage point in the back seat Pommes Frites followed the direction of his master's gaze and he, too, eyed their passenger with interest. Interest which was tinged, despite his feelings about the ground-sheet, with a certain amount of awe.

Thanking his lucky stars that he'd thought to open the roof of the car before they left – it would have been unbearably warm otherwise – Monsieur Pamplemousse glanced up the driveway as they passed the entrance to the school. There was nothing to be seen. The gates were shut.

'You are safe now.'

Fräulein Brünnhilde wriggled herself back up into a sitting position and readjusted the belt, removing a few loose dog hairs as she did so. 'I see you read the English

113

journaux,' she said, catching sight of the newspaper lying on the shelf above the dashboard.

Monsieur Pamplemousse felt a quickening of interest as he considered the remark, weighed it, analysed it, and began to wonder if perhaps his original theory had been right after all.

'You are interested in printing?'

'No. What is interesting about printing?' He received an odd look in reply.

'I only wondered, that is all.'

'It is a very strange question. Why do you ask if I am interested in printing?'

Monsieur Pamplemousse began to wish he hadn't. Fräulein Brünnhilde clearly had a very literal turn of mind, the workings of which were not enhanced by her phrase-book style of conversation. He decided he must be patient. In fairness, his own knowledge of German was minimal.

'Your spelling is not good, perhaps?' he asked hopefully.

'My spelling is very good. Why do you say my spelling is not good?'

'Because you would not improve it by reading that particular *journal,*' said Monsieur Pamplemousse with authority.

'Why do you say that? What is wrong with it! It is a very good *journal.*'

'There are many mistakes. Some letters are not where they should be. Sometimes there are whole lines that are not where they should be.' It was catching. Any moment now he would find himself drawing on an old English/French phrase-book he kept handy in case of an emergency. 'You have taken the wrong tooth out!' was one of his favourites. It was almost worth a visit to the dentist to try it out and see what happened.

'I wish to improve my vocabulary. All the girls speak English. It is hard to talk to them. They say things I do not understand, so all the time I am doing the crossword.'

'Ah, the crossword!' Busy with his thoughts, Monsieur Pamplemousse felt the warmth of a body against him as he negotiated a bend too fast. 'A bad-tempered worker gains in the beginning and gets something to eat. Nine letters.'

Fräulein Brünnhilde righted herself. 'What are you saying? I do not understand.'

'It is a clue from an English crossword,' he explained.

'Ah!' Fräulein Brünnhilde nodded. 'And what is the answer?'

'*Croissant*.'

'*Croissant*? I do not understand.'

Monsieur Pamplemousse changed down as they approached an even sharper bend. Ahead of them the Cornettes de Bises loomed large, marking the border between France and Switzerland. 'It has to do with a bad-tempered ant – a worker – and the cross which has an "i" in it.' He heard his voice trail away. He hadn't totally understood the answer himself and it sounded even less probable now.

'Why does the cross have an eye in it?' demanded Fräulein Brünnhilde. 'And why is the ant in a bad mood?'

Monsieur Pamplemousse felt tempted to suggest that perhaps it had been trying to explain crosswords to an idiot foreign ant, but he refrained.

'On Saturdays,' said Fräulein Brünnhilde unexpectedly, 'they have a prize draw. There is a token for the first one they open. With the token you can buy a book. They have never opened one of mine. I have never won a prize.'

'You like reading?'

'No. I do not like reading.'

'In that case,' said Monsieur Pamplemousse, 'it is good that you have never won.' Having delivered this remark he fell silent. The prospect of a picnic with Fräulein Brünnhilde was rapidly losing its attraction. He glanced across at her. She seemed to be breathing heavily, wriggling uncomfortably from side to side as though she was having complications beneath her tee-shirt. As she leaned forward to carry out some unspecified rearrangements and adjustments behind her back he couldn't help but notice the coastal mountains of California and the Appalachian Mountains of Eastern America resting impressively against the dashboard. Although they were jiggling up and down in time with the motion of the car they had none of the gay abandon one might have expected. Clearly they were being held in place by a superior form of restraint.

Averting his gaze and fixing it firmly on the road ahead, he reached out with his free hand for the safety-belt. 'May I help?'

His offer was rejected in no uncertain fashion.

'Please do not do that!' Fräulein Brünnhilde looked at him severely. 'I have met your sort before.'

Monsieur Pamplemousse wondered where. He felt aggrieved, both by the refusal of what had been intended as a genuine offer of help and by the sweeping generalisation that went with it.

'You are not to touch my top storey. It is *verboten*. You may touch my knees. You may touch my ankles. You may touch my bottom storey. Anything else. But not my top storey.'

Undecided as to whether he had received an invitation, a reproof, or the laying down of a set of architectural guidelines for future reference, Monsieur Pamplemousse lapsed again into silence.

Fräulein Brünnhilde spoke first. 'Are we going much higher?' she enquired. 'Heights give me problems. So do depths. I am best at sea-level.'

Monsieur Pamplemousse found the remark too cryptic even to think about. Holmes might have pondered over it, or perhaps Mr. Pickering. It sounded like one of his crossword clues.

'We are nearly there. I am taking you to a little place I know.'

'Is it where you take all your girls?'

'I have never taken a girl there before in the whole of my life.'

Monsieur Pamplemousse was able to speak with conviction. The only other time he'd been there was with Madame Pamplemousse when they had been exploring the area a few years before, and that was hardly in the same category. He still remembered it; most of all he remembered the profusion of wild flowers. Lower down the valley and on the hillsides fruit was still on the trees waiting to be picked, the grapes were yet to be harvested, but here, high up in the mountains, there would be wild geraniums, harebells, daisies and late crocus amongst the clover.

He turned in past a notice which estimated in hours the time it would take a walker to reach the next vantage point. Breaking off from the narrow track, he drove down a short dip and then up a grassy slope until he reached the top of a ridge where, if his memory served him aright, he knew there would be a view through a gap in the hills to Lac Léman, and beyond that again to mountain-tops eternally covered in ice and snow. He wasn't disappointed. The weather was on his side and the view was breathtaking.

Swinging the car round in a broad circle, he brought it to rest on top of the ridge facing the way they had come, its bonnet pointing back down the hill. Noting a strong smell of burning from the overworked brake-linings, he left it in gear and climbed out, followed by Pommes Frites.

'It is very beautiful here. It is a good choice.' Fräulein Brünnhilde appeared at his side carrying the groundsheet. She breathed in deeply, winced visibly, then touched his elbow with her hand. 'It is very romantic. The lake and the mountains.'

'It has always attracted poets and writers,' said Monsieur Pamplemousse. 'Especially the English ones. English poets are fond of lakes.' He drew on memories of past conversations with Mr. Pickering. 'It was outside the Hotel d'Angleterre at Sécheron that Byron first met Shelley. Another writer, Gibbon, finished a book called *Decline and Fall* at Lausanne.' He pointed towards the gap in the hills. 'Near there, where the lake is at its deepest, Shelley and Byron almost died in a sudden storm.'

Taking the groundsheet he shook it open and began laying it out behind the car. Along its sides there was a series of brass eyelets to which lengths of cord had been attached. He took the ones nearest to the rear bumper and began tying them securely in place, lifting up the edge of the sheet as he did so in order to make a barrier against the light south-westerly breeze.

'It is hard to think of storms on such a day as this. Storms are for bad days.' Fräulein Brünnhilde removed some pins from behind her ears, shaking her head as she did so. Her long, blonde hair glinted in the sunshine as it cascaded down her back. The effect was startling, like the sudden release of a waterfall, the transformation scene in a play.

Monsieur Pamplemousse cleared his throat, aware that Pommes Frites was watching too. He busied himself with a knot. 'Perhaps it was the fault of Shelley himself. Water always had a fascination for him. In the end he died in a boat which had been christened *Don Juan* by Byron.'

Fräulein Brünnhilde looked at him curiously. 'You know a lot about some things.'

'No.' Monsieur Pamplemousse went round to the side of the car and removed the carrier-bags. 'I know a *little* about many things. That is not the same. It has always been one of my problems. I am a picker-up of unconsidered trifles.'

Before closing the door he signalled to Pommes Frites to get back in. There were times when Pommes Frites got in the way if he felt so inclined. Or, not to mince words, if he got an attack of the jealousies. He looked as if he might have a bad one coming on. Pommes Frites obeyed the order with a marked lack of enthusiasm. He climbed into the car wearing his 'hard done by' expression.

Avoiding the unwinking gaze through the back window, Monsieur Pamplemousse began unloading the picnic, crouching as low as possible so as to avoid rubbing too much salt into Pommes Frites' wounds. He stood the bottles of Mondeuse and Evian and the cardboard tube containing the champagne in a neat row in front of the bumper, then reached into the second bag. 'Take this *gâteau de foies blonds de volaille, par exemple.* Some people might say that it does not matter how or where it came from; the fact that it is created from a *poulet de Bresse* means nothing to them. But to me, the knowledge that by law for the whole of its life, it will never have had less than ten square metres of land to itself, to run about on and to feed naturally, will also mean that its flesh will be juicy, and that will sharpen my appetite and thus increase my enjoyment.'

He took out two more packages and held them up. 'Knowing that this ham was smoked over pinewood and juniper berries high up in the mountains where the air is crisp, will add romance to the flavour. And when we follow it with this' – he unwrapped the *Reblochon* – 'the knowledge that the word *reblocher* means the last and richest dregs of milk from the cow's udder will not make it any more digestible, but it will warm my heart.'

'You are interested in food?' The thought was evidently a new one.

'If I am fortunate enough to live to be ninety,' said Monsieur Pamplemousse, 'and if I am equally lucky and continue to eat three meals a day it will amount to a grand lifetime's total of over one hundred thousand meals. It would be foolish not to be interested in something which has occupied so great a part of one's life and is in part responsible for its continuation. It would be even worse than economising on the bed in which one spends perhaps a third of one's existence.'

Fräulein Brünnhilde lowered herself carefully on to the groundsheet and lay back staring up at the sky. She appeared to be encountering a certain amount of difficulty in carrying out the manoeuvre, rather as if some hidden and opposing forces were at work, but at least she made herself comfortable.

'For me, sunshine is more important. That, to me, is food. Anything is better than being at the Institut.'

'Tell me about the Institut.'

She made a face. 'It is not interesting.'

'Everything is interesting,' said Monsieur Pamplemousse. 'I told you. I am a picker-up of unconsidered trifles. Tell me, for example, about the Sanatorium.'

Fräulein Brünnhilde sat up. 'Ah! You have chosen the worst thing. That is not a trifle. For three whole days I have been forbidden to enter my own sick bay. And for why?'

'For why?' said Monsieur Pamplemousse gently.

'I think it is that they do not trust me. There is something happening there they do not wish me to know about. But I will find out.' As she spoke, Fräulein Brünnhilde tapped her chest. For a brief moment she seemed to regret the action, then she recovered.

119

'In here I have a key. They do not know that. They have already taken away what they think is the only one. But in here I have a spare.'

Monsieur Pamplemousse eyed her thoughtfully. A key to the sick bay was what he most wanted at that moment. He had a feeling it would unlock many other doors besides. Getting hold of it might be another matter.

Reaching for a bottle of Evian he tore off the seal, removed the plastic top and slowly poured two glassfuls, adding some ice from the container for good measure.

As Fräulein Brünnhilde reached over to take one of the glasses her tee-shirt parted company with her skirt, leaving a large gap. For a brief moment he toyed with the idea of making a quick reconnaissance in the direction of Louisiana, a sudden pincer movement to establish what geographical problems any major invasion might encounter in Arkansas and beyond. But he was immediately forestalled. Fräulein Brünnhilde drew back, raising her glass as she did so.

'*Prost!*'

'*Balcons!*' It was a Freudian slip and one he immediately regretted. Fräulein Brünnhilde drew back still further. The moment had passed.

'You are thinking bad thoughts,' she said reprovingly. 'You are what is called a *tétons* man.'

'I am a man,' said Monsieur Pamplemousse simply, meeting directness with directness.

'Ah, men!' Fräulein Brünnhilde managed to invest in the word a wealth of meaning, not all of it bad. There was a certain wistfulness too.

'I appreciate the beauties of nature when I see them,' said Monsieur Pamplemousse defensively, 'and I like to savour them. If you were to ask a mountaineer "why do you wish to climb Mount Everest?" the answer would be simple. He would say "because it is there". To him that would be sufficient reason.'

'It is not sufficient reason in my case,' said Fräulein Brünnhilde firmly. She watched Monsieur Pamplemousse warily over the top of her glass as he busied himself laying out the rest of the picnic.

'The Herr Professor is a *tétons* man. He pretends he is a nature-lover, but he watches the girls with his binoculars through the changing-room window. He thinks no one knows. But I have seen him. I tell the girls they must keep their leotards on at all times.'

'Perhaps,' said Monsieur Pamplemousse, 'he is frustrated.' He helped himself surreptitiously to a *dragée*. Being surrounded day and night by nubile nineteen year olds must have its problems. Other diversions around the Institut des Beaux Arbres seemed conspicuous by their absence. He was glad he had left his own binoculars back at the hotel. Fräulein Brünnhilde might think the worst.

'*He* is frustrated? What about me? *I* am frustrated. You do not know what it is like being there all day long with no one to talk to except a lot of young girls.'

'Why did you go there?'

'I saw an advertisement in a German newspaper. It seemed a good idea at the time. Now, I do not think so any more. I do not like it there. I am unhappy. I am too much alone. Night-times are the worst.'

'What about the other men?'

'There are no other men.'

'Not even the ski instructors?'

'They are not there in the summer. They only return about now. Besides, they are different. I do not trust them.'

Monsieur Pamplemousse found himself wondering why. Perhaps in the Fräulein's eyes all men were alike, only some were more so. If the girls he'd come across the day before were anything to go by, he could see why the ski instructors had made such a contented group in the photograph. They had it made. And yet, contentment was a word which had many connotations. There had been something else as well. Some element he couldn't quite put his finger on. A certain hardness. As a parent he wouldn't have been entirely happy.

'I will ask you another question.' Fräulein Brünnhilde broke into his thoughts. 'Why is it that all the girls are blonde? Why are there no brunettes? Why are there no redheads?'

Monsieur Pamplemousse fell silent. It was quite true. At

121

first he had only half-registered the fact without actually giving it much thought, but subconsciously it had prompted his query to Guillard.

'Perhaps,' he said without conviction, 'it is a coincidence.'

'Perhaps,' said Fräulein Brünnhilde complacently as she lay back and folded her hands across her stomach. 'Perhaps not.'

Monsieur Pamplemousse leaned over to remove the glass to a position of safety, and as he did so he became aware of a strange phenomenon, a kind of amalgam of movement, of undulating breasts and rising and falling hands which didn't entirely relate to each other. It was hard to rationalise the feeling, but once again he was left with a distinct impression of opposing forces at work. He was also only too well aware of the fact that both tee-shirt and skirt were now very far apart indeed. Flesh, bare, white, warm, patently alive, lay within his grasp. He caught a glimpse of something metal.

It might be worth a try. The thing was if he tried and failed – if the key was attached to a chain, perhaps even some kind of primitive burglar alarm (and he wouldn't put it past her) – he might never get another chance.

Placing the glass down on the groundsheet out of harm's way, he was about to shift his position a little when he glanced up and realised that Pommes Frites was watching his every movement through the rear window of the car. Back paws straining against the dashboard, he was craning precariously across the back of the seats as he sought to obtain a ringside view of all that was going on. As he caught Monsieur Pamplemousse's eye he assumed one of his enigmatic expressions. When he chose, Pommes Frites could look very puritanical. It was something to do with the folds of the skin on his face and the deep-set eyes. Given suitable headgear he might well, at that moment, have passed for a Pilgrim Father catching his first glimpse of Massachusetts U.S.A. through a porthole in the side of the *Mayflower* and not caring overmuch for what he saw. It was, to say the least, very offputting.

All the thoughts of making a frontal assault on Fräulein

Brünnhilde were dashed from Monsieur Pamplemousse's mind. He eased himself back to his original position, wondering if perhaps it might be as well to prepare the ground a little.

'Would you care for a glass of champagne?'

'That would be very good.' She stirred lazily, almost disappointedly.

Pommes Frites watched with renewed interest as his master leaned back and reached over his shoulder.

It was, as it happened, the last coherent act any of them were to perform for some little time to come.

The peace of la Dent d'Oche was suddenly shattered by a violent explosion and Monsieur Pamplemousse felt the cardboard tube wrenched from his hand.

A passing *vigneron* from Epernay would have put his finger on the cause of the explosion right away. Given all the facts, a junior science master would have launched into a stern lecture on the inadvisability of storing champagne in the freezer compartment of a refrigerator rather than the rack inside the door. In normal circumstances, and given more time at his disposal, it would be true to say that even Monsieur Pamplemousse would have speedily put two and two together.

Gaseous liquid, solidified after its spell in the *frigo*, slowly warmed by the autumn sun, thoroughly shaken during the long and bumpy drive up the mountain, had come to life again, building up a pressure far in excess of its accepted norm of seven atmospheres, before finally rebelling.

That the bottle hadn't burst en route was a tribute not only to its makers, but also to those who had followed on in the wake of Dom Perignon, perfecting over the years the art of layering and gluing together bark from the Spanish *Quercus suber*, inventing machines capable of squeezing the resultant cork into something like half its size so that it could be driven into the neck of the bottle by a power-hammer, free to expand once again before being held in place by the wire *muselet*.

But there is a limit to everything. Unable to withstand the enormous pressures a moment longer, the bottle had, at Monsieur Pamplemousse's sudden movement, parted company with its base. Left to its own devices, it emerged from the tube in a manner which would have merited a spontaneous round of applause from Cape Canaveral.

Monsieur Pamplemousse's reaction was both swift and dramatic. Convinced that it was yet another attempt on his life by the Department of Dirty Tricks, deprived of any such nicety as a countdown, he automatically made a dive for the figure at his side, throwing his whole body on top in an effort to protect it. As he landed he felt a sharp pain in his chest. There was a gasp followed almost immediately by another, smaller explosion from somewhere beneath him. A low rumbling noise and what felt like the beginnings of an earthquake added to the confusion. Arms and legs encircled his body, holding him in a vice-like grip from which there was no escape, whilst a scream in his left ear momentarily blotted out any attempt at rationalising the situation.

Reaching out in desperation, he grabbed at the nearest available object, and as the rumblings and shakings and bumps grew worse with every passing second, held on to it for dear life.

But if the reasons for the original explosion were complex, the cause of the volcanic-like eruption beneath the ground-sheet was easier to pin down. Pommes Frites could have put his paw on the cause immediately. Or, to put it another way, one of his paws had triggered it off.

Not usually given to emotional outbursts, trained like his master not to show fear in the face of danger, Pommes Frites had been so startled by the explosion that in his haste to get clear he had used the gear lever as a springboard, pushing it into neutral as he executed a leap into the air of such Olympic proportions it had caused him to sail clean through the sunshine-roof.

The result was almost as spectacular as the cause and he stood watching the progress of events, looking increasingly unhappy as the car gathered speed and disappeared down the hill taking the groundsheet and its picnickers with it. He winced visibly as the car collided with a tree in the dip at the bottom and came to an abrupt halt.

For a moment he toyed with the idea of going for a walk. It was a nice day and he had an uneasy feeling his master would not be in a very good mood. But only for a moment. Loyalty coupled with a desire to find out what was going on finally won the day and he set off down the hill as fast as he could go.

Pommes Frites arrived on the scene just in time to see his master let go of the bumper and make an abortive effort to struggle into a sitting position. It was an attempt which was doomed to failure. Fräulein Brünnhilde's arms were still locked firmly in position.

Monsieur Pamplemousse gazed down at her in alarm. With her eyes tightly closed in ecstasy, her lips parted and an expression of other-worldly bliss on her face, she also looked, to say the least, a trifle unbalanced. Lopsided was the only word for it. California appeared to have suffered a major earthquake; Atlantic City had been pierced by a thin sliver of greenish glass to which a piece of label was still attached. Reaching down to remove it he became aware of a slow hiss of escaping air. He tried to push the glass back into place but it was too late. A deep depression was already settling over the area. As he braced himself for an explosion of wrath he noticed for the first time that her blouse was flecked with red.

'You are hurt?' Even as he spoke he realised that the blood was coming from a small cut to his chest.

Fräulein Brünnhilde uttered a low moan, waving her head from side to side. '*Mein Leibfraumilch!*' Her grip tightened. 'That was wonderful! The earth moved. Did you feel it? The earth moved.'

'Yes,' said Monsieur Pamplemousse cautiously. 'I felt it too.' All movement was relative. Speaking for himself he felt as if they were halfway to Evian.

'*Mein Beerenauslese!*' The breath was suddenly squeezed from his body as she tightened her grip. 'More! More!'

Monsieur Pamplemousse looked round for help but only Pommes Frites was there to answer his call. Pommes Frites averted his gaze. He was not without his finer feelings. There would be no help from that quarter.

'Love is a very inexact science,' he gasped, playing for time as he tried to regain his breath before the next onslaught. 'It is like the boiling of an egg. Success cannot always be guaranteed. The joy of getting it exactly right is not always easy to repeat.'

Fräulein Brünnhilde gave another moan and a shudder went through her whole body as she relived the moment.

'*Mein Trockenbeerepauslese*. It has never happened to me before.'

'I doubt,' said Monsieur Pamplemousse, 'if it has ever happened to *anyone* quite like that before.'

'*Mein Eiswein* . . . please . . .'

Monsieur Pamplemousse tried to distract her. 'Eiswein is made from grapes which have been left hanging on the vine until after Christmas. They are picked while still frozen. The wine is sweet beyond measure, but it happens rarely. Perhaps once in a decade.'

Fräulein Brünnhilde opened her eyes. He noticed for the first time how blue they were. 'Then let it happen again. Please let it happen again.'

'It is not yet Christmas,' began Monsieur Pamplemousse.

'Neither am I cold.'

'Perhaps,' said Monsieur Pamplemousse, bowing to the inevitable, 'we may do a deal. There are ways in which you can help me. But first you must let me go so that I can move the car.'

Fräulein Brünnhilde closed her eyes again. 'Do not be long. I cannot bear it if you are too long.'

'I will be as quick as I can,' said Monsieur Pamplemousse. Struggling free, he clambered unsteadily to his feet, signalling to Pommes Frites as he did so.

Pommes Frites jumped up wagging his tail. He sensed there was some kind of game afoot. Pommes Frites liked games and this one promised to be even better than usual.

8

A MEAL TO END ALL MEALS

The first half of the journey back down the mountain to the Institut des Beaux Arbres was conducted in silence. Pommes Frites spent most of the time gazing pensively out of the rear window, thinking thoughts, while casting superior glances at sheep grazing in the gathering dusk. Monsieur Pamplemousse was too busy concentrating on holding the 2CV in check with the handbrake to bother about making polite conversation. His mind was also racing on ahead to coming events. Now that he had marshalled his ideas he wanted to put them into action as quickly as possible. Speed was of the essence. Speed and confidence. Plus a reasonable amount of luck. The key to the Sanatorium was now safely in his pocket. He would have no hesitation whatsoever in using it. If necessary he would call in the local police. But that would involve lots of tedious explanations which would take time. Time was the one commodity he was short of. If all else failed, he would take it as high as he could possibly go. And if that failed . . . if that failed then at least he would have the satisfaction of knowing he had tried. His own conscience would be clear. Besides, he still had friends in the right *journaux*.

Fräulein Brünnhilde was busy with her thoughts too. 'Do you think the first time was best?' she asked suddenly. 'Or do you think the fourth?'

Monsieur Pamplemousse let go his concentration for a moment, long enough to glance across at her in wonder. She was like a child with a new toy, or a cat who had just discovered the existence of cream. It was a good job the cords attaching the groundsheet to the car had finally broken. They might still be at it.

'I think the third time was best.' He turned his attention back to the road.

'That is interesting,' she mused dreamily. 'I wonder why.'

Monsieur Pamplemousse didn't reply. It was not a moment to discuss practicalities. The simple answer was that food and wine after the second excursion had provided new energy to go with the second wind, and by then Pommes Frites had also got into the swing of things. Equally excited at having discovered a new joy in life, he hadn't even bothered to jump clear of the car. But by the time they set off on the fourth trip digestive tracts had begun to rebel, romance had flown out of the window.

'It was good that Pommes Frites had a puncture outfit. I have never before met a dog with a puncture outfit.'

'He is never without.' Monsieur Pamplemousse pulled hard on the brake as they approached a steep bend. Lights from houses in the valley below them were beginning to appear.

'And a cylinder of compressed air. That, too, is unusual.'

'It is for his kennel. He has an inflatable kennel. We do a lot of travelling together and sometimes he has to sleep outside. In the hot weather he prefers it.'

'Ah! There cannot be many dogs with an inflatable kennel.'

'As far as I know,' said Monsieur Pamplemousse, 'he is the only one. I had it specially made.'

'I had my *soutien-gorge* specially made. I sent away for it. It is also unusual. Have you met one before?'

'Never,' said Monsieur Pamplemousse. He had read of them. They had enjoyed a brief vogue at one time, or so he had been told, but he had never actually encountered one at first hand so to speak. Now that he had he could see why they had never caught on. If he ever met one again he would treat it with respect, sticking to sea-level, where the air pressure was normal. As the road levelled out and they reached a comparatively straight section he took advantage of the moment to glance across at his companion again.

'It is not necessary. In your case it is far from necessary. It is like gilding the lily.'

He felt a hand on his knee. 'You are very kind.'

'I am only speaking the truth.'

'It is good for my ego. The *soutien-gorge*, I mean.'

'What is good for the ego is sometimes bad for other things. Egos are like stomachs – they often grow too fat for comfort.'

Fräulein Brünnhilde looked down at herself. 'You think I should lose my egos?'

'I know you should. People are what they are. I have never met anyone yet who didn't want to change themselves in some way; a larger nose or a smaller one, or one which is straight, or to be thinner or fatter, or taller or shorter. And for what reason? It is like buying a book by a film star telling you how to become as beautiful as she is. It is pointless. If she thought for one moment that there was any possibility of it happening she would withdraw it from sale. Why should people always want to look like someone else? Everyone is different; that is part of the joy of life.'

'I shall keep them as a souvenir. You would like my egos as a souvenir?'

Monsieur Pamplemousse shook his head. 'It would not be a good idea. Madame Pamplemousse would not be pleased.'

'Ah!' Fräulein Brünnhilde fell silent again.

It would certainly not be a good idea. Doucette wouldn't be at all happy if she came across a pair of inflatable *doudounes* tucked away in his bottom drawer. Explanations would be tedious, prolonged and utterly unbelieved.

Again he felt a hand on his knee, lighter this time. 'I think Madame Pamplemousse is a very lucky person. Does she think she is a lucky person?'

Monsieur Pamplemousse weighed the question in his mind. It was hard to say. You could live with someone half a lifetime and still not know their true feelings.

'I cannot answer that,' he said at last. 'She looks forward to my coming home, that I know. But then, I think sometimes after a few days she looks forward to my going away again.'

'And you? Do you look forward to going home?'

'Yes. But then I also look forward to going away again. It is a good arrangement. We are not unhappy. It is the need to go back which is important. That, and the need to be wanted back.'

Another two corners and they were nearly there. As the perimeter fence came into view he pulled in to the side of the road and switched off the engine.

'Tell me.' Fräulein Brünnhilde took the photograph from her handbag and looked at it. 'Is it because you have no children that you are interested in this girl?'

Monsieur Pamplemousse considered the question carefully before replying. It was true in a way. Without his realising it and without ever having spoken to her, he felt he knew her and wanted to protect her. 'It is certainly not for the reason you might think.'

'That is all right then. I would not have liked that. I will help you.'

'Good.' He took the photograph from her. 'You know what to do?'

'Precisely.' She went over his instructions again.

'Excellent. You had better pack some things. Ask the girl to do the same. As for the other – we will work that out later.' He looked at his watch. It said 18.52. That it had survived the buffeting on the mountain was something of a miracle; a testimony to its makers – Capillard Rième. He might write to them. Except that it would be impossible to explain all that had actually happened. They would never be able to use it as advertising material.

'You had better check your own watch. I will be back here at 20.00 precisely.'

'I am sorry. My watch has stopped. It has 14.12.'

'In that case you had better borrow mine. I have my car clock. It is important that you are not late.'

He slipped the watch off his wrist and suddenly felt naked without it. Second only to his pen it was the personal possession he treasured most. As he slipped it over Fräulein Brünnhilde's wrist and began doing up the strap she gave a shiver.

'You are cold?'

130

'No. Suddenly a little lonely. That is all. After tonight I will not see you again.'

'If all goes well I will see you in Paris.'

'That will not be the same.'

No, it would not be the same. The cobbled streets of the Butte Montmartre would not lend themselves to such goings on. Doucette would be keeping a watchful eye on him as well.

'It is always unwise to try and go back; to repeat the unrepeatable.'

She gave a laugh. It was a good sign – the first time he had heard it. 'I have been thinking. I do not even know your name.'

'My friends call me Aristide.'

He felt the barest touch on his forehead; a butterfly of a kiss. Then the door opened.

'Thank you, Aristide. I shall leave my watch where it stopped. It will always remind me of a very happy after-noon in the mountains.'

He allowed her to walk a little way down the road before starting the engine, then caught up with her just as she was disappearing through a gap in the bushes. He fielded the second kiss in mid-air and mimed putting it into his pocket, then she was gone.

Pommes Frites gave a loud yawn and began moving about restlessly on the back seat. Monsieur Pamplemousse took the hint and stopped for a moment to allow him into the front. It still felt warm from Fräulein Brünnhilde. A moment later they were on their way again, each busy with their own thoughts.

It was late when Monsieur Pamplemousse finally entered the dining-room of Les Cinq Parfaits. The tables were full; the ceremony of the raising of the domes was in full swing; there was a buzz of animated conversation.

He was walking somewhat stiffly; joints were beginning to seize up, muscles making their presence felt, rebelling against doing even the simplest of day-to-day tasks like moving his legs. Even a long, hot bath hadn't persuaded them to behave otherwise. He paused by the window separating the *cuisine* from the restaurant. The scene on the other side of the darkened glass was reminiscent of the performance of a modern ballet. The *commis-poissonnier* partnered Gilbert in a *pas-de-deux* over some *truite*, sprinkling almonds over it like confetti with all the masculine delicacy and authority of a Nureyev. The *commis-rotisseur* and Edouard were limbering up in front of an oven, preparing themselves for their own particular moment of truth. Alain was just disappearing offstage with a large bowl.

There was a new face where Jean-Claude would normally have been; perhaps the *commis-pâtissier* was enjoying his big moment as a stand-in. He glanced at his watch. By now Jean-Claude would be well on his way to Paris. All around the *cuisine* the *corps-de-ballet* moved swiftly and with precision, gathering up dishes with lightning speed, conveying them to the *sous-chef* for final inspection and checking before handing them over to the waiters and thence to the diners in the other room. Of Albert there was no sign. Turning round, he caught sight of a white hat at the far end of the restaurant. He must be doing his rounds.

Monsieur Pamplemousse made his way towards his table. It was the cue for action. Again, it was akin to a ballet. Waiters preceded him. Greetings were exchanged in the correct pecking order. His chair was moved back and carefully replaced, the moment judged to a nicety. The napkin was whisked away, shaken open and placed on his lap. He ordered an apéritif – a Kir made with *framboise*; the house speciality.

The menu materialised, along with a bottle of the ubiquitous Evian – one more out of the six hundred million which left the factory every year. The *carte des vins* was placed discreetly within his reach, a plate of hot *friandises* appeared on the table as if by magic – slivers of sausage encased in the lightest of pastry. He tried one; it positively melted in his mouth. Jean-Claude's stand-in was making the most of his opportunity. The cast withdrew, leaving him to his *friandises* and his ponderings on the evening's events.

Doucette had taken the news that she was about to be

invaded remarkably well, entering into the situation with brisk efficiency. Rooms would be aired, beds would have to be remade. No doubt she would rush out and buy some flowers. There was no telling. Perhaps she'd sensed the urgency in his voice. Perhaps it was simply a need to feel wanted. As soon as he got back to Paris he would have to make other arrangements. Dinner accompanied by long, hot glances from Fräulein Brünnhilde would not go down well. There would be language barriers with the English girl. On the other hand, they might all get on like a house on fire. You never could tell.

First things first. He turned his attention to the menu. In all probability it would be his last meal at Les Cinq Parfaits. He must make the most of it. Tonight there would be no face at the window to spoil his appetite.

The whole operation at the Institut des Beaux Arbres had gone like a dream. In many ways it felt like a dream. Bluff had been the order of the day; borrowing the black boy who had shown him to Jean-Claude's room on the first evening, a happy thought. It had added the necessary stroke of realism. In the event Madame Schmidt had queried neither his sudden metamorphosis from being the emissary of a prospective student to that of a person of authority, nor the removal of Jean-Claude. Her husband had been more suspicious, asking for papers. He'd had to lean on him a little, adopting his long-practised 'I'm asking the questions' voice. 'Watch it, or it will be the worse for you.' It worked as it had always worked in the past. Pommes Frites had bared his teeth with great effect at the appropriate moment.

The taxi driver with his borrowed limousine had behaved magnificently; assuming exactly the right degree of studied indifference – of having seen it all before, leaning against the bonnet picking his teeth until required, his cap at a suitably insolent and rakish angle. He might have abducted people every day of his life. Perhaps he had in the past. The meeting with Fräulein Brünnhilde and the girl had gone without a hitch. Madame Grante would throw a fit when she saw the bill, but that was a minor problem.

A little way along the restaurant the V.I.P. was holding court. The table had been set very slightly and very discreetly apart from the rest. There were four other members of the entourage, each vying for the privilege of ministering to his wants; no doubt acting as bodyguards as well. He made a joke. Rolls of fat loosely encased in silken robes shook with laughter. It was echoed in turn by an obedient ripple round the table. Watching the scene over the top of his menu, Monsieur Pamplemousse couldn't help but wonder what would happen if one of them missed his cue. He wouldn't fancy their chances. What was it the chief had said about him?

'A *grosse légume* whose speed at acquiring untold wealth had not so far been matched by any show of finer feelings towards his fellow man.'

Behind the laughter there lurked corruption and decay. The black boy had said much the same on the journey up to the Institut. 'He make Idi Amin look like guardian angel on church outing.'

Even as he watched there occurred an incident which, although comparatively minor, served to underline the boy's words. One of the *commis*-waiters bearing a load of silver domes back to the kitchen passed perilously close to the great man's elbow and in swerving to avoid a collision inadvertently allowed one of them to fall to the floor.

The *Grosse Légume*, the flow of his conversation momentarily checked, half-rose and for a moment Monsieur Pamplemousse thought he was about to strike the waiter. The boy thought so too, and ducking in panic, he allowed the rest of the silverware to slide ignominiously off the tray.

The crash echoed round the room and for a moment there was a stunned silence. Then someone gave a nervous giggle in the way that people do in restaurants the world over at such moments and the tension was broken.

The *Grosse Légume*, sat down again and a broad smile filled his face. But it was a smile without mirth and it left a long shadow. At another time and in another place, it seemed to say, your life would not be worth living. The man was a *salaud. Un salaud de première classe.*

134

'*Vous avez choisi, Monsieur?*' The maître d'hôtel appeared at his side, pad and pencil at the ready.

Monsieur Pamplemousse came down to earth. He had already decided against a repeat of the *menu gastronomique*. It would be like trying to recapture the delights of his experience on the mountainside. On the other hand it was an occasion for a mini-celebration of some kind. What would Holmes have chosen? Oysters and a brace of pheasants, probably, followed by cheddar cheese and syllabub. He corrected himself, the latter two courses would have been in the reverse order in the English manner. He scanned the menu. All four items were conspicuous by their absence.

Running his eye down the *entrées* he had a sudden thought. Amongst those listed he noticed a starred dish – *soupe aux truffes noires* — the one that Bocuse had created specially for President Giscard d'Estaing's famous *Légion d'Honneur* lunch at the Elysée Palace in 1975. He had always wanted to try it. He glanced across at the list of *poissons*. At the time, Bocuse had called on other chefs to contribute to the menu. Sure enough, the Troisgros Brothers' *escalope de saumon à l'oseille* – a creation based on a happy thought by Pierre Troisgros' mother-in-law, was also listed and starred. He felt a growing excitement. There were more delights – roast duck Claude Jolly. He remembered that in the original lunch they had followed duck with cheese, then the first wild strawberries of the year. Jean-Claude's *Soufflé Surprise* probably hadn't seen the light of day then – but he could make do with some more of the *framboises*.

The maître d'hôtel nodded approvingly. '*Monsieur* is not in a hurry?'

'I have nowhere to go,' said Monsieur Pamplemousse simply. 'I have all the time in the world.' It wasn't strictly true, of course. But tomorrow was another day.

He picked up his copy of *The Hound of the Baskervilles* and was about to open it where he'd left off, when Albert Parfait hobbled into view.

Monsieur Pamplemousse looked up at the slowly approaching figure with a genuine sense of shock. In the

space of a few days the *patron* of Les Cinq Parfaits seemed
to have added another ten years to his age. There was a
stoop which he hadn't noticed previously, and his limp
seemed more pronounced. But as he drew near he saw it
was mostly in the eyes. The eyes were those of a man who
had suddenly grown tired of life.

'What news?'

'Your son is safe.' Monsieur Pamplemousse felt a
tremble in the other's hand as he took it, then the grip
tightened.

'*Merci.* I was almost beginning to give up hope.'

'I'm sorry I didn't tell you straight away. Time did not
allow it.'

Even as he spoke the words, Monsieur Pamplemousse
knew that they had a hollow ring to them. It was an excuse
rather than a reason. An excuse for an inexcusable omission.
Deep down he had been avoiding the moment and he wondered why. It left him with a strange feeling; one which he
couldn't entirely rationalise.

'I understand.' Albert Parfait relaxed momentarily,
allowed himself a brief smile, then the tiredness returned to
his face. It was almost as though he had been undergoing
some kind of inner battle, the outcome of which had
already been decided. 'When can I see him?'

'He is on his way to Paris for a few days. He has been
heavily sedated, but he is young and fit – the effects will
soon wear off. He will be back here as quickly as possible,
but for the time being it is as well if he is not around.'

'And the girl?'

'The girl is travelling with him. She will be staying with
Madame Pamplemousse. Pommes Frites is accompanying
them on the journey. They will be quite safe.'

He didn't mention Fräulein Brünnhilde. It was unnecessary. There would be the girl's parents to tell too. His heart
sank at the prospect.

'I am very grateful. Later tonight we will drink to the
occasion.' Once again there was a distinct tremble in the
hand. 'In the meantime, I will leave you to your reading
and to your meal. *Bon appetit.*'

Left to his own devices, Monsieur Pamplemousse picked

up his book again and gazed at it unseeingly, focusing his thoughts not on the jumble of words but on the scene around him and on Albert Parfait in particular. He had a strange sense of foreboding. Monsieur Parfait did not look a happy man. The news of his son's safety had revived his spirits momentarily, but it had been only the briefest of moments. Perhaps he was suffering the responsibility of success and wealth. It must have been a difficult week for him. First the disappearance of Jean-Claude, then the arrival of the V.I.P., whose presence he could hardly have welcomed at such a time. It must be a far cry from the comparatively modest hopes and ambitions he'd nursed when he'd first helped out in his *grand-mère*'s kitchen. He couldn't have dreamed in those far-off times that one day he would be hobnobbing with royalty, cooking for Presidents, playing host to the V.I.P.s of the world. All the same, it hardly accounted for his doom-laden manner.

Once again his thoughts were interrupted. This time by the wine waiter. He picked up the *carte des vins* and opted for a Hermitage – a bottle of Gérard Chave, one of the most meticulous of *vignerons*, whose land was so sheer the grape-filled *bennes* had to be hauled up to the top by a winch at harvest time.

Again his order met with evident approval. Then, having duly recorded it, the *sommelier* hovered for a moment, fingering his *tastevin* hesitantly. Clearly, he had something on his mind. Monsieur Pamplemousse raised his eyebrows enquiringly.

'I am sorry about the Château d'Yquem, *Monsieur*.'

'Sorry?' Monsieur Pamplemousse gazed at the man in amazement. 'But it was delicious. Sheer perfection. An unforgettable experience. I cannot wait to repeat it.'

'Ah!' A look of unhappiness crossed the *sommelier*'s normally dead-pan features. It was the kind of expression he must reserve for those rare occasions when he sniffed a cork and detected signs of the dreaded weevil bug. '*Monsieur* has not been to his refrigerator since this morning?'

Monsieur Pamplemousse thought for a moment. 'I have, but only briefly. I have been out all day.' It was true. He'd arrived back so late he'd even resisted the temptation of allowing himself the luxury of a drink with his bath. 'Why do you ask?'

'I am sorry, *Monsieur*. The room maid should have told you. On Monsieur Parfait's instructions we removed the second bottle. The wine should not have been withdrawn from the cellars in the first place.' He picked up the *carte des vins* and opened it at a page near the back. A neat red line had been drawn through one of the entries. 'As *Monsieur* will see, the '45 is no longer listed.'

Monsieur Pamplemousse digested the fact with mounting irritation.

'May I ask a simple question?'

'*Monsieur?*'

'If the '45 is no longer listed, then how was it that the night before last I was given two bottles when I ordered them. It was also my understanding that they were not the last.'

'There were three, *Monsieur*. Now there are only two. They were being held in reserve for a special customer. We will, of course, replace *Monsieur*'s second bottle with one from another year. Might I suggest the '62? *Monsieur* will not be charged.'

Monsieur Pamplemousse fixed the man with a stare. There were times when he would have dearly loved to announce his identity; hand over a card bearing the *escargot rampant*, symbol of *Le Guide*. 'I have another question. Would it not be true to say that in a restaurant such as Les Cinq Parfaits, a restaurant whose reputation is such that people come from all over the world to sample its *cuisine*, each and every guest should be considered special?'

'I agree, *Monsieur*, but unfortunately some guests like to be considered more special than others. It is the way of the world.' He allowed himself a brief glance at the table further along the room. 'We have to humour them.'

'Ah!' The penny dropped.

'He has a sweet tooth, *Monsieur*. The decision is not entirely ours.'

'*D'accord*. I understand.' It was the second time he'd

heard mention of a 'sweet tooth'. The phrase was beginning to grate.

'*Merci, Monsieur.*' The *sommelier* made to leave. 'If *Monsieur* will forgive me?'

'Of course.'

Monsieur Pamplemousse drained his Kir, helped himself to the remaining *bonne bouche*, then sank back in his seat while he awaited the arrival of the first course. It might be the way of the world, but there were times when the ways of the world didn't suit him and this was one of them. In truth, the chance to compare the '62 Château d'Yquem with its illustrious predecessor would not be without interest – he could hardly grumble. It was the principle, or lack of it, which irritated.

Another ripple of laughter from the offending party did nothing to improve his mood. At least they were approaching the end of their meal. The cheese trolley had been and gone, the table cleared in readiness for the next course. He wondered what kind of reception would be accorded the *Soufflé Surprise*. No doubt, to add to his feeling of injustice, it would be washed down with 'his' wine. He resolved to look the other way.

Seeing a flotilla of waiters approaching, their leader bearing a silver tray on which reposed the inevitable dome, he poured himself a glass of Evian and hastily cleansed his palate in readiness. At the same moment, through another door, the *sommelier* reappeared with his wine, reaching the table a moment before the others. The bottle presented, it was discreetly removed to a side table for opening and decanting. He sat up, preparing himself for the moment of truth, taste-buds springing to life with anticipation.

The junior waiters stood back in attitudes of suitable reverence as the plate was placed in front of him and the dome removed, revealing a deep earthenware bowl capped and sealed with a mound of golden pastry, puffed up like a gigantic mushroom.

Picking up a spoon, he pierced the top, breaking the flakes into small pieces so that they fell back into the bowl and released the smell. It was rich and woody, like nothing he had ever encountered before. A complex mixture; the result of combining a *matignon* of carrots, celery, onions, mushrooms, and unsalted butter with chicken *consommé, foie gras* and fresh truffles. A unique creation. No wonder Bocuse had been awarded the *Légion d'Honneur.* No wonder Monsieur Parfait spent so much on truffles every year. Both were fully justified.

He tasted the wine. Like the soup, it had been made with love. It was a perfect marriage. Automatically he reached for the notebook he always carried concealed in his right trouser leg and laid it on his lap, out of sight below the edge of the tablecloth. It was an occasion to record; one which would have met with Pommes Frites' wholehearted approval. He felt a momentary pang of guilt as he caught sight of the time on his watch. It was just after ten o'clock. By now Pommes Frites would have reached the *autoroute,* speeding on his supperless way to Paris. He made a mental note to ring Doucette as soon as dinner was over and remind her to put something out in readiness for his arrival.

He leant over the bowl again. Whoever said that the *bouquet* was often better than the taste would have had to eat not only his words, but the most heavenly dish imaginable. Spoon halfway to his mouth, he paused yet again in order to savour the deliciousness of the smell, and as he did so a frown came over his face. Heading in his direction was one of the page-boys, holding aloft yet another silver tray. He watched as the boy threaded his way in and out of the tables. What was it now?

He eyed a small sheaf of papers gloomily and, stifling his feelings, motioned for them to be left beside him. It was hardly the boy's fault. He was only doing as he'd been told. It was more his own fault for not having called in at the reception desk for so long.

Another spoonful of soup and he succumbed to temptation. There was a card from Doucette – a drawing of the Sacré Coeur – reminding him of someone's birthday. He couldn't make out the words in the muted lighting. Never mind, he would work it out later.

The thought occurred to him that Pommes Frites might be good at hunting truffles. He had a nose for scents.

Truffles might be just up his street. The *'egregious tuber-culum'* as Brillet-Savarin had called them; 'a luxury of kept women'. Perhaps one day, if they found themselves in Périgord . . .

There was a telex from the Director. The one he had spoken of on the telephone. Short and to the point, it said: CANCEL ORDER FOR *SOUFFLÉ SURPRISE* IMMEDIATELY. The girl in charge of the telex machine at Les Cinq Parfaits must be wondering what was going on. He hoped she hadn't relayed it to the kitchen first by mistake.

He picked up the envelope and opened it. It was a letter from Durelle. He skimmed through it quickly, then stopped halfway and began reading it again, much more slowly this time.

Merde! It was not possible.

His *soupe aux truffes noires* momentarily forgotten, Monsieur Pamplemousse read through the letter for a third time, still hardly able to believe his eyes.

'Aristide, you old *maquereau!*' it ran. 'How did you know it was my fiftieth birthday? You really had me fooled. When your bottle arrived and I saw the label I thought it's Aristide up to his tricks again. Trust Aristide to think of putting Pommes Frites' specimen into a bottle labelled Château d'Yquem '45. I even took it into the lab for analysis. Then when I opened it and discovered the truth I could hardly believe my eyes. Such wine! It was out of this world! If I had known I would have waited until you got back to Paris so that we could share it. I don't know what I have done to deserve such riches, let alone how I can ever thank you, but I am working on the problem. Your friend, Raymonde.'

Sapristi! He didn't believe it. It had to be some kind of a joke.

Picking up Doucette's card he held it up to the candle and reread the message on the back. The words confirmed what Durelle had said. It had been his fiftieth birthday.

He sat back in order to collect his scattered thoughts. He knew that he had taken the right bottle from the refriger-ator. Or rather, to be pedantic (not to say Holmesian) about it, he knew he had taken the one which he'd thought was the correct bottle, simply because it was where he had put it the night before. In his haste he hadn't examined it closely. The answer must be that in checking the contents, something she would do every morning as a matter of routine in order to see what had been consumed, the room maid must have inadvertently swapped the bottles over.

A second, more sobering thought struck him; one which caused a slow smile to spread across his face as it sank in. If Durelle had been sent a genuine bottle of the '45, then Pommes Frites' sample must have gone back into stock when the second bottle was withdrawn. And if it had gone back into stock and there was only one other bottle left, then it was a fifty-fifty chance it would arrive in the restaurant at any moment.

Monsieur Pamplemousse's smile grew wider. It would be rough justice if it did. He couldn't think of a more suitable recipient than the odious character at present holding court. His only regret was that Pommes Frites wouldn't be there to witness the event.

Polishing off the remains of his soup, he dabbed at his mouth with a napkin, then leaned back in his chair, anxious not to miss a single moment. Mathematically it might not happen, but if there was any justice in the world then mathematics would fly out of the window.

He wasn't a moment too soon. He had hardly settled himself before the *sommelier* appeared. Carrying a cradled bottle reverentially in both hands, he made his way across the dining-room towards the V.I.P.'s table. The formalities completed, the bottle presented and inspected, the label read and its inscription confirmed, he stood back and reached into his apron pocket for a corkscrew while those around the table voiced appreciation of their host's impeccably good taste.

Monsieur Pamplemousse's face fell again. He wished now he'd paid more attention to the remains of the soup instead of bolting it down without a moment's thought. He'd been living in cloud-cuckoo-land. Even if the bottle did turn out to be the one containing Pommes Frites' specimen, it wouldn't get any further than the opening. One sniff of the cork would reveal all; the other bottle would be sent for immediately. On reflection, it was just as well. The scandal if it turned out that Les Cinq Parfaits had served *pipi de chien* to one of the guests in mistake for a Château d'Yquem would reverberate around the restaurants of France for years.

Idly he watched the beginnings of a set and invariable routine he'd seen countless times before; the application of the corkscrew, its deft rotation, the swift but sure single leverage ensuring the clean removal of the cork, the passing of it under the nose . . .

Suddenly he sat up and leaned across the table, concentrating all his attention on the scene in front of him. Before the *sommelier* had a chance to complete his task, almost before the cork had left the bottle, Albert Parfait appeared at his side. There was a brief exchange of words and then Monsieur Parfait himself took over, removing the cork from the screw and slipping it straight into the pocket of his apron without so much as a second glance.

Monsieur Pamplemousse's eyes narrowed as a thought entered his mind and then emerged almost immediately as an inescapable conclusion. It could only mean one of two things; either the *patron* didn't trust his *sommelier* before such important guests, or there was something about the bottle of wine which might cause the V.I.P. to reject it. The former was so unlikely that he dismissed it, allowing his mind to race on ahead as he watched the wine being poured into a glass ready for tasting.

Unable to stand it a moment longer, Monsieur Pamplemousse snapped his notebook shut and sprang to his feet. A joke was a joke, but he couldn't allow it to happen. He *must* not allow it to happen. More than that, the evidence had to be destroyed. Albert Parfait was an idiot. Not only was the honour of Les Cinq Parfaits at stake, but also that of *Le Guide*, its contemporaries, even that of France itself.

Ignoring those around him, his stiffness forgotten, scattering the waiters as he went, Monsieur Pamplemousse reached the table in a matter of seconds and removed the offending glass from Albert Parfait's hand, placing it on a side table out of reach of the diners.

Their eyes met briefly. Failure was written large on

Albert's face; failure and something else. Desperation? A mute cry for help? Whatever it was there could be no time for speculation.

Before anyone had a chance to react, Monsieur Pamplemousse whisked the bottle from its cradle and upended it into a nearby plant container. The effect of his action was both immediate and impressive. He stared at the plant. Its leaves were turning yellow and wilting before his very eyes.

Marvelling at the potency of Pommes Frites' water, he turned towards the *Grosse Légume* and braced himself for the inevitable explosion. But hardly had he done so than there was a new diversion. Aware of a movement from behind, a movement which was followed almost immediately by a choking sound, Monsieur Pamplemousse spun round on his heels and was just in time to see a hand clutching an empty glass disappear from view on the other side of the table.

Attention, which a moment before had been focused in his direction, suddenly switched as glass and silverware and china crashed to the floor, overriding the dull thud which preceded it.

As those nearby craned their necks in alarm, an elderly man jumped to his feet and rushed to the rescue, bending over the figure on the floor with a professional air.

Monsieur Pamplemousse hurried round the table to join him. 'I think, *Monsieur*,' he murmured as he crouched, 'you will find it is only a temporary indisposition. The most it will require is the use of a stomach pump.'

The man looked up at him. 'On the contrary, *Monsieur*. I am a doctor and I think you will find on closer examination that Monsieur Parfait is beyond such aids. Monsieur Parfait, alas, is en route to the *grande cuisine* in the sky.'

9

APÉRITIFS WITH MADAME GRANTE

'Pamplemousse.' The Director held a sheaf of papers above his desk; heavily embossed notepaper, pink flimsies, yellow duplicates, sheets of memo paper. 'Congratulations are being showered upon you. They arrive by the hour. I trust I may add mine?' He released his grip and they fluttered down at varying speeds, like multi-coloured leaves in an autumn breeze.

Monsieur Pamplemousse inclined his head non-committally, but warily.

The Director salvaged one of the heavier pieces of paper. 'This one is from the Minister himself. He would like to see you later today – at your convenience. Word has also reached me from the Elysée Palace. Your name has been recorded. Even the *Grosse Légume* has let it be known that he wishes to honour you with a decoration – the Grand Order of the Star of something or other. It is accompanied by an invitation to become his chief food taster.'

Monsieur Pamplemousse shuddered.

'It carries a large salary commensurate with the post. The supply of wines would be without limit; the choice would be yours. Doubtless other pleasures would be at your command.'

'I think not, *Monsieur*.'

The Director breathed a visible sigh of relief. 'We would miss you, Aristide. The appointment is pensionable, but I doubt if you would live to enjoy it. You would also have suffered opprobrium from on high. Relations between our two countries are somewhat strained at present.'

'He has left France, *Monsieur*?'

'At the highest possible speed. He and his entire entourage flew out last night on a specially chartered plane. The visit to Les Beaux Arbres has been postponed indefinitely. Outwardly he took diplomatic umbrage, but in reality he is a very frightened man. Like all bullies he is a coward at heart.

'The soil in the pot-plant container at Les Cinq Parfaits is undergoing analysis. Preliminary reports suggest that there was enough poison in the bottle to kill a regiment. Whoever put it there was determined to make a good job of it.'

Monsieur Pamplemousse leant down and gave Pommes Frites' ear an affectionate tweak. At least his worst fear hadn't been realised. Responsibility for the contents of the bottle of Château d'Yquem rested elsewhere. He gave another half-suppressed shudder as the thought crossed his mind that he might well have tested the wine himself had he not been in such a hurry.

'One almost regrets your act, Pamplemousse. I realise it was done with the best of intentions, but had the poison reached the person for whom it was intended few tears would have been shed. As it is, the world of *haute cuisine* has been deprived of one of its most revered figures. The loss will be severe. It was a most unfortunate accident.'

'Accident?' Monsieur Pamplemousse closed his eyes for a brief moment while he pictured the scene in the restaurant. Albert Parfait's appearance that evening – the haunted look in his eyes; the final air of desperation. 'I do not think it was an accident, *Monsieur*.'

'What are you suggesting, Pamplemousse? If it was not an accident, then . . .'

'I am convinced he knew what the bottle contained. That was why he took over its serving, and that being so, one can only assume the drinking of it to have been a deliberate and final act on his part.'

'Surely not. By then, according to your own account, he knew his son was safe. The *Grosse Légume* would soon be gone. He had everything to live for.'

'Perhaps, *Monsieur*, "had" is the right word.'

'Elucidate, Pamplemousse.'

Resisting the very real temptation to say, 'Elementary, my dear Watson', Monsieur Pamplemousse racked his brains for the right words. Dishonour? Shame? Disgrace? Failure? Albert Parfait had probably known more of what was going on than most. If he'd known what the bottle contained then he must have been a party to its preparation, if only at arm's length. No doubt, pressure had been brought to bear: pressure from faceless people in authority whose names would never be known, leaving him to face the music. He must have seen the writing on the wall. He was no fool.

'I think he could see ruination staring him in the face. Not financial ruin. People would still flock to Les Cinq Parfaits whatever happened. What he couldn't face was the loss of all the things for which he had worked so hard during his life; the things he knew would have made both his mother and his grandmother proud. He couldn't bear the thought of losing face where it mattered most. His Stock Pots in *Le Guide*, his stars in Michelin, his toques in Gault Millau.'

'You think it would have come to that?'

'Michelin never award a third star to a restaurant simply for the food alone,' said Monsieur Pamplemousse. 'Nor, *Monsieur*, do we award our Stock Pots for that reason. The withdrawal might only have been temporary, but they would have been withdrawn and he couldn't face the thought.'

It was the Director's turn to fall silent. It had happened before, of course. There had been the famous occasion when a chef had committed suicide because of the loss of his only star in Michelin.

'Ours is a heavy responsibility, Aristide,' he said at last. 'The irony is that Les Cinq Parfaits will lose them anyway by virtue of Albert Parfait's own act.'

'Only if that act is made public, *Monsieur*.'

The Director gave a start. 'What are you suggesting, Pamplemousse?'

'I am suggesting that if Albert Parfait's death is put down

to heart failure – which covers a multitude of sins – then things will go on as before.'

'I am afraid that is not possible. I cannot agree. Knowing what I know, my conscience would not allow it.'

'In that case,' Monsieur Pamplemousse felt inside his jacket pocket and withdrew a folded sheet of paper. 'I am afraid, *Monsieur*, I have to tender my resignation. My own conscience would not allow me to continue.' It was the least he could do. The mental picture of Albert Parfait's last imploring look remained vividly in his mind. A cry for help if ever he'd seen one. A cry that he'd unwittingly ignored.

The Director took the sheet of paper and stared at it disbelievingly. 'What if I refuse to accept it?'

'That is your decision, *Monsieur*. I shall be elsewhere.'

'You realise what you are asking, Aristide?'

'If it is possible to hush up the business of the Institut,' said Monsieur Pamplemousse, 'as I am sure it will be, then doubtless it will also be possible to hush up the cause of Albert Parfait's death. Publication of the facts will do no one any good. Representations in certain quarters . . . a word in the right ear . . . I am sure you have many contacts, *Monsieur* . . .'

There was a long pause. 'And if I do? Will you allow me to tear up this ridiculous letter?'

'Perhaps,' said Monsieur Pamplemousse stubbornly. 'We shall have to wait and see. Jean-Claude will take over.'

'He knows about his father?'

Monsieur Pamplemousse nodded. 'I broke the news to him this morning.'

'How has he taken it?'

'It was a shock, although he had been expecting something to happen. It was the way it happened that bothered him most.'

'You think he is capable of becoming *patron*?'

'I am sure of it, *Monsieur*. It was his father's wish. He will rise to the occasion. Besides, he will not be alone. He will have the support of his brothers.' He took out his wallet and removed the photograph of the girl. 'He also has someone to work for and if all goes well, to help him. They have already been through a lot together.'

The Director took the photograph and studied it carefully.

'It was for her that Jean-Claude conceived his plan,' continued Monsieur Pamplemousse.

'She is very attractive, I agree. But why her? There must have been many such girls at the Institut.'

'When you are in love, *Monsieur*, it is always with the most beautiful girl in the world and always you fear for the attention of others. Jean-Claude knew the annual visit of the *Grosse Légume* was drawing near and he became more and more convinced that she would be amongst his targets. But short of abduction, he couldn't think of any good reason for getting her out of the way without bringing trouble on Les Cinq Parfaits. He needed something which would bring her parents running to her rescue without actually giving the game away. That was when he dreamed up the idea of the kidnap note and why it had to be in English. The timing was critical – it had to be immediately before the "visit". Unfortunately, just as he was about to put his plan into action something went wrong. Somehow or other, others got wind of it and panic set in. Getting rid of him for good was out of the question – he was too well known. Putting him out of action for a while in the Sanatorium was at best a temporary measure to keep him quiet while they tried to think what to do next.'

'I am curious to know what led you to the Institut so quickly,' broke in the Director. 'Locally, of course, I gather there had long been rumours about the place, but here in Paris there was nothing to connect it with Jean-Claude's disappearance. It was put down to all manner of things. At one point it was even suggested it might be the work of a foreign power. When you started your investigations on the instructions of certain people in authority, others started to panic. It had always been a case of the left hand not knowing what the right hand was doing. Orders were issued and then, as new facts came to light, promptly countermanded.'

Monsieur Pamplemousse gripped the arms of his chair

impatiently. '*I* am curious to know how such a situation could ever have been allowed to develop in the first place. I find it incredible.'

'Ssh! Aristide!' Putting a finger to his lips, the Director got up from behind his desk, crossed to the door, opened it and having looked out to make sure the coast was clear, indicated to his secretary that they were not to be disturbed.

Back at his desk he settled down again and made nervous play with a set of large ball-bearings suspended from a kind of stainless steel trapeze. In the silence of the office it sounded like the opening day of the National Boules Championship.

'Politics, Aristide,' he said at last, 'is a dirty game. In this case what probably began as a tiny favour on someone's part, a greasing of the wheels in return for a consideration, escalated beyond anything that had been contemplated. Greed is a very powerful incentive, and so is security. People who have grown accustomed to their creature comforts will often do anything within their power to avoid losing them. It begins in the cradle. Try taking a rattle away from a baby and see what happens. Instinctively the grip tightens.

'The situation a few years ago when Europe – the whole of the Western world – suddenly found itself short of oil was very different to what it is now. We had grown accustomed to turning on the heat whenever we felt cold. Hot water poured from our taps. Engineers designed bigger and better cars powered by fuel which gushed out of our petrol pumps. It was there. It would always be there.

'When all that suddenly disappeared for a brief while there was panic. Queues formed at garages. In America men were shot for the sake of a gallon of *essence*. People began to hoard coal and oil. Orders went out to take immediate action. Those we wouldn't normally have been seen dead with were suddenly courted as friends. Nothing was too much trouble for them.

'No doubt when the *Grosse Légume* first came on the scene instructions were issued by someone, somewhere, that he was to receive the very best of treatment. Doors would be opened; his every wish pandered to. And when he expressed an interest in food, what better place to send him to than Les Cinq Parfaits? If the Parfaits objected, so much the worse for them. Bureaucracy wields a very heavy bludgeon when it comes to the renewal of licences. It also moves very slowly and is resistant to change. Those original orders were never rescinded.'

'And when the *Grosse Légume* expressed an interest in the pupils at the Institut des Beaux Arbres?' Monsieur Pamplemousse remained coldly unhelpful. 'Did bureaucracy again turn a blind eye?'

The Director gave a sigh. 'Different people have different standards, Aristide.'

He stood up and crossed to the window, gazing down at the slate-grey rooftops of the seventh arrondissement. To the right lay the Hôtel des Invalides, to the left the huge mass of the Eiffel Tower; on the hill beyond, the white confection of the Sacré Coeur stood out in the sunlight.

'Two and a half million people are at work out there. At work and at play, engaged in the sheer business of living. In the Ile de France ten million. In the whole of France, over fifty-three million. Men, women, old people, children, babies; French, Moroccans, Algerians, Portuguese; Catholics, Jews, Protestants, Moslems. Perhaps, for those who were involved at the time, those who had been charged with the task of humouring the whims of the *Grosse Légume*, there was no choice – the scales were too heavily weighted in his favour; fifty-three million to one. Perhaps in the beginning it was a simple case of minor corruption. We shall probably never know.'

'It does not excuse it, *Monsieur*,' said Monsieur Pamplemousse stubbornly.

'No, Aristide.' The Director turned away from the window. 'It does not excuse it. It merely explains it. I do not agree, nor do I entirely disagree. I was not in the position of having to make a decision. It is like asking someone if they approve or disapprove of transplanting the heart of a baboon into a child. If it is someone else's child they will most likely get hot under the collar and say no. If it is their own child the chances are they will say yes. It was probably an on-the-spot decision, and once that decision had been made there was no going back.'

'A wrong does not easily become a right, *Monsieur*. Two, still less. There were many wrongs to follow. Nine at the last count.'

The Director shrugged. 'The second time was that much easier, the third probably a matter of little moment. By then it would have become a game; a matter of mechanics. The Department of Dirty Tricks were called in to help, and to them it was an exercise, a chance to flex their muscles and to pit their wits against others – it didn't really matter who – they do not have their title for nothing. The school was taken over; the original ski instructors replaced by their own men; the *Grosse Légume* made a patron. His visits to both Les Cinq Parfaits and the Institut des Beaux Arbres became annual events; a chance to restock his larder, so to speak. He has, as you probably gathered, a very sweet tooth; plus a taste for blondes, preferably young and Anglo-Saxon. He likes their fresh complexions and they are more docile than some of the Latin races. At the Institut he was guaranteed an inexhaustible supply.'

'Why did he not go to Britain in that case?'

'Have you ever tried to smuggle a schoolgirl through the British Customs, Pamplemousse? They are not noted for their sympathetic approach to such matters. Besides, it is a small island. They lack certain of our advantages; space, mountains, borders . . . It was very much simpler to get them over here first, and the very fact of their being away from home had many other advantages.'

Monsieur Pamplemousse sat in silence for a moment or two. Reaching down with his hand he sought solace in the warmth and comfort of Pommes Frites' left ear. He suddenly felt very tired and dispirited and for no particular reason he thought again of Albert Parfait. That made him even sadder.

'And the radiators of France, *Monsieur*? What of them?'

The Director eyed Monsieur Pamplemousse uneasily. He sensed from his tone of voice the need to tread a delicate line. 'That is not for me to comment on, Aristide. No doubt the Minister responsible will have more to say on the subject when he sees you. It is, in any case, a rapidly changing situation. I am told that by 1990, seventy per cent of all our energy will come from nuclear sources. We are rich in hydro-electric power. Beneath the Pyrénées near Pau lies the largest deposit of natural gas on the continent of Europe waiting to be tapped. Solar energy is already being harnessed and fed into our National Grid. Each year there is less and less need to pander to the *grosses légumes* of this world.'

'And in the meantime, *Monsieur*?'

'In the meantime, Pamplemousse, we must hope for mild winters. What has happened is over and done with. Life doesn't stand still. Tomorrow's problems are already waiting in the wings. The *Grosse Légume* will have to do his "shopping" elsewhere in future. In France he is *persona non grata*. Such a situation will not be allowed to occur again.'

'And what about his past shopping?'

'Moves are being made; pressures exerted behind the scenes. The government will not be idle.'

'And what will happen to the Institut des Beaux Arbres?'

'Questions, Pamplemousse, questions. I think you will find that as from today the Institut is "under new management". The "ski instructors" will be replaced by the genuine article. Its pupils will remain untarnished – at least until they go out into the world.'

The Director waved aside the problems. They were for others to solve. 'You still haven't answered *my* question. What led you there in the first place?'

Monsieur Pamplemousse considered the matter carefully before replying. Luck, he supposed. Luck, and a certain amount of tedious spadework. Attention to detail. He would like to have added a touch of Holmesian deduction, but it had been more a matter of being in the right place at the right time, as was so often the case. Plus, of course, Pommes Frites' temporary indisposition.

The Director glanced down at the huge bulk beside Monsieur Pamplemousse's chair. 'I trust he is fully recovered?'

'*Absolument, Monsieur*.' Pommes Frites' breakfast that

morning had been of gargantuan proportions. He'd had a lot of catching up to do. 'Had I not gone in search of him I would not have encountered the *doudounes*.'

'Ah, yes, the *doudounes*.' The Director perked up. 'I must say your red herring about looking for an illiterate female compositor with large *doudounes* was a masterly stroke, Pamplemousse. It had us all fooled. As a means of diverting attention away from your own activities it worked like a dream. Here at Headquarters, people were running around in ever-decreasing circles. Lists were compiled; descriptions circulated. The print unions were consulted; Interpol alerted. A photokit picture was painstakingly constructed, built up from the brief details at our disposal.' He reached down and opened one of his desk drawers. 'What do you think of this, Aristide?'

Monsieur Pamplemousse took a 20 x 25cm print from the Director and held it up to the light. The face looking back at him bore little resemblance to Fraülein Brünnhilde. She would not be at all pleased if she saw it. As for the rest – someone had had a field day.

'I would not like to meet such a person on a dark night, *Monsieur*,' he said.

The Director held out his hand. 'Blown up out of all proportion, eh, Pamplemousse?' Pleased with his own joke, he replaced the photograph in his desk drawer.

For a moment Monsieur Pamplemousse was tempted to say more, but only for a moment. A promise was a promise. That apart, he had a feeling it would provoke snide references to past cases; the *affaire* at La Langoustine involving Madame Sophie and the *gonflables* in particular. He could almost hear the Director's comments. 'There are those who would say you are developing a distressing penchant for inflatables, Pamplemousse. Were you by any chance frightened by some balloons when you were small?'

Outside, a clock began to chime. They both looked at their watches automatically. It was mid-day.

'There is a lot to digest, Aristide.' The Director reached for his telephone. 'I hope you don't mind, but I have asked Madame Grante to join us for a pre-*déjeuner* apéritif.'

154

Monsieur Pamplemousse's heart sank. 'Is that strictly necessary, *Monsieur*? I can explain the second dent in the other wing. As for the picnic, I agree it was somewhat elaborate, but there were good reasons . . .'

'The *second* dent, Pamplemousse?' The Director put his hand over the receiver. 'It must have been a very wide road sign.'

'I had another encounter, *Monsieur*. With a tree. Were he able to talk, Pommes Frites would bear witness that I was not to blame.'

'Ah!' It was hard to tell from the tone of the Director's voice whether he was registering understanding or resignation. A pained look came over his face. 'No, no, Madame Grante. It is not necessary to bring the appropriate forms with you. It can all be gone into later. This is a purely social occasion.

'It seemed like a good idea at the time,' he said with a sigh as he replaced the receiver. 'She is not a bad woman and she has a difficult job to do. I sometimes feel, Aristide, that she labours under the impression that while she is slaving away at her desk all day others like yourself are living a sybaritic life out in the field.'

'A gross misapprehension, *Monsieur*.'

The Director rose to his feet and crossed the room to a cupboard at the far end immediately below the portrait of *Le Guide*'s founder, Hippolyte Duval. 'I know that, Pamplemousse. You know it. But given the size of your present claims, claims that I am sure can be fully justified in the fullness of time, I feel a little P.R. would not come amiss.' Opening the door of a concealed refrigerator he withdrew a bottle.

Monsieur Pamplemousse gazed at it in awe. Even from the other side of the room the contents were immediately recognisable.

'Taste-buds on the alert as ever, Aristide!' The Director looked pleased. 'I have not forgotten my promise. It is the Château d'Yquem '45.' Placing the bottle carefully on the cupboard top, he unfolded a white napkin and made ready a corkscrew and three tulip-shaped glasses. 'It is a long time since I last tasted it.' Holding the glasses up to the light in turn to make sure they were scrupulously clean, he felt the bottle again. 'I hope it is not too cold.'

A knock at the door heralded the arrival of Madame Grante. In response to the Director's bidding she entered and gazed around the room, registering in one brief, all-embracing glance both its occupants and the array of drinking implements on the cupboard top. She bestowed on the former a thin-lipped, wintry smile. It was not, reflected Monsieur Pamplemousse, the kind of smile that would have raised the temperature of the wine had it been pointed in that direction; rather the reverse. Pommes Frites opened one eye and finding it greeted by a disapproving sniff, hurriedly closed it again.

'Ah, Madame Grante! How good to see you.' The Director's attempt to inject a note of *bonhomie* into the proceedings was not entirely successful. Nervousness was apparent in his voice. 'Please sit down and make yourself comfortable. I was just saying to Aristide that it is time we saw more of you.'

Madame Grante seated herself on a long, black leather couch near the door, straightening her skirt automatically as she did so. 'I am always available, *Monsieur*.'

She watched while the Director removed the cork from the bottle and began pouring the wine. 'Only a very small glass, *Monsieur*. Some of us do have to go back to work, you know.' The shaft, directed at Monsieur Pample-mousse, met with an unreceptive target. Turning back to the Director, she unbent a little. 'Unlike you hardened drinkers, I have to take care. One glass and I am not always accountable.' It was a joke she clearly kept for festive occasions – probably at office birthday parties and Christmas, and although it went unremarked by the other occupants of the room, it did not go unnoticed.

The Director looked even more nervous as he approached her, holding one of the glasses delicately by its stem. His eyes, as they met those of Monsieur Pamplemousse, clearly gave the green light for the other to take charge should the occasion demand it. As with Madame Grante's arrow, it fell on stony ground.

The second glass of wine deposited on a table beside

Monsieur Pamplemousse's chair, the Director seated himself behind his desk again. He held his own glass up to the light and uttered a deep sigh of contentment.

'Ah, such depth of colour, such bliss . . . it makes one feel good to be alive.'

'It looks very expensive,' said Madame Grante disapprovingly.

'My dear lady' – the Director sounded put out – 'of course it is expensive. Such wine can never be cheap. Grapes, infected by the "noble rot", are left on the vines to shrivel until they lose half their weight and are barely recognisable. Often they have to be painstakingly picked one by one; but the juice is lush and concentrated, rich in sugar and glycerine. Even then it is no easy matter. The wine is kept for three and a half years in cask, topped up twice a week . . . the result is overpowering – you can almost feel the weight.'

Seeing that Madame Grante remained unconvinced he swirled the contents round. 'Look at it. Note the deep, rich amber-gold. It is a luscious wine. It is like drinking a mixture of honey and *crème brûlée*. Would you say *crème brûlée*, Aristide?'

'It is an apt simile, *Monsieur*.'

'As for the bouquet . . . that is something else again . . .'

Raising the glass to his nose, the Director held it there for a brief moment while he inhaled deeply. '*Sacré bleu!*' The glass fell from his nerveless hand as he jumped to his feet. '*Mon Dieu! Nom d'un nom!* Have you smelt it, Pamplemousse?'

Monsieur Pamplemousse reached for his own glass, but before he had time to put it to the test there was a choking sound from the direction of the door. Looking round, he was just in time to see Madame Grante, a handkerchief already to her mouth, disappear through the opening. The slam as the door swung shut was echoed seconds later by another.

Pommes Frites, wakened by the commotion, rose to his feet. He peered at the half-empty glass on the table, gave it a proprietorial sniff, then stared at his master in surprise.

Avoiding his gaze, Monsieur Pamplemousse looked the

Director straight in the eye. 'Did you say you *bought* this wine, *Monsieur*?'

'No, Pamplemousse, I did not say that. I made no mention of where it came from.' The Director sounded irritated. His voice was defensive. 'It was, as a matter of fact, a gift from Les Cinq Parfaits. It arrived this morning and I am told it was their last bottle. It seemed only right that you should share it.' He picked up his glass again and eyed the contents dubiously. 'What do you think can have happened to it? You have a nose for these things.'

'I think it is a little over the top, *Monsieur*.'

'A little over the top? It is *incroyable*. I have never smelt anything like it. It reminds me of that old *pissoir* near the Métro.'

'An even apter simile, *Monsieur*.' Monsieur Pamplemousse crossed to the cupboard and picked up the bottle. 'Perhaps the journey has unsettled it.'

'You think we should give it time?'

Monsieur Pamplemousse looked round the room. 'I think, *Monsieur*, it is yet another bottle destined for the pot plant.'

The Director watched unhappily while Monsieur Pamplemousse performed the task. 'This is becoming a habit, Pamplemousse.'

'At least Madame Grante will appreciate that life in the field is not all roses.'

The Director chuckled. 'She will not be querying your P39s for some while to come. Do you think she is all right?'

'I think she will recover.' Monsieur Pamplemousse decided against any further explanations. He'd had quite enough for one morning.

The Director joined him at the cupboard. 'Shall I open something else? I have a Beaumes-de-Venise. I am told that locally they drink it as an apéritif.'

Monsieur Pamplemousse shook his head. 'If you will forgive me, *Monsieur*, I must go. I have to get back to Montmartre. I may watch a little *boules* on the way while Pommes Frites enjoys the fresh air. I must not be late. Despite his troubles Jean-Claude has promised to prepare a

Soufflé Surprise. Madame Pamplemousse is taking his mind off things in the kitchen.'

'I admire your stamina, Pamplemousse. I must say I have been quite put off my *déjeuner*. Besides . . .' The Director hesitated. 'I have another matter to deal with. One which requires a certain amount of delicacy in its handling. A complaint has been lodged.'

'A complaint, *Monsieur*?'

'Yes, Pamplemousse, a complaint. You are exercised by what happened at the Institut des Beaux Arbres. I am exercised about something that happened at Les Cinq Parfaits on the night of your arrival. It seems that one of the advance guard – a lesser wife of the *Grosse Légume*, mother, nevertheless, of twins – was attacked by a fetishist of the very worst kind. A fetishist whose bizarre tastes defy classification.

'Picture the scene, Pamplemousse. It is night in a strange country. This poor, defenceless woman, knowing not a single word of the language, decides to take a stroll in the woods, her two infants suckling at her breasts. Suddenly, when she reaches the darkest part of the forest, she is pounced upon by a pervert. A pervert, Pamplemousse, who not content with waylaying her, begins to gloat over the innocent, down-covered heads of her charges, pawing at them like an *homme* possessed. It is scarcely credible the lengths to which some people will go in order to assuage their base desires.'

'Was she able to provide a description of this man, *Monsieur*?'

'No, Pamplemousse. It was a very dark part of the woods.' The director gazed at him. 'But it seems there was a dog involved. A very large dog.'

Monsieur Pamplemousse returned the gaze unblinkingly. Pommes Frites did likewise. 'Perhaps, *Monsieur*, it was a case of mistaken identity. As you so wisely said earlier, sometimes things get blown up out of all proportion.'

The sun was shining as he came out of the offices of *Le Guide*. There was, nevertheless, more than a hint of autumn in the air. Pommes Frites paused to leave his mark on a tree. He was obviously back to his old self. More Muscadet than Château d'Yquem.

Monsieur Pamplemousse stopped to call in at a *charcuterie*. It was good to be back again on his own territory. As with Holmes at the end of *The Hound of the Baskervilles*, he was about to turn his thoughts into more pleasant channels. He ordered a selection of cold meats for lunch; a *saucisson* or two for the first course. Doucette was preparing a *blanquette de veau*. Then it would be Jean-Claude's turn. Afterwards, if the others went out, he might show him his record collection.

A little further along the rue de Babylone he called in at a *fleuriste* and bought a bouquet of freesias for the girl, suddenly realising as he did so that he didn't even know her name. In his mind she would be for ever Diana. He bought another small bunch for Fräulein Brünnhilde and a bunch of red roses for Doucette; it would establish demarcation lines.

Pommes Frites waited outside the shop for a while and then ran on ahead and waited by the car. He, too, was pleased to be back home. It signalled a return to normality, to walks at set times and his own basket at night. Given a day or two to settle down, his master might even stop calling him Watson.

ALLISON & BUSBY CRIME

Jo Bannister
A Bleeding of Innocents
Sins of the Heart
Burning Desires

Brian Battison
The Witch's Familiar

Simon Beckett
Fine Lines
Animals

Michael Bond
Monsieur Pamplemousse Afloat

Ann Cleeves
A Day in the Death of
   Dorothea Cassidy
Killjoy

Denise Danks
Frame Grabber
Wink a Hopeful Eye
The Pizza House Crash

John Dunning
Booked to Die

John Gano
Inspector Proby's Christmas

Bob George
Main Bitch

T. G. Gilpin
Missing Daisy

Russell James
Slaughter Music

J. Robert Janes
Sandman

H. R. F. Keating
A Remarkable Case of
   Burglary

Ted Lewis
Billy Rags
Get Carter
GBH
Jack Carter's Law
Jack Carter and the
   Mafia Pigeon

Ross Macdonald
Blue City
The Barbarous Coast
The Blue Hammer
The Far Side of the Dollar
Find a Victim
The Galton Case
The Goodbye Look
The Instant Enemy
The Ivory Grin
The Lew Archer Omnibus
   Volume 1

The Lew Archer Omnibus
   Volume 2
The Lew Archer Omnibus
   Volume 3
Meet Me at the Morgue
The Moving Target
Sleeping Beauty
The Underground Man
The Way Some People Die
The Wycherly Woman
The Zebra-Striped Hearse

Priscilla Masters
Winding Up The Serpent

Jennie Melville
The Woman Who Was Not There

Margaret Millar
Ask for Me Tomorrow
Mermaid
Rose's Last Summer
Banshee
How Like An Angel
The Murder of Miranda
A Stranger in My Grave
The Soft Talkers

Frank Palmer
Dark Forest
Red Gutter

Sax Rohmer
The Fu Manchu Omnibus
   Volume 1
The Fu Manchu Omnibus
   Volume 2
The Fu Manchu Omnibus
   Volume 3

Frank Smith
Fatal Flaw

Richard Stark
The Green Eagle Score
The Handle
Point Blank
The Rare Coin Score
Slayground
The Sour Lemon Score
The Parker Omnibus
   Volume 1

Donald Thomas
Dancing in the Dark

I. K. Watson
Manor
Wolves Aren't White

Donald Westlake
Sacred Monsters
The Mercenaries
The Donald Westlake Omnibus